Enamoured

The Enslaved Duet. Book Two.

giana darling

giana darling

The Enslaved Duet. Book Two.

Copyright 2021 Giana Darling
Published by Giana Darling
Edited by Jenny Sims
Proofed by Ellie McLove
Cover Design by Najla Qamber
Cover Model Santi Wane
Cover Photographer Wong Sim

To Damma.
For raising me, loving me, and supporting all of my dreams.

"How can I be substantial if I do not cast a shadow? I must have a dark side also if I am to be whole."
— *C.G. Jung, Modern Man in Search of a Soul*

Playlist

"Hurts Like Hell" —Fleurie
"Castle" — Halsey
"Nocturne" — Blanco White
"Don't Forget About Me" — CLOVES
"Wasting My Young Years" —London Grammar
"Waiting Game" — BANKS
"La Traviata / Act 1: Libiamo ne'lieti calici" — Verdi
"Killer + The Sound" — Phoebe Bridgers & Noah Gundersen
"Primavera" — Ludovico Edinaudi
"Addicted" — Jon Vinyl
"Go Fuck Yourself" — Two Feet
"The Night We Met" — Lord Huron
"Start A War" —Klergy & Valerie Broussard
"To Build A Home" — Cinematic Orchestra
"Bad Guy" — Billie Eilish
"The Devil Within" — Digital Daggers
"Control" — Halsey
"Smother" — Daughter
"If I had A Heart" — Fever Ray
"Chains" — Nick Jonas
"To Be Alone With You" — Sufjan Stevens
"Siegfried Idyll" (Cosima's symphony)— Richard Wagner

Part One

SOLD

NON DECOR, DECO. I AM NOT LED, I LEAD.

Chapter One

ALEXANDER

*E*veryone who was anyone in British society was at my wedding. Even the royals had sent Prince Alasdair as their representative. It was the event of the season, of the fucking decade, and everyone worth their salt was in attendance. Everyone, that was, except for my bride.

"What do you mean?" I ground out. "Where the bloody hell is she?"

Riddick blinked, his hands locked behind his back, his feet braced apart like a soldier before his general. "She's gone, milord. No one has seen her for the past hour. I had Rupert check the cameras, and they went haywire half an hour before that. He's only just got them back online."

"Can he recover the footage?" I asked around the swell of rage rising tidal strong in my chest.

Someone had done something to Cosima.

To my wife.

I was seized by the primal urge to stalk around the crowded gardens and crush the pastel-clad guests littered across the grass like flowers under my foot until they confessed who'd taken her. I wanted to read their confessions in their blood, spilled from the hammer of my fists and the weight of my fury.

I wanted each one of them to die for even existing at the wedding when my bride did not.

"We…we can't be sure. Whoever tampered with them knew what they were doing," Riddick admitted, his eyes cold with his own fury.

My implacable manservant had developed his own obsession with Cosima.

I didn't blame him. How could I when I felt savage with longing for her at every hour of the day, even in those minutes when I was buried deep inside her.

I could never get close enough, fuck her long enough, plant myself deep enough.

In her head, in her heart, and in her sweet, tight cunt.

And now she was gone.

"That doesn't exactly narrow down the list of suspects, Riddick," I growled lowly. "It could be anyone in the Order, a disgruntled ex-employee even."

"You want it to be Dante," Riddick noted because he knew me well.

I wasn't a man who had friends, but if I had been, Riddick would be the best of them.

"Yes," I seethed, my hands flexing so hard I could feel the tendons pinch with strain. The pain grounded me. "Everything in me believes it's him, but I will not be ruled by emotion. If he is the one who took her, she shouldn't be in any danger. If it's someone else, if it's someone from the Order lashing out at me for some imaginary infraction, she could be dying as we speak."

I ignored the way my heart tripped over the notion of anyone causing her pain but me. It had been foolish to marry her, but I'd been foolish enough before that to believe marriage was the only way to protect her from the monsters I'd brought into her world.

Sherwood was somewhere in the crowd, no doubt ready to read me the riot act for going against The Code.

I didn't give a flying fuck. I'd given Cosima my name in marriage because there were more forces than the Order at work against us. The name Davenport was a shield, the titles of Greythorn and Thornton a lance and sword. I'd caved in to the compulsion to make sure she was armed for battle even when I couldn't be there to protect her.

Sherwood wouldn't kill me. He couldn't afford to. I was one of the wealthiest, most influential men in Great Britain. The Davenports had been founding members of the Order of Dionysus, and each generation had sat on its council.

So they wouldn't kill me.

Blackmail, harass, and maim me, potentially.

But any of those were less objectionable than the idea of Cosima being exposed to the harsh elements of my world. I'd dragged her into hell with me, but I would not leave her alone in the dark.

My stomach cramped at the idea of her alone there now, somewhere dank and black where even her considerable light couldn't keep her mind safe from its taint.

"Alexander."

I whipped around to glare at my father as he strolled toward me, adjusting the cuff on his impeccable white dress shirt as if it wasn't already perfectly aligned by his valet.

Years of latent bitterness sank roots in my gut and gave birth to fury.

I stormed up to him before he could freeze and slammed my fist across the strong line of his nose hard enough to feel the bones break like eggshells under my knuckles. Blood erupted from his nostrils and sluiced down the fine linen of his suit. Before he could recover, I banded my fingers around his throat and pushed him brutally against the wall of the house.

I hefted him into the air so that my hand was an iron bar holding him aloft. His face went pink, then mauve, and shifted into a satisfying shade of purple.

I still had the taste of my wife on my tongue, sweat on my face, and my father's blood on my fist. Fury had turned me heathen, and I didn't give a single fuck.

"Where in the bloody hell is she?" I seethed in Noel's purpling face.

He blinked at me, dispassionate even as I squeezed my fingers tighter around his neck.

"Tell me, or so help me, I will rip you apart with my bare hands where you fucking stand," I seethed, wishing each hard-bitten word was a bullet in his diabolical brain.

"So"—he wheezed—"dramatic."

My hand pulsed tighter against his neck. I wanted to snap his spine like a biscuit between my fingers and watch the bone crumble to dust at my feet.

But another stronger instinct urged me to let him breathe.

I spent my entire thirty-plus years being fashioned into my father's son. I was born, built, and programmed to operate under his system. Despite the abominable way he treated his slaves, the hurt he'd doled out to my mother with his various affairs, and the unethical way he ran his businesses, I felt bound to him elementally, vitally. If I was a great tree, he was the earth that bound my roots. I could never escape him, and to hope for release was to hope for death.

Without consciously deciding to do so, my fingers uncurled from his hot throat.

"You will tell me where my wife is," I said with my voice in my burning gut. "You will tell me now."

"You always were impulsive," Noel scolded calmly as if we were sitting in his office, and I was just a young lad. "I never could find a way to beat it out of you."

"You never could find a way to do many things. This estate was mortgaged to the gills when I graduated from Cambridge. Your marriage was a sham from its inception. You are a man with a title, but little wealth or real political power."

"I am a member of the most powerful society in the land," Noel said, his eyes finally flashing.

I fed off his anger, letting it stoke the flames of my own. "The Order is the most *corrupt* power in the fucking land, as you well know. In large part because of your influence over it."

Noel went still in a way that was dangerous. I'd always found that stillness could be considerably more threatening than action. It was the fear of the unknown that made the potential energy coiled in stillness so much more frightening than the kinetic.

"Watch how you speak of the Order, son," he said quietly. "It is not the type of organization that takes lightly to slander, nor is it one that accepts defectors."

I narrowed my eyes at him and stepped forward to loom over him with my excess three inches of height. "And I am not the type of man who takes rejection or evasion for an answer, especially when loyalty is called into question. I'll ask you once more, Noel, where the fuck is my wife?"

"I told you not to do this. I told you your enemies would smell your blood in the water if you were so weak to take a slave as your wife."

"And I told you," I growled, feeling the frenzy of panicked

rage erode my iron shields. "Our name would make Cosima safer than anything else could, even keeping her in the relative security of slavery. It was too late to keep her from their notice."

I knew the way the Order of Dionysus worked because I'd been pledged to the secret society since birth without my contest, my will signed over by my father in a binding, eternal contract.

They wanted Cosima for themselves, or they wanted her destroyed.

She was a poor choice for a slave, in the end.

I'd wanted her to end Salvatore and my turncoat excuse for a brother, but I should have known she was too glorious not to glint brightly from the shadows. She drew covetous glances, inspired lustful aspirations, and turned me from a player without weakness to a king constantly in check.

To see her was to want her, to know her at all was to be enamoured by her.

I'd bought her as a weapon to use against my enemies, and she'd become the ultimate tool for my destruction.

To mitigate the disaster, I'd married her.

It was against the rules of the Order. They expressly forbade intimate relationships with slaves. They were property. Livestock. Nothing more, and maybe something even less. To marry a slave was to marry the cow you sought to slaughter. It was the worst of all sins and punished mercilessly by the society. A chap I'd gone to Eton with had been castrated for the crime of loving his slave over a decade ago, but it was punishment no one would soon forget.

"If they'd done away with her, you'd know, son. The Order wants you to know *why* you are paying a price for your disobedience. I will say, Sherwood was just speaking with Willows and Canby about your insolence. I believe there was talk of punishment. If not for you," he said with a slow, sly smile that spread poison as an oil slick across the otherwise placid cast of his face, "then for her. Maybe it's a good thing she's run away."

"She hasn't fucking run," I snapped.

Cosima never would.

I'd broken her the way God had broken his fallen angels, tearing the wings from their backs and blinding them to the light of heaven. But she had endured. More than that, she'd bloody well thrived, taking to my sinful explorations and tainted lifestyle as if she had been born for it.

She was the bravest person I knew. No brand of adversity would take her from my side. Not unless she didn't want to be there.

And she did.

At least, some voice in my chest that I'd never listened to before whispered to me that she did. That she was made for me in a way that had to be cosmic.

It was appropriate that her name meant beauty of the cosmos because, to me, that was exactly what she embodied.

The beauty of all living things.

My chest ached and burned as I thought about all the times I'd wanted to say something like that to her but refrained. Poetry and emotion were for the poor and the uneducated, my father and tutors had always preached.

It was only with Cosima that the idea of being impoverished and stripped of my massive wealth and considerable influence seemed almost preferable if it meant I'd be free to... to be with her.

"She wouldn't run," I repeated, stepping up to my father again and pushing my hand against his heartless chest to keep him pinned. "Not unless someone made her."

"Women are weak. You think she could handle the kind of man you are? Women are for using, Alexander, not cherishing. Have I taught you nothing?" Noel sneered.

"You taught me everything about the kind of person I don't want to be," I said through my gritted teeth. "If you think your manipulations will keep me from finding out who took my wife from me, you're sadly mistaken. Not only will I find them, but I will also end them with my bare hands."

To highlight my point, I wrapped my hands once more around his throat, squeezing so tightly that I could feel the bones in his vertebrae grind together.

He let me.

Ominous premonition rolled down my spine.

For my entire life, my father had always been one step ahead. I'd seen him put into impossible positions with his creditors as a boy, with testing, power-hungry members of the Order as I grew old, and somehow, each time, when it seemed the end was near, he'd slipped out of their hold and come out on top.

If he was letting me punish him now, it was because it served his purpose.

Disgusted, I let him drop to his feet, then kicked them out from under him with a lazy sideswipe so that he fell to the grass against the house.

He glared up at me, more disturbed by the effect of the dirt on his Spencer Hart suit than by any violence I'd done to him.

"It's pathetic how much you've let this woman get under your skin." He sneered at me as he adjusted his cuff links. "No son of mine should be so affected by a woman, even if she is comely."

Comely?

The word was entirely too meek to describe her. She was magnificent from the ends of her midnight black hair to the tips of her thick, dark lashes. She was the most beautiful creature anyone in her life had ever had the good fortune to clap eyes on, and all of that, that considerable glory, was mine.

Not just because I owned, broke her, and used her.

But because intrinsically, fucking elementally, she belonged with me.

I growled low in my chest. "You're clearly no help to me. I'll find out who took her if I have to threaten every person of influence at this wedding."

"This *sham* wedding," he reminded me. "You only married her in a misguided effort to dig yourself out of the deep, dark hole you'd gotten the both of you into, correct?"

I gritted my teeth and gave him a terse nod.

He didn't deserve to know how I felt about my slave.

My *topolina*.

My wife.

"They'll kill you for loving her," he told me as he languidly gained his feet and flicked a piece of grass off his grey bespoke suit. "They'll kill you, and you know it, so do us both a favour and don't get the heir of Greythorn killed for something so idiotic. Stalking around like an enraged bull in a china shop will only get you murdered and your precious slave lost for good. They're just looking for a reason to take you down a peg or take you out entirely. Ever since you took that beating for Ruthie, they've been watching and waiting."

"Her name is Cosima," I corrected pointlessly.

He waved his hand through the air as if it didn't matter.

"If the Order did take her, you're better off lying low and playing the dedicated soldier so you can figure out who did it."

I exhaled roughly, side-eyeing Riddick where he stood off to one side, ready and waiting for any directive. He looked pissed right off but also conflicted.

We both knew Noel was right.

As much as I hated my father, as much as I'd had to live with him and be groomed by him as dictated by British upper-class social mores and secret society directives, but mostly because someone had fucking killed my mother, I knew life was a game.

A complicated game of chess that only the very best could succeed at.

And if I wanted to beat the Order when they had the most

powerful pieces on the board, then I'd have to play the long game.

Which meant doing exactly what Noel said.

Playing nice until they cocked up well enough for me to capitalize on it and end them.

For fucking good.

"Happily, I have a solution that won't end in your execution," Noel offered blasély. "Wentworth has petitioned for divorce from his wife and plans to run away with his slave. I've known this for some time, but I was waiting for the right time to make it known."

"Of course." Noel never gave an inch of himself or his knowledge away unless it would earn him a mile of leeway and influence.

"Unfortunately for the poor chap, he's grown careless as the date of his departure looms, and he made an error. An error that I happened to catch on film."

I stared into my father's eyes and noted how empty they were, like a steel room filled with stale air just waiting for someone to accidentally wander into. A holding cell. A torture chamber.

The eyes of a man without a heart.

I wondered painfully if those were the eyes Cosima had seen staring back at her in my face as I broke her into submission those first few weeks in the ballroom.

"Wentworth was one of the men who tried to claim Cosima at The Hunt," Noel mentioned casually, only the sly cast of his eyes sweeping in my direction gave away that he knew he was putting the final nail in Simon Wentworth's coffin with his words.

"Why would he do that if he's as in love with his slave as you claim he is?" I retorted.

"Why have you done so many horrible things to your slave? You know as well as he did that you are constantly watched for misconduct. They've been keeping tabs on him since he sent his wife to live on their Irish estate so he could be alone with the slave. It was the right call to capture and bed someone else at The Hunt, a call *you* should have been smart enough to make yourself. I believe he was almost successful in claiming your little mouse before another man knocked him from his horse and nearly beat him to death in a stream... think about what the man would have done with her if he hadn't been interrupted?"

It was sheer manipulation.

Grossly obvious, crude as a prehistoric tool chipped roughly out of stone.

Yet it still found its mark.

"Set it up."

Growing up, I'd always been drawn to the study of the classics, the great epic poems by Homer and Virgil, the Olympic gods, and the tragic, heroic stories.

I'd always identified with Hades the most, a hero who'd drawn the worst prize and been stuck as king of a dark, desolate kingdom he wanted no part of yet still ruled fairly over.

But it was the relationship and difference between the two gods of war that had always seemed most apt for Noel and me. I was quick to anger, though I'd curbed my impulsive actions over the years, a man of rapid decision-making and immediate execution like Ares. My father like the Goddess Athena, studied and patient, with the ability to formulate a plan and implement it over years, even decades.

When it came down to it, there were very few times Ares beat Athena.

I knew I had to change and adapt in order to best him.

The resentment that had been planted and germinated as a boy, taken roots through the cruel teachings of my adolescence and been only temporarily stunted after the death of my mother when I was eager to make peace with the only parent I had left, burst into riotous bloom.

Finally, I had a fully formed reason to take down my father.

That reason had eyes the colour of gold bullion and a soul purer than freshly driven fucking snow.

So, I smiled sharply at him as he wiped the blood I'd spilled from his cruel mouth. "Set it up," I repeated. "I'll show the Order just how loyal I am, and I'll enjoy doing it."

They strung him up between two trees. I wondered idly why they didn't use the dungeon or the exercise room as they had in the past, but I was too blind to the cold flurry of my own rage to think fully on it.

Maybe I should have.

I wasn't a man of feeling. I'd been raised to think emotion was akin to a normal man's sin, and that sinning was my right as an earl. I was better than petty sentiment but worthy of satisfying my every need, no matter the cost.

And my need at that moment was violence.

I wanted to channel all my considerable devastation at the sudden loss of my wife on our wedding day by decimating the bastard strung up between two ash trees.

He was a poor bloke without the intelligence and artifice

to pull off his greatest crime against the Order by loving his slave. A crime we shared.

I studied his defeated posture as I slid the end of a cat-o'-nine-tails whip through my hand. His dark head was bowed between his shoulders, a gash on his cheek dripped blood to the grass from where one of the brothers had beaten him into submission enough to get him strung up like a Christmas goose.

In years past, I wouldn't have spared a thought as to whether he deserved what was coming to him. My fundamental apathy had always extended to the Order. It was my father's domain, and only his will kept me tethered to it.

Now, the heart of me had woken from its lifelong slumber, and I felt moved by the wretched bugger hanging from his wrists. No doubt, his slave was already dead, taken care of by one of the society's discreet and deadly acolytes who only ever operated from the shadows and never showed their faces at the Order's social events.

There were so many paths that could have led to me between those massive ash trees, broken by love and punished by people who could never understand such a feeling.

It was ironic that I was to be the one to punish him for it.

"Are you sure you're up for this, old chap?" Martin Howard asked me affably with a chummy pat on the back.

He was not a friend.

He was the brother to Agatha Howard, a woman the Order and Noel, more specifically, had urged me to marry for years.

They were part of the most ambitious and callous family in British noble history, and I'd always found the lot of them incredibly distasteful.

Anyone that hungry for power was never going to achieve it, at least not for long.

Like the ouroboros, they would only end up eating their own tail.

I shot Martin an impassive look and continued to slide the whip sensually across my palm. The feel of it in my hands was right, like a pitcher with a baseball or an artist with a brush. This was my tool of trade, a weapon I wielded with both precision and passion to create a masterpiece on a woman's body.

Like the many I had made on Cosima's golden brown skin.

Wrath burned any lingering misgivings I had clean from my mind.

I had to show the Order I was just as heathen and unfeeling as they were.

I had to prove I was on their side until the bitter end so that when I discovered which one of the motherfucking men took Cosima from me and went after them, they wouldn't see it coming.

"Of course, you're ready," Martin guffawed. "You were born ready for this society, with a father like Noel."

"*Acta, non verba,*" Sherwood proclaimed as he stepped away from the masses of Order men at my back to speak with me.

The wedding was long over, the guests sent home without explanation for why the bride had suddenly retired early for the night.

"Action, not words," Sherwood translated like the haughty arsehole he was even though he knew both Martin and I perfectly understood Latin. "Prove yourself as one of us after this disgrace of a wedding, Davenport. This man flagrantly disobeyed the primary rule of this society. Do not fall in love with your slave. They are meant to slake the temptations of your body and purge the demons from your mind, but they are *never* worthy of our regard."

"I'm aware of the rules," I said drolly.

Sherwood and Howard shared a quick look.

My unflappability in the face of my own transgressions

that almost directly mirrored those of the bugger to be punished confused them.

Was I an idiot, they wondered?

No, Alexander Davenport, Lord of Thornton and heir to the Dukedom of Greythorn, was one of the wealthiest men in the United Kingdom and had amassed one of the highest-grossing media companies in the world.

Dumb, I was not.

So what other explanation could there be for my bone-deep calm?

Well, he clearly hadn't loved his slave.

Not if he was this unruffled by the disappearance of the slave and by his punishment of one who had committed that very crime.

I could see my manipulation snare them in its web, and I moved in for the kill.

"I married the slave as the final nail in the coffin of my contempt for her father. He killed my mother, but before I killed him, he knew what it was to have someone he loved wholly and completely taken from him."

They didn't know Amadeo Salvatore wasn't dead. I doubted even Cosima knew I was aware of her ruse.

No man as clever as the Napoli *capo* went into a situation unarmed out of concern for his estranged daughter.

It was a set-up, and though amateurly thought up, it was fairly well-executed.

The fact of it was, I didn't much care.

There was very little to make me believe anymore that Salvatore was the one who killed my mother. There was little motive, and my own gut coiled at the idea.

It was wrong.

I had more important things than Salvatore on my mind at the time, but I knew where he was when the time came to confront him.

Now that Cosima was gone, finding her was my only

focus, and Salvatore was at the bottom of my list of suspects based on one simple fact. Not even her birth father could have convinced Cosima to run away from me hours after we'd married.

Snapping the whip forward with complete accuracy, I broke a branch arching above Simon Wentworth's prone form and watched as leaves fell over him like macabre confetti.

"Let's begin," I intoned, just as mightily as Sherwood, striding forward and taking my place behind Wentworth's back.

Unlike mine, his was smooth and unblemished. He had never been punished for defending a woman as I had for Yana and Cosima.

Unbidden, I wondered what kind of man he was, and remorse scored through me like talons over my innards. Then I remembered that he had tried to claim Cosima in The Hunt, and anger blazed through me, eradicating the wounds.

"Just do it," he whispered brokenly. "She's gone, and I don't…I don't want to *be* anymore."

"Disgusting," someone called out.

Another spit at him.

"Pathetic wanker," someone else shouted.

"Silence," I ordered, the boom of my voice like a sonic bomb quelling every noise in the vicinity.

Even the wind died suddenly, and the animals obeyed, frozen in the trees like ornaments.

I let the banked rage at losing Cosima overcome me as I lifted my arm and brought the deadliest whip in my arsenal down on Simon Wentworth's back.

His screams exploded in the silence, louder than my command, filling the quiet like a waterfall into a cup, his agony so forceful it seemed to tear through my eardrums.

I continued ceaselessly.

My mind focused not on the wet thwack and thud of the whip on his torn back or his banshee wails but on the face of a woman who was young enough to be a girl but wise enough to be a goddess.

I thought of the way she slept curled in my arms as if I was her protector. For a girl with a life filled with monsters, the idea that she thought I could keep her safe from harm was so heady, it made my head fucking spin.

I thought of her hair wrapped around my fingers as she babbled on about her day cooking with Douglas, attempting needlepoint with Mrs. White, and fencing with Riddick. How those words gave life to my house, to Pearl Hall, in a way nothing ever had before. How her words made my house a home.

I thought about Cosima until my arm was weak with strain and my white shirt was stained with red like a Jackson Pollack painting. I thought of her as Simon Wentworth's breath turned to a wet rattle, and then I thought of her as my mind seized with the knowledge that this person she had turned me into could not live with beating Wentworth to death for committing an act I was guilty of myself.

"Davenport?" someone called.

I realized that my arm had dropped, and I was heaving for breath as I stared at the mutilated mess I'd made of the man before me.

"Can't stomach it?" Sherwood asked smugly.

If I couldn't, I would be signing my own death warrant.

I looked up at him, trying to veil the hatred I felt for him and his well up like a spring river over the protective banks I'd erected over the years.

"I have a better idea," I said softly, dropping the whip, ignoring the way my hand cramped into a curled position from holding it so tightly for so long.

The Order watched wearily as I moved around Wentworth, dropping to my knees before I called to Noel, "Bring me a knife."

My father strode forward as if he had been prepared all

along for this exact eventuality, a gleaming hunting knife with an ivory and golden handle already brandished in his hand. It was the knife passed down the Greythorn line since its inception in the 1500s.

The handle was warm as he passed it over to me, his eyes cold with violent pride as he placed his other hand on my shoulder, and said, "That's my boy."

That's my boy.

Proud of me for one-upping the Order's prescribed punishment to one even more cruel, even more steeped in the society's brutal history.

I cut my gaze from my father and looked up at Simon Wentworth, whose face was pale as a blank page and just as undone.

"Do it," he mumbled. "End me."

"I won't," I told him, my voice strong enough for the Order to hear it. "Because you don't deserve it. For the crimes you've committed against the Order of Dionysus, you'll be gelded."

There was a collective gasp and hum of approval from behind me, but Simon Wentworth's eyes only widened as he panted and gaped at me.

"This is for trying to rape my wife," I said quietly, just for him.

And then I fit the knife up behind his balls and *cut*.

Blood poured over my hands, wet and warm like a Satanic christening while Simon's screams rent the fabric of the air again and again until they stopped with a whimper, and he fainted in his bonds.

I stepped back, turned with the bloody knife, and wiped it on my father's shirt before he could move out of the way.

He bared his teeth and growled at me, but I was already stepping away, handing both the knife and the offender's wet mass of testicles to Sherwood.

"Your price for the crimes committed," I told him,

layering my voice with meaning as I pinned him in place with my glacial regard.

I took primal satisfaction from the way the rail-thin older man paled.

"The price is paid," he murmured. "Welcome back to the fold, brother. We have many plans for you."

And I—I thought darkly, mind racing—*for you.*

Chapter Two

COSIMA

"You don't have any experience," I heard for the dozenth time in less than two weeks. "I'm sorry."

I blinked at the man wearing the regulation visor and polyester vest. My mouth was twisted into something between a sneer and a smile, misaligned by bitter humour at the idea of a pimply faced teenager telling me I had no experience.

I wanted to lean across the table and wrap my hand around his throat as I recounted just how much experience I had with nightmares he was too pure to even dream up. I wanted to watch his eyes bulge, the whites redden with fireworks of burst blood vessels as I squeezed and said my dirty words. As I told him about my rape, The Hunt, my wicked beating at the hands of the world's wickedest man.

Then I wanted to sit back and watch him gasp for breath, scrubbing his hands over his face as if he could erase the images I'd implanted in his mind, and ask him calmly if he still thought I was lacking in *experience*.

I didn't do any of that.

Defiance wasn't me, it was the Cosima of before. Before my father sold me, before Alexander bought me and wholly owned me, before his father ruined me.

I was too well trained to lash out against the bonds society had strapped me in, too tired to execute the violence boiling in my heart, and too desperate to waste my energy on another rejection.

So, I smiled at him, knowing it was the most beautiful thing the boy would see in his day as a cash register attendant at a cheap chain restaurant.

He blinked hard at the sight of me, and it gave me a sliver of comfort.

"Thank you for your time," I said softly before I pushed back from the table and left the cramped restaurant.

Sometime during my failed interview, it had begun to rain over the streets of Milan. I stepped out into the elements, tilting my head up into the knife sharp spray of water, loving the way it hurt, needing the way it grounded me to my new reality.

I wasn't a slave anymore, but I didn't feel free.

I had more obligations than before.

Dante and Salvatore had uprooted their organization to restart in America, and their money was spent establishing their hold in the city. They didn't have extra to support a family of five, though they tried.

I'd left England without the assurance of a continued allowance for Mama and my siblings. There wasn't even an account for my ex-owner to deposit into anymore. Dante had worked his illegal, technological wizardry and dissolved the Lombardi family of Naples from the anvils of Italian history. If anyone in Mama and Elena's new life in New York, or Sebastian's in London, or Giselle's in Paris decided to look into the Lombardi clan, they would find nothing.

I didn't know what Alexander thought of my disappearance, if he assumed I was dead or hated me enough for my escape that he'd forgotten me entirely, but he hadn't come for me in the month I'd been gone. I tried not to focus on why he hadn't and whether he just couldn't find me or he didn't want to.

I'd made my decision, and I had to live with it.

So, it was back to work for me. Sebastian was working on a film with the revered movie star Adam Meyers, so I knew a windfall was coming for us, but until then, I had Giselle to put through her remaining two years in art school, and now, Elena's law school.

We were too poor to even take out a loan. How does someone secure an investment when they have no equity?

The only thing of value we had, that we'd ever had, was me.

I tried to model, but I'd been out of the game for a year, and Landon Knox's blackmark against me still lingered in Milan and echoed out into the rest of Italy.

I couldn't secure an agent, let alone a go-see or photo shoot.

Even my beauty, it seemed, couldn't help us now.

My eyes stung as I blinked up into the rain, and I wondered idly if I was crying.

I could have been, though I wasn't a crier, but I doubted it.

It seemed that running away from the only man I'd ever loved hadn't ripped me open like a raw wound as I thought it might. Instead, it had calcified me. Where I was once warmth and light, I was only sinew and blood, stripped of metaphor and emotion, a human vessel without animation.

Oh, my family still gave me comfort. I was free to Face-Time with them every night, to see the small but comfortable brownstone Mama had made a deposit on with the last of the money I'd sent her, to see the tender, excited way Elena handled her new law school textbooks for her first semester at NYU, to watch Giselle as she painted intricate works of art as easily as breathing while she gabbed to me about how much she loved Paris, and finally, most beautifully, to discover the face of my brother as he talked about the woman he had fallen in love with.

I could have moved to any of their cities. It would have been an incredible comfort to wrap myself in their love as balm against the sucking black hole of missing and misery that lay in my chest where my heart used to be, but I didn't.

First, I didn't want them to see how broken I was. They would have questions I didn't have answers for, and they wouldn't let things lie if it looked like I was in pain.

I had to get a handle on myself before I could go to them.

Secondly, I needed a job. I thought, given my previous experience in Italy, that it was the obvious place to do so.

I'd been wrong, but I'd sent the bulk of my money to my family members, and I didn't have enough to book a flight even if I wanted to. I was crashing on my friend Erika's couch and that was getting old quick because she had a boyfriend who was gross enough to hit on me whenever she wasn't home.

So there I was, stuck in Milan with my sorrow and without a hope.

I tilted my head back farther, letting the rain pelt me in the face. I could feel the rush of water drenching my black wrap dress, sluicing over my hair like a religious cleansing, a rebirth, or a baptism. I was lost to religion forever, but I enjoyed the metaphor. My fingers unfurled and my palms rounded so that I would feel the rain run through my fingers.

I just stood there like a crazy person, smiling because I was free to stand there like a crazy person, and no one was going to stop me.

I'd fought so hard for so many things that had escaped me, but this, this freedom, was something I would never *ever* take for granted.

"*Scusi,*" a cool, slightly accented voice interrupted my reverie. "*Stai bene?*"

I righted myself and took in the frankly gorgeous man before me who was nearly as waterlogged as I was. His dark copper hair dripped over his forehead, partially shielding the vivid, nearly electric blue of his eyes as he peered down at me in concern. He was tall—not as tall as Alexander or Dante, but I'd yet to meet anyone who was—and trim but fit beneath his trench coat.

If I'd been a normal girl with a normal past, I might have blushed and flirted with such an attractive stranger.

But I wasn't that girl.

In fact, the primary reason I found myself drawn in by him was because of the aloof cast to his mouth and the stern set of his features. Even though he was clearly concerned about the crazy woman happily getting drenched in the rain, he didn't really care.

That apathy stirred something in me, a strange combination of empathy and allure.

I answered him in English, just guessing at his accent. "I'm fine, thank you. I enjoy the rain."

His lips twitched, drawing my attention to the firm, perfectly formed mouth. "I wonder if it might be better enjoyed from the café behind you, maybe over a hot *caffè latte*? I'm not sure if you are aware, but your teeth are chattering."

I froze and noticed that my teeth did not follow suit. "Oh."

His mouth pulled even higher in the barest hint of a smile.

"Allow me?" I stared at him as he offered me his coat, putting it around my shoulders before gently leading me over to the small café beside the restaurant I'd applied at.

"Do you normally like to play with life and death by standing out in the freezing rain?" he queried drolly as he stepped forward to grab the door for me.

A surprised laugh bubbled up as I thought about it. "Not in this particular way, no, but you'd be surprised how often I straddle that fine line."

He cocked an eyebrow at me, a hand hovering over the small of my back in an old-fashioned gentlemanly way as he led me into the café and over to a small table. "You look like a goddess from the underworld. I don't find that surprising at all."

I beamed at him, surprising even myself with the vividness of my expression. His comparison had solidified my regard for him.

Anyone who likened me to Persephone, I decided, had an unerring sense of character.

"And you the miraculous Hermes who could cross into the underworld unscathed to rescue me and take me back to my mother?" I asked him, testing him because only someone well versed in mythology would know the details of Hades and his Queen's story.

His eyes twinkled even though his lips stayed flat. I took him for a man who didn't smile often and wondered what I would have to do to change that.

It was a surprising thought, but I let myself have it because I'd been obsessing over the wrong man for so long, it felt good to care even momentarily about a good one.

"Unfortunately, I think I am the messenger who will be forced to take you back to *my* mother," he explained as the small bell above the café door sounded and a beautiful dark-skinned woman swept into the room.

I recognized her immediately and not only because she

was fairly well known in the fashion world. I knew the perfectly coiffed head of caramel highlighted waves and the gorgeous slant of her cheekbones because I had met her before.

Willa Percy had been a judge at the St. Aubyn panel when I'd auditioned what seemed like a lifetime ago.

And she had *not* been very kind.

I pursed my lips in a mirror image of hers as we took each other in.

"Cosima Lombardi," she said slowly, dredging up my name from the depths of her memory. "Intimissimi campaign, if I'm not mistaken?"

"You're not."

She eyed me, then her son, though clearly not biologically as he was red-haired and only lightly tanned. "If you are attempting to sleep with my son to get me to patron you, you'll be sadly mistaken."

"Willa," my new friend protested, partially standing to glower at her. "Sit down and be silent if you don't have anything kind to say. I ran into this…I ran into Cosima." He tasted the name, rolling it properly the way Italians do and then did his lip twitch smile before continuing. "She was outside in the rain, and I offered her a coffee to warm up. Neither of us had any idea of our ties to you, and frankly, I still doubt either of us *care*. Really, Mom, you think too much of yourself sometimes."

My mouth gaped a little at his strong tone and audacity, but surprisingly, Willa sat down on the chair he pulled out for her and accepted his kiss on the cheek with only a mild sniff.

"Go get us those coffees, will you?" she asked him, patting his cheek and inciting a grimace from him.

A little giggle escaped at seeing them interact. This man was older than me, strong and sure in his movements and actions in a way that spoke of inherent confidence and unflappability.

He reminded me, in small ways, of Alexander.

And those small ways were both just not enough and enough to make me feel comfortable around him.

"Now, what's a girl like you doing out in the rain looking like a drowned rat?" Willa asked me pointedly as she unwound her Hermes scarf and opened her sleek designer raincoat.

"Enjoying my freedom," I told her honestly because I didn't know her, and I had nothing to lose.

Not anymore.

"Is freedom a euphemism for unemployment?" she asked me pointedly, scraping her scathing brown gaze over my seated form. "I haven't seen or heard of you in any circles in months."

"I was living abroad for a while," I hedged.

"Modelling?"

I shook my head but didn't explain even when she shot me a frustrated look to continue.

"Career suicide to be gone so long. Models age quicker than dogs, my dear. You're what now, twenty?"

"Nineteen," I told her as her son returned with three lattes.

He frowned at me as he handed over the small warm mug. "Jesus, you are young."

"How old are you?"

Willa pinned me with a glare. "I thought you were not trying to sleep with him?"

I shrugged one shoulder indolently, completely unnerved by her rudeness.

"Stop it, already. The mama bear act was old when I was seventeen," he told her.

Willa pressed her lips together.

He shot her a fond, slightly exasperated look and then turned to face me as he pushed back his rapidly drying hair. "I am nearly as rude as my mother. My name is Daniel Sinclair, but please call me Sinclair. It's lovely to meet you, Cosima."

"French?" I asked, identifying his accent much more easily when he spoke English.

He inclined his head slightly. "*Mais, bien sûr.*"

"I don't speak French, but I do understand that. How many languages do you speak?" I asked.

"Four fluently," his mother said proudly. "He also has an MBA from Columbia and owns an up-and-coming real estate development company in New York City. Perhaps now you can see why I'm protective?"

"I can," I agreed, fiddling with the handle of my cup, imagining what it would have been like to have a mother who had gone to bat for me. "And I can't blame you for it. I wish I had a protector like that."

I looked up at them after a beat of silence and found them watching me, twin expressions of reluctant tenderness on their faces.

"I'm not to be pitied," I told them as I wrung out the ends of my drenched hair onto the tile floor beside me. "You don't know my story. You aren't to know if it's a tragic one."

"No nineteen-year-old girl should have so much sadness in her eyes," Sinclair said, his beautiful blue gaze cool and serene as twin lakes. "I don't need to know your story to know that."

"Ah, and we hit on the real reason you offered to buy me coffee," I said with a self-deprecating quirk of my lips.

"No," he said slowly, locking eyes with his mother who shook her head slightly and sighed. "I bought you a coffee because you are a beautiful woman who looked like she could use a kind word. I'm offering to be your friend and maybe, to protect you the way my mother protects me because of those sad golden eyes."

"Why in the world would you do that?" I asked, instantly suspicious of his altruism.

If my time at Pearl Hall had taught me anything, it was that no one did anything without getting something in return.

The world was a hellhole masquerading as a field of dreams, and I wasn't a naïve girl frolicking through the flowers anymore. I was a warrior with a blade, and I'd cut down anyone who tried to drag me farther into that hell again.

"We're a family who takes in strays," Willa surprised me by responding, throwing down a few bills to pay for our drained coffees.

"Especially beautiful ones," Sinclair said with such an audacious wink that it made me laugh.

"You better come with us," Willa said with a dramatic sigh. "I'll have to do something about your hair if we want to get you back to work."

"I'm not cutting it," I snapped, my hands flying to the thick, inky wet mass of it.

My hair was my security blanket, my crown when I would otherwise be without one. Even Alexander hadn't tried to take it from me, and I didn't know what I would have done if he'd tried.

Willa rolled her eyes as she ushered us all out into the rain straight into a waiting car, the driver holding the door open for us.

"Darling girl, I would never. Your hair will be your signature when I catapult you to stardom."

"It will be her eyes," Sinclair argued as he helped me into the clean leather interior. "I have a feeling her money eyes have taken her places before, and that won't stop now."

Chapter Three

ALEXANDER

The sight of her hit me with the force of a nuclear wave.

My back slammed into the plush leather car seat as my chest decompressed, my heart swollen and beating against the confinement.

She was achingly beautiful.

It was the only way to describe the acute sensation her beauty stirred in the beholder, the breath-stealing, blood warming impact one had at the sight of her.

My muscles locked against the urge to throw the door to the Bugatti open and stalk over to her where she stood looking lost and unforgivably alone of the street corner outside the Piazza Mercanti in Milan.

I'd spent hundreds of pounds directing resources to find her. Finally, after five weeks of searching, they found Cosima in Milan because she'd sent the bulk of her savings to her mother in New York City and the transaction had pinged on our radar. From there, it was easy. She was living in a cramped apartment with a fellow model and her lecherous boyfriend. No one in Milan's varied and thriving fashion circle would work with her thanks to the damage Landon Knox had done to her before she'd become mine. She was broke and broken, all because of me.

But I'd put into action events that would help her, even if I decided not to get out of the cold car and catch her up in my arms like a captured water nymph.

Sherwood was a gormless arsehole if he thought for one minute I would follow his directives like a good little lamb and let the best thing that had ever happened to me slip through my fingers.

Cosima was *mine*.

She could exist across the world. Hell, she could be transported to another fucking planet, and she would still be owned wholly by me.

Contractually, spiritually, physically, and fucking emotionally.

Every drop of blood in her body was tainted by my dark, seething obsession with her, and she didn't even know.

I hadn't had a chance to tell her.

We'd been playing a game too dangerous to take for granted.

I'd fought hard, in the only way I knew how, to silently, swiftly move my pieces across the board when the odds were stacked heavily in the Order's favour.

For a brief shining moment—when Salvatore was lying shot through the chest in a hotel room in Rome, and I was about to wed the woman I knew in my bones was my reward for a life of painful servitude to my father and his demons—I thought I might have even done it.

Outsmarted them.

The shrewdest, wealthiest, most corrupt group of men in Britain.

Of course, I hadn't.

My hamartia had always been pride.

I believed in myself enough to *try* to eliminate the problem, but in the end, my failing had come from exactly that pride blinding me with arrogance.

The magic Cosima had brought to my life was just that, an illusion created by the cruel hands of the puppeteers and masterminds who ruled us both.

I stayed seated in my car and watched her through the mirrored streaks of rain obscuring the windshield. She had her chin tipped up as water peppered over her face, lips parted and eyes closed as if she was preparing for a baptism.

I knew differently, though.

She might have been homeless and alone, sodden on some street corner like a forgotten whore, but my topolina wasn't focused on any of that.

She was glorying in her freedom.

I could tell by the sad but awed tip of her lips and the reverent way she opened her hands to the sky to collect the drops in her palms.

That last time I'd seen her in the rain, I'd fucked her in the mud in a field of poppies my mother had planted behind Pearl Hall.

Seeing her like that again, wet and ruined, made me want to do it again.

Then again, any time I looked at Cosima, no matter the inappropriateness of our surroundings, I wanted her.

I'd never wanted for anything in my entire life yet, I'd never *wanted* anything the way I wanted her. I felt her absence from my life like a limb lost in war, blasted away by a bomb, the shards of shrapnel still digging and twisting painfully deeper into the salvaged tissues.

At that moment, after days without contact, I was frankly mesmerised by the sight of her.

She was more alive in the tableau of bittersweet misery and joy than I had been in any moment of my life before and without her.

It was intoxicating enough for me to risk everything for her.

Even my own safety.

I checked the gun hidden neatly under my arm in the holster beneath my bespoke Armani suit, and then did a quick survey of my surroundings to make sure my path to her was clear.

I was taking my wife home with me.

Sherwood and Noel could bombard us with threats like the London Blitz, but I didn't give a fuck.

I'd shield her with my own body and throw my entire fortune like a golden shield up around us if it meant keeping her at my side, on her knees but proud just as she was meant to be.

Only, as I swung my eyes back to her, I noticed two things that gave me pause.

A man standing on the opposite street corner from Cosima, his copper hair wet with rain, his trench coat drenched in the deluge but still obviously expensive. He stared at my wife with a cocked head, mesmerised as any red-blooded male would be by the sight of her on that street like some queen finally freed from the underworld.

Jealousy burned like a straight shot of whiskey to my gut.

He looked at the ground, then back up at her, and then he was moving with purposeful strides across the road.

It was only then I noticed the man who had been partially obscured behind a parked tram. He was tall, reed-thin, and pale like wax paper, so quintessentially British it made the hair on the back of my neck stand on end.

It was his hand, though, that highlighted the threat.

His arms folded over a suited chest, hand resting just under his left armpit where a slight bulge was noticeable through the material.

He was palming a gun.

Adrenaline sluiced over me, my legs aching with lactic acid that urged me to charge out of the car and kill the bastard for following either of us.

The Order had sent someone to take care of us if we disobeyed orders.

Despite my show of loyalty by castrating Simon Wentworth, they still didn't trust me. Indignation burned through me, chased on its heels by the inferno of betrayal.

That they knew where she was to send someone indicated they were the ones to take her from me.

I felt the insane urge to tip my head to the sky and howl like a beast with rage. Instead, I pulled my knife out from my pocket, flipped it open, and stabbed it into the passenger seat of the hundred thousand-pound Bugatti.

The act of violence calmed me enough to take stock of Cosima again.

As I deliberated how I could instantaneously kill each member of the Order, the strange man reached Cosima and began to pull open his coat.

I had my gun out of its holster and in my hands, leveled at the threat in the next instant, my breathing calm and cool as I narrowed my sight at the threatening bastard.

Would they really be so bold as to take her out on a bloody street corner?

No. I told myself to relax and lowered the weapon as the man took off his trench and handed it to my wife.

The Order operated in the shadows, illusive and

ephemeral as the spectre of a demon sent from Hell. They wouldn't cause a scene.

The bastard-in-wait across the street was a sleeper agent. He wouldn't pull the trigger unless Cosima gave him—and therefore the Order—reason to do so.

Right now, she was safe.

If I stepped into the picture again to claim her, I'd be placing her in imminent danger. If we somehow escaped this gunman, there would always be another threat around the corner.

Sherwood and the rest were not the kind of men who let flagrant rule breaking go unpunished.

I thought back to the difference between Ares and Athena, of how cool logic and careful planning always prevailed over hot-headed action. I wondered if I was strong enough, clever enough to think hard and long, to craft a plan so precise and perfectly honed I could use it like a lance to drive it through the heart of my enemies and hers. *Ours*.

I watched distractedly as the redheaded man spoke with Cosima, obviously trying to comfort and coax her toward a café to get out of the rain.

She laughed, her head thrown back and her hand snapping out to brace herself against his arm as if the weight of his hilarity was too much to bear.

The man looked down at her hand on his arm and then back up into her gorgeous face made even more gorgeous by the rain and good humour, and I knew he was caught.

It only took a moment, a glance, to be hooked by her beauty, but the moment she allowed you a glimpse of her vital spirit, it was like a bludgeon over the head and the end of any protestations.

He would help her.

I could see it in the way he led her into the café, leaning down to better hear her lyrical voice.

I wanted to kill him.

And not even quickly, simply by shooting him with the cold gun in my lap.

I wanted to rip him apart with my bare hands just for touching her, for even thinking about caring for her when she was my responsibility.

But then I looked over at the minion across the street and saw him watching my car, squinting across the distance into the dark interior.

He couldn't see me, but if he did, the work I'd done to convince Sherwood I was indifferent to Cosima would be undone.

And it couldn't be.

If I really wanted the best for Cosima, I'd leave her alone to carve out a better life for herself. One that didn't involve my dark tastes, my sadistic father, the cursed Order, or the past four years of a debt that should never have been hers to settle.

She'd helped me enough.

Salvatore was dead. The Order was appeased now that I'd taken part in their twisted games. They had ammo for blackmail should I choose to go against them, which was really why they participated in things like The Hunt and The Trails in the first place. To get dirt on the wealthiest, most powerful men in the United Kingdom and save it for a rainy bribe-ridden day.

Cosima was only ever meant to be a tool, and she'd fulfilled her purpose.

It should have been easy to let her go.

So why did my chest feel on fire?

Why could I hear the bones snapping and cracking as flames ate away at them, as my organs shriveled up to soot and ash?

Why couldn't I fathom a life without her?

I hit my head against my hands wrapped around the steering wheel and knew in the way I normally instinctively knew about changes in the stock market and trends in media that I'd never be able to get over her.

How did someone get over a person who had fundamentally changed their life?

I was strong. I'd been made into a man of intellect and steely determination. I could quit any addiction if I set my mind to it, maybe even my obsession with the girl with gold eyes.

But I didn't want to.

And that made all the difference.

I thought about that as I got out of the car, slipping silently through the small crowds down the street toward the man stalking Cosima. As I passed him without drawing his notice and then doubled back when another tram arrived to obscure us from the street to catch his thick neck in a chokehold and drag him farther into the alley. I thought of her silken skin as I wrapped my hands around his neck while he struggled and went red, then white with the effort and failure to breathe, and then I thought of her beautiful sorrow as she stood in the rain, rejoicing in the drops as I sharply turned my gloved hands to the right and felt the Order's sycophant's spine snap between my hands.

After I threw him into an overflowing dumpster, I took one last glance at my wife sitting in the small coffee shop drinking tea with her new strange savoir and a woman I'd called only hours before, and somehow curtailed my possessive rage and encompassing grief enough to get back into the car and drive to the airport.

Then, I thought about her still as I caught my private jet back to London, as Riddick picked me up in the Rolls and drove me straight to 10 Downing Street. Security tried to detain me before Prime Minister James Caldron himself stepped through the famous lacquered black door and crossed his arms over his chest at the sight of me.

"Alexander, you git, what brings you to my hovel?"

I stared at my old uni roommate with the familiar comfort of my implacable mask affixed to my face, and said, "I have something of a story to tell you, James, and at the end of it, you're going to help me take down one of the most corrupt organizations in the U.K., and you'll go down in history for it."

James stared at me for a long moment, his stare almost as aloof as my own. He didn't come from money the way most of my Cambridge compatriots in Trinity College had, but he was all the sharper for it.

It was just that razor wit that had driven a wedge between us after graduation when James had tried to recruit me to help his mechanisms in parliament, and I'd told him, quite honestly, I wasn't a man who did something for nothing.

"Why now?" he finally asked.

I felt the wedding ring I'd taken off, thrown into the lake behind Pearl Hall and then had retrieved after the Order had left, burning a hole in my pocket as I locked eyes with him, and said, "They took something from me. One thing that might have meant everything."

Chapter Four

COSIMA

I saw him. A year into my separation, a full twelve months into my self-imposed rehabilitation project to rid myself of his influence on my mind, body, and soul, I saw Alexander Davenport at Bulgari's annual Fashion Week party in Milan.

I stepped into the gilded room and felt the hair on the back of my neck stand up in the oddly static air. There was a ripple of awareness down my spine as I descended the marble steps into the crowded ballroom, that animal awareness I'd learned to hone like an alarm bell to tell me when I was being watched.

I was alone, unaccompanied by one of the few men I kept on rotation as potential dates to such functions. It was more impactful, I'd found, to enter the room as a beautiful woman unencumbered by the weight of a man at my side. It took confidence and power to arrive as an unaccompanied female, and I'd learned to take every opportunity to show power when the occasion arose. So, when I wanted to make an entrance, as I did that night because I was the star of not one, but three fashion house catwalks that week, I did it solo.

My eyes swept over the masses of gorgeously attired people, noting the fashion moguls I should talk to and the models I should avoid. I wasn't expecting my gaze to snag on the brilliant warmth of a head of golden hair.

I paused on the last step, my stilettoed foot hovering just off the ground as I clung to the bannister and let my eyes devour the man I hadn't seen in twelve months.

He was holding court unlike anyone I'd ever seen before, surrounded by a flock of avid admirers who stared at him, readying to hang onto his every word even though he gave them none. Instead, he stood quietly, proud, and perfectly groomed as a lord of the realm warranted. He was the most beautiful, powerful man anyone in the room had ever seen, and he knew it. People spoke at him, trying to lure him into conversation with pretty, flashing praise and the scintillating scent of gossip, but he remained unmoved.

Until something in the pressure of the air around him must have shifted, penetrated by the hot knife of my regard.

Instantly, his spine stiffened, and his eyes snapped to mine like powerful magnets clipping together. It didn't matter how many people stood between us like sheaves of paper stacked between our magnetized bodies. At that moment, it seemed the only two people in the room, in the universe, were us.

Instinctively, my body gathered itself to run. Not away from him, but toward. I wanted to throw myself across the room into his arms and then slide to the ground on my knees and beg him to take me home.

Home to Pearl Hall.

Home to wet and dreary England where I knew no one, but him and his.

Home was where he was, no matter how hard I'd tried to convince myself for the past twelve months it wasn't.

After all my hard work, the hours of therapy and meditation, the countless self-help books, and I was right back to where I'd been before.

My heart and body were slave to Alexander Davenport.

I opened my mouth to say something, lowered my foot to take the first step in his direction when his eyes went from smoke to stone, and his gaze cut away from mine.

I felt that knife's edge of his disregard cut me off at the knees, and I sank gracelessly from the last step to the ballroom floor, clinging to the rail to keep from falling.

Unhooked from his eyes, I noticed what he had turned to look at. Not what, but *whom*.

A gorgeous woman with hair like spun sunlight stood at his side wearing a smile as bright as the diamonds wrapped around her throat and a dress that was nearly as expensive.

She was the golden queen to his golden king.

They looked so perfectly suited, his arm wrapped tight around her hips, her hand pressed lightly to his chest, that for a moment, I wondered if they were real.

Alexander ducked his head to listen to something she spoke quietly in his ear and then broke into a smile like sunbeams cutting through clouds to bathe her in unfiltered warmth.

God, but he'd never smiled at me like that.

Not once, not *ever*.

I'd had private moments with him, small intimacies I collected like charms on a chain around my wrist but seeing him with her like that made them feel cheap and fake.

Nothing like the diamonds she wore around her arms that I knew instinctively that he had gifted her.

"You look thunderstruck, Cosi," Jensen Brask murmured as he took my elbow and gently pulled me into his side for stability. "What has happened?"

I placed my shaking hand over his forearm where it linked with mine and took a deep breath to settle my rabid heartbeat.

"Someone I once knew," I explained to the man who had taken me so thoroughly under his wing since I'd re-entered the modelling world heralded by the great Willa Percy. "I thought I saw a man I once knew, but it was just a trick of the light."

Or of the mind.

I wondered with a sinking gut whether my time apart from Alexander and the horrors we'd live through together had only distanced me from the pain of the memories and gilded them with a love and magnitude that had never really existed.

Jensen's platinum blond brow puckered, but he knew me well enough not to push me for answers. "Why don't you come meet some of your admirers then, my beautiful girl? There is nothing like the flattery of shallow people to make one feel better about themselves."

I laughed, as was his intention. Jensen might have been one of the most famed fashion house directors in the business, but he was not idle or vainglorious. He believed in hard work, dedication to the craft, and a rigorous level of self-discipline. He was a study in control, and I longed to model myself after him.

He held me close as we made the rounds, our laughter pretty and perfectly formed, canned like the giggles after a sitcom joke. He knew how to play the game, and he'd taught me well how to do it too. If he sensed my discomfiture as I moved around the room, aware of every shifting angle between myself and Alexander like a star orbiting the sun, he didn't say.

But I knew he was aware because of that hold on me, tight and comforting, as if he knew I felt safer shackled than I did free.

"Did you see him?" a woman I'd met countless times whose name I could never remember expressed excitedly at one point two hours after my arrival. "Did you see the Earl of Thornton?"

I stiffened, a gazelle downwind of a predator.

Jenson calmly patted my arm. "I did."

The woman touched her blond updo self-consciously as she looked over our shoulders, presumably at the man in question. "Isn't he the most handsome man you ever saw?"

Somehow, instinctively, my charm arose to save the day. "My brother would take umbrage with that. He's awfully vain, but I have to admit, he has good reason to be."

Jenson and the other man we were with laughed.

"He is ridiculously good looking," my friend and artistic director agreed. "It irks me to no end that he refuses to campaign with you for St. Aubyn."

I shrugged a shoulder because we'd had this conversation before. "He doesn't like standing still if he doesn't have to. Acting is more his gig."

"*Gig.*" Jenson shook his head at me, but his small smile was fond. "You're becoming more American every day. I wish I could lure you back to England."

Never, I thought fiercely even though a secret voice I tried to mute whispered, *Maybe one day.*

I was hyper aware of Alexander's placement in the room. Unwittingly, I found myself angling my body and shifting my feet to keep him in my orbit, to feel the gravitational pull he exuded to its maximum effect.

Just being in the same room as him made me ache for the feel of the hard marble of the ballroom floor beneath my knees.

"Who is the woman he's with?"

My throat closed up as I waited for the answer.

"Apparently, that's Agatha Howard, of Castle Howard and the Earl of Suffolk Howards," one of the women helpfully pointed out. "She's been one of Britain's most eligible catches since she came of age. It was rumored she was supposed to marry the younger Prince Alasdair, but who can blame her for choosing Lord Thornton instead, hmm?"

No one. No one could blame her because while Prince Alasdair was a freaking *prince*, and at twenty-five, already handsome enough to be an international heartthrob, Alexander was, well, like a god. Someone so viscerally powerful and unflappably cool that he incited the urge to kneel and prostrate oneself before him on the off chance he would bestow you with a cutting look from those quicksilver eyes.

"He's one of the most powerful men in the nation," Jensen pitched in. "His influence, if he chose to use it, would be unparalleled, but he doesn't take part in politics."

"Why not?" I asked before I could help myself.

I was weak. There were Google alerts set up for Alexander Davenport, Earl of Thornton, heir to the Duke of Greythorn on my computer. I knew he owned the largest media company in England, Davenport Media Holdings, that consisted of a large radio network, news station, and popular culture magazine. He focused on work, he rarely dated, though he was seen out with a variety of upper-class women, and he donated regularly to a rotation of charities.

Six months ago, he'd appeared in an article in *The Guardian* because he'd donated two million pounds to STOP THE TRAFFIK, a United Kingdom-based charity to help victims of sex trafficking.

I didn't know how he got that one past the Order, or if they all thought it was amusing he'd donated so hypocritically.

Despite my righteous anger at his duplicity, reading that article had given me a brief flare of hope.

Maybe he cared.

Maybe he regretted the awful things he had done to me and put me through, enough to scour the globe for me in order to beg for my forgiveness.

"Not a political type of bloke, I think." The man shrugged. "Though I must say I'm surprised you haven't met him. He likes to keep his finger deep in all his pies."

Jensen shot him a disgusted look at the metaphor. "He specifically asked not to be involved with St. Aubyn anymore, beyond the obvious financial obligations."

A chill started in my toes and worked its way like creeping ice across a pane of glass over my entire body.

"What?" I breathed.

"Davenport," the man, I thought his name might have been Franklin, clarified. "He owns the House of St. Aubyn. His great-grandmother started it in the 1920s and most recently, his mother ran it before...before her untimely death."

Alexander owned St. Aubyn.

Dread pooled in my stomach as everything clicked together.

He'd been outside my auditions for the brand when I'd first met him, when I'd unwittingly saved his life and basically thrust myself into his clutches.

The scent. The one I'd been made to wear the entire time I was at Pearl Hall, the one that seemed to smell like me but amplified, the one I'd discovered was a recent, highly popular debut of the company's first signature fragrance.

It was modelled after me. Alexander had created a perfume based on my scent and named it *D'oro*, or *Gold*. For my eyes, my money eyes.

My breath wasn't moving properly through my lungs. I could feel it waffle and whimper through my parted lips, wavering as it went down so that somehow, I wasn't getting enough oxygen. I felt precariously light-headed.

What did any of that mean?

Jensen mistook my shock. "His lack of involvement has nothing to do with you being the face of our brand, Cosi. He's a busy man, and he doesn't have time to play with all his toys."

I almost gave myself away at his apt comparison. I almost protested that I wasn't just *one* of Alexander's toys. I was his favourite.

Or I had been.

I thought of prissy, perfect Agatha Howard and wondered if she knew how to take a spanking, if she could make him come with just her mouth and throat as I could.

Possessive rage lit me up like I was dry kindling.

Why the fuck hadn't Alexander come over to claim me now that he saw me? What other reason could have dragged him from his dreary homeland to mine, to some insipid fashion event when he hadn't shown up at any before, even for his own House of St. Aubyn?

He must be here to claim me, I thought wildly, my heart beating at the door of my chest, waiting for Alexander to somehow answer the knock from all the way across the room.

"He's a right arsehole, if you must know," Franklin said as he sipped his champagne, and I decided that I instantly liked him. "My flatmate went to uni with him and told me he'd never met a man so full of his own bullshit."

That startled a laugh from me, a loud burst of hilarity that I didn't bother covering politely with my hand. The moment I did, the air around me went static with electricity, and I knew Alexander had heard me.

I remembered how he'd loved to hear me laugh; how much I'd fought to make him express his humour that way too. I remembered that I'd made him laugh eighteen times on the one birthday I'd spent with him.

My chest felt lighter with hope.

I was one of the most successful up-and-coming models in the fashion industry. I had already saved up enough money for a down payment on an apartment in New York City close enough to Elena and Mama in Little Italy that I could walk to their brownstone, but far enough away to grant me some peace. I had friends. I had autonomy. I'd worked so hard for all of it, sweat and sobbed and made myself sick to secure a better life for myself.

And at that moment, I wanted to give it all up again for the most enigmatic man I'd ever known just on the off chance he'd want me back.

Before I could help myself, I turned around, my gaze unerringly finding his through the mass of beautiful people. He stood at the opposite end of the room, as far from me as he could be in the shared space. It wasn't an accident. One look at his cold face, his distant eyes as if he was gazing at a stranger and not his runaway wife, solidified my awareness of his contempt for me.

My breath left my body as if I'd been run into by a sixteen-wheeler.

"Cosima?" I was vaguely aware of Jensen touching my arm. "Are you all right, love?"

No.

No, fuck me, but I wasn't all right. I wanted to close my eyes and curl into myself in a dark place so that I could cry into my knees in peace.

One year of shoring up my defences, one year of speculating how Alexander would have reacted when he'd found out I was gone.

One year of waiting for him to find me and drag me back to his underworld dominion.

And now this.

Indifference so acute it seemed to cut me off at the knees.

Alexander shifted his gaze from mine as if looking through

a ghost and then gently leaned down to press a kiss to Agatha fucking Howard's perfect golden head before he turned on his heel and swiftly made his way out of the room.

Before I could stop myself, I was following.

A few people tried to impede me with polite conversation, but it was like I was underwater, submerged so deeply in my desire to interact with Alexander again that I couldn't hear anyone else. I rushed up the steps and out the door into the cool Milano winter night, scanning the Piazza del Duomo for a tall man with a crown of golden hair.

I caught the glint of it out of the corner of my eye and watched as Alexander strode purposefully to the massive white cathedral itself even though it was closed and locked for the night. He shook hands with a man who appeared out of the shadows and then pushed through the massive central bronze doors into the holy space.

I wondered how he didn't catch on fire.

Swiftly, I ran down the steps on my six-inch Gucci heels, thankful that years of modelling had made me sure-footed as I navigated the cobblestones.

I was out of breath when I reached the looming gothic doors, terrified that someone would appear out of the night to stop me from chasing after Alexander.

No one did.

The cathedral was empty and resplendently gothic in the murky moonlight spilling in through the multitudes of windows. I could hear my steps ringing out across the marble, echoing against the vaulted ceilings and depressed altars.

I felt like a sacrificial virgin voluntarily walking toward her own slaughter, but I couldn't bring myself to give up the chase as I searched the massive structure for him. I stopped before the statue of Saint Bartholomew with his flayed skin wrapped around his exposed flesh like a stole, as if he was proud of his vulnerability, pleased with his sacrifices. I reached out to run a finger over the smooth marble of his skinless muscles and shuddered with empathy.

I half expected to find Alexander behind the altar to the right of the sculpture, a curved knife in his hands and cloak over his head, waiting to kill me and offer me up to the Order's god of wine and revelry.

He wasn't.

Instead, the door to the stairs leading up to the roof was slightly parted, a cool wind whistling through the crack like a call for me to enter.

I counted the steps as I ascended in the pitch dark, focusing on the two hundred fifty footfalls instead of the growing anticipation churning through my system like acid, eating away at me from the inside out.

Would he be happy to see me?

Had he lured me away from the party so that he could claim me properly as his own once more after over a year of frantic searching for me? Would he punish me with his hand against my ass and my knees against the unforgiving marble as penance for my sin of running so we could move on from this place together, cleansed and reborn together again after his punishment?

I didn't know how that would work. There was still Noel and the Order to consider, still my family and the secret of Salvatore's continued existence after Alexander had supposedly killed him.

Still so many secrets, ones better off left undiscovered.

I'd unearth them all with my bare hands until the skin peeled and cracked and bled if it meant Alexander would pluck me out of the limbo my life had become and take me back home with him.

The door creaked as I pushed it open, then banged against the wall so loudly it sounded like a gunshot.

Alexander wasn't startled.

He stood in the middle of the roof on the narrow flat platform between the soaring buttresses and complicated carved spires.

I felt like peasant entering a king's throne room, and my knees nearly buckled before they could carry me across the roof into his space. The cold window broke my flesh into ripples, and my nipples beaded in the sheer fabric of my dress. I could feel my pulse settle deep and heavy in my groin, a slow beat like a kick drum at a pagan ritual thrumming through my body from my center.

Alexander did not move. He didn't even blink. He just watched me cross the space to him as if he had known all his life we would one day meet on the roof of the most famous cathedral in Italy under the cover of stars and a yellow moon the same shade as my eyes.

I opened my mouth to say his name, but, "Master," emerged instead.

Old habits—old programming—were slow to die, apparently.

Alexander blinked then, a slow click of his thickly lashed eyes like the mechanical movement of a shuttering lens.

He'd never seemed less human than he was then.

I stared at the cruel god before me and knew how utterly inane my fantasies of his reciprocated love had been.

"Stop searching me," he said finally, his voice slicing through the air, calculated as a whip strike against my back. After all this time, he still seemed able to read my mind. "Stop the searches, stop the waiting and wishing like a heartsick fool for me to return to you and bring you back to Pearl Hall. It won't happen, and it's frankly pathetic that you're pining after your abuser like some doleful victim. Honestly, I thought you were better than that."

I recoiled, my heel catching in the stonework oddly as I stepped back so that I went careening to my knee.

Alexander didn't bat an eyelash.

"You own St. Aubyn," I accused him in a stronger voice

than I would have thought I could manage. "Did you send Sinclair to me? Willa Percy?"

Had he orchestrated their entry into my life? Was he the reason I'd had a place to stay in New York City while I recovered from my heartbreak, the reason Willa Percy had decided I would be a much better fit for St. Aubyn than the girl they'd hired a year ago after I disappeared?

Alexander crossed his massive arms over his tuxedo-clad chest and blinked at him. "You think too much of yourself. Why would I waste my time on a slave? Let alone one who reneged on her contract and disappeared without a trace."

"You found me now," I said defiantly as if that changed anything. "You've found me, and now what?"

He shrugged, such a casual gesture that it seemed wrong on his broad shoulders.

Alexander wasn't a casual man, so the mannerism felt wrong.

Contrived.

Hope fluttered again in my chest.

"I could sue you for breach of contract?" he suggested coldly.

"Is that all you want to do?" I asked, eyeing him closely as I stood up and stalked closer to him.

I could see a muscle leap in his jaw, and it made me feel like a queen.

His breath froze in his throat for a brief second as I pressed my breasts to his chest, ran a hand up the silky lapel of his blazer, and then wrapped it around the side of his neck so I could feel his pulse against my palm.

When I looked up into his eyes, the remoteness was gone, replaced with a ferocity that made me hot with want and cold with terror.

"You married me, Xan," I said, my words landing like soft blows. "You once told me that if you ever felt moved to marry, it would be because you wanted to give your future wife your protection and the promise of your undying love. You said you would always care about her, about *me*, no matter what happened."

We were silent as my words glittered in the air around us, wrapping us in their magic, in their complete and utter beauty.

Alexander wasn't a man of many things, but I knew he was a man of his word.

He couldn't marry me just to cast me aside.

"I think you're forgetting the part where you ran from me," he said, his hand shooting up to catch me around the neck in a firm grip. "I think you are forgetting that you embarrassed me in front of Britain's elite and made a fool of me when I put myself on the line with the Order of Dionysus to *protect* you."

"I had my reasons," I breathed tightly through the pressure around my throat. "Trust me, Xan, I didn't want to leave you."

"Even if you didn't, I don't care. You were amusing while it lasted, but you've been gone for months now, and I've found myself new amusements." He watched the colour drain out of my face, his words affecting me more than his stranglehold ever could. "You mean nothing to me, Cosima Lombardi. You were a slave, a nothing I made into a momentary something, but your time is done. Stop obsessing over me, move the fuck on, and if I ever hear of you saying my name, ever see you step a single *foot* in England again, I promise you there will be consequences. None of which you will like as you have before."

"Xan," I tried again only to cry out as his other hand fisted at the back of my hair, and he started to drag me to the side of the roof.

I screamed as he thrust me over the balustrade so that I was dangling precariously over the piazza below me, bracketed by gargoyles jeering at me from either side of the spires.

My eyes were wide with shock as I stared up into Alexander's emotionless expression. I was gripping his wrists where he held me instinctively.

In all our experiences together, he had never threatened me like this. To hurt me just for the sake of hurting me, to scare me enough to fear for my life.

I couldn't fathom why he was doing it, not with my body flooded with adrenaline and my mind overrun with fear.

The only option that seemed available to me was simple.

He truly didn't care.

His rejection burned in my heart, but I'd come too far to give up without a fight. I'd hurt him, I'd run from him, and that would have seemed like the ultimate betrayal and rejection. He needed to know I trusted him, that I hadn't wanted to go.

With my eyes locked on his, silver and gold, I held my breath and slowly let go of my death grip on his wrists so that the only thing keeping me from tumbling back into space was his grasp on my neck and hair and my ankles hooked tight over the balustrade.

"I didn't want to leave you, Xan," I told him in a voice like a splitting thread as I bared my entire self to him. "I've never felt happier, more complete in my entire life as I did the moment we were declared man and wife. A year later and I still miss you so much it feels like a constant echo in my soul."

I felt like raw, tenderized meat hanging from a hook in my spine as he held me half suspended over the edge of the Duomo, but I didn't move.

I didn't even breathe.

Instead, I watched a flurry of emotions turn Alexander's eyes from angry smoke to the storm clouds and rainwater of despair and finally, achingly, to wet concrete. I knew any second they would set into stone, and I would be done, locked out of his head and his heart forever.

"I love you," I told him, and it was the truest thing I'd ever known. "I love you, Alexander."

Back to rainwater for one deeply profound moment, where those wet grey eyes fell from mine to my lips in cool trails like drops against my cheek. I saw the agony in his eyes, felt the emotion mirrored in my own, and thought he would crush me to his chest, wrap his strong arms around me, and never again let me go.

And then...

Stone.

Cold, grey intractable granite like the cliffs in the Peak District that rose around Pearl Hall like a sea of rocky waves.

He was gone.

Gone to me forever.

He pulled me back to my feet and dropped his hands from me as if I was toxic.

"Not a word, not one sight of you. Is that understood, slave?" he asked me.

I blinked at him, trying to keep a tenuous hold of the calamity of emotions in my throat that threatened to drown me like a tidal wave.

He took the blink for what it was, shocked acceptance. Then, just when I thought he would stalk away and disappear from my life, he lunged forward, drove his hands into either side of my hair above my ears, yanked my head back and kissed me so hard I knew it would tattoo my lips blue with bruises. I gasped as he bit my bottom lip so hard it broke the skin and the tang of blood erupted between us. He collected it with one searing swipe of his tongue and then thrust it deep inside my mouth as if feeling the cataclysmic amount of pain in my body wasn't enough, he wanted me to taste my own heartbreak too.

My hand flew to my busted lip as he stepped back and then away, turning on his heel and striding off with brisk intent as if he hadn't just shattered me open on the roof of

Milan's Duomo, as if he hadn't left me bloody and irrevocably broken.

He didn't look back.

And after another hour spent weeping into my knees in the dark of the rooftop's spires and stone creatures, after I collected myself enough to see through my blurry eyes and walk down to the Piazza to catch a cab… after all that, for the next three years, I didn't look back either.

Part Two

DANGER

NON DECOR, DECO. I AM NOT LED, I LEAD

Chapter Five

COSIMA

Three Years Later.

The flash of cameras nearly blinded me, but after over three years in the spotlight, I knew how to dodge the light and duck into the darkness. I tipped my chin down, the silky hair tucked behind my ear slipping out to curtain half of my face from the roped-off crowd of photogs and reporters lining the red carpet.

It was my first time back in England in almost four years. I'd always claimed that wild horses couldn't drag me back to the godforsaken country, but my brother being nominated for his first BAFTA was reason enough to make me a liar. I flew in the day before the awards show, and I had a return ticket for the crack of dawn the morning after. Less than thirty-six hours in the country. Definitely not enough time for Alexander Davenport to sniff me out and punish me for stepping foot in his country against his explicit orders.

Alexander Davenport could go fuck himself.

"Miss Lombardi," a reporter called as I emerged from the limo and accepted my brother's hand. "Is it true you and Mr. Matlock are engaged?"

Sebastian wound my arm tightly under his, pulling me so close I could feel the warmth of his hip against my side.

I didn't like personal questions.

I didn't take interviews, and I didn't engage in idle gossip.

Ironically, that made the rumor mill churn faster, harder. Gossip about the mysterious, beautiful Lombardi twins ran rampant across tabloids and celebrity news.

Where had we come from, who did we love, what did we live for?

The only thing that was clear was our futures.

We were rising stars on the meteoric ascension to a permanent position in the sky of fame and success.

"Sebastian, do you want to address the rumors that you and your sister have a more than platonic relationship?"

My twin turned to iron, freezing in our slow progress down the red carpet. I could feel him weaponize with rage, the appalling accusation honing the edge of his ever present but latent anger.

I didn't attempt to wield or shield him.

Sebastian was a much better actor than I could ever dream of being.

He shot the audacious reporter a smile that was inherently charming, veiling his wrath with the pretty costume of his smile. "You've clearly watched too many episodes of *Game of Thrones*. I'd suggest finding something more worthwhile to occupy your time. Perhaps genuine journalistic research?"

His cutting remark delivered, Seb tugged me forward to the X marked out on the carpet where we were meant to pose for a series of photographs.

He tucked me into his side and stared down at me with a stock issue smile as the *click* and *clack* of cameras rattled around us.

"Ignore them," he told me sternly.

I looked up into his golden eyes, counting the striations in his irises the way I'd done my entire life. His eyes differed from mine only in that minute way, spikes of sunlight instead of my pinpricks of burnished bronze.

"I don't care," I said softly, beaming at him so that the catcalls that followed would drown out my words. "It's them who are sick, not us."

Sebastian's smile thinned, his own demons daring him to accept that for the truth.

In some ways, I believed my words.

I certainly wasn't in a relationship with my brother, nor engaged to Mason Matlock, or a closeted lesbian with my best friend and fellow model Erika Van Bellegham. None of the rumors were true, no matter how fucked up they created them to be.

But I *was* sick.

Only my disease was terminal. It ate away the marrow of my bones until I was hollow, fragile as a small bird perched on a branch in a gale, but unable to fly.

It infiltrated the chambers of my heart, corroding and calcifying the arteries. The organ still worked, still pumped hot blood through my limbs, but it didn't *feel*.

Joy was a glass half empty no matter how marvellous the news or accomplishment because I was a woman half alive.

The other portion of my heart, of my soul, was still buried deep within the underworld, cradled in the cruel hands of a man who had stolen me away years ago but never really let me go. It echoed in the antique rooms of a home on the other side of the Atlantic and ghosted across the landscape of a place called Pearl Hall.

Alexander Davenport had held me prisoner in his dark kingdom and coaxed me to eat of the forbidden fruit so that now, so many years later across so many miles, I was still intrinsically shackled to his domain.

Even after the cruel goodbye in Milan.

Even after extensive hours of therapy with one of the best woman's trauma psychiatrists in Manhattan.

Years later, an ocean of time between me and the island of my servitude, and I was still empty and indentured to the past.

"I suppose whatever helps us sleep at night," Seb murmured, pulling me from my thoughts as he turned us into a new pose for the shouting cameramen.

"You help me," I told him before we shot twin gleaming smiles to our captive audience. "Always."

Our progress along the carpet was slow and mind-numbing, but I didn't mind being Sebastian's arm candy. After years of hard work, my brother had finally established the kind of success usually found in a Hallmark movie. His first film, written and starred in by his truly, had been an international success, first at Cannes Film Festival, and then in America where it was optioned by Sony.

Now, he was one of the hottest commodities in Hollywood.

I smiled blankly at the third woman to interview us about Sebastian's feelings on his first BAFTA nomination and second Oscar nomination in as many years. I tried to ease the strain from my smile and knew I'd succeeded when the cameraman blinked owlishly at my expression.

"No one special?" the seasoned reporter asked, a gleam in her heavily made-up eyes.

Sebastian flashed her one of his megawatt smiles, the shine making the reporter blink dazedly. "Anyone can be special for a night."

"A little birdy told me you refused to be tied to Tate and Savannah Richardson's latest project despite their best attempts to seduce you into taking the lead role." I watched her swallow hard, her resolve to mine a potential trove of gossip deeper than her desire to bed my handsome brother.

Seb tensed just slightly under my arm. He didn't like any mention of Savannah Richardson. She'd had many names in her storied life, but despite Sebastian's superlative charms, she had never worn the name of Lombardi, and now he couldn't stand the sound of her in his ear.

Before he could respond, the entertainment reporter swung to me with a wide, faux-innocent smile, and said, "Mason Matlock was seen walking out of Tiffany's with their signature Robin's egg blue bag just yesterday. Do you approve of your sister's future husband?"

"Speculation is the indulgence of the lazy," I told her coolly, channelling my inner Elena, trying to be as aloof and unflappable as my eldest sister. A little voice told me I was also tapping into the influence of my ex-Master. Only Alexander Davenport, lord of the freaking realm, could deliver such scathing condescension so effortlessly. "Mason is a good friend, nothing more."

"You speak as if marriage is off the table."

I pressed my thumb to the bare ring finger of my left hand where I constantly felt the phantom weight of a gold ring I once wore for less than four hours.

"It is," I said, staring into the camera, wondering if my husband was watching. "I won't ever marry."

Not again.

Legally, I couldn't, not without a divorce to the Earl of Thornton, heir to the Dukedom of Greythorn and one of England's wealthiest estates. That was something I would never do. I'd left as Noel had wanted, and nothing would coerce me into getting in touch with Alexander.

I'd considered it countless times over the years. At first, I'd wanted to call him for the simplest of reasons. For permission to come when I touched myself at night, desperate for the level of pleasure only he could grant me. For the right to even leave the house and talk to men who weren't him.

I missed him when I dressed in the morning, hating the way I fit the clothes to my curves instead of dressing his edges. I craved him during the after-work rush, seeing businessmen hurry home and knowing that across the pond Alexander would be doing the same thing only I wouldn't be there on my knees to greet him.

To say my new life in America had been an adjustment was a gross understatement.

I'd been miserable.

The events of the past four years were indistinguishable, my teardrops running the ink in the pages of a diary I'd taken to keeping just to mark the time.

Before Alexander and after Alexander.

Before, my life had been sad, but I'd had no context to deepen my despair.

Now, now, I knew exactly what I was missing.

And horror of horrors, it was the cold bite of a whip wielded in the ruthless, exacting hands of a Dominant and Lord named Alexander Davenport.

My therapist called it Stockholm Syndrome. She told me I felt the most betrayed by his inhumane goodbye in Milan because I'd grown unhealthfully attached to the cage he'd constructed around me, that my continued melancholy was a side effect that would eventually wear off as I readjusted.

Three years of therapy and nothing had changed.

Sebastian ushered us past the rest of the reporters, greasing our way with his slippery smile and a few well-placed winks. We both stopped just inside the hotel's luxurious lobby and mutually decided on a recessed corner near the elevators to take a moment of peace before going upstairs into the ballroom.

My brother let out a gusty exhale as he leaned back against the marble wall and drew his collar away from his neck with a hooked finger.

"You're more on edge than I've seen you in a long while," I told him, frowning up into his face as I noticed the strain around his eyes and mouth, the deep bruises from lack of sleep beneath his golden gaze.

He closed his eyes. "Leave me be, *mia bella sorella.*"

"Seb…you can talk to me." I told him something he already knew in his bones.

He peeked at me through one squinted eye. "Oh? Just as you talk to me?"

It was my turn to sigh.

We were still close in a way only twins could ever understand. His presence in a room alone brought me unquantifiable comfort, and the touch of his hand to my shoulder grounded me like lightning through a steel rod.

But things had changed.

We'd only been apart for fifteen months, but those months had been compressed with rapid, irrevocable change. Change so significant it had altered us as individuals and as confidantes.

I was no longer that woman who shared every intimacy with her family, who babbled about her day happily in the carefree manner of a bubbling brook. Now, I was shadows and secrets so dark they were like black holes sucking at everything else light in my life until it was diminished or devoured.

Those black holes ate up the words to describe my particular brand of pain, and the memories that had made it so before I could even think to voice them.

"There's nothing to say beyond what I've told you." I tried to placate him even though I knew he would frown before he even did, disgusted with my bald-faced lie.

I placed a soothing hand on his arm and tried again. "Really, whatever is in the past can stay there. You can only be haunted by the past as long as you keep the door open into your present."

"Don't feed me fortune cookie *cazzate*. You don't want to talk to me, fine, but don't be a hypocrite and incite me to share with you what you won't share with me."

I bit my lip, wondering if I should say what I'd been desperate to say since I'd run into him on the street outside Club Dionysus in London three years ago. "Does your unhappiness have more to do with Savannah and her new husband… or the handsome actor I saw you walking with in London?"

My brother went still.

Goosebumps rippled across my flesh because the threat in that stillness reminded me so much of Alexander.

I knew instinctively, I'd been wrong to go there.

But as I opened my mouth to apologize, Sebastian cut his blazing yellow eyes to mine.

"If you speak to me again about them, I won't hesitate to delve further into exactly what you were doing with the Earl of Thornton in England when you'd just told Mama, the girls, and me that you were working in Milan. I won't be considerate of your secrets any longer, and I'll drag them kicking and screaming into the light for everyone to see."

"You're threatening me?" I asked, my voice soft with shock.

Sebastian had never spoken to me like that before. Never looked at me with barely constrained violence in his tiger eyes and fury so quick on his lips.

"No," he said after a long moment of vibrating rage. I watched him pull himself together second by second, sucking a deep breath through his lips and then exhaling as if performing an exorcism. "No, Cosi, I would never threaten you. Please, just…just don't speak about him, *them*, and we won't have any problems."

"I'd tell you if it wasn't dangerous," I confided in him,

stepping closer to press my palm to the hard angle of his jaw. "I'm just trying to protect you."

And myself.

A muscle in his cheek jumped as he ground his teeth, but he put his hand over my own on his face and then kissed my palm. "That's exactly the stuff of my nightmares. That my beautiful, sweet sister had to do the unspeakable to get us out of that Neapolitan sinkhole."

"The past," I reminded him as we both silently decided to step back into the crowd to find our seats for the ceremony. "Should stay in the past."

Seb squeezed my hand, and I looked over to see his face exposed like a raw nerve, bloody skin and muscles peeled away to reveal the ugly truth of his own experiences. A second later, someone called his name, and his habitual expression of levity slid into place.

I stood quietly at his side as he introduced me to industry acquaintances and lingered to talk to close friends. They only wanted my smile and a long perusal of my body clad in a red bustier corset lace and silk gown by Oscar de la Renta. I liked to wear red; it reminded me of wet poppies and spanked asses, of strength and lust, and memories that ached in a good way like a massage to sore muscles.

I was happy to play dumb and pretty as I chewed over my brother's obvious heartbreak regarding a *man*. He was so easy in his masculinity, in his love of women in whatever shape and size they were packaged in that it had honestly never occurred to me that he may be bisexual. I didn't think he was gay, not with the obvious way he appreciated females and their forms, but the fact that the mere mention of a man could so clearly unhinge him made me believe he had to have been at least a little in love with him.

I wanted to know the story. I wanted to know why he lusted after Savannah Richardson even as he seemed to revile her very name, and how Sebastian had become attached to her ex-husband, mega-movie star Adam Meyers.

But I wouldn't press.

It was in my nature to dig and delve past people's boundaries. I was an emotional archeologist, dissatisfied with anything less than the naked, vulnerable truth of a person. But I would never force my best friend, my brother, to unveil his past when he wasn't ready.

It would have to be a story for another day.

Maybe a day when I could share my own with him too.

As if my thoughts had summoned him like a demon from Hell, a British accent I recognized from years ago though even then I'd only heard it a few times, rang out with wit behind me.

I froze, as if not moving would make me invisible to him.

Without turning around to face him and the threat he posed, I silently but swiftly moved through the crowds of people, mingling amid the red velvet theatre seats to a hallway that led to the ladies' restroom.

A few women were gathered in front of the mirrors, checking their makeup and gossiping, but I ignored them to wet some paper towel and hold it to the back of my neck in a foolhardy attempt to calm myself.

I wanted to run. Out the door of the theatre, out of the city and straight to the imposing grounds of Pearl Hall where we could lock the gates against intruders from the past. Where Alexander could protect me from men even more evil than himself as he had before.

My back ached with phantom pain as I thought about those twenty-five lashes he'd taken for me, as I thought about the blood and the sacrifice of that moment.

I'd thought Alexander would do anything to protect me. *Cazzo*, he'd even married me to do so.

But he wasn't here.

He couldn't be, and he didn't *want* to be.

It was just me.

So I stared at my ashen face in the mirror, blinked my fake lashes hard over my frightened eyes, and filled them with determination instead.

If I was being hunted, I would fight.

I didn't need Alexander or Dante or Salvatore to protect me.

I could damn well do it myself.

With a bracing inhale, I bent to part the high slit in my gown even further and took the SOG Salute mini folding knife from my garter belt to palm it in my hand. It had been a gift from Dante, engraved with a quote from Sun Tzu's *The Art of War*, a book he had forced on me when I first moved to New York.

"Appear weak when you are strong, and strong when you are weak."

He wanted me to be prepared even though I'd teased him for being paranoid. For once, Dante hadn't found me amusing.

I was grateful then for his overprotectiveness because if I was going to face a man I'd believed to be dead for the past four years, I wanted to be armed and ready.

He wasn't waiting for me in the hallway when I emerged from the bathroom, and I wondered if he'd even spotted me in the crowded theatre.

I shouldn't have wondered.

The disciples of the Order of Dionysus were sharks. They could smell blood in the water.

Sharp pain burst through the back of my skull as a hand reached out and yanked brutally on the strands so that I went reeling backward.

Hot breath fanned across my face as I was turned and then slammed against the wall with a hot body pressed chest to thighs to mine.

Lord Ashcroft's floppy sand-coloured hair hung in his

sneering face. He was shorter, my height, so we were eye to eye, mouth hovering so close to mouth.

"No Thornton to save you now, pet," he taunted me, pulling on my hair so tightly that tears sprang to my eyes unbidden and sluiced down my cheeks. "No one to tell me I can't take what I want."

"You want the woman who got you strapped to a chair made of iron spikes? The one who got you bludgeoned over the head during The Hunt?" I snapped back.

The weight of my little knife was cold and heavy in the palm I had caught between our bodies. I tried to wiggle it free, and he pinned me with his hips.

"Such a little slut, trying to get at my cock already." He dipped his head and ran his nose along my throat before tracing the same path with his tongue. "I've thought about taking you countless times over the years, but I never thought I would be so lucky as to bump into you right here in London. What a silly little chit you are to come back into the lion's den."

"Are you really going to rape me against the wall at Royal Albert Hall?" I asked before turning my head sharply, ignoring the flash of pain at the back of my head, so I could bite savagely into his earlobe.

He cursed viciously and slammed a knee up against my groin so hard, I doubled over into him.

"You have no idea how much I would love to do just that. I dream about the memory of your sweet, filthy mouth around my cock, and I cannot wait to test out your cunt. But I have all the time in the world to use you up, pet. Do you know why?" he whispered into my ear as he nuzzled my hair.

"*Vaffanculo!*" I spat at him.

Fuck you!

He laughed and ground himself against my thigh. "You will, you impatient minx. You will beg me to fuck you because if you don't, I'll sell footage of you and your precious ex-Master fucking on the floor of Pearl Hall's ball-room." He snickered as I froze against him. "Oh, didn't you know? Every brother of the Order is made to film the first time he breaks and takes his slave. We have a little friendly contest each year to see who can take them the most viciously."

His tongue lashed out against my ear, and then his teeth were there. "Alexander did a good job with you—I've jerked off to the footage many times—but I could have done better. I *will* do better. If you don't want me to ruin your shining career by showing the world just what a slut you are, you'll agree to be my new slave."

No.

I was done.

I was done with men and their power playing, their conceit and barbarity. I wasn't just a pretty pawn to be sacrificed and passed around by the will of another more influential player.

I was Cosima Ruth Lombardi.

Born August 24th 1998 in Napoli, Italy, to Caprice Maria Lombardi and Amadeo Vitale Salvatore.

I was not a victim.

I was a survivor.

And there was no way in hell that I would kneel at the feet of anyone ever again unless it was by my choice alone.

Schooling my face into the sultry smile that had made me famous, that had graced the covers of *Sports Illustrated* and *Vogue*, I rubbed my lower body against Ashcroft's to distract him from the hand I freed from between us.

I pressed my lips to his ear and clicked my tongue to cover the *snick* of the knife unfolding. "You don't need to blackmail, sir. I'm just a slutty vessel for cock, and I'm desperate to be used like a rag to catch your cum again and again."

He hesitated over my words, doubting my sincerity even as his hard cock throbbed against my leg.

That hesitation was his weakness, so I capitalized on it with my strength.

Men.

They always underestimated me.

Quick as a flash, my knife was at his throat, directly under my lips. I slid the blade tight up against his skin and watched blood bleed like a ruby necklace.

For a moment, I yearned for the weight of my gold and ruby Davenport collar across my neck.

"You'll leave me alone, Ashcroft," I threatened softly as I dug the blade deeper and watched his skin part like butter in an inch-long gash. I felt vampiric, drunk on blood lust. I wanted to lap up the red and spit it in his face to give him a literal taste of his own fucking medicine. "You'll leave me alone, or I swear to your unholy god Dionysus that I will find a way to gut you like a fish."

"You don't scare me," he retorted, squeezing his fingers tighter in my hair. "Are you really going to slit my throat at Royal Albert Hall?" he mocked.

I dragged the blade around the side of his throat, lengthening the wound.

"Sometimes the worst monsters hide in the prettiest packages," I sneered at him, then shifted slightly so that I could violently jab my knee into his balls.

I stepped out from the wall as he doubled over, cupping his groin and moaning like the pathetic sack of shit he was.

"You've been warned," I said as a parting shot before turning on my heel and somewhat miraculously walking away from him without looking back.

I made it to my seat beside Sebastian just at the lights dimmed in the colossal theatre and the host of the evening, Graham Norton, stepped out onto the stage to a flurry of cheers and applause.

My stomach roiled and toiled like the storm over the high seas, and my skin was clammy with stress sweat. I felt sick and giddy with fear and triumph because I knew that even though I'd bested Ashcroft this time, I was on his radar again, and the Order was made up of hunters who never ceased their chase.

He would find me again, and I had to be ready for it.

"Cosi?" Sebastian asked softly. "What's happened?"

Sebastian could always see my inner turmoil even more than my mother and sisters could. We'd always had the strange ability that seasoned sailors have, to read the stars and find direction in them when no others could.

"Did someone hurt you?" he demanded, sitting up in his seat so that he could suspiciously scan the dim theatre from visible threats.

"No," I said, surprised by the strength in my voice. "Someone tried to get handsy with me, but I know how to defend myself."

Sebastian peered at me as the crowd around us laughed at something the famous British comedian and talk show host said in his opening monologue.

"I should have been there," he said, and it was about so much more than just that one incident. "I never should have left you alone."

I shrugged and patted his hand on my thigh so he would know everything was fine.

I wasn't bitter about the sacrifices I had made for my family. Given the choice, I would do it all again in a heartbeat. But I'd learned an important lesson from those martyred choices, and it wasn't one I would soon forget.

At the end of the day, the only champion I could count on was myself.

So, if Ashcroft was gunning for me, I would have to be the one to stop him.

Chapter Six

COSIMA

*A*nyone who says the life of a model is a glamourous one has clearly never woken at the crack of dawn and then spent hours on their feet in the freezing mid-autumn wind in Central Park wearing a leopard print minidress, two pounds of face makeup, and so much hairspray I was worried I'd draw satellites into my orbit. I'd been back in the city for less than twelve hours, and I was already at work.

"That's it, darling," Beau Bailey crooned to me as I arched my back and pressed my breasts against a tree. "Let me see those curves. I want tension! Give me tension."

I kept every muscle in my body snapped taut and focused

on keeping my face relaxed, my eyes heavy-lidded and my mouth parted slightly in the unfurling bloom of a newly budded rose.

My spine would ache tomorrow, my feet were already throbbing, and my head pained from the weight of heavily styled hair, but I loved it. I loved putting my good looks to better use than being some man's pretty face or some Master's indentured slave.

The money I made from modelling put food on my family's table. It had sent Giselle to the most prestigious art school in France, Elena to law school at NYU, and purchased a home and a business for Mama.

The thing that had brought me so much misery growing up in Napoli, that had eventually led me to sexual slavery, had become my saving grace. It had taken years of therapy to realize that the tool everyone had used so long against me could be wielded by my own hands.

So I loved it, the endless boredom and rigorous physical exhaustion of modelling.

It wasn't some great passion of mine to stand in front of the camera or strut down a catwalk, but the things it permitted me to do—the travel and the riches—were enough to make it seem like the best job in the world.

Besides, the tedium of modelling gave me more than enough time to think obsessively over my past or, today, over Ashcroft's threat to expose a sex tape of me to the world.

I hadn't had time to tell anyone, and I wasn't sure if I would.

Dante or Salvatore were the obvious choices, but I hadn't seen the former in nearly a month, and the latter was supposed to be dead, so I didn't like to pull him out of seclusion for any old reason.

I supposed if there was ever a *good* reason, though, Ashcroft was it.

"Okay, let's break for a moment," Beau called out, and

immediately, half a dozen aides swarmed the posing models to bring us water and thick wool coats to ward against the chill.

"How's she doing?" Beau asked, strolling over as his first assistant traded out his camera lens and set up another tripod.

Beau was my sister Elena's best friend and had been since I first introduced them at a Prada event two months after moving to the city. He was flamboyant, outgoing, and deeply charismatic. My sister was stiff, formal, and unerringly conservative. They were a strange duo but an inseparable one.

"You'd know better than I do," I told him as I wrapped myself up in an oversized men's coat and pulled my masses of curled hair out of the lapel. "She hasn't spoken to me about the adoption in weeks."

Beau worried his plump lower lip as people flowed around us like a river over rock. "Between you and me, I'm worried Sinclair's heart isn't in it."

I sighed because that had occurred to me many times over the course of the past three and a half years too.

Sinclair was one of my best friends. The man who had changed my life as irrevocably as Seamus or Alexander, but in every way good where they were bad. He'd given me a place to stay in the city while I'd gained my feet, a private reprieve away from the scrutiny of Mama and Elena so that I could get my bearings again. He was the only man in my life who had never wanted anything from me, and the love I had for him because of that was almost fiercer than any other.

I'd only wanted the best for him when I finally introduced him to my gorgeous, driven eldest sister. They were both beautiful, successful, and mad with ambition. When they started dating, it had seemed inevitable.

But the cracks showed early. Sinclair wasn't a man who smiled much, and neither was my sister. I'd hoped beyond hopes that they would find humour and happiness in each other, but I'd forgotten the concept of yin and yang. They were too similar, and those likenesses canceled out the right things and emphasized the wrong.

In the years they had been together, they'd only become more professionally driven, more emotionally distant.

But Elena was too steeped in her desire to have a baby to see that Sinclair wasn't right for her, and my dearest friend was too inured in the mundanity of his life to realize he wasn't really *living*.

Of course, Sinclair's heart wasn't really into adopting a baby. His heart hadn't been stirred since we'd met so long ago in Milan.

"Do you think Elena believes the same?" I asked him.

He continued to chew on his bottom lip. "I think she's thrown off by...everything. Sin's been gone more than not with work, and you know how she feels about Giselle. Now that she's back, I think she's a little worried you'll pick Giselle over her."

I rolled my eyes. The rivalry between my sisters had started from such an early age that I honestly couldn't remember a time when it didn't exist.

Giselle was dreamy and sensually beautiful with exaggerated curves like our mother and the deep red hair of our father. She was naïve and pure, gentle and whimsical. Even though she was older than Sebastian and me, we had always taken it upon ourselves to protect her from the more horrific aspects of our impoverished life in Napoli.

Elena resented our protectiveness. She was a fierce soul who had been broken more than once and who had allowed her fractured heart to calcify in order to guard herself from further harm. She hated Giselle's wistfulness, her impractical artistry, and her bohemian allure because Elena herself was none of those things, and somewhere deep in the secret recesses of her mind, she wished she was more like that.

Then, of course, there was Christopher.

The man who had obsessed over Giselle but settled for

Elena and used her up like a snotty tissue before casting her aside.

As much as I might have wished their relationship was different, because I loved them both indelibly and it was a strain on the rest of the family, I knew nothing would ever change.

There was too much history there.

"She's being ridiculous," I said finally. "I won't be insulted by her worry, but I won't entertain it either. I've been there for her through everything"—through Christopher's abuse, through law school, through Sinclair, and through her miscarriage—"and that will never change."

"You're letting her live with you," he pointed out.

I took a deep breath as my irritation mounted and tried to remind myself that he was just looking out for Elena. She had so few friends, and she alienated herself so much from the rest of the family that I was happy that she at least had Beau as a champion.

"Giselle needed a place to stay while she settled in. She's been alone in Paris without any family for four years, and I'm rarely at home as it is. It was an obvious solution, and I won't feel guilty about making it. You know I love them both."

Beau sighed and pulled on the perfectly stylized curl hanging over his forehead. "I know. I think she just wishes that for once, someone would choose her feelings over Giselle's. You've always put her first." At my glare, he amended, "All of you have."

"That's not true," I said through gritted teeth, feeling the piercings I still couldn't bring myself to take out flare with the memory of the pain, and the brand on my ass that no amount of expensive skin treatments could eradicate burn like a fresh wound. "I've sacrificed for everyone in my family, and I would do it again. Even if that were true, though, Beau, don't you think she could see it as a compliment? Giselle was never as strong as my steel-souled Elena. If we let her feel the impact of our cruel lives a little more, it was only because we knew she could handle it."

Beau nodded reluctantly. I wanted to spit at him, to rage against his guilt trip because who was he to judge? Had he ever asked himself why Sebastian and I were put on the front lines of our family when we were the youngest? Had he ever wondered what we had to do to get Elena out of Italy and into NYU law?

No. Of course not.

Because people see strength in a person, and it blinds them to their need to be compassionate with them.

Just because I was strong enough to handle the worst of things didn't mean I didn't want or need help.

"Miss Lombardi." Someone interrupted my silent wrath to tap me on the shoulder.

I looked over at one of the interns for *Vogue* and smiled instantly. "Yes?"

She stared up at me as if she wanted to be me. "Um, someone is here to deliver something for you."

I frowned at her but followed as she led me to the edge of the cordoned-off area where a man in a suit stood with his hands behind his back. He had the bland look of a servant and the outfit to match.

A shiver shot through the base of my spine and reverberated in my teeth.

"Miss Lombardi?" he asked in a clipped, monotone British accent.

I nodded, unable to summon my voice.

He produced a silver tray from behind his back with thick card stock folded and sealed with red wax atop its shiny, unblemished surface.

I would have recognized the seal anywhere. Sometimes, I actually found it, tucked into architecture in the city, pressed into a pattern on a popular fabric, or hidden in works of art.

The Order of Dionysus was one of the oldest secret societies in the world, and though they were based in England, their reach extended across the globe.

I stared at the lock with the blooming red flower caught in its loop and felt my stomach plummet like a runaway elevator to the base of my belly.

When I didn't immediately reach for the envelope, the manservant frowned. "Lord Ashcroft instructed me to tell you that if you do not open and obey his summons, he will be forced to send someone for you."

Send someone for me meant *forcibly* take me.

I gritted my teeth and snatched the summons off the tray, ripping it open with shaking hands.

FUTURE SLAVE,

I EXPECT YOU AT MY HOME IN ONE HOUR. FOR EVERY MINUTE YOU ARE LATE, YOU WILL BE PUNISHED. UNLIKE YOUR PREVIOUS MASTER, I DON'T REQUIRE THAT YOU ENJOY THAT PUNISHMENT. TRUST ME WHEN I SAY YOU WANT TO BE GOOD. WEAR RED. I KNOW HE LIKED YOU IN THAT COLOUR.

YOUR NEW MASTER,
ASHCROFT

I stared up at the manservant, seething and impotent with rage. I wanted to throw the invitation in his face and tell him to go hell, but I wasn't that stupid.

Not anymore.

If Noel had taught me anything, it was that these men played games, and everything was just a move across the board leading them to greater power, greater success.

Ashcroft hated me for embarrassing him, but more, he

hated Alexander because he was endlessly jealous of him. This was about revenge, and honestly, it wasn't smart.

I knew that even if Alexander didn't care about me anymore, even if he never had to begin with, he was not a man who liked to share his things.

He would end Ashcroft for taking up with me.

All I had to do was find a way to make the situation known to him.

And maybe, a little voice I'd learned to subdue in the back of my mind that spoke from my heart said, in doing so, he would reclaim me himself.

I shoved the idiocy from my mind and sought another end goal, finding it almost too easily.

Ashcroft was proving himself to be an impulsive *stronzo*.

Maybe he would slip up and expose something I could use to take him down.

To take the Order down.

I flipped the ripped invitation onto the tray and tilted my chin at the servant.

"Tell him I'll be there with bells on."

*U*nsurprisingly, Ashcroft's New York City home was on the Upper East Side in a four-story stone town-home with vines gone red with autumn bursting across the façade. A liveried butler opened the door for me when I rang exactly one hour later and led me through the opulent, antique ridden interior to an office at the back of the house where Ashcroft sat behind a desk smoking from an honest to God wooden pipe.

Lord, but the man took himself too seriously.

He studied me for a long moment through the curling smoke as the butler closed the door on his way out. I felt his regard like greasy fingers running over my skin.

"You aren't wearing red," he noted.

"I was working when you 'summoned' me. In order to make it here on time, I had to come straight from the shoot," I explained, waving a hand over my heavily made-up face with three leopard print spots drawn beside my eyes. "I also have to meet my family for our weekly lunch date in two hours. If I miss it, they'll probably call the police."

I'd changed out of my minidress into black jeans, a pink silk camisole, and a blazer, unhappy that my nipples could clearly be seen through the thin material in the cold room.

Ashcroft licked his lips salaciously as he studied them. "I'll have to punish you for that nonetheless."

I tried to control my breathing to keep the sick swell of bile in my stomach at bay. The idea of him touching me, let alone assuming the role that had once been Alexander's, made me want to throw up until I passed out.

"As it is," he continued idly, "I have something else in mind for the moment. I have work to do, but I thought it might be nice to have some eye candy while I do so, and my maid is away with some family issue so..." He nodded to the neatly folded clothes on the ottoman beside the leather couch to my left. "Change."

I swallowed as I walked over to lift the tiny black and white frilly edged and collared maid's uniform. "You're joking, *si?*"

He adjusted himself obviously as he shifted in his chair and leered at me. "I never joke about sex. Change. I want to see the body Alexander risked his arse for and take pleasure in knowing it's mine now."

I swallowed thickly, trying to find that almost forgotten space in my mind where I could block out the nightmarish reality of my life and focus just on my breath, on the peace inside the chaos. It was harder than it used to be, the steps there coated with cobwebs and dark with disuse.

I took deep, even breaths as I shed my clothes and quickly donned the humiliating costume.

"Ah," he groaned in delight. "Look at those full breasts. Such a delicious thing."

Thing.

Fuck him.

I breathed deep and tried to remember why I was doing this.

To keep from being blackmailed.

To keep the job I'd come to enjoy that put food on my table and money in my family's coffers.

To get Alexander back.

To get enough dirt on Ashcroft and hopefully the Order to destroy them.

My spine straightened as I finished buttoning the dress and looked directly into Satan's greedy eyes.

"Come here," he ordered, leaning back and spreading his legs, indicating the space between them.

He watched me carnally as I walked over and stopped just outside of his reach.

"On your knees, slave Ashcroft," he demanded, reaching out to slap me lightly across the face for my insolence. "You know better than that. Knees, *now.*"

I dropped, my head angled low so my eyes were trained on

the ground, my knees folded and my hands palm up over my thighs.

Submission coursed through me like a lightning strike.

I gasped at the sensation of being bent and folded like origami into shape by another person's orders and then burned with the shame of knowing how deeply it settled something eternally restless inside me.

I didn't want to feel this way with Ashcroft, and I knew it was only a tremor compared to the quake of rightness and longing I felt with Alexander, but it still disgusted me.

I glared up at him instead of bowing my head in proper submission and watched as Ashcroft laughed.

"You can defy me as much as you want to, little thing. I'll break you in nice and slow." He leaned forward to grasp my chin painfully. "After all, we have all the time in the world. No one is here to save you now."

I didn't need anyone to save me, but myself.

He didn't need to know that, though, especially when I hadn't yet figured out how to work this to my advantage.

"You'll clean for me now. I don't have time to play at the moment. Then next weekend, I'll take you to Club Bacchus for The Trials."

"The Trials?" I dared to asked.

Ashcroft leaned down further, shifting his hand so that it collared my throat tightly. "Think of it as the Order's annual Best in Show. Do you want to know what that is, sweet thing? I have a feeling with prime stock like you, I'm in for the ultimate prize."

I kept stubbornly mute.

He chuckled and then lashed his tongue across my pressed lips before biting the bottom one. "I'll debut you as my new slave, put you through your paces on stage for everyone to see, and then the council will vote on which slave is the most desirable, the most beautifully broken in."

"Fuck you," I lashed out before I could control it. "I won't be displayed like some kind of dog you trained for your amusement."

"Ah, but you will," he reminded me, reaching over to his desk and dropping a folder open at my knees. Glossy sheets of photos spilled out over the floor, showing Alexander and me in the black, white, and gold tiled ballroom at Pearl Hall. Some had him chasing me across the room, others had him pressing me into the floor, my mouth open in shock and then progressing to full-blown desire. They were graphic and horrible, a visual reminder of the first and only time Alexander had taken me against my will.

My heart thundered, and my cunt grew heavy.

I remembered the thick, acutely agonizing feel of Alexander's big cock between my thighs, sliding wetly through my pussy as he fucked me in the ballroom, in the Hall, in the stables, in the greenhouse, and in the wet crush of poppy at the back of his estate.

I closed my eyes, hating myself for missing it, but mostly for missing *him*. The man who had bought me to collect me like a token bauble and then forgotten me so easily when I fled.

My shame deepened because it was his complete and utter rejection of me three years ago in Milan that rankled me most and not any aspect of my year of slavery with him.

"So you see," Ashcroft said smugly, bringing me back to the present, "you will be my obedient little bitch because you have too much to lose if I let these little photos free."

I swallowed the knife's edge of rage in my throat, feeling it slice my insides. "I'll do it, but I'm warning you, Ashcroft. You won't live a long and healthy life if you go through with this. I'll kill you myself before the year is out for doing this to me."

He laughed uproariously, tossing his mousy blond curls back and holding his belly as he laughed and laughed.

I visualized slicing open that exposed throat with the letter opener on his desk and felt momentarily better.

"Have you not learned this yet, little slave?" he asked, genuinely curious as he looked down at me. "You are less than nothing. The only value you have is the one that is placed on you by men more powerful than yourself. Alexander might have made you feel like his little countess when he married you, but you are nothing but a *slave.*"

We stared at each other, my breathing hard with the effort to stay calm and not throw myself at him in a violent flurry. His eyes were almost kind as he let his truth settle around my wrists and ankles like the weight of phantom chains.

I knew he was wrong. I wasn't nothing.

I was Cosima Ruth Lombardi, the wife of an earl, the sister of a famous actor, upcoming criminal lawyer, and incredibly talented artist, daughter to one of the most wanted mafiosos in Italy, friend to the New York Camorra's *capo*. I was loyal and brave, beautiful and kind.

And I was *smart.*

No one had ever told me I was, but I'd learned to believe in myself that way.

I was smart enough to trick Ashcroft into believing he held me in check and then use his arrogant mistakes to execute a Fool's Mate and defeat him in the end.

All I needed was patience and maybe a little luck.

So I smiled at him beatifically. The smile that Willa Percy had used to launch the second phase of my career, the smile that had once so briefly wooed the most powerful Lord in England.

I watched Ashcroft blink, capitulating to my beauty, letting it make him even dumber than he already was to think he could own me.

I imagined my inner strength like an invisible shield coating my skin, protecting it from the vile man before me who I had to lull into a faux sense of security.

"Yes, sir," I said because my mouth wouldn't form the

word *Master* to this false Dominant. "I understand, and I am sorry for my attitude. How can I make it up to you?"

Ashcroft grinned slowly like the cat that ate the canary and widened his stance. "I know exactly how you can make it up to me."

Chapter Seven

COSIMA

Almost two hours later, I rushed out the door of Ashcroft's house once again in my street clothes, his semen washed off my chest from where he'd jerked off on me after spanking me with a wicked metal ruler for being late and leaving early. My ass stung, my heart ached, and I'd never felt dirtier, not even after Ashcroft had raped my mouth at Pearl Hall when I'd thought he was Alexander. It wasn't much, he'd really barely touched me, and I realized that I got away easy. A spanking, his cum on my skin, and an hour of acting the maid with a duster and broom was trivial compared to my previous trials, but it hurt so much more.

I knew why. I didn't need my therapist to say words like Stockholm Syndrome and PTSD to know that it felt so wrong because it hadn't been Alexander.

I felt weak and exhausted as I stood on the sidewalk, blinking owlishly as I tried to gather the tattered remains of my self-control around me. All I wanted to do was go home to the apartment I had painstakingly saved for and curated with beautiful things and snuggle my cat Hades from the warmth and comfort of my bed.

But it was Sunday, which meant family lunch at Mama's restaurant in Soho. It was an unspoken rule that unless Sebastian or I were out of town working, we were all required to attend on pain of death by glare from our matriarch.

So, I stepped to the edge of the curb to hail a cab to Mama's part of town.

"You look appalling," a familiar European accent called out from behind me.

I sighed heavily before turning around, both relieved and anxious at seeing Dante again after a few weeks without contact. We were close but only so much as our jobs allowed.

There was hardly a month I didn't have to travel for a shoot or walk, and even while I was home, I encouraged my agent to book as many go-sees and campaigns as possible. Idleness was not good for my mental state.

Dante was busy with *the Family*.

He'd been in New York City for nearly four years, and he'd already amassed considerable power. He tried to keep me out of the loop on the details, but I knew from Salvatore that he had usurped the old head of the Camorra to become capo just last year.

Things were different for the mafia in 2019. It wasn't the eighties anymore, and the mafia was much quieter, less showy than their older counterparts. That didn't mean they were any less powerful. Police and intelligence agencies had diverted resources once aimed at curtailing mafia activity toward the newer, greater threat of terrorism, and Dante operated happily from the vacuum created by that.

He was leaning against an iron lamppost the way he was known to do, his ankles crossed and massive arms folded over his even bigger chest. No matter how long I'd known him or how often I saw him, his sheer size and overwhelming beauty always took my breath away.

It was still early enough in the day that the ink shadowing his hard-cut jaw was only a hint of the half-inch pelt it would become after dinner, and it perfectly contrasted with his full, ruddy lips. They twitched as I studied him, amused by the way I always needed a minute to order my thoughts after being hit with his beauty.

Leaning against that pole in a black suit with an open collar black button-up and his thick hair pushed back from his forehead, he looked especially gorgeous—the definition of tall, dark, and handsome.

And dangerous.

So, so dangerous.

I swallowed thickly before smiling at him. "Dante, you know better than to sneak up on me."

My guilt trip didn't provide the distraction I'd hoped. His sensual smirk slid through the shadow of his beard as he straightened and strolled toward me, stopping only when we were toe to toe. I had to tip my head back steeply in order to maintain contact with his pitch-dark eyes.

"*Tesoro*, you know I never *sneak* like some *teppista*," he chastised me with a roguish smirk. "I called out to you so that you would know I was here, but you were too lost in your waking nightmares to pay attention. What has you looking so wrecked?"

I wrung my hands before I remembered that he knew it was my nervous habit and then awkwardly jerked them to my sides before shrugging a shoulder. "Nothing much. Jet lag."

He cocked a brow. "Jet lag? From the woman who travels

so much, she has trained herself to sleep at the drop of a hat? I do not think so. Now"—he leaned down, his sharp citrus and warm pepper scent filling my nose—"tell me the truth."

A cab rushed down the street, and I took advantage of it by flagging it down. I pulled open the door, told the driver the address, and then flipped my hair over my shoulder to attempt an innocent smile at Dante. "I'm late for lunch with my family, and you know how they get."

He stared at me with such warmth and gentle amusement, I felt it in my chest. That was, until he moved forward and pushed me into the cab, following so closely after me, I felt crowded by his big body even in the three-seater space.

"What are you doing?" I demanded.

"I'm taking you to lunch, and you are telling me what has you looking like someone ran over your hellacious demon cat."

"Hades is not a demon cat," I snapped, falling into our old argument. "He just doesn't like you because he has good taste."

"Does he?" he asked drolly. "If that's the case, it seems his mistress doesn't. You know you love me."

I rolled my eyes, but Dante's familiar banter was exactly the remedy I hadn't known I needed. There was something about my rapport with him that brought me comfort the way no other relationship could. Maybe it was because he had seen the worst of my trials, that he had saved me from Ashcroft and another disciple of the Order at The Hunt, or that he had spent years with my father, years I had missed out on. For whatever reason, he was my closest confidante, my *only* confidante, and I viewed him like a brother and a best friend.

He shifted closer, his full lips parted in a smile that made my heart skip a beat, and a little voice asked me if my feelings weren't as platonic as I thought they were.

"I barely tolerate you, and you know it." I sniffed haughtily, turning away to hide the smile I was sure he could hear in my voice.

His huge hand landed on my thigh, squeezing until I looked back at him.

"Cosi, tell me what's happened. How can I help if I don't know who to harm?"

I almost choked on my giggle. "*Cazzo*, Dante, when did you become such a mob boss? That was like something straight out of an Al Pacino movie."

"You know I don't watch those stupid mob movies." He scoffed. "I'm still recovering from when you forced me to see *Goodfellas*."

"Hey, that's an American classic."

"Good thing I'm not American then."

We smiled at each other for a long minute that knit my torn edges together seamlessly. The dirtiness I'd felt after leaving Ashcroft felt washed away by Dante's love and attention.

"Tell me, *tesoro*," he urged softly, reaching over to brush a lock of errant hair out of my face.

I closed my eyes, trying to block out his beauty while I talked about something so ugly. "Ashcroft found me."

Instantly, the air went hot and metallic as if the car itself had caught on fire.

"When?"

I winced because I knew he would be furious with me for what I was going to say. After Alexander had dismissed me permanently in Milan and told me never to set foot on English soil again, I'd returned home more broken-hearted than ever. It wasn't as if I could turn to my family. They didn't know what I'd been through or how I'd fallen for my own personal villain.

Only Dante and Salvatore did.

They'd been stone-cold furious on my behalf. Honestly, it had gone a long way to repairing some of the damage

Alexander had inflicted on me. It reminded me that even though I was damaged and depraved, there were two people who loved me more than anything. Salvatore had even proven he loved more than his own life by staging his death to end Alexander's vendetta against him as peaceably as possible.

They were going to freak when they knew I'd been back to England.

And they would both know because anything I told Dante would inevitably be passed on to my birth father.

"Sebastian was nominated for a BAFTA," I muttered. "It was a huge accomplishment for him, and he has...his own issues with that country. I had to go with him for moral support."

Dante stared at me, breathing in such a controlled way I knew he had to be counting back from ten in order to stay calm with me. I had told him I wasn't fragile a million times, but no matter what I said, he still thought I'd had enough violence and aggression to last a lifetime.

It was the other reason he kept his mafia business separate from me.

"I know you love your family. In fact, I know it more than most people will ever have the opportunity to. But, Cosi, that was just an exercise in stupidity! The Order has people *every-where*, but London is their fucking hub. How did you think you could get away with that?"

"I was there for barely twenty-four hours," I snapped. "I doubt Alexander has someone stationed at London's central surveillance hub just waiting to catch sight of me setting foot in the city."

Dante arched both brows and pursed his lips.

I hesitated as he meant me to.

It was difficult to put anything past Alexander. If he wanted something enforced, he would go to any means to see it through.

"I didn't see him, anyway. It was just pure bad luck that Ashcroft was at the awards and ran into me," I argued.

"You think Alexander is the only one keeping an eye on you? I know Frankie and I did a fine job erasing you from Italy and your old life, but you kept your name, and you're a fucking international supermodel, Cosima. It's not rocket science to find you. How do you know Sherwood wasn't the one to send Ashcroft?"

I thought about the way Ashcroft has acted, sly and giddy with it like a child who had stolen another boy's toy.

"No, Sherwood didn't send him. Honestly, Dante, I think it was purely coincidental."

"You can't know that."

"No...but given Ashcroft's plans for me, I think I can guess."

Dante's body expanded even more until I thought his muscles would tear through his expensive suit like the Hulk.

"What. Is. His. Plan?" he demanded through clenched teeth.

"Ugh, sorry to interrupt," the cabbie said in a thick Bronx accent, "but we're here."

I peered out the window at Osteria Lombardi and felt relief pluck a resonant chord in my chest.

"Listen, we can talk about this later, but I have to go," I told him, leaning forward to press a kiss to his bristly cheek.

He snagged my wrist gently before I could make it out of the car, but his face was creased with conflict as he mulled over his words.

"I try to give you space, *si*? I try to give you freedom to live the kind of life you want to live because you were so long in a cage, and not just one owned by my brother. I try, Cosima, when all I want to do is stand guard like a sentry by your side every single minute to make sure life cannot fuck with you anymore. So have a care, hmm? Take pity on this overprotective guy, and promise me, when I come to you next, you'll tell me what happened, and you'll let me help."

I paused, my throat thick with unshed tears.

"You're not alone in this," Dante said, his own voice thick with emotion. "You won't be alone ever again. Not with Salvatore and me on your side, *bene*?"

I nodded jerkily, then let out a deep exhale to settle my hummingbird's heart, pounding rapidly yet so fragile in my chest.

"*Va bene*," I agreed softly, before moving quickly out of the cab, dashing at the wetness under one eye as I moved to the sidewalk.

I didn't look back as the cab pulled away, but the crowded streets of Little Italy wouldn't have afforded me the room to turn around anyway.

Mama's restaurant straddled the line between Little Italy and the trendier Soho, the perfect place for her intimate, upscale Italian restaurant. She drew in a combination of the city's wealthy, elegant couples and deeply traditional Italian-American neighbors.

Italian-Americans were not like native Italians. The immigrants had packaged the culture of Italy pre-World War II and put it in a time capsule, cracking it open after passing through Ellis Island and settling in the small rectangular neighborhood of Little Italy in New York City. They spoke in broken, bastardized Italian, different than even the most obscure dialects back home because English underscored it like a highlighter, turning accents into mockeries they'd made famous with cartoon characters like Mario. They were only American enough to set them totally apart from Americans and barely Italian enough to pass for it if they ever re-entered the mother country.

My siblings and I didn't like to spend time there in that cramped neighborhood slowly shrinking under the expansion of China Town. It felt claustrophobic and tragic, like maybe we'd worked so hard to escape Napoli only to wind up right back inside another version of it.

But Mama loved it.

She wasn't an old woman, but she was set in her ways, and her ways were just as antiquated as the Italian-American ideal. She believed in the outward strength of patriarchy and the secret skillful workings of the matriarchy. She spoke Italian whenever she could get away with it, and though she wasn't bigoted, most of her employees at Osteria Lombardi were Italian or Italian-American because of it.

She'd escaped a small world, a world that was a cage, only to carefully lock herself inside another one. It made her feel safe, I knew, but it also made me feel sad for her.

We weren't on bad terms.

We could have been, and part of me even thought we should have been, but I took too much pride in my ability to intellectualize and understand a person and their motivation to truly blame her for her past.

Especially given that both her mistakes had come from falling in love. First with the wrong man at the right time, and then the reverse with the other.

She wore the weight and the indignity of those decisions every day in her dark eyes, her demons making the brown seem black with shadows.

At first, when I'd moved back with Salvatore and Dante at my side, she had been quiet, almost shy with shame around me. She knew I knew the truth about my parentage, and she wondered when I would strike out against her, and more, when I would tell Sebastian and take another child away from her.

But I didn't tell anyone.

My year of slavery and its contrast of deep horrors and tender mercies went into a locked box in the farthest reaches of my soul and stayed there, untouched.

It was a defence mechanism, maybe even an unhealthy one, but I wasn't going to castigate myself for it.

I'd been through enough.

So had my family.

I didn't need to throw a bomb into the middle of my family just as we were all reaching for each other and our dreams.

Still, Mama and I existed on my terms. She walked on eggshells around me, and a small, horrible part of me enjoyed that. She deserved some discomfort for telling lies, for ruining my life before it had even started.

Without her, I wouldn't have been a pawn to the mafia or to Alexander.

But it was also why I cut her so much slack...because without her, I wouldn't have met Alexander.

And no matter what, I'd always treasure my connection with him.

I pushed through the wooden doors of Osteria Lombardi, inhaling the yeasted scent of focaccia and semolina dough as I walked across the dark wood floors to the back of the restaurant. It was a traditional space, exactly how you would imagine an elegant Italian eatery right down to the bookcases stocked with regional wines, the exposed brick walls, and the old, weeping candlesticks at each table.

I loved it there. It was the manifestation of a dream Mama had dreamt her whole life and never believed would be possible. Sebastian and I had made it so through hard work and sacrifice.

Just being inside those four walls made all of it—the pain, the separation, the scars both physical and unseen—so fucking worth it.

"*Mia bella figlia,*" Mama called out operatically as she pushed through the sliding doors from the kitchen to see me. "Come give your mama some love."

Obedient as any Italian to their mother, I hustled over to

be embraced in her sweet basil and semolina scented arms, crushed against her bosom with both cheeks bussed in the traditional Italian greeting.

Satisfied, she pulled back but kept her arms around me and studied me with a fierce frown on her handsome face. "You look dead on your feet, *piccola*. Sit and let Mama feed you."

I followed her to our family table at the back of the room and allowed her to fuss over me, holding out my chair and taking my purse.

"You let me fix you something, *si*? You need more meat on your skinny bones, Cosima. It's not so good to be skinny like this. No men like a woman with so little to hold, *capisce*?"

"*Si, Mama*," I allowed even though I had enough meat at my tits and ass to warrant being featured on *Sport's Illustrated* despite my slim limbs.

Mama and Giselle had the same lush, deeply curved bodies that most men drooled over, whereas Elena and I got the long, lean forms of our fathers.

I'd once thought we both inherited it from Seamus, and it had taken me a long time to realize I much preferred being genetically tied to Salvatore.

"Why did you marry Seamus?" I blurted out, freezing Mama like a bug in amber.

Her wide, light brown eyes blinked at me as her mouth opened, then closed.

I leaned back in my chair and crossed my arms, deciding to follow through with my spontaneous interrogation. In the three years I'd been reunited with her, I'd yet to ask any of the hard questions. Honestly, I even avoided talking about it too much with Salvatore because every mention of Mama just made him deflate like an old balloon.

"I deserve these answers," I reminded her, not unkindly.

With a heavy sigh, she sank into the chair beside me. "I knew this day was coming, but to have it here now, it is still difficult. Seamus was exotic, *si*? So fresh and different. I liked this. My father was a fisherman when this was still big industry in Napoli. He was very popular and always had big parties. During one party, Seamus was there with locals he met at the university. My father was so traditional, and I wanted different for myself. Seamus was from *America*. It was so glamourous for us Neapolitans who had never been beyond Roma. He spoke with an accent, and he had this fire hair, yet he knew so much about Italy that I did not feel stupid when we spoke. He found me almost right away and stayed with me the whole night even though I was just sixteen and not the most beautiful woman at the party."

She stared down at her soft, worn hands, gently fingering the slight indentation that still remained from decades of wearing a wedding ring.

"We married quickly in those days. My father, he did not mind Seamus in the end, but he died just after I was pregnant with Elena. He might have helped when Seamus started to gamble and drink..." She shrugged. "My mother, she was long gone to a sickness. There was no one left. When Seamus started to become...the man you remember him to be, it was too late to turn to anyone. There was no one left, you see?"

My heart constricted with empathy. Wasn't that exactly how I had felt when Seamus first told me he was selling me through the mafia to the highest bidder to repay his debts? As if the only person with the power to do anything was myself?

"I had Elena and then Giselle. I was just a girl really and I had few skills, but good hands in the kitchen. In Napoli, you know this is not so special. It is the men who own the restaurants, and we had no money to open one anyway. Seamus did not like me to work. A traditional Italian family, this was his dream." She laughed bitterly, her eyes glazed as she stared over my shoulder at her past. "He got one more typical for Napoli than he could have dreamed of, *si*?"

I nodded tightly, trying to swallow the burn of my mama's tragic story.

"I was walking by the docks to buy the fish for dinner one day when I saw this man," she said, her voice dipping into low, velvet tones as she began the part of the story where my real father came in. "He was very tall and very big across his chest like a man who works with his hands for a living. I liked this. He seemed...*esperto?*"

"Capable," I offered.

"*Sì*, so capable. It was very different from my husband with his books and his words. This other man, he looked at me, Cosima, for such a long time that I stopped to watch him look at me. I had Elena on one hand and my baby on the other hip. He looked, and then he just walked to me like this." She used her arms, swinging them firmly, her brow lowered in mock concentration. "He walked to me, and he said his name, *Salvatore*, and did I want to get coffee right now with him."

I could imagine that. My strong, determined father seeing my beautiful mother across a stinking fish market and deciding then and there to have her.

His sense of conviction was something I admired and aspired to.

I thought of my plan to dispatch of Ashcroft, and my resolve hardened.

"I went. Then the next day, I went once more. This was again and again until I was so *innamorato* with him, I couldn't see beyond his golden eyes." She smiled softly at me then. "The eyes he gave my twin babies."

She had been enamoured with him.

There was something about her word choice and the way she spoke about Salvatore that panged in my heart like a gong. This was the way I'd felt about Alexander.

Both men had entered our lives like a storm, and where there should have been only devastation in their wake, there was beauty too in what remained.

"Why didn't you just leave with him?" I asked the million-dollar question, and it tasted metallic on my tongue.

The dreaminess in her eyes snuffed out.

"He was *le mafie* and not small, *capisce*? He was rising like this." She slapped her hands together. "One day, we walked with my babies. I was pregnant with you, but just, and I had not told him this. A man from another *mafia*, *le Cosa Nostra*, he attacked us because Salvatore had done something. He took the knife here," she said, pressing a hand to her upper right shoulder. "And my girls, they were not hurt, but I was inside here." She moved her hand again, this time to her chest over her heart. "I knew this was no life for my babies. Seamus, he was involved because of the cards and the money. But Tore, he was involved because he *liked* this life, and I knew he would not leave it."

She shrugged as if her shoulders were waterlogged. "I asked, we fought, he begged, and I cried more tears than one person should in one lifetime, but this is life, *uh*? We make decisions, and this was mine." She stared at me again, squaring her shoulders and tipping her chin in a way that was so *me*, it made me want to cry. "You can judge me for this, *piccola*, but this I will not ever regret. Look at what we have today because of this choice."

I was still too mired in her story to argue with her that we were exactly where we were that day, sitting in her restaurant in the America of her childhood dreams, because of *me* more than her.

I could give her pride. It would hurt no one to let her have that after everything she had been through.

The door at the front of the room ricocheted opened, heralding calls from my brother as he commanded the space. Mama snapped out of her melancholy to hustle up to him and squeeze him even more tightly than usual.

He frowned at me in question over her smaller form,

stroking her hair softly to comfort an ailment he couldn't understand.

I shrugged one shoulder, unable to give voice to her story.

Or my own.

Were all love stories inherently tragic?

Was that what made them so epic? Not the gentleness of connection between two souls or the comfort of their union, but the inevitable loss of it at some time or another.

I wondered if I loved Alexander in retrospect more than I ever had while I was with him, and I came up blank.

My emotions toward my Master were too convoluted to untangle. Most of all, when I thought of him now, all I felt was grief and embarrassed hatred.

I tried to pay attention as Sebastian sat down, then as Giselle and finally Elena joined us for lunch, but my mind was lost to musings.

I had a degenerate Lord blackmailing me for sexual favours, a worried mafioso and soon-to-be worried father on my hands as well as lingering, eternally unresolved feelings for the man who had once owned me.

I figured, even though my family didn't know it as they gabbed about Elena's plans for adoption and Giselle pretended too hard that she didn't care about them, then as Sebastian stormed out because of Elena's rude inquiries about Savannah Richardson, they could damn well cut me some slack for being distracted.

COSIMA

"**No.**"

"Listen to me, dear heart." Jensen Brask tried to reason with me over the speakerphone as I stood in the bathroom preparing for a charity event that evening. "We *need* you. Clemence Bisset has dropped out because she had an anaphylactic attack! It's not like I planned this, but you really are our only hope to keep this campaign on schedule. You cannot tell me you don't care about St. Aubyn. I know after that Bulgari afterparty you resigned from your spokeswoman role because you 'had your reasons,'" he said, slightly mockingly. "But this is one of the best fashion houses in the world, and it's the one that gave birth to your stardom. You *owe it* to us to substitute for Clemence."

I sighed so heavily, I blew my powder brush off the sink sill and onto the floor. After picking it up, I braced my hands on either side of the porcelain basin and looked into my tired yellow eyes.

There was really no way I could risk going back to England. Once in the past four years had been one time too many. I wasn't foolish enough to think that I could survive another visit without drawing the all-seeing eye of the Order.

"Laying on the guilt trip a little thick there, Jen," I accused him as I resumed carefully contouring my eyelids with dark brown and gold shadow. "You know I will always be grateful for what you and St. Aubyn did for my career, but I was serious when I said I would never work for the brand again."

Alexander Davenport owned the fashion house. There was no way I was going to have anything to do with any aspect of that man or his business.

He'd made it clear to me I had no role in it either.

When I'd first discovered the connection, I thought he might have set the entire thing up with Willa and Sinclair, that my duo in shining armor had been sent from the lord of the manor.

But there was no way.

I'd been ridiculous to think he cared about me enough to ensure my safety and success even after I'd abandoned him.

Even hearing the name St. Aubyn made my stomach ache.

"No, Jensen, I'm sorry, but I just cannot."

"What if I told you the shoot wasn't in London proper? You'd fly in and a driver would pick you up directly to transfer you to Cornwall. We're doing an indoor/outdoor shoot on the cliffs of the Jurassic Coast. The theme is very Heathcliff and Cathy."

"Wouldn't that mean the moors of the Peak District?" I asked, because I knew just how atmospheric those rolling hills of purple and red heather could be.

Pearl Manor was there, nestled in the landscape like the setting for every great British literary classic.

"The cliffs are more cinematic. Honestly, Cosi, I wouldn't have called you if you were not my last resort. The shoot is in two days, and we'll be going to Hell in a hand-basket if we can't make this work for the next fall catalogue." A long pause then he said, "Do I have to make Willa call you?"

I worried my bottom lip as my chest went to war with conflicting emotions. Jensen and Willa had been my mentors for so long. I didn't need the additional guilt from Willa to know that I was beholden to them eternally for their generosity.

If lack of desire to return to the birthplace of so much of my misery was the only thing keeping me from accepting the contract, I would have caved in immediately. I didn't like saying no to the people I loved. In fact, I abhorred it.

Still, this was my safety on the line, and that was something I had learned the hard way not to take for granted.

"I can't. I'm sorry, Jen, I really am. If things were different, if it wasn't in England, I would do it in a heartbeat. I hope you know that."

He sighed heavily, but when he spoke there was a smile in his voice. "What if I told you Xavier Scott was doing the shoot?"

I squeezed my eyes shut. Xavier Scott was a household name, and as a photographer, that was saying something. He did everything from the royal family's photos to *Vanity Fair* spreads and *National Geographic* covers. He was *the* man behind the lens.

And he had never, not once, consented to work with me.

He was that famous. He chose his own models.

"He wants me?" I breathed like a child being told they could meet Santa Claus for the first time.

Jensen chuckled like the cat who ate the canary, knowing I was locked in. "He did."

"*Cazzo*," I swore under my breath, then said, "Fine. I'll be there, but Jensen? I want a flight at the latest possible time and the first one out of there when we wrap."

"Cosi, are you in some kind of danger if you go to England?" he ventured, suddenly somber.

"No," I countered immediately, infusing my voice with a smile. "Only in danger of bringing up a past I would rather keep buried. Do not worry, *bello*, I'll be fine."

I hung up after exchanging more information about the particulars and let my head drop between my shoulders in defeat.

I was an egotistical maniac for going back into the den of my monsters.

More than that, I was a masochistic, fatalistic lamb willingly walking to my slaughter because a small, dark sordid part of me hoped one of those monsters *would* find me.

"You look fancy," Giselle said, appearing in the mirror behind me as she leaned against the doorframe and took in my black lingerie and dramatic makeup. "Big plans tonight?"

I slid vermillion red lipstick over the thick curve of my bottom lip and then carefully painted it into the exaggerated bow of my top one. "Nothing too exciting. I'm going out with a friend."

My sister hesitated, then moved deeper into the room to sit on the edge of my bathtub. "Would that friend happen to be *the* Mason Matlock?"

I sighed heavily, turning to face her worried expression. "What have you heard about Mason?"

"Just the rumors that he wants to marry you. I didn't even know you were dating anyone, Cosi," she said, hurt softening her voice like a bruise.

"I'm not dating Mason. When I first came to the city, he was a good friend to me, and occasionally, when he needs a date to a function, I go with him. As his *friend*."

She blinked her huge pale grey eyes at me eloquently, obviously not believing me.

"I know you have your secrets," she said before pausing for a pregnant moment. "We all do. I'm just saying, if you like this Mason or if he helped you out through our…leaner years, I won't judge you for having a sugar daddy or whatever."

Laughter erupted past my lips like champagne, frothing through my fingers as I tried to hold it in. How I wished my secret was as simple as trading my time and some sexual favours for patronage like some muse from the 1800s.

What would my sweet, innocent sister say if she knew I had sold myself through the broker of my father and the mafia we all hated so dearly into sexual slavery?

"*Dio santo*, Gigi, you have a brilliant imagination," I told her when I recovered enough to speak.

She shrugged bashfully, pink highlighting her lightly freckled, tanned cheeks. "I'm just trying to be open-minded to show you that I don't care if that's what you do or even what you like. I think I proved today when I told everyone I wanted to do a show based on human sexuality that I'm not a puritan like Elena, but I just wanted to be sure."

No, my boho sister wasn't like my prudish Elena, but she'd also had one lover in her life, and he was a sweet Canadian boy who wouldn't know bondage and sexual mastery if it kicked him in the balls.

I walked over to take her sweet face in my hands and smooth my thumbs across her high cheekbones. Her gentle, sensual beauty hit me in the chest with pride. She had so much to offer the world, her boundless heart and optimism, her artistry and talent. I felt the echo of my sacrifices in my chest as I looked at her as I was reminded once more of her endless potential, and I knew I'd done right by her.

That didn't mean I was *ever* going to tell her what I'd done to help her find possibilities in this life.

I pressed a kiss to the corner of her mouth. "*Ti amo, bambina.*"

"I'm not so innocent as a baby anymore, Cosima," she protested, pushing me back so that she could look into my eyes. "You don't need to coddle me. What did you mean earlier when you said you've been sad, used, dumb, and very nearly dead?"

It was my fault for being so dramatic. Giselle had announced she was doing a sexual study for her next art gallery showing, and my family had exhibited mixed reactions. To show her I was on her side, I'd immediately volunteered to be her first model, and when we had returned home from lunch, I shed my clothes and revealed a few of the secrets punched into my flesh.

I was lucky she hadn't been able to discern the brand on my buttock, the twin lions roaring beside a shield of gold depicting pearls, thorns, and poppies.

Normal people didn't voluntarily mar their skin with a red-hot branding iron, and even my considerable imagination was not enough to come up with an excuse for that.

Explaining the evolution of my relationship with my body was simple compared to that quandary.

"I only meant this; I was born with inherent value because people enjoy beautiful things and my body grew into a pretty vessel others could admire and lust at. Over the past few years, I've learned that people think a pretty girl is hollow, and they will try to fill me up with their desire and their greed, with their power and control like a puppeteer with a doll. I'm not so strong I've never succumbed to the headiness of their longing for me, not so sure I didn't allow myself to be bent and reformed in a shape that suited them because it benefited me, but also, sometimes, it turned me on."

I peered up at her through my lashes and saw her intensity, as if she was a lightning rod readily absorbing every single one of my electric words.

"There is power and sensuality in submitting to a formidable man," I said with a brief shrug, turning back to the mirror to unravel my long black hair from the big red curlers they were held in. The curls spilled like wet ink over my bare shoulders. "There is also sadness, stupidity, and at the darkest spectrum of it, danger. This is what I meant."

I watched Giselle swallow thickly in the mirror behind me. "You're speaking of BDSM, right?"

A one-shouldered shrug that sent my hair sliding sensuously over the bare skin above my corset. Even talking about the act of dominance and submission set my womb to aching, my core fisting in a yearning, mournful clench.

"In all its forms and many expressions," I agreed before sliding her a coy glance. "Is this something you are interested in, Gigi?"

Her blush flared across her face like a neon warning sign. She prevaricated, stepping closer to filter her charcoal-stained fingers through my hair to break up the curls.

"You know the man I told you about from Mexico?" she started quietly. "He made me feel as if the door to my pleasure could be unlocked as easily as saying 'yes, sir.'"

She shivered slightly behind me, either in remembrance of a fantasy or with anxiety at divulging such a sinful secret.

I reached back to grab her arms and wrap them around my torso in a backward hug. I could see the uncertainty in her eyes, the same questions and longings I had struggled with for so many years.

Was there weakness in submission?

Shame in pain?

I knew the answer was no because I had been broken and reformed around that simple concept. It was a natural expression of desire that went beyond the sexual. In submission, I found self-assurance, generosity, and peace for the first time in my life.

As much as I wanted to reassure her, it wasn't a question I could answer for my sister.

Sexuality was too individualistic to blanket with bromides.

So, I hugged her arms tight to my tummy and stared into her beautiful face in the mirror.

"I'm happy to hear you have found a man who excites you, especially after that dullard Mark from Paris." She giggled at my words, and tenderness suffused my chest like fumes from a chemical high. "Just remember the power of *no*. The Dominant is not the only one who makes the rules, *si*?"

She bit her lip and nodded, her gaze caught on something tucked in the farthest reaches of her mind. I took advantage of her distraction to entertain the real possibility that had been lingering at the corner of my preoccupied thoughts that Sinclair could very well be the man Giselle had found in Mexico.

I knew he'd once dabbled in the scene because he was the one who had urged me to try to find another Dominant when I confessed I'd been involved in a relationship of the kind in England.

I knew Elena detested kink with a bitter kind of verve that would take years of therapy and/or a very strong, resilient kind of man to temper and reform.

Sinclair wasn't that man. They didn't have a relationship of trust and passion, but of drive and mutual admiration.

But Sin was the type of man who would fall head over heels for the siren's call of my beautiful, vivacious sister, and he was just sinful enough to indulge in that desire even when he shouldn't.

"Be careful, hmm, *bambina*?" I called to her softly.

She blinked, refocused, and then frowned as the doorbell

rang, heralding the arrival of my escort for the evening. Her eyes dropped to the high cut of my corset, her gaze tingling over the branded skin of my bum before they cut back to mine.

"You too, Cosi, you too."

Chapter Nine

COSIMA

The opulence of a New York City high society function was not dissimilar to those of the upper crust elite and the Order back in England. The women were filled, covered, and sparkling in millions of dollars' worth of plastic surgery, and brand-name designers and jewels while the men all wore a variation on the classic suit and tie as if individuality was frowned upon in such circles. It was. This was the major reason that Mason Matlock, one of the wealthiest men in New York and the heir to a coffee chain franchise, used me as a very pretty beard. Bigotry was frowned upon, but still, those who were too different often felt the brunt of society's sharp tongue, and Mason didn't want to have to deal with the fallout. His mother's family was also Italian and Roman Catholic, so I had a clear understanding of his situation. I didn't think he was a coward for hiding, not when I had been hiding for so many years. We all had our crosses to bear, and I was happy to help my friend carry his once in a while.

The noise was calamitous for such an elegant function, but I was grateful for it; between the band and the gossiping, there was little need for me to speak with the man standing next to me at the bar.

"You look beautiful." Wesley Longhorn gazed down at me with deep admiration, and I wished, not for the first time that night, that my dress wasn't quite so low cut and that Wesley wasn't quite so tall.

"Thank you," I murmured and smoothed a hand down the corseted front of my gold crystal Versace dress.

"So what's it like? Being a model." He took a large sip of his scotch and winked at me. "I can tell just by looking at you, that you're a party animal."

"Can you?" I asked coolly, my back ramrod straight with tension.

"Oh, yeah." His hand found my waist and smoothed down over my hip. "A girl like you has got to love a good time."

I struggled not to roll my eyes, but it was getting increasingly difficult. The truth was, men like Wesley Longhorn, son of one of the biggest talent agents out there, abounded in the industry. Tossing a drink in his face, as satisfying as it would have been, would only hinder my career, not his.

I had experience with men worse than him, and I knew how to handle them.

So, I smiled beatifically at him. "The truth is, with my husband and two kids..." I watched his facade fall feature by feature until his classic all-American face was melted like cheddar cheese. "I don't have much time for going out. And

I'm always on the lookout for a good sitter; do you like children, Wesley?"

I was still laughing when Mason appeared moments after Wesley had scampered away. He stared at me questioningly, but when I offered no explanation, he smiled.

"I leave you for five minutes, and you get into trouble."

I pouted up at him. "You leave me for five minutes, and I *find* trouble. What else do I have to entertain me while you are gone?"

Mason's face creased into his familiar smile as he laughed. He was thirty-seven years old, much older than me by anyone's standards, but his seasoned good looks reminded me subtly of Alexander's experienced appearance, and I had no doubt his age was the very reason I found him so attractive. His dark brown hair was brushed away from his forehead to emphasize the square cut of his jaw, his Roman patrician nose, and his dark eyes.

We had first met one night a month after I'd move to the city, when I'd been especially tired of my robotic existence and caved into my curiosity by visiting a local BDSM club. *The Bind* was an exclusive establishment run by one of Sinclair's old friends, which was how I secured an invitation. I'd gone alone, unsure what I was looking for but needing something to settle the wild restlessness in my soul. It was there I'd found Mason, arguing with a man who was trying to strap him into a saddle horse. I'd intervened, getting in the large Dominant's face until a club monitor arrived to escort him out. Mason and I spent the rest of the evening drinking at the bar and talking about our mutually dissatisfying love lives and large mixed Italian families. We'd been friends since then.

"I'm so glad you could join me tonight," he was saying in his deep, methodical voice, thinking through each word before he uttered it. "You always brighten up these things."

I rolled my eyes at him. "Mason, these 'things' are important. For you and me."

He sighed heavily. "My uncle *did* say he was proud of when I told him we were still seeing each other, though he put the pressure on to make the rumors a reality and get a ring on your finger."

I laughed in solidarity because we both had complicated relationships with our father figures, leaning in to press a kiss to his cheek. A camera phone flashed as someone took a photo of us, but that was the point of these things. Mason had helped my celebrity by toting me around town when I'd first arrived, and I continued to help with his overbearing, homophobic family by being his date.

His lips pursed, but he relaxed when I put a hand on his arm and led him back to our table to take our seats. When he placed his on top of mine, he looked down at me with somber eyes. "You are important to me too, Cosima, and I can tell you're unhappy. Even more than normal, which I have to note, is saying something."

I looked away quickly, slipping my hand from his grasp. "You barely know me."

"I've known you for two years. I'd say that's a considerable length of time," he countered, his voice stiff with irritation.

He deserved more than my irascible defensiveness, but I found myself protesting again. "I'm just your arm candy, Mason. Chill out."

Suddenly his arm was on mine, and I was wrenched around in my seat until I faced him fully, my knees locked between his own. His expression was cold with brutality. "Don't you dare. Don't do yourself and our relationship a disservice by pretending this is a transaction and not an emotional connection. I'm here as your confidante just as you are mine. What is wrong with you that you can so easily forget that?"

I yanked my arm from his hold, avoiding the condemnation in those icy eyes. Normally, I could control my unreasonable desire to distance myself from the people, specifically men, in my life, but I was thrown so far off-kilter by the events of the past few days, I felt as if I'd been put through a wood chipper. Pieces of my scarred past, tumultuous present, and dreams of my future lay scattered around me like debris, and I had no idea how to make sense of the chaos.

"Forgive me?" I asked Mason softly, crossing my legs and leaning over in my chair so that I could cup the side of his neck. "I'm on edge tonight."

"You could talk to me about why that is," he suggested mildly, still angry. "I know you don't like to talk about your past, but has something or maybe someone come up again? You know you can tell me anything, right?"

I sighed and turned to my glass of red wine for solace like any Lombardi woman would.

Mason and I were silent as dinner started, and a well-dressed master of ceremonies took the podium to speak about the cancer charity we were supporting. I played with my food instead of eating it even though one of my favourite New York chefs was catering the event. There were too many things on my mind to absorb the magnificent evening. My heart was set to rapid pounding, knowing the risk I was taking to go to England even though I hoped it would pay off by posing for the most famed photographer in the world.

"Hey." Mason's soft voice interrupted my thoughts, and I looked up to see his face creased with something edgier than concern, something like anxiety. "Are you still up for this? We can always go home."

I shook my head adamantly. "No. I know this is important to you, so it's important to me."

He nodded curtly, but he was frustrated with me for being so tight-lipped. I shrugged off my fretfulness and focused on the night ahead of me. Mason's first love, his high school best friend and secret boyfriend, had died at twenty-three from brain cancer, and now that Mason had money and influence in the city, he was one of the charity's biggest patrons. Which was why I had agreed to be "sold" for a date night to the highest bidder to raise money for the illness.

The irony of voluntarily selling my beauty again was not lost on me, but my therapist had assured me it was a viable way to "take back my power" and rewrite a traumatic experience into one that was positive and altruistic.

I thought it was a load of crap, but I wanted to be supportive of Mason, and I was experienced at playing on my beauty like a maestro with her instrument.

"Ladies and gentlemen, distinguished guests," the emcee declared dramatically. "I am privileged to announce the items we have for auction tonight. Please remember, the proceeds go to a very worthy cause." I tried to focus on his explanation of the charity, but pins and needles played against the skin on the back of my neck. Frowning, I turned slightly to brush the itch away when I spotted him. The Earl of Thornton, Alexander Davenport sat at one of the main tables in front of the stage, his legs crossed with one arm slung casually across the chair next to him where a pretty young woman sat chatting to him. The very same blonde goddess I'd seen him with last time in Milan, Lady Agatha Howard. I couldn't see his eyes from where I sat, but I knew without hesitation that he was staring at me.

Hope and fear churned in my gut. I pressed my fist to my mouth as I fought through my nausea.

"Too much wine?" Mason murmured, his eyes still on the emcee.

I shook my head, my eyes inexorably linked with the man across the room. I could feel the anchor pull painfully in my soul as our connection snapped taut and vibrated with energy. He was wearing an all-black ensemble, but for the gold silk pocket square. Even from so far away, he quite literally took my breath away.

What the hell was Alexander doing at this charity event?

I swallowed convulsively and tried to take my eyes off the

gold pocket square. Was it too much to think he wore it as a subtle reminder that he owned me and my golden eyes?

"And now the moment we have all been waiting for," the emcee crowed. "Everyone, please welcome to the stage the lovely ladies and gentlemen who have volunteered themselves for the auction!"

That was my cue, but I remained arrested in my seat, staring at the silver coin eyes I hadn't seen in so many years.

"Cosima, what are you waiting for?" Mason whispered, nudging me with his thigh.

I watched as a slow smile spread across Alexander's features, and only when he gave a slight nod of his head did the enchantment snap, and I found myself free of his hold.

Shame coursed through me like volcanic heat, and I tasted the ash of my old dreams on the back of my tongue.

He wasn't mine to want anymore, and the feelings of unwitting desire he still stoked in me were deplorable reminders of my own lingering need for a sexual satisfaction only he could give me.

I stared daggers into the back of his head as he turned to smile winningly at Agatha fucking Howard.

"Who is that?" Mason asked sharply, more alarmed than he should have been as my friend and fake fiancé as he followed my eyes to the other table.

"No one important," I said flippantly with a big smile as fake and functional as fabric flowers.

With a languid smile, I rose to my feet just as the last few volunteers mounted the stage, and I pressed a long, lingering kiss on Mason's surprised lips. I could feel the eyes of the room watching me as I pulled away and walked unhurriedly up to the stage where the other women eyed me with varying looks of annoyance. Surprisingly and horrifyingly, it was Agatha Howard who seemed the most amused by my tactics. Her blue eyes sparkled as she grinned at me sashaying through the tables.

"Excuse us for a moment, folks," the emcee asked as he watched me climb the stairs. "This one is worth waiting for, and I do think she knows it."

I beamed at him as I passed, and when he offered his powdered cheek for a kiss, I complied. The swell of catcalls and whistles buoyed me. Let Alexander see just exactly what he had been missing the past four years.

The auction began with a petite brunette at the other end of the line, and I realized that I would be the last woman called.

"You did a remarkable job," Agatha whispered in her incredibly posh British accent. "The anticipation is just going to build now that you're last."

I shot her an uneasy look, trying to gauge her intentions. Unfortunately, she was British to her core, and she'd been raised to be perfectly poised and opaque. "Thank you. Though, I'm sure the men will spend all their money on you, and I'll be stuck with the leftovers."

She snickered like a schoolgirl at my testing compliment. "I have a feeling the man I came with will be leaving with someone else."

Sweat broke out on the back of my neck, and my hands itched to be wrung together, but I maintained my composure through sheer willpower.

What the hell was this bitch's game?

"Agatha," she told me with a small smile. "It's a pleasure."

"Cosima," I murmured reluctantly and watched as her lips twitched with mirth.

"Do I have twelve thousand dollars for the toned and tanned Wesley Longhorn?" the emcee prodded. A woman in the audience jumped in the air as she raised her paddle, and everyone cheered when he was sold to her.

"She overpaid," I muttered.

Agatha sniggered again. "Don't make me laugh," she said sternly. "I'm up."

Four men bid on her instantly, and she preened visibly as each struggled to outbid the other.

My gaze sought out Alexander in the crowd, idly swinging his paddle between his index finger and thumb even though his companion was currently being bid on by other men. He wasn't looking at me, but I felt the same fission of alarmed excitement race through my core.

"Sold! For thirty-eight thousand dollars," the emcee yelled over the applause as Agatha's suitor fist-pumped in triumph.

"Wish me luck?" I asked as she walked past me off the stage. I was still wary of her friendliness, but I found myself drawn to her; my curiosity always seemed to outweigh my sense of self-preservation.

She hesitated and shook her head, the locks of her pale hair like moonshine under the spotlights. "You won't need it."

I swallowed nervously when the crowd quieted down, reminded of the way the Order had leered at me as I was presented as slave Davenport in Pearl Hall's lavish dining room. It was harder than it should have been to remind myself this was an entirely different scenario. Sucking in a bracing breath, I placed one hand on my hip and smoothed the other down my side from the small of my waist to the long line of my upper thigh. My palm was sweaty against the sheer fabric and my heart thundered loudly in my ears, but I could tell that I had everyone just as enthralled as they had me.

"Now, the pièce de résistance," the emcee laughed and abandoned his podium to approach me with his microphone. "I know this isn't protocol, but I just had to ask you…" His black-lined brown eyes were wide with sincerity. "Do you wake up looking like this?"

I laughed with the audience and looked down at the man before me coquettishly. "Very few people know the answer to that, *bello*."

"Well!" He turned to the audience, the ultimate showman, and swept his arm toward me. "Maybe this Italian goddess will give up her secrets for a price? Let's start the bidding at two thousand dollars."

Immediately, Mason's paddle was up, but so too were seven others. I watched in delight and horror as the price continued to rise and rise. My eyes sought out my admirers, but the harsh stage lights made it difficult, and finally, I stopped straining to see. The bidding reached thirty-four thousand dollars before Mason's last competitor gave in.

"Going once, going twice," the emcee sang into his microphone.

"Fifty thousand dollars."

A gasp went up amid the attendees, and chatter broke out as everyone searched for the calm voice offering to buy me for such an exorbitant price. They didn't have to look far. Alexander Davenport, Earl of Thornton, leaned against the bar to the left of the stage, lazily presenting his paddle.

Our gazes snagged and locked together again. I found myself in his gaze, lurking in his metallic grey eyes like a vision of the person I truly was; strong, beautiful, and graceful as I knelt at his feet with my head tipped down, eyes blazing with inner fire from between the dark curtains of my hair. My legs wobbled as I battled the urge to go to him. I didn't know what I would do if I gave in to the impulse, if I would sink to my knees like a sandcastle collapsing into waves or if I would punch him in the throat for thinking he could usurp my life again. It was a dichotomous sensation I hadn't experienced since I'd last seen my husband three years ago.

"Fifty-one thousand dollars," Mason returned, his voice coarse with shocked anger.

There was almost no way he would let someone else win me in the auction even though he was oddly reticent about paying for me. He had been approached about auctioning me off for a date night fundraiser before, but always adamantly refused despite my consent. It was only because of the charity's connection to his first love that we were participating tonight. Mason was also deeply protective, and the idea of a stranger paying such an exorbitant price to take me on a date would raise all his red flags.

Unfortunately, he didn't know that the man in question was technically and legally bound to me in holy matrimony.

"Give up, Mr. Matlock." Alexander's crisp British voice carried perfectly over the large ballroom, though he didn't seem to shout. "She's mine. Fifty-five thousand dollars."

Alexander, on the other hand, had proven before that he had no problem paying for me. It seemed the husband I hadn't seen in years had come back to claim me.

My heart wedged itself in my throat and throbbed like something cancerous.

"Going once, going twice…" Everyone was wondering about us; the supermodel on the stage and the gorgeous Brit they didn't know but desperately wished to meet. I didn't care. For better or for worse, I was thrilled when the master of ceremonies announced, "Sold to the suave British man for fifty-five thousand dollars."

Everyone erupted in applause, but I remained rooted to the spot as he slowly began his way toward me, his gait coiled and powerful as he stalked to the edge of the stage and offered his hand.

"*Topolina*," he said quietly, just for me. "Come to me."

A whimper worked at the back of my throat, and inexplicably, I wanted to cry. I never thought I would hear his cold voice cut the simple word *topolina* into something like a diamond for me ever again.

There was no room in my head for logic and questions. I was filled to the brim with static shock, and my brain was misfiring.

The only thing I could focus on was the stern form of his beautiful face and the look in his eyes that clearly stated *mine*.

On wobbly legs, I carefully made my way to the stairs and took his offered palm. A current of chemistry electrified my fingers as he clutched them, but I beamed at the photographer who raced up to catch our expressions.

"And now the lucky ladies and gentlemen who successfully bid on one of our volunteers will take the floor for their hard-earned dance," the emcee crooned as the podium was moved and a piano accompanied by a string quartet began the soft strains of "Primavera."

As we were already on the dance floor, Alexander wasted no time in pressing me into his arms. Even though we had only danced together once, years ago at Grammar House in London's Mayfair square, we moved like ballerinas tangled together in a music box, inevitably in sync. The strong scent of him engulfed me, transporting me to the cool misted cedar forest behind Pearl Hall. I breathed it in deeply, surprised by how much I still loved the smell despite the painful memories it evoked.

When I looked up into his eyes, he was watching me with that steady, possessive regard he'd mastered.

"What the hell are you doing here?" I breathed.

I was thrilled he was there to ask the question and terrified of the answer.

"You know, polyandry is illegal both here in the United States and in Britain," he said almost conversationally, but each word bit into me with vicious teeth. "Does this Mr. Matlock you plan on marrying know that he is about to commit a felony?"

Anger crashed into me so brutally, so completely that I felt suffocated by it. I was consumed by a wall of fire, the flames eating every ounce of oxygen from the air before I could drag any into my lungs. Black spots popped through my vision, and I swayed in Alexander's firm hold as I tried to get a grip on the utter devastation of my own humiliation and fury.

"Are you," I said slowly, focusing on the formation of each word so that I wouldn't scream. "Are you seriously here in New York, seeking me out after you made it *painfully* clear you never wanted to see me again…after years of radio silence…*to threaten me?*"

His hands flexed against me, my body tugged forward until it was plastered thigh to thigh and chest to chest against his own. I could feel the magnetic thump of his heart against my cheek before I wrenched myself as far out of his hold as he would allow.

"You are not the master of your fate," he reminded me with glacial eyes. "I am."

"Not for over three bloody years," I countered, whisper-yelling so that the glistening couples spinning like metallic tops around us wouldn't be privy to my personal hell.

"Since you saved my life on that godforsaken day in Milan, and I felt you just like this pressed to me as I pressed you to a wall, you've been mine. Whether or not you knew it. Whether or not you *like* it."

"Fuck you, Lord Thornton," I spat at him. "I've lived my own life, and I've made a success of it without you."

"You have not," he said, his words a sexual, sinister hiss. "I sent Willa Percy to you that wet day in Milan. I forced Jensen Brask to take you on as the new face of St. Aubyn when the beautiful Jenna Whitley was already signed to the task. I made sure the Order had no reason to stalk you longer than was necessary to prove you were nothing to me. I kept you safe every single one of the one thousand two hundred and eighty days we were apart."

He hauled me closer still, his hand sliding down my spine to press intimately into my lower back, his face coming within an inch of my own so I could feel his hot breath on my lips.

"There has not been one single minute since you ran away from me at our wedding that I have not sought you out and cared for you from afar. Everything you have done is because *I* bloody well willed it. And now I discover you mean to marry another man?" His mouth pressed hard to mine, stamping them in a way that would leave the bruise of his possession on my lips for everyone to see. I fought the urge to lick open the seam of his lips and taste the ambrosia I knew I would find on his tongue. "I will not allow that."

"You have no right," I said too loudly, my voice crackling with the fire I felt eating at my heart. "You have no fucking right to come here and say these things. You were the one who told me there was no place for me in your life!"

"I told you once before, my beauty," he sneered. "Even a predator is prey to something. I had things to take care of before I could reclaim you, but now you've forced my hand. I will not have you with another man. Not even if my body was cold and dead in the ground, would you belong to someone other than me."

Rage built in my chest, the smoke of it robbing my voice of any power as I said, "I hate you, Xan. I fucking *hate you*."

"Since when have I cared about your feelings, *topolina*? I'll have you either way."

The crack of my hand across his face cut through the smooth, emotive music and quiet conversation in the hall. Pain exploded in my palm, igniting the bonfire of hurt and horror that lay like dry kindling where my heart should have been.

He turned his head slowly from where the force of my blow had bowed it, his silver eyes blade cold. Then his hand snapped out and wrapped tightly around my throat, his thumb digging into the brutal beat of my pulse.

"Love me or hate me," he echoed the words he had spoken the first day I'd consented to kneel for him. "Either way, I've been on your mind since the day you met me, and I'll be there until the day we die."

"You don't own me anymore, Alexander. If you want me to kneel for you, you have to *earn* it."

The hand around my throat pulsed in time with my heart-beat as if to prove to me he was so attuned to my needs, he could read what was in my heart.

"I will," he vowed.

"You could never make up for everything that's happened, and I have no faith that you'd even know how to try," I said, the truth and lies so wrapped up in each other, I couldn't tell where one began and the other ended. "So I can tell you confidently to go straight back to hell," I snapped even though the feel of his hand collaring my throat made my pulse drop straight and heavy between my thighs.

"Don't believe you can fool me into thinking you don't want to rule there by my side."

"I never should have fallen for your manipulations," I rushed to say, needing to fount the anger before it ebbed into lust under the hot touch of his hand on my pulse. "You've always been the villain in my story, and you always will be. If you really care for me at fucking all, you'll leave me alone to live my new life without you."

People were circling too closely to us, aware of the animosity sparking in the air around us, drawn to the chaos of our reunion. I could see Mason powering through the couples, his face set to stone after witnessing my anger.

"Think of this as a courtesy call," he said dispassionately, completely unaffected by my vibrating anger or the growing unease of the people around us. "You are my wife, for better or worse, and I'm coming for you, Cosima, to inaugurate you at my side where you belong. You can run," he taunted, angling his nose along the line of my throat before sinking his teeth into my neck on either side of my jugular. "But I think we've proven that I'll always find you."

Abruptly, he stepped away from me, releasing his hold so that I stumbled slightly on my high heels and instinctively reached out to grasp his arm to steady myself.

His smile was a weapon thrust into my chest. "Oh, and *topolina*? If you let that man touch you, I'll kill him with my bare hands and make you watch."

Chapter Ten

COSIMA

I listened to Verdi.

He was the favourite composer of both my fathers, Seamus Moore and Amadeo Salvatore. I grew up listening to the dramatic strains of his operas played over the tinny old radio in our tiny yellow house in our tiny life in Napoli, and then I learned lessons I should have been taught as a child from my birth father in his olive grove while Verdi played over the speakers set up at the terracotta patio at the back of his house.

His music was the soundtrack to my operatic life, and it soothed me as I cooked breakfast before dawn the morning after the charity event and hours before I had to leave on a plane bound for England.

I sang along softly with Violetta as she spoke of *sempre libera*, being forever free, even as she wondered if she was in love.

I had spent the last three years trying to teach myself how to be free, to no avail.

At first, I'd wondered if the ties that bound me to my past were just too strong, that I was weak in the face of my trauma.

But as time moved slowly on like the drip of cold molasses into a cup, I realized just how wrong that assumption was.

It wasn't that I was weak and traumatized.

It was that, sick as it might be, I was enamoured with the sins of my past.

Yes, I'd been sold and hunted like a fox destined for death. But Alexander had been there to save me, to claim me with his body in the dirt and the stamp of his ownership bruised into my skin.

After the revelations of last night, I knew that it was his machinations that had brought my "good luck" into fruition after running away from him three years ago.

How could I possibly reconcile the unbiased fact that Alexander Davenport was a cold-hearted villain with the irrevocable knowledge that to me and *for* me alone, he was also the world's most unlikely saviour.

I hated him for his interference. I'd wanted, no *needed* so badly to make my life my own.

But I knew it would have been nearly impossible without him.

As the clerk at that horrible fast food restaurant had said, I was deeply unqualified for even basic work.

Still, Alexander may have given me the means to make a name for myself in the world, but I was the one who had put those advantages to good use.

My life was my own, vibrant and fully drawn even if it existed in a frame of Alexander's making.

Strangely, I was okay with that.

"A bit early for Verdi, isn't it?" Giselle asked from behind me.

I spun to face her with a genuine smile despite my inner turmoil. There was no one who made me feel as at peace as she did. I could feel the noose I'd been wearing around my neck since Ashcroft reappeared in my life, the one that had tightened inexorably when Alexander showed up last night, fall lax around my collarbones at the sight of my pretty Giselle wrapped up in grey and cashmere in preparation for the cold autumn morning.

"It is never too early for *il maestro!* Although, I would argue it is way too early to be looking so cute." I cocked my head to the side as I watched her cheeks stain with a blush. "Where are you off to?"

She smiled softly; the expression so intimate that it panged somewhere in my heart. I'd never seen her with such a secret wealth of contentment, such a secret pasted to her lips.

To my knowledge, she had always shared everything with me. Giselle was the only one of us Lombardi's with an open heart and innocent past.

"Sinclair," she said before clearing her throat as she dispensed ice into a glass from the fridge. "Daniel invited me fishing. I told him the other day at lunch that I had enjoyed it when I was in Mexico, and he got pretty excited about taking me." She rolled her eyes, but they danced with amusement. "Who would have guessed such a buttoned-up guy would be a fishing geek?"

I tried to temper my grin as I turned back to my stewed tomatoes. It was now almost painfully obvious that my sister and Sinclair were having an affair. I wanted to be furious with them, but I'd seen Sinclair when he returned from Mexico and the very air around him had been luminous with newly found contentment. To look at Giselle now as she spoke about him, it was obvious she felt the same.

My heart twisted as I thought of my beautiful, misunderstood Elena and what this would mean to her even as I knew I wouldn't get involved.

Everyone has their own dramas to play out, and this was their own, for better or for worse.

Finally, I said, "*Massive* fishing geek. He enters the Bass-master Elite Series on Oneida lake every August, and I'm pretty sure he takes his executives on their annual business retreat in Mexico just so he can get in some fishing."

Sinclair had tried to take me fishing dozens of times over the years, to varying degrees of success. I laughed lightly as I told her, "He's taken me out before. Let's just say I'm more comfortable on land. I'd take horseback riding over fishing any day."

I thought about Helios, the gorgeous Golden Akhal Teke mare Alexander had gifted me toward the end of my stay at Pearl Hall. She crossed my mind frequently because I hoped beyond reason that she was still stabled at the manor, taken care of like a princess by their able groomsmen and waiting, impossibly, for my return home.

I hadn't ridden since leaving her. It felt like a betrayal the same way practicing BDSM felt like a betrayal of my relationship with Alexander.

"Why are you up so early?" Giselle asked, pulling me out of my reverie.

I scooped some *shaksuka*—a Middle Eastern stewed tomato and egg dish I'd learned from Douglas during my days at Pearl Hall—into a bowl and handed it to her with a kiss on the cheek.

"A model dropped out of a Ralph Lauren shoot in England," I fibbed, keeping my eyes averted as she took a seat at the kitchen island. There was no reason to lie. Giselle didn't know enough about St. Aubyn or Alexander Davenport to know their connection to each other, let alone to me, but I was wary after a lifetime of coincidences that had always turned out to be too good to be true. "I have to be in Cornwall tomorrow."

"You don't seem too enthused, and that doesn't really explain the early start."

I shrugged as if I didn't feel the siren's call of England like a lullaby luring me to my future death. "I hate England. I leave later today, but I couldn't sleep thinking about it."

"That's a bit extreme, isn't it?" she asked with a light laugh. "I mean, the entire country? What did the Brits ever do to you?"

My answering smile was sharper than I would have liked, but happily, Giselle was distracted by the ping of her phone. I watched as a stunning expression of excitement and joy broke across her face like sun piercing through clouds.

"I have to go," she told me without looking up from the text glowing on her screen.

She shoveled the last forkfuls of food into her mouth, then raced to her green gumboots to tug them on. I watched bemused as she finally spun to me and granted me a brief squeeze.

"If I don't see you before you leave, I'll miss you," she murmured into my hair.

"I will be back in three days. If it was any other brand, I wouldn't be going at all." I kissed her soundly on the cheek, then pushed her away. "Now, be safe and enjoy your day. Sinclair can be a charming bastard when he wants to, so I'm sure you'll have a grand adventure."

She smiled tremulously at me, then quickly ducked out the door.

I stood frowning after her for a long moment, trying to pinpoint why her expression had bothered me so much.

It was only hours later, after I'd showered, packed for

England, and was reading curled up on my couch with Hades that I realized why her smile had resonated with me.

It was the same one I recognized from my own face whenever I thought about Alexander.

I tried to dismiss it as my own bias spilling into my perceptions, but I knew Giselle would never continue to pursue a taken man unless she was very much in love with him.

Which meant Elena's future was looking decidedly grim. I resolved to spend more quality time with my eldest sister when I returned, as if somehow my love would buffer the blow of her upcoming heartbreak.

I was still distracted when a raucous knock sounded on my door, and someone cursed loudly in Italian from the other side.

My heart jumped into my throat as I pulled the door open and saw Dante leaning in the frame, his big body bowed with pain and his teeth gritted and gleaming from his sweat-soaked face.

"*Madonna santa*! Dante, what happened?" I demanded as he dropped his bunched-up jacket to the side table.

I stepped under one of his heavy arms to begin the process of dragging him into the house. He was over six feet five inches and quilted with dense muscle from his hands to his toes. It felt as if I was lugging a car behind me as I led him into the kitchen and propped him up on a stool at the island.

"Start talking, *capo*," I ordered harshly as I took his white shirt between my teeth and ripped it cleanly in two.

"So eager to see me shirtless that you couldn't wait to grab the scissors?" he asked drily, only a slight edge to his voice giving away the pain he was in.

I hissed as I saw the oozing wound in his left abdomen. "*Cazzo*, a bullet wound?"

He shrugged one shoulder, then groaned at the pain. "I'm an easy target."

"Because you're a fucking idiot?" I snapped.

"Because there's so much of me to aim at," he countered with a lopsided smirk.

I rolled my eyes at him as I snagged a clean dishtowel from the drawer and pressed it a little too hard against his wound. "Hold that tightly while I get some more supplies. You're lucky I'm always prepared. Seamus taught me nothing if not how to stitch up a broken man."

"My heart's been broken for ages, and you haven't seen to fixing that," he muttered petulantly.

I lightly slapped his shoulder as I moved out of the room into my bedroom to grab the comprehensive first-aid kit I hid there.

"*Cazzo*, Dante, I don't know why you don't just—" I froze in my journey back to his side when I caught the look on his face.

"Cosima," he purred, his Italian accent thick as mink pelt. "We have a visitor."

My eyes shot to Giselle who stood in blatant shock at the entry to the kitchen. The tin kit dropped from my suddenly listless hands to the kitchen counter.

"What are you doing here?" I demanded, too startled and defensive to curtail my tone.

"Um, I live here. What is a man doing in our kitchen with a *bleeding wound?*" she countered with a previously unheard-of amount of sass.

Dante settled farther back on the stool, leaning his back against the wall as he made himself comfortable enough to enjoy watching our show.

I shot him a dirty look, then sighed as ran my hands through my hair agitatedly. "I...Listen, Giselle, I need you to leave. Right now."

Both Dante and Giselle seemed bewildered by my demand.

"Are you kidding me right now? I'm not leaving here like this!" she cried out, her hand flying forward to indicate the wounded, highly amused mafioso sitting at our kitchen island.

"You are," I said, channelling Alexander so that my voice brooked no argument. There was no way in hell I was making Giselle privy to Dante's life and Made Man drama. We'd had more than enough of that growing up in the armpit of Napoli. "You are going to go out for the afternoon and enjoy the city, think about your show, and see friends. You will absolutely *not* say anything about this to *anyone*, and I will text you when you can return to the apartment."

Giselle's mouth opened and closed, useless with anger, before she finally found her voice and her forgotten Italian instincts. "Cosima!"

I crossed my arms, braced my feet apart like a general impatient with his given orders being flagrantly disobeyed, and waited for Giselle to yield.

It took longer than I thought it would, but finally, with one last wounded, confused look, she whispered, "Cosima…"

It was an entreaty to know more, to trust her with the weight of my secret so I could share the load.

She had no idea how heavy the weight of my many secrets was, and there was no way, if I had any say in it at all, that she ever would.

"*Parta,*" I ordered. "Go."

I hated the wrinkle between her red brows as she backed away so much that I turned before she could, focusing on sorting through the med kit so I wouldn't have to watch.

"So strong, *tesoro,*" Dante said quietly, his voice tender as the hand he swept down my back. "Do you ever wonder if one day, you'll break?"

"*Stai zitto,*" I muttered at him, telling him to shut up.

His chuckle fanned softly over my face as I bent down to clean the wound with alcohol and antiseptic.

He didn't move an inch when the burning liquid encountered his ragged flesh because this was not his first bullet, and it wouldn't be his last.

"Call Salvatore," he gritted out between clenched teeth as I pressed fresh gauze to the wound and efficiently wrapped it around the sloping v of his torso.

I nodded, moving into the bedroom to grab my phone so Dante wouldn't hear me tell his pseudo-father what a fucking idiot he was. Vaguely, I was aware of Dante moving past the view through my open bedroom door, but then the phone connected, and Salvatore's rough Italian accent came through the phone.

"Cosima, *mia ragazza*. To what do I owe this pleasure?"

I let myself close my eyes for a moment to feel the gravel of his voice in my ears. He lived outside the city on a vineyard in upstate New York where he led a quiet life under the name Deo Tore, so I didn't see him as much as I would have liked. He visited infrequently because he was smarter and more diligent than most. Being dead in the eyes of the Order and the law was important to him and to whatever plans he had with Dante, so even though I knew he would rather live in the city, if only to see me and pester Mama until she took him back, he stayed away.

It seemed silly to say I missed him. I really barely knew the man whose DNA I shared and wore so proudly in my features, but I did miss him with an acuteness that didn't slacken even in his presence.

Perhaps, I still ached for the loss of him in my early years, and I didn't think that would ever change.

"Dante got himself shot," I tattled, somewhat joyfully because I always felt like a child around him.

He huffed out a chuckle. "Not badly, I'm sure. For such a big buffoon, he is a hard one to target and kill."

"*Tocca ferro*," I muttered, the Italian equivalent of knocking on wood to avoid tempting fate.

Tore laughed. "He can't be too bad if you're speaking to me so calmly. What happened?"

I moved into the kitchen again, frowning as Dante walked through the living room from the front door with a gun in his hands.

"Don't you think you should put the gun down? I'm still not convinced you didn't accidentally shoot yourself," I told him solemnly.

He flipped me the finger and then winced as he settled himself on the stool again. "Give me the phone. I've had enough of your sass. Can't you see I'm injured? Why don't you try healing it with some sugar instead of this vinegar?"

"*Raggazzi*," Salvatore's voice sounded loudly through the phone, and we both grinned as I put it on speaker between us.

"What happened, *capo*?"

Dante's humour evaporated, and the air went hot with rage.

"di Carlo's boys," Dante sneered at the name of the Cosa Nostra *capo*. "They're becoming fucking bold. Walked right into the Bronx warehouse and demanded they be cut in on the Basante Colombian deal."

Salvatore laughed, a rough exclamation of incredulity. "Guiseppe di Carlo was always a *stronzo*. How did they get to you, huh? Are you losing your edge out here in cushy America?"

"*Vaffanculo, vecchio*," Dante cursed light-heartedly as he called Tore an old man.

"Listen, boys," I cut them off before their banter could escalate further. If left to their own devices, I'd known the two of them to continue insulting each other for hours. "Yes, Giuseppe di Carlo is a prick, but he's also the leader of the biggest crime family in New York."

Both men snorted indignantly at my assertion, but I powered on. "Is there no way to make nice with him and his?

As much as you both love power, you can't want a mob war right now. Not with everything else going on."

"Everything else?" my father barked out, suddenly furious that anything could be happening in my life that he wasn't made aware of. He might have only been my acting father for the past four years, but he took the job extremely seriously, especially because we'd both agreed not to tell Sebastian about their connection yet.

"Dante, what the hell is my daughter talking about?" he demanded.

I rolled my eyes because he didn't even try to hide the fact that Dante was meant to report every detail of my life to him.

"She had some trouble with Ashcroft, the man who—"

"You think I don't remember the man who orally raped and assaulted my daughter?" he snapped. "Cosima, *figlia*, you don't come to me with this? Have I done something to deserve such treatment?"

"Well, nineteen years of neglect is a pretty large black mark," I retorted, angrily cleaning up the rest of the medical supplies and throwing away the bloody bandages. The cabinets banged loudly as I stormed around the kitchen. "I am capable of handling my own problems."

"Capable has nothing to do with it." Dante lurched forward with a wince to snag my wrist and tug me closer. "We are your *famiglia, tesoro*; it's our right and duty to protect you. Why do you refuse to let us do what is only natural?"

I refused to look into his burning black eyes. On the surface, they were the same depthless black as every mafia man without morals I had ever met, but sometimes, caught at the right angle or looking at me the way he tended to do, they were beautiful to their core.

It was a deeply confusing juxtaposition that I wasn't in the mood to endure.

"I don't need any saviours. I'm strong enough to handle

things on my own," I said, my voice so cold it immediately froze the air between Dante, the phone, and myself.

"I came to you because I needed help. Does that make me weak?" Dante asked softly, curling the arm on his undamaged side around me so that I was pressed to his inferno of warmth.

"No," I muttered petulantly. "Though getting shot in the first place makes you pretty damn dumb."

I looked up into his smile because like the sun, it was impossible to ignore.

"Good, now that that's settled, explain to me what the plan is."

"Who said there was a plan?" I asked innocently as I moved out of his grasp to pour him a glass of whiskey and grab the bottle of ibuprofen.

Salvatore snorted. "None of us are that stupid, Cosima. If you didn't want our help, it's because you have your own agenda. Now, kindly tell us before I die from the suspense."

I rolled my eyes at his dramatics even though they always warmed my heart because they were so much like my own. "Fine, it's not much of a plan, but the intent is there." I sucked in a deep breath because I knew they were going to hate what I had to say. "I want to take down the Order."

Immediately, the two men burst into raucous discord. I crossed my arms with a beleaguered sigh and waited for them to wind down a bit before I interjected to explain.

"It was my own fault, but I went to London with Sebastian to support his nomination for Best Actor at the BAFTAs and Ashcroft saw me there. He's blackmailing me into being his new slave."

"With what?" my dad asked, right down to brass tacks even though I could feel his fury through the phone.

"Apparently, there are photos and video from the night Alexander took my virginity in the ballroom."

Dante cursed a blue streak of English and Italian words and then thumped his fist loudly on the countertop. "I should have remembered…maybe I could have slipped in to take the tapes when I went to Pearl Hall for your… union."

"You knew?" Salvatore yelled.

"It's not your fault," I placated Dante by placing a hand on his thick forearm. "You couldn't have known."

"But I did. It's the practice of the Order of Dionysus for each lord to record themselves taking their slave's virginity. They have to submit the tape to the council, and then they are, well, fuck, *graded* on their performance. Anyone found wanting—maybe the Master is too gentle or the girl too eager—is called before the council to testify."

"Because if either of those things happen, it might seem like the Master and slave are in love," I concluded hollowly.

Every predator is prey to something.

Alexander's warning reverberated through my head as everything locked into place. I'd been so shocked by the way he had hunted me across the ballroom, held me down and rutted into my untouched sex like a ruthless beast when he had been relatively kind to me in the days following my first dinner. It had seemed needlessly violent because, honestly, we both knew he could have had me willingly after a few more days or with some carefully tended touches to my traitorous body.

Why he'd needed to take me like a marauder, his spoils had always confounded and hurt me.

But now, of course, it was so clear.

They were watching us.

Not just the Order through the cameras I'd known were pinned throughout the ballroom, but through *Noel* who was their eyes and ears on the ground.

God, but we'd never stood a chance against their mechanisms.

Dante reached out to give my hip a comforting squeeze. "Does this make things better or worse in your memories?"

I blinked slowly, then again rapidly to cut the string tethering me to that past. "It makes things different."

"Yet you still want to take the Order down for him," he stated, cutting through my mask with the exaction of a scalpel.

My chin thrust forward as I stared down my nose at him, emulating Elena's haughty poise. "Is it so impossible that I might want to take them down for myself? They ruined my life, not to mention the lives of so many people I love."

"Like Alexander," Dante needled ruthlessly.

"Like *you*," I snapped.

He held his hands up like twin white flags of surrender, but I was on edge with defensive irritation, and nothing could soothe that restlessness. I knew from experience the only way I would be able to relax again was under the clinically cold hands of a seasoned Dominant.

And not just any Dom, but Alexander himself.

Unbidden, an image of him from last night branded itself in my mind's eye; the thick wave of golden hair pushed from his forehead like a crown, the cold metallic bite of his eyes as he pronounced me *his* from across a crowded room. Being in his arms again had felt like magic, like something I'd concocted so long in the cauldron of my heart I still couldn't believe it had come true.

"You know he doesn't love you," Salvatore reminded me, his voice flat and factual, not unkind. "He was raised by monsters to be a monster. There is no love in a heart like that. If there was, he would have come for you at some point over the last half decade."

It would have been a good time to confess to them both that Alexander had come for me, but I didn't want to deal with the fallout. If they thought he might reappear again, they'd have Dante installed at my side every minute like a shadow.

I wasn't sure they were worried about safety so much as

worried that if given the chance, the way I hadn't been given three years ago on my wedding day, I might stay with him forever.

My stomach ached with the force of my conflicting emotions. I could be honest with myself by admitting that seeing Alexander again had brought my staid black and white life once more into vibrant colour, but I was also smart enough to wonder if that was healthy or not.

He was my captor, my abuser.

My father's sworn enemy and my best friend's ostracized older brother.

A shrink's worst nightmare.

I had my own life I'd worked so hard to make full and happy in New York. Alexander showing up out of the blue shouldn't have undermined that the way it did.

But God, I hoped beyond hopes I would see him again.

I was enamoured with him eternally as if I'd been cursed, and I had no clue how to find the remedy.

"I can help, if you insist on getting information on the Order," Dante interrupted my thoughts to say. "I still have connections I could call on…Why don't you let me set up a meeting with a man I know who might be able to help us get some answers?"

"Ren," Salvatore spat the name like a curse. "Such a man doesn't do something for nothing."

"No," Dante mused as his eyes washed over me like hot water so that my skin seemed to steam. "But I have a feeling he'll do this for us."

"Good. You do that, and I'll do my thing with Ashcroft."

"No. It's too dangerous and unnecessary. What do you hope to find?"

"He likes to dress me up as his maid and have me clean the house, so I'm sure I can find some incriminating evidence."

Salvatore cursed through the phone, and I heard the smash of a glass.

"Cosima, you need to be careful with Ashcroft." Dante shifted on the stool to pull me between his legs and take my face in his hands. I closed my eyes because, for the first time in years, I couldn't bear to look at him and see the ways he resembled Alexander. "Don't put yourself at risk for a man you've romanticized in your memories."

"This isn't the first time I've put myself at risk for the ones I've loved. Ashcroft isn't a danger to Alexander right now, Dante; he's a danger to me and my family. I won't have my career ended by a scandal, and I won't have him hurt my loved ones to get to me. If Ashcroft wants me, he can have me. He just doesn't know yet that he won't ever be able to handle me."

Chapter Eleven

COSIMA

I was blindfolded.

For the first time in years, my sight was taken from me, and I was half naked before a man.

Only this wasn't a scene with my Master.

This was professional, a shoot for one of the top clothing brands in the world.

The air in the studio was clinically cold to keep my nipples beaded behind the delicate silks and satins of their expensive lingerie. The man instructing me to bend, curve, and smile was not my Dominant with a whip, but my director with a camera. One of the most famous in the fashion world.

Professional, not personal.

But as I sat on an uncomfortable antique wooden chair that reminded me of something from Pearl Hall with my legs spread to expose the placket of the black lace panties I wore and the leather harness encircling my hips and thighs like a kinky bracket for my sex, I went wet.

My pussy began a slow, steady beat like a kickdrum of dancing feet against the earth.

I tried to focus on the set of my matte painted wine-red lips and the angle of my head as I tipped it back in pretend ecstasy so my hair fell behind me like curls of sooty smoke. This was my job, my livelihood. There was no reason to feel aroused by bondage and my own mild discomfort.

I'd moved on from those desires.

I'd moved on from Alexander fucking Davenport no matter what he said.

The flight to London had been long and sleepless, the drive in the luxury Town Car too reminiscent of Alexander's Rolls Royce to be relaxing. Even the scenery out the rain striped windows evoked memories I couldn't defend myself against. By the time we arrived at Kynance Cove, I was a mess of clammy skin and frayed nerves.

Jensen had taken one look at me and sent a masseuse to my change room before I got into hair and makeup.

It hadn't helped.

The only thing that quelled my unease was the cold crush of the briny winter wind off the Lizard peninsula as I climbed the rocks to the grassy outcrop in one of St. Aubyn's statement gowns. Xavier Scott was a seasoned professional with a vivid eye for cinematic shots, and we'd wrapped up the first half of the shoot in under six hours.

Then a quick full makeup and hair change had me sitting in the godawful, erotically familiar antique chair in the cold chamber that reminded me too much of Pearl Hall's ballroom.

Six long hours stood between me and the safety of my hotel room with my emergency vibrator and a pair of particularly vicious nipple clamps, and six minutes into it, I was already unravelling.

It was an empty set because I would be mostly nude for the duration, and it was so silent I could hear the click of the Xavier's expensive loafers across the polished concrete floor as he circled me with his camera.

I'd been working with him for hours outdoors, but as he moved closer behind my closed eyes, I was surprised by the scent of him.

Cedar and pine, a wildfire dampened by cool, wet British air.

I'd never smelled that fragrance on anyone but my Master.

I sucked in a deep breath through my shock parted lips and tried to rationalize the odour.

The photoshoot was dredging up old memories.

Suddenly, his hands were on me, lifting and spinning me to face the chair before pressing into the base of my spine so I was bent over it. His palm slapped on my inner thigh, prompting me to spread my legs wider, my weight precariously balanced on the razor thin edge of my six-inch stilettos.

I bit my lip as he moved me like a doll into position. It was so hard to ignore the wet moor, cold forest air scent of him. Coupled with the way he moved me so perfunctorily, my lusty thoughts were impossible to suppress. My skin broke out in gooseflesh, and I shuddered delicately as the hand on my lower spine slid up my back to rearrange my hair in a curtain to the left of my cheek.

It wasn't unusual for photographers to pin me into positions with their hands or their cold orders, but this was the first time it gave me such an animal thrill.

I told myself it was his smell. It was a conditioned response my body had to the fragrance of Alexander, how it warped so fluidly into the scent of Dominance.

Finally, he stepped back, and the rustle of fabric let me know he'd crouched almost level with my raised bottom. The shutter *click, click, clacked* rapidly as he took shot after shot, moving around to the front when he was finished to capture the catch of my red lip in my teeth and the obscene swell of my breasts as they threatened to spill out of the half-cups.

Then he was moving me again, turning me, pushing me into the chair and hooking my legs over the arms so my entire scantily clad sex was exposed to the harsh bite of cold air. He arranged me so I sprawled like a broken toy in the hard angles of the chair; head back, mouth parted wetly, arms akimbo.

Maybe not a broken toy...

A used one.

Fucked hard and left to wallow in the aftershocks and exhaustion of her satiation.

I could smell my arousal and hovered on the tense wire of lusty hope and shame, if Xavier could see it dampening the placket of my thong.

The click of the camera and his shoes against the floor were the only sounds for long minutes as he continued to silently photograph me. The silence and the punctuated noise were driving me crazy.

I wanted him to say something. Anything.

Just to prove what my crazy mind was more and more convinced of.

That it was Alexander at my side and not Xavier Scott.

Only, the press of a thumb to the slight indentation in my plump lower lip paralyzed my thoughts.

I dragged in another lungful of that heady scent through my open mouth and unconsciously swept my tongue across the pad of that thumb.

His taste exploded in my mouth like ambrosia.

"Master?" I breathed, too entranced to worry I was wrong and face the embarrassment of asking such a question.

I wanted it to be him with every fiber of my being. My

body vibrated with coiled energy just waiting for release. Specifically, for him to release it from me with his wicked words and cruel, calculating hands.

"Master?" I asked again, stronger this time.

Desperate.

Needy.

High on the idea of him in my space.

"*Topolina*," he breathed against my lips. "Are you ready to kneel once more for your Master?"

Momentarily, I thought I was dreaming.

One of those inescapable nightmares when you know it isn't real, but the knowledge does nothing to shield you from the terror.

I often dreamt of Xan returning to claim me over the years, and it always started with those haunting words.

Are you ready to kneel for your Master?

Psychologically, I was more than ready. I felt as though I had never got up off the floor of the white, black, and gold ballroom after the first time I'd knelt there.

Rationally, the idea of kneeling ever again made my brain seize and short circuit like an overworked hard drive.

Then another touch filtered through the chaos in my mind, cutting cleanly through it like a hot knife.

Rough fingers ran up between my lace-covered breasts where they wrapped one by one around my neck and gently squeezed.

A collar.

My throat ached but not from the pressure. I wanted to lean into the hand, feel it band stronger, tighter, and intractably against my skin. I wanted a physical one without an escape latch. A permanent one tattooed into my skin.

One that showed everyone I was owned by Alexander Davenport.

The collar was there already under my skin, burning at all hours of the day so even when Alexander had seemed convinced I didn't belong to him, my body had said differently.

"What are you doing here?" I mouthed more than said.

His lips skimmed and bumped my own, firing off electrons under my skin that made my mouth feel static with current. It took everything in me not to jerk forward and feel the electricity erupt in a real kiss.

God, I wanted a kiss.

He'd stamped me with his brand of ownership at the charity event, bitten me when he'd cut me out of his life in Milan, but I hadn't been the recipient of Alexander's masterful kisses for far too long, and my body felt starved of them.

"I told you, you can run, but I'll always find you," he murmured against the skin of my cheek as he skimmed his nose into my hair and breathed deeply. "I could find you with my eyes closed, my ears plugged, and my nose stopped up. I can *feel* you before I know for sure you are even in a room. If predators have natural prey they are born to chase, you are mine."

"Xan," I breathed because that was the word that seemed to echo through my mind with every beat of my rapidly increasing pulse. "Please, don't play with me like this."

"Like this?" he asked cruelly as he plucked both my nipples and twisted.

I hissed but shook my head, desperately wishing I could see him to read what he would try to keep hidden in his eyes. "No, please don't play with my emotions like this. I don't understand."

I didn't. I was hopelessly confused, tangled up like yarn curdled on a loom.

My heart stuttered and chugged in my chest, a failing engine that wouldn't survive the test Alexander would no doubt put my body through if I let him...

Maybe even if I didn't.

Heat sluiced from my brain to my groin where it pooled between my legs.

"I'm not playing, *topolina*. When I use your body like this"—his hand cupped hard between my thighs, tight enough to feel the heavy pulse that beat through my pussy like a war drum—"it is the way a painter wields his brush or a sculptor his clay. You are mine to use, to mould into something more beautiful than before. It is no game. It is *art*, and you are my canvas."

"Not anymore," I whispered brokenly even as I thrust my chest forward when his fingers left my nipples.

"Always," he promised darkly and then his lips were sealed over my own and his tongue was thrusting like a lance through my shields and into my mouth.

I hummed instinctively as the taste of him hit me like hot whiskey and burned a path down my throat and straight to my core where it burned and burned.

He ate at my mouth like a glutton at his last meal before death, hungry to the point of devastation, desperate to the point of pain. I loved the bite of his teeth into my lower lip, the way he dragged them over the plump flesh like a wood scraper carving his name into the inside of my mouth.

He owned me in that kiss as if I had never been lost, as if every moment we were apart was only a period in a series of ellipses that was always going to lead to more of *this*.

Him and me.

My brain wildly tried to calculate how to deal with this latest development, but I was so wholly overwhelmed by the taste of him, the scent of him surrounding me like fog on the moors, and the feel of his big body hovering just out of my reach, a taunt, a possible present for good behavior well earned.

"Hush, my beauty," he ordered softly but no less commanding. "Stop that beautiful brain. Stop the questions and the need for answers. Be with me again and let it be as simple as that."

I whimpered because I wanted with my entire body to acquiesce to his control and give in to the weight of desire in my sex, but I couldn't find the latch to open the cage on my thoughts and set them free.

Reading my mind in the way only he had ever been able to do, Alexander straightened and stepped away, the air that rushed between us glacial cold.

When he spoke, it was in the carved stone tones of domination. "I think you need to remember who is in control of you, *topolina*. Who here is the mouse and who the Master?"

His hand snapped forward and slapped against one of my scarcely clad breasts. The *smack* resounded through the empty room and made the slight pain all the greater as the sharp sting sank deep roots in my chest and added to my feverish burn.

"There are consequences to your actions," he said almost conversationally as his shoes clipped away from me. "Are you ready to reap their reward?"

I didn't answer, my ears strained so hard to discern the soft sounds he made rustling in a bag that they felt as if they burned with the effort.

Despite my exertion, I startled when the soft kiss of suede tassels tickled over my collarbone and then settled over my shoulder. I shivered as Alexander bent over my back and whispered hotly in my ear, "Are you ready for your punishment, wife?"

I didn't ask him any more questions. They burned the back of my tongue, but there was no impulse sparking in my brain to ignite them and toss each burning arrow of thought at his head, to watch him drown in the bonfire of my rage and pain.

I was already too far gone to submission. The cool calm of it sluiced over my tongue and down my throat, dousing the questions and banking those fires. I could hate him later, force him to make sense at another time.

For now, I was free to be his.

Being his meant I could have him in the only way he'd ever let me.

As his submissive.

"Yes, Master," I said, and the words slotted into something inside me like a key in a lock.

And when Alexander coldly commanded, "Present yourself for me. I want to see how you've changed since the last time I touched your cunt," I felt the lock *click* and the door swing open.

There was a space in my mind that was inaccessible to me. Another plane, another dimension, whatever you wanted to call it, it was a place that transcended the restrictions of thought and social constructs. It was the setting of pure sensation.

Try as I might over the years, I'd never been able to reach it on my own. A vibrator on my clit, a thick dildo wedged into my tight ass, and four fingers stretching my cunt. Clothespins on my nipples, e-stimulator pads on my groin, and a few vicious slaps to my engorged sex. Even a few misspent nights at a well-known BDSM club where trained Dominants took me in hand with my favourite whips, and toys, everything short of sex, until I was a quivering, striped mass of flesh.

Nothing unlocked that elusive door to that taboo but delicious place.

Nothing but Alexander and his special brand of mastery.

A shudder wracked my body that had nothing to do with the cold room.

When I didn't respond quickly enough, Alexander twisted his hand in my hair and pulled me off the chair so that I collapsed to the ground on my knees. Instantly, instinctively, my head bowed gracefully, my spine straightened, and my hands met like a necklace clasped behind my back.

"Pretty as ever," he said in that soft tone with those hard-bitten words that always seemed louder than he spoke them. "But I always preferred you adorned in the jewels of my possession, both against your flesh in diamonds and rubies and stamped there in bruises and love bites."

I groaned breathily as he sank his teeth into the junction of my neck and shoulder and sucked hard at the skin so it bloomed beneath his tongue. When he disconnected with a loud sucking smack, the wet cooled deliciously on my skin and peppered my flesh into goosebumps. He touched the spot with the tip of the flogger he held in his hand and pushed until I hissed in pain.

"A poppy on your skin," he murmured as if lost in thought and desire. "I used to see the poppies behind Pearl Hall and think about the time I fucked you into the earth there."

"Yes," I hissed softly because I thought of the same thing whenever I saw my favourite bloom, forever tainted by the memory of Alexander and the way he fucked me goodbye.

I bent my neck deeper like a swan seeking sleep, only I was seeking the deep, darkly delicious bite of Alexander's bite into my neck. I wanted him to plant a garden of bruises under my skin, water them with my tears of pain, and watch them bud under the possessive heat of his gaze.

I wanted him to use me as a canvas to give voice to all his darkest desires.

Use me, fill me up, make me yours from the inside out.

I'd thought the words were contained in my head, rattling around loudly, but confined to my own mind. They were dangerous words to give a man who had proven he would come and go but keep our strings attached so that I was always linked to him, always his even when he didn't want me.

I would never have said them out loud if I'd been in my right mind.

But I wasn't.

I never was when Alexander's hands were shaping my body into his art.

"I am going to use you up. I'm going to mark your tongue with the taste of my cock and your skin with the print of my palm. I am going to fill you. I'm going to hold you down with my hands and my teeth and impale you on my cock so you feel the burn of me between your thighs for days. But you know already, you've been mine inside and out since the day we met."

A whimper leaked from my parted lips, shamefully eager for the future he described and pathetically forlorn that it was already occurring.

"But first," Alexander's words chipped off his posh tongue like shards of granite. "You are going to prove to me just how much you missed your Master. Just how eager you are to be my willing slave again."

"I am no one's slave," I slurred almost drunkenly, spurred by instinct but blurry with longing.

"Ah, that is where you are fundamentally wrong. You see, your enslavement to me has nothing to do with currency and contracts, and everything to do with your willingness to be used by me. Owned by me in every way I may wish to possess you."

One of his corded arms was suddenly belted diagonally over my chest, angling down my stomach so that he could cup my entire slick sex in one big palm. I was pinned by him, to him, surrounded in his heat and cool forest fragrance. It had been years since I'd been so close to another human being, and the fact that it was Alexander reclaiming my body in the way only he knew how made my brain spark and short circuit with exquisite lust and something more, something intangible that settled my bones better beneath my skin as if they had been broken and improperly reset until that moment.

"You told me I would have to earn your submission again, but that's not the truth, is it, my beauty? I need to earn your trust again, your tenderness, and your depthless heart. But your submission? Ah, that is intrinsically mine. The way the moon owns the tide and the sun owns the sky."

I opened my mouth, to protest maybe, or more probably to beg him to fuck me however that came, even if it fucked up my mind and heart at the same time. My heart ached from the hammer punch of his sweet, uncharacteristic words. I needed something to take me out of my head so I could steel myself against his emotional attack and focus on the physical. He unclasped me, and I fell forward sharply, his release as impactful as a car accident thrusting me forward.

The sharp whisper of the leather cutting through the air as I righted myself quieted me a second before I would've spoken, and then I was groaning from the sweet pain of the flogger against the bare skin of my back.

He beat me soundly, only seconds between each slap of the soft tassels digging like knife points into my flesh. The pain of the flogging built like hot bricks, one by one, into a wall of burning pleasure against my back.

I stayed folded in the shape of his desire, turning red with the colour of his lust beat into my skin, and I felt more at home in myself than I had in years.

I needed this, to bend until the point of breaking just to feel how far I could stretch, just to know I was doing my best to please someone worthy of my effort.

And Alexander was worthy.

No matter what he had done, my body and soul, my spirit were his to command just as I'd promise both of us they would never *ever* be.

But I was too far into subspace to think of the err of my ways, to reprimand or shame myself for the wants that had been too long woven into the fabric of my character to unstitch and respool.

So by the time Alexander stepped away from the throbbing ache in my back, I was exactly how we both wanted me to be.

Empty, but alive with purpose for one single thing.

The will of my Master.

"This first time, I won't hold back," he promised over the clank of a belt buckle falling open and the sensual rasp of a zipper being teased apart. "But you'll take everything I have to give like a good little sub, won't you, *bella?*"

Then the hot, hard tip of his cock brushed across my lips, painting them in the brine of the cum beaded there. I moaned from deep in my clenching gut as my tongue traced the taste of him over my mouth. He halted my efforts with hard hands woven into my hair, pinning my face at exactly the distance and angle he needed to use me best.

"Open your mouth and keep it open. I want to use you until you're drooling and choking all over my cock, and then I want you to gag for it."

A shiver juddered through my torso as my lips fell open. My hot, panting breath fanned over his length, and I wished acutely that I wasn't blindfolded so I could see the way the thick veins in his cock pulsed for me.

Instead, I felt them rub over my tongue as he used his hands in my hair to leverage me onto his cock until it was wedged at the back of my throat. I swallowed around him, humming the secret lyrics of my pleasure as I tended to his dick, as he sawed it over my lips the way a violinist controlled his bow. The sounds we made together like that were obscene; the wet suck of my lips against his skin, the hot whorl of my breath churning over his length each time he pulled out of my throat, and the faint vibration of my constant, babbling moans and groans. We filled the empty, cavernous room with the music of his Domination and my submission, and I'd never heard a more satisfying symphony.

Finally, he pried my tightly drawn lips off his dick with a loud *pop,* and my subsequent groan of disapproval.

"Did you miss your Master's cock in your throat?" he asked me coldly.

I squirmed on my knees, the cold studio air against the arousal sliding down my thighs from my overheated pussy. His meanness aroused me the way no tenderness ever could. It amplified him until he seemed giant with power, Herculean with strength.

"Yes, Master," I said, all breath and wet, smacking lips. "I don't know what I did without it."

A small part of my brain realized how shameful my actions were; I was a woman scorned. Where was my right-eous wrath and fury? Where was my backbone?

It was ramrod straight in the perfect posture of a submissive.

It wasn't just Alexander using me at that moment to wring out his own pleasure. It was about me using him for *my own*. I needed the cruelty and the objectification, maybe even more than he needed to dole it out.

This was about him proving to me, in his own way, in our secret language of flesh and fetish, that he could still fill all the cracks in my heart with gold. Give purpose to my masochism and a swift death by climax to my worries and my doubts.

This was a Master taking care of his slave in the most elemental way he knew how.

Alexander moved one hand from my hair, pushing the blindfold off my face as he did so, and then over my tear-streaked cheek to slide two fingers into my mouth.

I sucked feverishly at them, my eyes nearly rolling back into my head at the pleasure of having the taste of his skin on my tongue again. When I recovered, I looked up at him, hungrily devouring the sight of him looming over me like a lord demanding reparation from his vassal. The power dynamic made saliva pool at the sides of my mouth and wet leak from my swollen sex like an overturned jar of honey.

"You are mine," he swore solemnly as he pulled his fingers

out of my mouth and wrapped them around the root of his long cock. I kept my eyes tipped to his as he slowly fed it to me, inch by steel inch until I couldn't breathe around the fullness of him buried to the balls in my throat. "You are mine in every conceivable way. Mine to use." He pulled out to the tip of his head and then thrust back into the warm cavern so hard I choked around him. "Mine to worship." Another thrust. "Mine to own."

Spit dripped from my lips and splashed against my furled breasts.

I was so close to coming, I gyrated against the air, looking for even a mild current to swirl through the room and break open the cap on my bottled desire.

Sensing my desperation, Alexander stepped forward so that the smooth leather of his loafer was pressed tight to my drenched sex.

"Fuck yourself hard. Show me how wanton you are just for me." His strong voice was like the press of a hand around my throat.

I watched his smoking grey eyes as I began to hump against his shoe to the time of his thrusts into my mouth. The smell of our sex perfumed the air like a drug I couldn't help dragging deep into my lungs. I was light-headed, intoxicated by the fierce desire stamped across his face, the way his soul blazed so brightly from his usually opaque pewter-toned eyes.

There was no one else in the world for either of us but each other.

The thought cut through the ribbon of sense that tied me together so that every inch of me unravelled and unfurled as I orgasmed for him. Alexander watched as I screamed around his cock so deep in my throat, as I ground my clit into the leather, seeking more friction against the smooth swell, and then with triumph in his eyes he tipped his head back and punched a shout at the ceiling loud enough to echo through the room as he came.

And came.

He drowned my mouth in the hot, salty liquid, and I gulped him down greedily, an alcoholic after years of abstemiousness pouring herself a drink.

Before he finished coming, he pulled out and painted my cheek with the last two ropes of his cum. I gasped for breath, my clit throbbing like the heart of a hummingbird. Alexander used the opportunity to smear his fingers in the seed on my skin and slide it over my tongue.

"How do I taste, *topolina*?"

I hummed lustfully around his fingers, so gone to my desire that my inhibitions had been ground to dust. I wanted to roll onto my back, spread my legs open, and beg him to fuck me. I wanted to get him hard with my mouth again and nuzzle him with my cheek just to get closer to the musk and salt scent of him.

His soft, dark chuckle brushed over my skin in a silken caress. I bit my lip to stop my protest as he stepped away, but he was back before my anxiety could build, his legs pressing into the tender skin of my back. Shivers coursed down my spine as his big, abrasive hands slid over my collarbones, collecting the thick veil of my hair on either side so he could move it off my neck.

I sucked in a deep, sharp exclamation of breath when a cold weight settled around my throat and closed with an audible *tsk* under my hair.

I didn't need sight or touch to know that Alexander had collared me.

My pussy felt heavy, pulsing with a deep, dull throb that made it impossible to concentrate on anything but that and the cold bite of metal around my neck.

"This is who you are," he whispered into my ear, tracing the gold thorns around my throat so that I shivered. "Not just a slave, a trinket to own and flaunt and punish, but my slave, my *topolina*, a woman so beautiful it makes me ache. A warrior so powerful Joan and Artemis would shudder at your feet. Do you know how it makes me feel to make you sweat and cum and cry? It makes me feel like a god, fierce enough to deserve you, and a peasant, wholly unworthy of such a magnificent gift."

Every inch of my skin tingled with fear and hope. I wanted to close my eyes and absorb his words like a neglected plant exposed to light after too long in the dark.

But he was right. I didn't trust him.

He hadn't kept me safe from Noel, from the Order.

He hadn't ever loved me back.

There was still too much at stake to give myself over to him the way I had in those last months at Pearl Hall.

My family, Ashcroft, Salvatore and Dante…least of all, my heart.

"Please," I gasped softly in benediction. "Please, Xan, let this be enough."

He stilled at my use of my tender name for him, and for a moment, I worried he would be angry I broke the scene, furious that I would deny him even though it had been years, and I didn't owe him anything.

But then he pressed his palm over the large ruby sitting in the hollow of my throat and planted a lush, open-mouthed kiss to my pulse point.

"For now," he agreed darkly. "But the day I demand it all is fast approaching."

I didn't ask him why.

Why now?

Why at all?

Why even after all these years me?

I swallowed the burn of them as they lodged in my esophagus. I wanted this—his hands on my body, his cock inside me, his words breathed against my skin—too much to deny myself the wonder of it now. I could let it be goodbye. The proper goodbye I hadn't been able to have when Noel beat me and chased me off Pearl Hall estate and out of the country. Tears scorched the back of my tender eyes, but I blinked them back and committed myself to the moment. If this was the last time I ever enjoyed sex and intimacy, I would indulge as excessively as Dionysus with wine.

Sucking in a deep, bracing breath, I tipped my head to the side to expose more skin to Alexander's wandering lips.

He took it for the acquiescence it was.

"Thank you, *bella*," he breathed as if accepting a blessing from a priest. "Now, I missed your exquisite body, and I don't intend to ever go a day without seeing it again, even when we are distanced. Spread your legs for me and show me that gorgeous cunt," Alexander crooned as he stepped back and reached for the camera he'd abandoned on a side table to the left. "I plan to photograph it before I fuck it raw."

Chapter Twelve

COSIMA

*H*ave you ever woken up from a dream already crying because you know it was just a dream and the loss of it was so real you feel it like a hiccough in your heart?

That was how I woke up the morning after Alexander commandeered my photo shoot.

I was curled the way a cat would, my head tucked into the curve of my arm, my legs pulled tightly into my chest as if I could protect myself from harm by occupying as small a space as possible.

It didn't make a difference to the man behind me who

cupped me like a ladle, the bowl of his hips tight against the sphere of my ass, his front knit skin to skin against my back, his hands and feet tangled with my hair and toes as if he had to possess me from top to bottom even in slumber.

And he was asleep.

I could feel the soft caress of his short, deep breath against my bared neck and the weight of him so heavy against me like a leaden bracket.

More than anything, I wanted to turn into his arms, touch my fingertips to the steep curve of his thick eyelashes, and breathe in his every breath after he took it.

Then, I wanted to spend the rest of the day in the faintly lumpy bed at the quaint bed and breakfast my agent had booked me on the Lizard Coast while Alexander taught me new and difficult ways to worship him.

But I wouldn't do any of that.

My heart felt newborn in my chest, too weak and too small to sustain the stress of my adult body and mind. I pressed my fist to my ribcage and felt it flutter weakly, a butterfly suffocating trapped in a jar.

I needed distance to build back my walls, to construct a fortress better than the one before so I could survive living without Alexander again. My heart clenched just thinking about leaving him in this bed, let alone spending one day or a dozen strung together without him by my side.

How was it possible to love someone so much when you hadn't spent any time with them in years?

Was it true that whatever souls were made of, two could be constructed the very same? One heart cut into two and pressed into separate chests with the hope that one day, they would find each other.

I didn't think God or science or the universe were that romantic or that cruel, but I couldn't come up with a plainer explanation for my continued and absolute adoration of a man I'd once called my captor.

My therapist might have said Stockholm Syndrome again, the catch-all excuse for loving someone in a position of power who took advantage of you.

Yes, Alexander had taken advantage of me, but some secret, mammal part of me yearned for him to take more.

He sighed in his sleep, and I cranked my head awkwardly to watch his brow pucker in a way that cracked open the planes of his face and revealed how much closer to forty he was than thirty. There was silver peppered in the gold hair over his ears, but it was still a thick, soft pelt across his crown. Otherwise, there was very little evidence of the last four years in his face or the hard, perfectly cut and proportioned body that was pressed so intimately to my own.

I had to get out of there.

Carefully, I leveraged myself onto an elbow and searched the room. My clothes were folded and placed on the seat in the corner because Alexander was an exacting Dom, and he took pleasure in ordering me to do something for the sake of seeing me obey. My luggage and purse were stacked beside it, and my phone lay overturned on top of that.

It would be an easy getaway as long as he didn't wake up.

And Alexander was an apex predator; there was no way I'd get out of his grip without waking him and falling into the trap of his domination again.

Metal winked in the crack of light spilling in through the curtains and I turned farther to see my ruby collar and the discarded leather and metal cuffs Alexander had used to bind me into complicated folds after we'd returned to the room last night.

My cheeks burned like twin stove elements as I remembered the way he'd chained me to the brass headboard positioned on my hands and knees with my ass in the air and my cheeks parted like the pages of a book under his big hands. He'd eaten at my crease for an hour, using his teeth, tongues, lips, and fingers until I was dripping juice down my inner thighs and humping back against his face in desperate need of *more*. He had taken my mouth and pussy at the studio, photographing me for his pleasure in profane, graphic ways that still made my core tighten like a fist, but he waited for the plushness of a bed to claim my ass again. I'd forgotten, somehow, how an anal orgasm ripped me apart from the inside out and left my muscles frayed like split wires.

I shook off the memory even as my pussy dampened and clenched with need. I couldn't afford to give in to my lust if I wanted to get away from Alexander.

And I did.

Whatever pretty words he had spoken last night had long dissipated in the cold light of dawn. I didn't know what his game was, but I knew there was one. Every step of our relationship had been a carefully calculated move across the board. I didn't yet know what this one led to, but I was finally smart enough not to let him force me there.

Working quickly and quietly, I leaned over to the bedside table and hooked the cuffs over a finger. I held my breath as I slowly slid the padded leather over one of his wrists, untangled his fingers from my hair so I could thread the chain through the brass headboard rail, and then fastened the second cuff to his other wrist.

The second he was secured, Alexander's eyes flashed open like headlights, pinning me in the high beams, frozen and frightful as a deer.

After a brief, furious second of connection, we both burst into action.

I scrambled back from his body on my heels and hands, crab-walking to the end of the bed so that his reaching fingers couldn't grab me.

"Cosima Davenport," he growled, paralyzing me not because of his venom-laced tone, but because I hadn't heard my married name in years and only then, once from his own lips.

Even in my current state, I loved the sound of it.

"What the fuck is it that you think you are doing?" he asked me, enunciating each word like bullets shot from the cold chamber of a gun.

I blinked at him and bit my lip. "I'm leaving."

Fury darkened his face so savagely, he looked more monster than man.

"You will absolutely *not*."

I gritted my teeth against the intractable demand in his voice and began to hum under my breath as I slid off the bed and quickly donned my thick rust-coloured sweater and silky oyster beige skirt.

"You will uncuff me in the next two minutes, Cosima, or I will make you very dearly sorry for your disobedience," he promised darkly.

I hummed louder, ignoring the way my pulse raced like prey sprinting away from its predator. I continued to shoot him quick, short glances as I dressed just to reassure myself he was still sturdily locked to the bed.

His eyes blazed with rage so bright it made my belly quiver.

"Hear this, *topolina*," he said, his voice so low, so filled with the gravel dredged up from the bottom of his stony core that I could barely discern the words. "If you think locking me up will stop me from reclaiming you, you are pitifully, sorely mistaken. We have things to discuss, you and I, things I hoped to bring into the light this morning. But if you insist on being *foolish*..." The word slapped me across the face, but I continued to tug on my knee-high boots as if I didn't feel his scorn like a handprint on my cheek. "The next time I find you, I'll cuff *you* to each leg of the bed and beat your pussy until you cry every single one of the tears your body has to offer me, and then I will fuck your sore, ravaged pussy and smear my cum in the cuts across your arse. Then, when you are wrecked beyond thought or further feeling, I'll bundle you up in my arms and hold you there until you *bloody well listen to what I have to say*," he roared.

But I was already hastily dragging my suitcase to the door, wrestling it open, and hesitating in the doorway to take one last thirsty look at the lord in my bed. He was sitting upright, the large muscles in his arms coiled rope under golden skin as he strained against the cuffs, his abdominals so clearly defined they looked like a checkboard just waiting for my tongue and fingers to make a game of it.

My mouth went dry at the sight of him. He was sexy and regal somehow even bound, a lion you knew was seconds away from breaking free and devouring you whole.

"Please," I told him with quiet desperation. "Don't come for me again. I don't want a half-life with you. I don't want to be your secret or your slave. I'm tired of existing in the dark, dismissed to your shadows. I know now that I deserve the light, and I swear, Xan, even though I can't handle this—*you*—if you come for me, I might cave, and I will never *ever* be satisfied with what you have to give."

Alexander stared at me, his mouth pursed tightly, a lock of golden hair caught on his eyelashes, but all he did was watch as I slowly backed out the open door and then closed it on his face.

I slept on the plane, not because I was exhausted and emotionally spent, but because my back ached each time I shifted in my seat, and I couldn't stop thinking of the beautiful, hard man I'd turned away from again. He hunted me, a predator even to my thoughts. Finally, thirty minutes into the flight, I succumbed to weakness and took two sleeping pills.

The flight attendant had to wake me up with a brisk shake that reminded me instantly of the state of my back, and I was up, groggily walking off the plane.

I was still out of it when I saw the man standing outside of the arrivals gate holding a sign written with my name. It was the same man who had delivered Ashcroft's missive to me in Central Park. I recognized him not because his features struck a chord of remembrance, but because he was so completely forgettable with his bland features and pale British colouring, I knew instantly he was a servant of the Order.

"I'm not going with you," I told him as I stopped by his side. "I just returned from less than thirty-six hours in a completely different time zone, and I'm knackered. Tell your employer to beckon me in six hours after I've had a nap."

His hand shot out as I went to move by, clutching my bicep in a bruising grip.

"I think you'll find, slave Ashcroft," he jeered quietly. "That my employer has a heavy hand with a whip when he's been kept waiting."

"I think you'll find that so do I," I retorted, using one of the moves I'd been taught in self-defence class over the years to twist my arm out of his hold, catch his dislodged hand, and then leverage it back against his wrist.

He hissed with pain, rage animating his stoic face.

I leaned in close to softly jeer at him, "Touch me again and I promise, I'll kill you."

He cursed as I released him, but dutifully stooped to take

my bags from me and lead me to the waiting car parked illegally at the curb.

"No wonder Davenport let you lose," he muttered as he opened the door for me.

I ignored him, but my chest panged with guilt as I thought about Alexander locked to the bed back in England. I had no doubt Riddick or the innkeeper would find him before long, but he would be furious and maybe even embarrassed at the predicament.

I was prepared to deal with Ashcroft. I had plans for him just as he had ones for me, and I knew I didn't *need* Alexander there with me to hold my hand while I plotted.

But I would have preferred it.

Though, knowing Alexander, I wasn't so sure he wouldn't storm into Ashcroft's Upper East Side home, slit his throat, and then raze it all to the ground.

I was a woman; therefore, my plan was slightly more understated, but hopefully just as deadly.

Ashcroft was waiting for me in the foyer of his townhome, hands held behind his back and feet braced like a general expecting his orders to be obeyed.

Before I had even crossed the threshold, he demanded, "On your knees, slave."

I gritted my teeth as I folded myself to the ground.

"Good little thing," he praised, petting my head the way one would a dog.

A deep breath helped to quell my more imminent rage. I was there because he was blackmailing me, but I was also there to learn from him all there was to know about the Order.

I didn't know what was going on with Alexander or why he was suddenly back in my life with a tenacious vengeance, but I did know that even if we weren't together in any way ever again, I still wanted to end the Order.

They had made him into a monster, so I was going to become theirs.

"I didn't give you permission to leave the country," Ashcroft said mildly as his hand jerked a hank of my hair back brutally. "You'll have to be punished for that."

Honestly, that was fine with me. Ashcroft was a true sadist; he didn't need to fuck me to take his pleasure from me. He only needed my sweat, my tears, and a little blood. Then again, his reluctance to fuck me might have stemmed from the damage he'd garnered from his stint in the Iron Chair at Pearl Hall. I'd seen the mangled bend of his cock and his horribly scarred scrotum. Riddick and Alexander had not been kind to him after he'd forcibly taken my throat.

"I had to work," I demurred as I blinked tears from my smarting eyes.

"Maybe I should move you in with me. Get myself a permanent little slut and maid to do all the dirty work around here." He stepped close so that the hard length of his dick pressed to my cheek through his slacks. "Would you like that?"

I looked at his feet in answer, unable to bend and contort myself into the origami folds of submission I usually fell gracefully into at Alexander's feet.

The memory of his cold voice like a collar around my throat, his will a chain-link leash ruthlessly guiding me through the obstacle course of his desire made my throat go dry.

"That's more like it," Ashcroft said, flicking my hardened nipples. "I would beat you so fucking soundly bent over my desk, but The Trials are tonight, and they need each slave unmarked before the start."

The Trials.

I'd heard of them before, in my past life as slave Davenport, but I didn't know what they entailed. Alexander hadn't participated in The Trials at Club Dionysus the year he owned me in England because I'd only just been broken.

I didn't know how Ashcroft could delude himself into thinking he could put me on display, and I would happily obey his demands like some trained bitch at a Best in Show.

"I know you'll obey beautifully for me," he said, reading the expression on my face and sneering at it. "Or I'll not only release the tawdry photos of Davenport fucking you into the ground, but I'll also give you over to his father."

His sinister laughter rang through the foyer like the track to a bad B-list movie.

My skin broke open in gooseflesh, and I fought the urge to wrap my arms around myself as a protective shield.

As much as I had missed Alexander over the last few years, I had been that much more relieved to be away from Noel.

You could still see the faint silvery trace of scars on my back if you caught me in the wrong light, and when I dreamt, it was often of the vicious beating he and his third son had bestowed upon me as a wedding present.

The very mention of Noel's name was akin to invoking the devil.

"I see you understand the gravity of your situation now." Ashcroft tipped my chin and leaned down so that his smug, fleshy smile was all I could see. "Noel wants you. He's mentioned offhand enough times at the Club that he would pay handsomely if someone turned you over to his possession. It seems he didn't get enough of you when you were Alexander's pet. Apparently, the Thornton is not very good at sharing."

No, Alexander wasn't, which was only one of the reasons he had warned his father to never lay a hand on me.

Of course, Noel hadn't heeded that threat, and to this day, I doubted Alexander knew just how much physical damage, not to mention emotional trauma, his dad had wreaked upon me.

"Such a shame Noel can't be there tonight to watch you perform for me." He dragged his fingers down the side of my face and sifted them through my hair. I held my breath as I prayed he wouldn't catch sight of the poppy Alexander had planted under the skin of my neck.

"Though, he would take you away, and quite honestly, I'm not done with you yet. You have all this golden skin I've yet to mark." He hummed contemplatively as if cataloguing all the future ways he would hurt me.

His dispassionate malevolence reminded me of all the other truly vile men I'd met before. It was surprising how intrinsically boredom and evil were linked together. I wondered if the men of the Order were not so wealthy as to be idle and not so emotionally vacant as to need cruelty to fill them up if there would even be an Order to begin with?

"You will stay here until tonight. I have a girl who does hair and makeup coming for you, and before then, you'll don your sweet little maid's uniform and see to my house, won't you, slave?"

"Yes, sir."

He petted my head again, then twisted his fingers in the locks and yanked me into a standing position again. His sneering face was hot against my own as he plastered our cheeks together and spoke into the corner of my mouth. "Please me tonight and when I bring you back here for a night cap, I might not have to reintroduce you to the bullwhip. Do you remember that, sweet slave? When Landon Knox peeled the pretty skin off your back in long, golden ribbons?"

He felt my shudder and laughed like a drunkard, intoxicated by my fear. I caught myself on the wall as he tossed me away and then struggled not to spin around to attack him as he strolled down the hall to his office with his hands in his pockets, whistling.

I reminded myself that I had a plan, and that plan would one day lead not just to the destruction of Ashcroft himself, but the entire Order of Dionysus.

With that thought running through my mind like a meditative chant to drown out the agony of my anger, I hurriedly donned the ridiculous maid's costume and started to explore the three-story townhome. The arrogant and entitled were bound to be careless with their belongings, and I was eager to discover what he could be harbouring.

He had a sex room done up entirely in black, the floors polished concrete stained dark in places with what I was sure was blood, the walls covered in slick black paneling that gave the entire place a dark, antiseptic feel like a nightmarish doctor's room. He had trays of tools, not just the normal Dom's paraphernalia, but vials of drugs, syringes, thick piercing needles, scalpels, and medical clamps. The entire aesthetic reminded me that Ashcroft was a rather prolific chemist, and it churned my gut to think of all the ways he might torture a woman with this kind of equipment.

There was nothing to be found there but fodder for nightmares, so I quickly moved on, cleaning the rest of the house in my stupid costume with a feather duster, mop, and broom. My hands smelled of artificial lemon, and my body, still aching from Alexander, creaked and moaned as I moved over the huge space.

I was tempted not to clean at all and merely hide away to waste time, but the criminally bland servant who had picked me up trailed me through the rooms to ensure I worked.

By the time I reached Ashcroft's office, vacant while he was dressed by his valet for The Trials, I was depressed by my lack of findings and weary enough to weep.

I wanted to give in to self-pity and curse God for continuing to heap trial after trial on my heart. It pained me to admit that the worst of those lately was spending the day and night with Alexander in London knowing that it was goodbye.

But something in the memory clicked in me like the shutter of a camera, and I realized with giddiness exactly what Ashcroft's blackmail gave me in opportunity.

"I have to use the toilet," I told the servant as I hesitated at the office and began to wander down the hall to the last door at the end of the hall by the back door. "I'll just be a moment."

He scowled, but remained where he was, ostensibly organizing Ashcroft's life on an iPad.

I was careful to control my gait as I walked into the bathroom and locked the door, only letting a smile break through the crust of sorrow on my face when I was alone with myself in the mirror.

Hurriedly, I took my phone out from where I'd wedged it into my garter belt and dialed a number I knew by heart.

"*Tesoro?*" Dante asked. "You are returned from the isle of the beasts?"

He always had a derogatory nickname for his homeland, and it usually made me smile, but I had too much on my mind to find him charming.

"Listen, could you do me a favour?"

"Anything," he replied resolutely.

His readiness did something funny to my heart, a palpitation of glee.

"Good, I need some kind of small camera. Like a nanny cam? Those exist in real life, correct?"

Dante laughed, warm and loud. "Yes, Cosi, those exist in real life. Dare I ask why you need one of these?"

"More than one. Ideally, I'd like six or seven."

"Does this have something to do with Ashcroft?" he demanded, and there was a murmur of voices in the background in response.

I bit my lip. It wouldn't do to lie because Dante could sniff out dishonesty like a police dog did a bomb, and honestly, I couldn't think of another viable reason I would need hidden cameras.

"Yes, it does. I need you or one of your…men to meet me in the next hour and a half with the cameras at this address," I said, rattling off Ashcroft's information. "Can you have them meet me by the back entrance? Just text me when they arrive. I won't respond, but I'll feel the vibration on my thigh and find a way to get to him."

"Cosima, are you in his house right now?" he growled.

"Well, obviously."

"Don't be fucking smart with me right now. Fuck your cameras, I'm coming myself and bringing some guys. We'll take care of that *figlio di puttana* ourselves right now."

"Dante, no," I said sharply. "If you want to come wait outside the door, I can't stop you. But I have an idea here, one that could lead to ending the Order, and that is important to me. Not just for myself because of every single way they've tried to ruin my life, but for other women too. No one deserves to be sold into a society that will use, humiliate, and harm them for their own amusement."

He hesitated, the puffs of his angry breath blowing heavy through the phone.

"Fine, I'll send Frankie. If you need any help at all, though, you call me. Even if you can't talk, you call, I'll answer, and I'll be there before you know it, okay?"

"Agreed," I said before lightening my tone in an attempt to keep him from worrying about me. "But really, Dante, you don't need another bullet wound. At this point, I think you are more metal than man."

"Understand this and understand it well, Cosima," he said in a voice like Alexander's, in a way that reminded me the big teddy bear I knew he could be was also one of the most dangerous mafia men in the country. "I would take a hundred more bullets for you until my blood ran lead if it meant you were safe from harm."

"Dante," I exhaled as his words found purchase in my chest. It was only one word, his name, but I thought it relayed how very much I loved him and how very awed I was that he loved me that way in return.

Noel hadn't ruined the hearts of all his sons.

Only Rodger and, maybe, Alexander.

The thought made my heart pinch, but I forged on.

"I have to go. I've been in here too long. Send Frankie and I promise I'll call you when this is all over, *si*?"

"*Si, tesoro mia*," he agreed in the same tone I'd used with him, one that ached with tenderness, vulnerable as a bruise. "Be safe."

I ended the call, flushed the toilet, and ran the faucet before I slipped out the door and returned to the office. The unimpressed servant gave me a narrow glare, but I smiled jauntily at him as I resumed my cleaning duties.

Later, when I was finished my chores, and I was seated in front of the vanity being beautified by a woman who spoke only Russian, my phone vibrated, and I excused myself once more to the restroom.

No one stopped or spotted me as I crept down the stairs and out the back door.

Dante's right-hand man and the only member of his crew that I was ever allowed to interact with greeted me with a large, boyish smile.

"Frankie," I greeted, kissing both his stubbled cheeks.

"Cosima. These are ready to go. They record video until they reach their max storage point. I didn't have time to set up a live feed, so these will have to do for now. Will you be able to retrieve them at some point?"

I nodded, taking the dime-sized cameras in my hand. "Thank you for this, Frankie. Tell Dante not to worry."

His lips twisted in a grimaced smile. "Yeah, that's not gonna happen with you in the lion's den, but I'll pass that along to give the other boys a good laugh."

"I know what I'm doing." I'm not sure why I felt the need to tell the almost stranger that when it was really every single other man in my life who needed to hear it. Still, Frankie respected me enough to go somber for a moment and scrutinize me with his wet, black eyes. Eyes that had seen death and blood, corruption and greed so big it swallowed people's entire lives.

It was those eyes that blinked, then smiled at me. "Sure, babe, I believe it."

I swallowed thickly, surprised by how much I'd needed someone to have faith in me, and then punched him lightly in the shoulder before heading back inside.

I planted one in the bedroom I'd been given to use to get ready for the night. Another in the hallway on the second story and another in the open doorway of Ashcroft's room. There was one pressed to the wall behind a ficus plant in the entryway and then another, finally, in Ashcroft's office in the eye of black marble carved wolf.

I placed it there as I moved toward Ashcroft where he sat leaned back in his chair like the entitled lord he was.

"You look beautiful," he praised as his hot, greasy gaze smeared over all the skin exposed by my gold satin lingerie.

I smiled at him with words in my eyes only Alexander had ever been able to read; *I am so much more than my beauty, and one day soon, you will find that out.*

Chapter Thirteen

ALEXANDER

Eighteen hours after Cosima had abandoned me for the second time, my anger had yet to abate. I could feel it coursing through my veins as thick and chemical as opium in my bloodstream. Even Riddick, whom I had finally identified as my closest friend in the last four years, was careful around me in the hours after she'd left, barely speaking a word unless it was to confirm travel plans.

To say I was royally aggravated by her flight was a gross understatement. I was both angry with her for running and with myself for believing she would obey out of hand.

It had been four long years since Cosima had come to heel

for me, and she'd spent countless hours in therapy, in meditation classes, reading self-help books written by self-aggrandizing gurus to get over her compulsion to serve me.

I should have known.

But my elation had made me sloppy. I was a virgin on her wedding night, knowing I was finally going to receive the gratification I so deserved, the union I'd worked toward for years, and I'd underestimated the fact that my bride was still a reluctant one.

She did not know the myriad of ways my life had changed since she had up and left me the first time.

She didn't know the sacrifices I had made.

The men I had extorted, threatened, and maimed to achieve my goals.

The estate I had given over to Noel like a gift and a prison so that I would know where the Devil lived even as I sought to end him.

She didn't know anything, my little mouse.

As per usual, she had been kept out of male mechanisms for her own safety, and it had led to a less than satisfactory ending for us both.

It appeared I had to learn that lesson one more time before I vowed never to repeat it again.

By the end of this night, Cosima Davenport would know exactly where I stood, and therefore where she did too because whether she cared to admit, we were unequivocally linked; two planets locked in orbit.

I'd had a plan, a damned good one that had been cooked up in the Prime Minister's office in the middle of the night after returning from finding Cosima in Milan so many years ago over godawful coffee and endless conversations about politics, morality, and revenge.

In that precise plan, I was not to contact Cosima until it was all over.

She was my reward at the end of my hero's journey.

Unfortunately, though I had undertaken the path of a hero, I was still drawn to villainous tendencies, and the moment the tabloids had splashed her supposed impending union to the git Mason Matlock, my good intentions had crumbled to ash.

There was no way, even over my dead body, that I would allow anyone to lay claim to the woman I'd already made my own. I would kill every single man who so much as dreamt of making her theirs. Cosima was and always would be *mine*. Even if she didn't know it.

I hadn't planned to approach her so brutishly at the charity ball either, but my Cosima had been so utterly ravishing, there was no other proper course of action but to publicly—perhaps stupidly, given the covert nature of my life for the past four years–buy her once more.

It was largely symbolic, exchanging money for a date. I had no desire for one measly night with her, nor did I feel the need to ask or barter with anyone for the privilege, but I thought it made a very nice, if somewhat dramatic, gesture.

Especially after the way I'd turned her away in Milan. The look of her priceless, stunning face breaking into thousands of fine cracks and fissures when I'd so ruthlessly dropped her heart to the roof of the Duomo and crushed it beneath my heel would haunt me for the rest of my life. It was a necessary evil. The Order kept minute track of Cosima for the first year of our separation, delving into her internet history and the habits of her new life in New York. So did I. And it was obvious to both parties that Cosima was still hung up on me, her endless therapy appointments, Amazon book orders, and the one ill-fated visit to a BDSM club were more than evidence of that.

So to ensure that she was safe, I had to crush her.

There was no greater torture than loving a woman and being unable to have her. The only thing that had alleviated any of the pain over the past four years was making progress against the very Order I'd come to infiltrate that night.

I had enough information on most of the Order to put away some of the most powerful men for life, including Noel, who was on house arrest in Pearl Hall for his corrupt dealings with the Falmouth Port Authority.

The end was nigh and a better man, a stronger man, would have stayed away from Cosima until it was over.

But I wasn't a stronger man.

I was completely wrecked by the weight of Cosima in my chest, the anchor and chain that pulled taut across the time and distance between us.

There was no way she was marrying another man.

No way, now that I'd have her submission and her reluctant capitulation, that I could go another bloody, agonizing day without her.

Which brought me to the door of the Order's New York City hub, Club Bacchus, to flagrantly thumb my nose at the society and take back what was mine.

Women hung like ornaments from the ceiling, strung up in gold chains, diamond ropes, pearls on strings of reinforced carbon fiber so that the beauties didn't fall to the floor in a tangle of riches. They were suspended in shapes, each bound in a different pose by beautiful loops of Shibari bondage. A redhead dripped from the air upside down, her hair a flaming arrow, her feet cuffed to a wooden bow with her knees out-turned and bare pussy displayed. They had made her into the symbol of a bow and arrow, the hunter's classic weapon.

Another spun slowly with her neck bowed, back arched until her head nearly connected with her pointed toe like a ballerina twirling in a music box. She was caught up in a yard of shimmering pale pink chiffon, three lengths of which wrapped around her throat and kept it strained backward in a fruitless attempt to meet her raised right thigh.

They would have been beautiful strung up like that if they

had consented to it. As it was, I could read the fear in their glassy eyes, smell the metallic tang of their stress sweat under-cutting the leather-tainted air of the club.

There were fifteen girls festooning the lavish interior of Club Bacchus, trapezoids of light from the gently swaying chandeliers cutting their skin into fragments of gold. Men traced those yellow shapes over their skin as they mingled throughout the cavernous room, drinking scotch and chatting amiably with their companions as they ogled and molested the women on display.

I had no desire to join them.

Most of the men wouldn't know me by sight, but some would, and my entire plan rested on remaining anonymous until the last moment.

I slipped through the shadows at the edges of the blue brocade walls until I found a velvet upholstered chair with the perfect vantage point of my target.

My beauty was strung up in gossamer chains of gold, thousands of them that bound her breasts into swollen peaks, wound over her belly and between each thigh so that her legs were bent under and spread, exposing her pussy to the cool air of the room and the hot eyes of its patrons. Her arms were folded over her head and covered so completely in gold, it seemed she wore them like a crown.

She was the only woman in the entire room who stared boldly from her bondage, who tipped her chin as much as the ropes allowed so she could look each of her lecherous admirers in the eye and damn them all silently to hell.

A goddess in chains was still a goddess.

No amount of maneuvering or lording over her would change that.

My God, but she took my fucking breath away.

I snapped my fingers at one of the blokes walking around with a drink tray and snatched someone else's whiskey for myself. The boy pursed his lips but didn't utter one word of protest as he pulled away and resumed his duties.

He knew his place better than Cosima did, and she'd had years of acrimony and male dominance under her belt.

I wondered as I sipped the Laphroaig twenty-eight-year-old scotch, if her inability to break was the reason I had become so enraptured by her. There was nothing brittle or hollow about her submission, nothing that cracked under the force of another man's will.

She was too warm, too elastic and self-contained to snap like that. Instead, she bent, twisted, and swanned into the shapes dictated by my domination. It made the beauty of her submission utterly heady and shamelessly intoxicating because it was not just a random, broken woman I had at my control, but one of substance and verve who chose to obey my commands.

There was mutual respect for the power each of us yielded in the exchange.

If you had asked me years ago, the first time my father had forced me to whip one of his slaves, if I would ever revere a woman the way I did my wife, I would have thought you were crazy.

But secretly, the truth of it would have resonated.

I hated the way Noel treated his slaves, and as soon as I was old enough to withstand a beating in their place, I'd taken it.

My entire life, I'd believed that I was hardwired to be the exact replica of my father. That my nature would always outweigh the nurture my mother had displayed.

As I sat in the dark of the hedonistic club drinking scotch, planning to dismember the man who stood beside Cosima like her false god, the relief that coursed through me felt like a baptism.

I wasn't fool enough to think that my feelings for Cosima washed away the blood on my hands or the countless shady dealings I'd been made to witness as part of the Order. I was still, intractably and always, the villain, characterized that way before birth by my father.

But if I'd had a heart, I would have loved Cosima with every facet of it.

If I could be a hero, in any way for any stretch of time, it would be to save the woman I'd been calling my own since the moment she saved my life in a Milanese alleyway five years ago.

The lights dimmed across the club as one of the hanging slaves was unbound and led to the main stage for the first exhibition of the night. The men lingering around the room in groups found their seats for the show, but not before taking their last lingering touches of the displayed slave girls.

One man, ruddy like an Irishman, cupped Cosima between the legs and then licked off his fingers one by one.

The rage churning in my gut was not hot or volcanic. It was glacial, colossal shards of ice cracking off into frothing arctic waters. It cast a clear, cool light on my thoughts as I mulled over the way I would kill that Irishman for touching my beauty.

She might have run from me—and she would pay for it—but no matter the distance or time between us, Cosima Lombardi Davenport was mine.

I did not want her to have a life with others, dialogue or even monologue separate from me or my name. I didn't want to spend one single moment more without her understanding that my ownership had nothing to do with money changing hands or contracts signed, and everything to do with the way one soul could possess another.

Call it witchcraft, call it enchantment, but whatever it was, I had surrendered to it a long time ago.

She would too, just as soon as I extracted her from the perilous situation she was tangled up in with Ashcroft.

Riddick appeared silently beside me, feet braced and hands clasped behind his back like a soldier awaiting orders.

"She's up next, milord," he murmured as he stared with dark rage at Ashcroft running a hand down Cosima's inner thigh.

"Patience, Riddick," I told him even though a shard of icy rage pierced my throat painfully as I tried to swallow it down. "You know what to do with him when the time comes?"

He nodded curtly, blatantly unmoved by the sexual display of dominance and submission taking place on the stage. The echo of the slave's sobs throughout the room were nothing to the man who had stood by my side for years.

Only the quiver of Cosima's thigh as she struggled away from Ashcroft's lingering touch made the tin man fill with feeling.

I knew because the same feeling echoed within myself.

Finally, the first lord finished with his slave, and there was a smattering of applause. No one was enthusiastic about the performance. It had lacked screams, blood, and begging, the three cornerstones on The Trial's grading rubric.

"Now, gentlemen and slaves, I know we've been waiting to see what Ashcroft will do with the supermodel, and I am sure it will be delectable. Ashcroft and slave, please take the stage."

I watched, not breathing, not even blinking as the man untangled Cosima briskly from her chains and then hooked a leash through the leather collar at her throat before forcing her to crawl after him up onto the raised dais at the back of the room.

My body moved like smoke through the shadows, silently making my way up the stairs to the left of the stage where I lurked behind the navy-blue curtains. A hand slipped into the silk lined pocket of my blazer and carefully grasped the syringe between my knuckles.

Ashcroft said something to the crowd that made them

laugh as Cosima folded to her knees in the perfect submissive posture.

I uncapped the plastic lid and shifted deeper into the cover of the velvet drapes.

Ashcroft's shoes clicked like the timer of a ticking bomb as he crossed the black lacquered stage toward me to retrieve some of the plethora of tools laid out on the sideboards backstage.

Click, click, click.

He appeared parallel to me; his profile sharp with excitement for what was to come. There was a smile on his lips, twisted like his lust into something ugly.

I wiped it from his face in one smooth swoop as I stepped from the blackness, wrapped my arms sinuously around him, and then squeezed like a python. My prey froze in fear before the struggle began, but it was really no struggle at all.

I hooked my leg around his feet so that I could leverage his stumbling step forward back against my chest, holding him closer, suffocating him harder.

"You dare to touch what is mine, Ashcroft?" I hissed into his ear, just loud enough to be heard over the thundering rush of blood to his head.

"Not yours…anymore," he managed to wheeze.

My god, but I wanted to rip him apart right then and there, twist his spine until it cracked and everything inside him spilled open like candy from its papier-mâché holding.

"Cosima is and will always be mine," I told him calmly, focusing on my breath so that I didn't kill him too quickly, and end all the fun I'd planned for him. "But even if she wasn't, I would kill you all the same for blackmailing her as you have, for daring to touch a woman so much better than your pathetic self."

Then, before he could infuriate me to murder, I plunged the tip of the needle I held in one hand deep into his neck and pushed the drugs into his system.

Ten seconds later, he was out.

Riddick stepped out of the dark to catch him as I let him fall forward out of my arms.

"Keep him in the Iron Chair until I get there," I reminded my manservant and friend. "Somehow, the bastard retained his ability to get an erection after the last time he sat on the spiked throne. See to it that the same mistake isn't made again."

I turned on my heel before Riddick could respond. The crowd outside the stage was beginning to murmur at the delay, and I didn't want to give them any reason to investigate. Quickly, I gathered my tools and strode into the light of the stage.

There was a collective gasp at the change of Dominant, but no one rushed the stage to stop me from continuing the show. Things like this happened. We were all lions in a cage filled with a limited supply of meat. There were no rules to curtail our natural aggression and need for dominance, so only the strongest thrived.

And I was strongest of them all.

Cosima knelt with her head bowed, her veil of glimmering black hair almost blue under the spotlights. She didn't know why the audience had gasped, but the tight set of her shoulders and the bracing set of her toes against the floor spoke to her readiness to prepare for the worst.

Nearly naked and bound, my beauty was still a gladiator.

Music pulsed like a heavy heartbeat over the speakers as I wrapped the leash around my palm and used it to force Cosima up onto her knees to lessen the strain on her neck. Bowed into me, mouth parted like a split cherry, I felt myself get hard at the sight of her.

"Are you ready for your punishment, wife?" I asked against her damp lips before running my tongue down her jawline and sinking my teeth hard into her neck.

Her gasp punched into the air like an exclamation mark as

her body swayed even closer to mine. I watched her golden eyes turn up to mine and go black with shocked relief and dark desire.

Yes, I told her with my eyes, *this was what she deserved for locking me to the bed and running away from me.*

Again.

She deserved to be punished in whichever way I saw fit, and I deserved to watch her struggle to meet each demand as recompense.

Her eyes flared, hot as the center of a flame. I could read the angry question in that heat as easily as ink from a page.

Why are you not rescuing me from this place?

My answering grin sliced through the left half of my face and filled my chest with a different kind of cold.

Not one of rage, but the cool metallic edged precision that comes from stepping into Domination.

I dragged her closer by the leash instead of leaning down myself because every action from here on out was meant to emphasize the power discrepancy between us.

I led, and she followed.

"Because, *topolina,*" I responded to her unspoken demand, "I am not your saviour come to take you away to a fairy-tale land. I am your Master, and *this?* This is my domain."

Her shiver ran through the leather leash into my hand, a steel rod transporting the lightning current of her desire straight through my flesh.

The power of the moment was so tangible, I could feel my very skin hum.

Without warning, I released the tension on the leash, but instead of collapsing to the ground in a tangle of ungainly limbs, Cosima floated like silk to the ground in the perfect pose of obedience.

Her composure was the only response I needed to know she wanted this, *needed* this, as much as I did.

In the complicated dance of our recoupling, this was the

main combination of moves. All I needed to do was lead, and my beauty would, always, inevitably, follow.

A small silver table on wheels like you might find in an emergency room was set up to one side of the stage where I'd deposited my toys as I walked past, and I returned to it then. Ostensibly, I organized the implements there as if musing over the scene I planned to see out with my slave. In reality, I needed a moment to look at her again, folded into submission so impactful that it seemed to hit like a flaming arrow through my chest.

I took in the heavy weight of her perfectly formed breasts, the ruddy brown tips of her nipples puckered in the deliberately cold air. They were large breasts, edging toward profane on her slight frame, her tiny waist and flagrant dip beneath the swells, her hips rounded but slight as they narrowed into the longest legs I'd ever seen. She was perfection. Not because she met the standard definition of beauty as measured by media and modern ideals, but because there was a painfully attractive duality to her form; confidence and power stamped into every dip of her curves while every hollow held the youthful vulnerability of someone much less seasoned than her tragic experiences had made her.

Looking at her like that reminded me in acute ways I'd been blind to see before, that tending to her the way I would was the greatest of all my considerable gifts and responsibilities.

Carefully, I removed my suit jacket and laid it over the table before methodically rolling up the sleeves of my dress shirt.

"Who may we say is performing?" one of the judges asked from their long table at the center of the room.

I could see a slave bent over under the table servicing him, his cock glistening and alien in the blue light of the club.

As carefully as I folded my blazer, I collapsed the vibrancy of my affection for Cosima into a small, pressed package and tucked it into the farthest reaches of my mind so that when I turned to face the room full of men I planned to eviscerate to ash, all they would see was one of their own.

An arrogant lord who believed that everyone should bend the knee to his powers and persuasions.

"I am Alexander Davenport, Earl of Thornton, heir to the Duchy of Greythorn. And this," I said as I crossed to the woman I planned to spend the next hour breaking apart and the next century putting back together, "is my slave."

Chapter Fourteen

COSIMA

*H*e had me trussed up and tied down in a series of complicated knots by rope as silky and black as my hair. It slithered over my skin and then constricted; a snake wrapped unerringly around its prey. It provided the same curiously meditative euphoria that a near-death experience lends; that clarity and almost morbid anticipation that can give dying men an erection. I was naked but for those ropes, and they seemed to confirm my nakedness and highlight the utter exposure of my body to the masses.

I was panting by the time he finished methodically binding me into position, breasts cinched so tightly they were ruddy swells like desert rock, feet trapped wide apart with only my toes braced against the ground, arms bound in a single plait over my head, connected to a lowered hook from the ceiling. My cunt was utterly exposed, the frigid air like pointed teeth on my delicate flesh, the greedy eyes of the men in the club hot as a branding iron against my clit.

It was wrong to be aroused by such blatant humiliation. I was made up like a doll for the pleasure of my Master, to be flaunted like a prize in front of spectators and panelists who would judge me for my sexuality, my obedience, and the gradation of my submission.

It was wrong to so easily—no—*greedily* submit to his domination when only hours ago I'd convinced myself I would never capitulate to his attentions again, but a small part of me knew even then how wrong I was to cast that intention in stone. An unassailable symbiosis existed between us, like the moon with the tides. Everything I was seemed tied to his will. I wondered dazedly if the fight I'd been waging against my baser instincts for the past four years, struggling to live again after years of survival, had been a hoax I'd concocted for myself. There was never any question in my heart that I would ever defy the inexorable pull of Alexander Davenport if he should call for me, but I'd thought he never would again, so I'd fooled myself into thinking I wouldn't heed the order if it came. My body on the ground, pliant and ready as wet clay to be moulded into the shapes of his desire underscored the wrongness of my thoughts over the last near half decade.

It was wrong, but it felt deliciously heavy in my sex, as heady as a drug through my bloodstream. If I wasn't tied down to metal spikes skewered into the stage floor, I would have drifted away into subspace before he'd even really begun to reclaim me.

No, it wasn't the spikes that kept me secure.

It was my Master, the weight of his gaze on my body like

hands at my throat and on my hips, spurring me to submit harder, please him better.

It wasn't about The Trials, about proving to anyone else that he was the best Master and I the best slave. I still didn't know exactly what he wanted from me outside this reunion of flesh, but I was too relieved by his dismissal of Ashcroft, too overwhelmed by my continued thirst for him to focus on anything but the rich intent in Alexander's gaze.

Whatever his end goal was, this scene was about beginning to re-establish the expired trust between us in the most elemental way he knew how—by showing me with his cutting words and cruel hands how far he could take my body into pleasure so powerful it splintered into exquisite pain without taking me over the edge into true embarrassment and hurt.

It was a game and also not a game because his talent was a calling, and my response was as intrinsic as the natural turning of the tides. It seemed so trivial to the men watching us, judging us, but in the small bubble of close air that surrounded my Master and myself, nothing had ever felt so poignant.

I was finally back where I belonged.

Finished with his Shibari masterpiece, Alexander appeared before me, his body partially shielding me from the audience at his back. I knew it was deliberate, as was the marked absence of a blindfold. He wanted me to feel seen because the beauty of my submission to him was worthy of notice, but not be totally exposed because the sight of my intimate folds and creases was for my Master's perusal only. He wanted me to see, but only so that I would watch the way his eyes changed from smoking gas to liquid cold waters straight to punishing stone.

He was accentuating our connection even in a room full of people I abhorred.

I stared into those pewter grey eyes and watched as his firm, full mouth pressed into a grimly pleased line.

The touch of his fingers to the outside of my groin startled me because I had been so enthralled by his gaze, and I shuddered as he drew a path down the sensitive crease where my thigh met my pubis to the tender skin of my inner leg. His skin was colder than the frigid air, as if he was carved from ice, and as his fingers slid down my inner thigh, goosebumps flourished in their wake.

I swallowed thickly as he pulled his fingers away and brought them between us to show me the way they glistened wetly in the light.

"So wet and I've yet to really touch you," he taunted me as he smeared my juices against my breasts like I was a human rag. The degrading touch sent a sharp throb of pleasure through my core. "You love being used by me, but let us not forget, this is a punishment."

Sharper than bee string, harder than a slap to the face, Alexander's palm connected with the fragile inside of my thigh. Pain burst in small shards through my senses, fracturing then pooling in my groin.

I moaned and squirmed in my roped-off pose.

"Keep still while I beat you," he said, and while his words were an order, his tone was bored, as if my obedience was route. "You know you deserve this, *sposa in fuga.*"

Runaway bride.

His Italian words reverberated off my heart like a gong, and the look of stern displeasure superseded by genuine hurt on his aristocratic face prolonged the echo.

Before I could comprehend how his regret might have changed things, his hand found my opposite thigh again in a biting slap.

Then again. Back and forth between each thigh, his palm heating the skin in rhythmic increments; the sharp initial slap, the dull burn, then again, the slap harder, the burn deeper, tunneling through my legs like new nerve endings.

I rocked into his thrusts unconsciously, tipping my hips to

give him greater access to me, hoping wantonly that his hands might find my cunt.

"You are leaking all over the place," he noted, his palm smacking damply against the evidence. "Perhaps I'm not making my point properly."

His eyes snagged mine, his pupils blown wide so that the grey only thinly framed the wide abyss of dark want at their centers. I could read his arousal in the kick of the pulse in his throat, the way his Adam's apple scraped against the skin when he swallowed thickly around the surge of desire cresting through his belly. The scarce evidence locked under his cold control made me pant even harder.

Then our connection broke as he angled his hand up instead of across and landed a cutting slap directly over my cunt. I almost collapsed to the ground as pain went spiraling into whorls of pleasure inside me, but Alexander's hand on my pussy stilled me, cupping the wet flesh so intimately I could feel the slight chafe of his callous against the sensitive skin as strongly as sandpaper.

With his other hand, he pinched my chin and leaned close so that his black eyes dominated my vision. "You are going to keep completely still as I turn this pussy red and raw with my hand. I know you'll want to come, my beauty, because you love it hard like this, but you are not to orgasm until your Master wills it. Is that understood?"

"Yes, Master," I breathed as his fingers played at the wet entrance of my sex, dipping just inside my flesh, the three points of his fingers stretching me with their width.

I tried to grind down on them, but then they were gone, my hips twisting into empty air. My groan was loud, prompting the men I'd forgotten were watching us to laugh quietly at my obvious lust.

I thought it was probably a rare thing to see one of the slaves so blatantly enjoying the ministrations of their masters. A very small dark and forgotten corner of my psyche perked up under their regard. I was a vain woman after all, and I'd always loved male attention, even when it was tainted with avaricious lust. Maybe even especially then. The exhibition was strangely tantalizing, not because I felt the men deserved to see the intimate beauty of my union with Alexander, but because a dark part of me loved to be treated like this by my Master.

Like his wanton, needy slave.

He spanked me until my pussy throbbed harder than my heart, until I keened and begged shamelessly for his cock to fill me up and take away the ache.

Then, when I couldn't take any more, there was the thick stretch of large plastic cock burrowing into the swollen folds of my pussy. Alexander carefully pushed me down on it with a firm hand over my hip, the other holding the toy still between my legs, unmoving so that I had to be the one to fuck myself down on it. He wouldn't take me, he told the crowd and me, unless I could prove I was worth the fucking.

So my hips churned as well as they could in the tight bindings, the lightly abrasive rope cutting over my hips the way Alexander's punishing fingers used to, the slight chafe arrowing straight to my sex, increasing the tempo of its throb. I was panting and sweating with the effort to fuck that thick toy, whimpering slightly because it was just *not* enough to get me off, even with the added sensation of Alexander's cool metallic eyes cutting into my skin like the edge of a blade. There was a wet, sucking slide that sounded clear through the room from my efforts, and it lacquered my skin with the blazing heat of a blush.

"My poor slave can't orgasm like this," Alexander taunted, his eyes narrowed at me in twin expressions of disappointment and derision. "You need to be filled up with more, don't you? You want to feel me claim each one of your tight holes."

My moan wrecked the passage of my throat, raw and rumbling. "Yes, Master."

"Such sweet words on your filthy lips," he praised, pinching my chin to tip my head up so he could bite, then lick at my mouth. He tasted of heat, slightly metallic and rich like the warmth after swallowing certain spices. I wanted to luxuriate in that hot cavern, moan into it as he fucked his tongue over mine, but he pulled away with one last searing suck, and my mouth went suddenly cold, tingling from the abuse.

"You need your Master between these pretty red thighs?" he asked coolly.

Yes, yes, yes, I chanted and moaned and pleaded.

He asked me again. Slapped me again just over my clit. Plucked at my nipples relentlessly until they felt like forged iron, hot and torturous on my chest.

"You want me to fuck you in front of everyone, in front of anyone I chose?" he asked as he squeezed the thick, mouth-watering length of the erection tenting his slacks.

I licked the drool from the corner of my mouth. "Yes, Master."

"Tell me why, little mouse."

I knew what he wanted, not just because I was a good slave, but because I'd been in love with the man. I knew he wanted more than just my body at that moment, but I rebelled against giving him the rest. I didn't know his plan, what he would do with my capitulation and my heart if I granted them to him.

Smack.

Another slap made my pussy convulse around the girth of the toy inside me almost painfully. My clit throbbed so strongly, I was afraid I would come just like that, shattering on the sharp edge of his meanness like ceramic thrown to the floor.

I whimpered loudly as he wrenched the plastic cock from my cunt and tossed it to the floor, leaving my hips churning restlessly over the empty air.

"Tell me, wife," he ordered darkly, stepping into my body

with his thigh against my sex so that the material scraped over my raw nerves like a match to a striking board. "I've waited five years to hear you say it, and I won't wait a moment longer. Give me what we both need to hear you say."

His eyes were silver mirrors duplicating the desperation and longing I felt reflected in my own. A whine leaked from my parted lips.

"Tell me, little mouse," he repeated, his eyes hooks drawing me into him inexorably, dragging me through his wake until I was caught up in his net.

"Because I want everyone to see that I belong to you," I said, not a whisper or a roar, but a statement that moved through my body like a spiritual awakening.

"Yes," Alexander hissed, unbuttoning his trousers, unzipping, and then—I gasped because I was so far gone to him—his gorgeous, weeping cock. "You belong to me."

And then he stepped up with his cock grasped almost violently in his fist, the other hand clamping down over my hip, and he surged inside me in one long, searing thrust.

I screamed at the ceiling as my head threw back and my pussy detonated in an orgasm so strong, I saw stars dance against the top of the club. He fucked me hard, pounding into my spanked and swollen cunt proprietarily, uncaring of my pleasure in his entitled quest for his own climax. It only proved to send me higher, and when he sank his teeth into my neck, holding me there as he fucked me like an animal breeding its mate, I came again, screaming my throat raw as he claimed me.

When he came moments later, it was with a roar, the beast at the heart of him exposed for me to see and feel against me. I loved the thrill of it, of fucking a man so much like a dangerous animal, of being bound up by his orders and tied down to his mercy.

My mind was lost to the plush, velvety texture of quiet that followed a spectacular orgasm, but I was distantly aware of Alexander pulling out, his semen and my wetness leaking obscenely down my thigh. Then he did as he'd once done after fucking me in the poppy field at Pearl Hall, he smeared our combined juices into my achy, distended cunt all the way back over my asshole and up onto the bare skin of my pubis. I gasped as he smoothed the last of the dampness against my lips and then swooped in to kiss it brutally off my mouth.

He turned to the audience after tucking his wet, half-hard length back into his trousers, his eyebrow cocked and arms crossed as he idly demanded, "Well?"

A man stood up, adjusted his erection in his suit pants, and said, "There are still more pairings to exhibit…"

Alexander condescended to giving the man one of his patented arch looks.

"But, well, yes, you both were incredible, Mr. Davenport. We'd be happy to include her with the girls used at the club for special occasions. She heeds your direction beautifully."

"The only one who touches my slave's sweet mouth and tender cunt is me. Next time you inquire, I'll cut your bollocks off, is that clear?"

The judge shot a look at the rest of the panel but nodded. It was clear they had no idea who Xan really was, that this New York branch hadn't heard of the legends of the unconquerable Earl.

"Oh, and please," Xan said, smiling his predatory smile. "Call me Lord Thornton."

We didn't leave right away. We weren't allowed, and while Alexander was the kind of man who only listened to demands when they suited him, he relented and tucked us both into the dark recesses of a corner table to watch the remaining "performances." He had cut me out of the ropes, washed away my sweat and grime with a warm, damp cloth in one of the back rooms, and wrapped me in his huge dress shirt so that I didn't have to stay in the minuscule lingerie set I'd arrived in. I belted it at my waist and laughed at the way it covered a decent portion of my legs and drooped over my hands.

Alexander had watched me laugh, then tucked a lock of hair behind my ear before ushering us back out into the club.

Now, I sat on his lap as many of the other slaves were doing, but I had his shirt covering my body and a blanket a server had unearthed from somewhere that smelled of oak barrels keeping me warm. Alexander cradled me; there was no other word for it. He tucked me into the crease of his body and his right arm, my cheek propped on the bulge of his pectoral, my legs curled up against his chest. I could feel his strong, steady heartbeat against my cheek, and the hard planes of his muscled body bracketing me like armor.

It was an illusion dreamed up in my lingering subspace, but I thought I might never have felt so safe.

We didn't speak, and I didn't attempt to. It wasn't the time or place, and I was desensitized to Alexander's long, heavy silences even after all these years. He was content to hold me, and I was more than content to be held.

Of all the things I'd missed about being Alexander's, I'd missed his physical affection the most. In some ways, it was more eloquent than his cultured, highly educated words ever could be.

I was drifting into a post-climax nap when Alexander turned to concrete. My eyes snapped open, instantly alert as someone slipped into the shadowy space beside us.

She was speaking before I could get a sense for who she might have been, but her words made it impossible to mistake her for someone else. "Master Alexander, I-I I am sorry to b-bother you when you are with…s-slave."

Yana.

Her sweet Russian accent and nervous stutter only high-lighted her delicate, almost fragile beauty, like a flower that would be too soon out of bloom. It shocked me how young she appeared given that she had been Noel's slave almost three decades go. There were scars highlighted on her skin in the blue light of the club, and fear worn tightly in the skin around her eyes, but otherwise, her slight build and ethereal beauty made her seem no less than twenty-five. It was no wonder she was popular with the men of the Order. She looked built to be broken, a clay pigeon constructed just to be shot open.

"Don't worry yourself, Yana, I asked you to meet me here."

I looked up sharply at him, jealousy so acute in my chest it felt like a poison dart punctured right through my heart. He placated me with a hand smoothed down my hair, wrapping familiarly in the strands.

When I looked back at Yana, her huge almost translucent

blue eyes were trained on his fingers in my hair as if she was witnessing a miracle enacted by God.

I supposed affection from a Master was exactly that to a woman so inured to the cruelty of slavery.

"I-I am happy to s-see you, Master, b-but I do not know what you w-w-would want from me," she admitted in a timid voice, her eyes trained on Alexander's neck and never straying higher out of engrained respect for his superiority over her.

I wondered if she even knew how deeply grey and enchanting his eyes could be.

"You are slave to Master di Carlo now, aren't you, Yana?" Alexander asked.

I stiffened at the name of the Cosa Nostra's crime family boss. He was part of the Order?

"But he's an Italian-American?" I accused without filtering myself.

"The American faction of the Order works a little less discriminatingly than its British counterpoint. There are no titles here, only wealth and power. Di Carlo is enough of both now that he warranted an invitation, and as part of his initiation, he was gifted his first slave." He tipped his head to Yana.

I blinked hard, my mind scrambling to make sense of the pathway of connections. It felt like a significant reveal, but I couldn't fathom how di Carlo being part of the Order was exactly momentous.

"What the American Council didn't understand," Alexander continued as he eyed Yana's bruised, frail form with hard eyes. "Was that a man built on wealth is not necessarily one of old loyalty or integrity. That a man like that could be bought."

"By who? You?" I asked and watched as Yana flinched at my audacity.

"Perhaps," he said, sipping his scotch. "Or perhaps by another. Yana, maybe you can shed some light on the matter?"

She licked her lips, quick and nervous, then did it again. Her entire body seemed filled with quick, brittle energy as if she would break and do so willingly at any provocation. Pity bloomed in my chest, overtaking my previous jealousy.

Alexander might have taken a beating for her as a boy, but he hadn't been old enough or caring enough to save her completely.

Not the way it seemed he had once tried and might attempt again to do for me.

"H-he was sponsored by a man," she admitted, eyes rolling around the club like loose marbles, searching for someone who might spot her betraying her new Master. "He and his n-nephew. He wanted badly to be in Order, b-but he waited a very long time. H-he had to d-do something f-f-first for this man."

She swallowed hard and leaned forward to look right into my eyes, her own filled with almost savage apology.

"H-he had to k-know you and r-report on you," she admitted.

Alexander turned to stone beneath me, so it felt I was entombed in concrete.

"By who?" I whispered, so afraid of the answer I barely dared to ask the question.

Yana shuddered violently, then finally, her fear of the name she spoke more than the fear of Alexander, she lifted her eyes to his and said, "Master Noel."

Chapter Fifteen

ALEXANDER

"She didn't know anything more," I told Alexander, trying to calm the barely leashed fury that threatened to overtake him as he sat beside me in the Town Car, furiously texting someone.

Yana had disappeared almost immediately after her confession when the council had finally concluded The Trials and announced Alexander and me as the winners. She hadn't wanted to be punished for being outside her Master's orders, and I couldn't blame her for it. In fact, I was sure if it wasn't for Alexander taking that whipping for her as a boy, she wouldn't have ever dreamt of slipping out of di Carlo's house in the first place.

The last thing she had said of any consequence was that di Carlo would be sitting a card game in Little Italy at an underground casino the next night, and only then, after Alexander used his Dominant voice on her.

It wasn't much to go off, but it was enough to leave me reeling.

Noel had been keeping an eye on me through a spy for years through the Cosa Nostra family, and it made me sick to my stomach to think of all the information he might have gleaned.

"She knows more," Alexander bit out, the harsh lines of his face made steeper by the bright light of his phone screen as he glared down at a message. "If not, she could if only she wanted to."

"She risked her safety by meeting you there. You should have asked her to meet you more discreetly," I chastised him.

His eyes swept from the phone to where I sat beside him, pinning me in place so forcibly I couldn't even draw breath. "There isn't much more discretion for a slave wearing an unlockable collar and shackles around her wrists and ankles than Club Bacchus. No one notices slaves there, no one will have noticed one more, especially one as meek and well trained as Yana. It was safe as I could make it and necessary too."

"It was risky, probably for both of you," I countered, turning to find solace in the streets passing like blurred, dark watercolours passing out the window.

His scoff was haughty, so condescending I didn't have to see his face to know how his brows would be raised, his mouth puckered like an exclamation mark punctuating my stupidity. "I shuddered to think how you may react if you knew just how many 'risks' I've taken over the past four years to see you safe."

I swallowed the thick swell of longing in my throat and nearly choked on the impossible obstruction. Alexander's hand collected the spill of hair down my back and wrapped it unerringly around his palm until my head was forced to turn his way to lessen the tension and my mouth parted on a slightly gasp of pain. He was waiting for me, his eyes glittering like the sheen of a knife's edge as they cut into the heart of me.

"There is no one I wouldn't kill for you. No crime I wouldn't commit or atrocity I wouldn't instigate if it meant keeping you safe and keeping you mine."

"I'm not yours," I told him, more breath than sound.

I hated the way my body defied me in favour of him even in that small way.

He had his hooks in me so deep that they were embedded in my DNA.

"You are," he said simply, an irrefutable fact. I sucked in a breath through my teeth as he banded a hand across my lower back and snapped my torso forward into his. My curves submitted to his hard lines, and I hated how beautifully we fit.

I bit my lip but didn't argue because my body betrayed me more readily than my words could ever defend me. I decided a change of topic was a better strategy and pulled out of his hold to give myself needed space to think more clearly. "Did you know Noel was watching me?"

His eyes burned like arctic ice against my skin. "Of course. He's not a man who lets his prey run loose and free. Unfortunately, I only recently realized how obvious it was that he had been keeping an eye on you…I only needed to ask who he could have used to accomplish such a thing to think to seek out Yana. After all, she has been one of his most powerful tools of trade for a long, long time."

I wanted to tell him that Noel had been the one to send me fleeing four years ago, that he had beaten me within an inch of my sanity and forced me to run.

But I wouldn't, not when I didn't understand why Xan had finally returned to me after all this time.

"Why are you here, Alexander?" I asked him, suddenly so weary that the words felt misshapen and heavy leaving my lips.

His golden brow knotted, and his fury slithered through the car like smoke, thick and carcinogenic. "You can honestly doubt my intentions after everything I'd said to you in the last thirty-six hours?"

"Is there really any doubt that I would?" I countered, my own anger creeping through my exhaustion. "You've played me like a yo-yo for years. I have no idea of your real intent. How could I?"

"You once told me you loved me," he reminded me ruthlessly, suddenly in my space, both hands twined in my hair so my face was pinned against his, nose to nose, eyes nearly crossed as they connected. "And I once promised I would take that from you; your love, your body, and your devotion. I'm a man of my word, Cosima. I've come to take what you've always wanted to give me."

"Are you trying to tell me you love me?" I demanded because he was still crafting puzzles with his words and my wary heart needed confirmation.

I would not give in to less than his reciprocity.

He stared at me still, his eyes working beneath his heavy lids, his jaw so taut I worried it would break under the strain.

But he said nothing.

I gripped my hands over his wrists like shackles and forced him tighter to me so he could see the way my eyes glowed, how something inside me wanted to reach out and eat him up entirely. Devour his power and his essence until he was all mine.

"How can I forgive you for everything you've ever done if you won't give me access to your heart? Or the very least your mind? I cannot begin to fathom your motivation over the past few years, and I'm so fucking tired of trying. *Why are you here, Xan?*"

He was quiet for so long, only the heavy drag of our combined breaths punctuating the gummy silence, that I worried he wouldn't respond. And then what would I do? I'd come too far to give in to him again without his meeting me halfway.

I needed some tender, vulnerable piece of his soul or else all my fragile, sandcastle dreams of more with this man would crumble irrevocably into dust.

"Please," I whispered fiercely. "Give me something."

"I want to give you everything," he bit out almost before I'd finished speaking, his voice thunder and his eyes flashing like lightning. "I've wanted to give you everything since nearly the moment I laid eyes on you so beautiful and brave. Do you know what it is like for a man used to power and spoils when he is helpless to keep and worship the one thing he wants most?"

I didn't breathe. My heart, for one long, agonizing minute, didn't beat.

I existed on the precipice of his words, staring into the dark future hoping a soft landing would meet me after the jump.

"If I had a heart, Cosima, I know I would love you with every facet of it," he breathed with almost violent tenderness, his hands so painful in my hair and his eyes so wonderfully tender on my skin my heart didn't stand a chance against the contrast. "But I was born without one, and I don't know if something like that can grow in a man like me. If it could, I know it would for you."

A sob bubbled up my throat and burst between us. Xan ground his forehead hard against mine, somehow knowing the pain and the savage passion in his gaze would keep me from dissolving.

"You are mine, *topolina*," he vowed with the same solemnity he had spoken his vows at our wedding. "I know this because everyone is a slave to something, and I am enslaved by you."

My mouth was over his before I'd made the conscious decision to kiss him. He tasted of heat, slightly metallic and rich like the warmth after swallowing certain spices. I wanted to luxuriate in that hot cavern, moan into it as he fucked his tongue over mine, but he pulled away with one last searing suck, and my mouth went suddenly cold, tingling from the loss.

He rubbed his thumb over my swollen bottom lip and then nipped it before smiling his rare smile that broke open every hard plane of his face and made it almost boyish.

"I'm back because I couldn't stay away, even if it was the safer, *saner* thing to do."

"Safer?" I asked, shivering slightly as I thought of Noel watching me all these years, every memory tainted by the possibility of his eyes on them.

Metal shutters slammed shut behind his eyes, and suddenly, the lord and master was back. He pulled away slightly, a muscle in his jaw jumping.

"We've arrived, Lord Thornton," the driver said over the intercom.

Alexander was out of the car before I could demand more answers. Even when he opened my door for me, his face countenanced no conversation, and he ushered me quickly into my building as if a threat lingered around every corner.

I wondered now if they actually did.

"Xan, what's going on?" I asked, pushing back against the hand driving me at the base of my spine as we made our way to the elevator bank. "What did you do with Ashcroft? What do you know about Noel watching me? I swear I'm going to scream if you don't stop being an enigmatic piece of shit."

His eyes darkened as he tugged me into the elevator and hard into his body so that he could band both hands around my hips in a crushing embrace. "Speak to me like that again, *topolina*, and I will remind you right here in this elevator where any of your neighbors might see exactly what happens when you disrespect me."

I shivered with lust even as my anger still coursed through me. "Then respect me enough to tell me the truth of everything that's happened. I feel as if I don't understand the events of my own life even as I've been living it."

His stern expression didn't soften, but his expressive eyes went burnished with pride and tenderness. "Always so brave, little mouse, standing up to creatures greater than you in the jungle. So brave and beautiful." He dipped to press a soft, almost fluttering kiss to my lips and then pulled back so I could see his eyes as he said, "I wanted to tell you everything on the Jurassic Coast, but you ran away from me as you seem liable to do. If you show me your home and promise not to run again, I promise to tell you the truth."

"The whole truth?" I pressed suspiciously.

His lips twitched microscopically to the side, a small tell giving away his amusement. "The whole and nothing but, my beauty."

"Deal." I took a determined step back out of his embrace and offered my hand to shake on it.

Another lip twitch, this one nearly a full grin. He clasped his big, worn hand in mine and stroked his thumb over the delicate skin of my wrist. When I stepped to his side, a careful distance between us so that I could center my thoughts, he didn't try to breach it, and I appreciated his restraint more than I could say.

I felt strange knowing Alexander would see my home. It was my happy place, a collection of rooms that vividly catalogued all the multifaceted aspects of my soul. I'd bought into the building because it was a pre-war historic New York City landmark, and the palatial caramel marble lobby and scrolling woodwork reminded me of Pearl Hall. The apartment itself was rich with vibrant colours, the living room the colour of my favourite Italian wine, the bookcases delineating that primary space from the office behind it were thick black structures filled with books, relics from my childhood home in Naples and photos of my family since moving to New York. A handful of Giselle's paintings were on the walls, and some of my favourite framed portraits from fashion spreads I'd done lined the hallway leading back to the kitchen. I had a clay pitcher of wine forever filled to the brim on my island, a tradition started years ago at Mama's house, and an easel set up by the small French doors that Giselle used to craft her masterpieces. A half-finished painting was propped there of a woman bound Shibari-style by locks of her own hair.

It was a space as intimate as the inside of my heart, and it frankly alarmed me that Alexander and his scalpel sharp eyes would have access to it all.

This was the person I had become in every carefully culti-vated vase and colour-coordinated fabric choice. I wasn't sure how he would react to seeing an autonomous me because it was never something he'd had to face.

Alexander read my hesitation at the door and stilled my fumbling hands as I searched for the right key with a large, heavy one of his own. I watched as he took the key ring from me and easily found the correct one to slot into the gold lock. His smile was slight, but smug as he opened the door and placed a hand on my back to usher me inside.

"I knew where you lived before you finished signing the papers," he told me, his lips against the shell of my ear, tick-ling the thin skin so that I shivered. "I might not have been beside you for the past four years, my beauty, but I still made sure you had everything you'd need."

"I needed you," I told him in a moment of intense honesty.

My skin went hot and tight with embarrassment, but Alexander only pulled me inside and then pressed me to the door as it closed so that he could pin me against it in a hot, punishing kiss. I groaned into his mouth, slipping my hands into the short, silky strands at the back of his head to hold him to me.

I wanted answers almost as badly as I wanted his kisses, but the latter still trumped everything. It felt as though I existed only under his touch, an apparition made whole by his will and his alone.

Alexander froze against me so suddenly, I kissed his unmoving mouth for a moment, making out with a statue. When I clued into his paralysis, I moved my head back the inch it took to meet the wall at my spine and noticed the gun trained to Xan's golden temple.

Before I could tilt my head to see who yielded the weapon, Dante's tangled British-Italian accent slithered low through the room. "Step back from Cosima and keep your hands at your fucking sides."

"Dante—" I started exasperatedly, moving forward to block him from Alexander.

His black eyes cut to me, sparkling and hard as chips of obsidian in his glowering face. "Move another inch, Cosi, and I'll put a bullet straight through his soft temples."

"Dante, don't be a *stronzo*," I snapped even though I obeyed his order and held myself still.

Alexander merely stood, strong and immovable as a tree being threatened by a slight breeze as if the gun at his head was nothing but a mild nuisance. He stared at me with a flat face and eyes gone black with predatory instinct.

"What the fuck are you doing in New York City, Alexander?" Dante demanded, his stance just as firm, his face just as implacable.

They had never looked more alike.

The air was distorted like blown glass with the waxy waves of their anger and animosity.

A secret, animal thrill worked its way down my back and sparked in my sex.

"I'm here for Cosima. What the fuck are you doing lurking in her apartment like a bloody thief?"

"I have a key," he retorted smugly, grinding the gun into Xan's temple as if to physically rub it in.

"She's my wife," Alexander reminded him in a tone like a gavel strike before moving so sharply, I couldn't discern the series of movements that had Dante's gun knocked to the ground, skittering over the wood floors, and both men in a fierce grapple on the ground.

Alexander emerged on top and pounded one large fist brutally into Dante's side, somehow knowing exactly where his brother had been shot a couple weeks ago. Dante's breath punched out of his lungs, but he twisted his massive body even as he struggled to drag air into his lungs and leveraged his torso to sock a blow directly to Alexander's chin that had him reeling back. He took advantage, pushing him back with a push to both shoulders so Xan fell to his ass and Dante scrambled over him, pinning him to the ground to growl in his face.

"You motherfucking, selfish prick," he bellowed into my husband's face, spittle flying, face vermillion. "You couldn't stay away, leave her to her peace?"

"You think what she had was peace?" Alexander said, the ice to his brother's fire, laying calmly beneath his hulking adversary as if he had chosen to lie down and wasn't pinned there. "You think she could ever have peace without me?"

"Egotistical maniacal *bastardo*," Dante spat. "You really think she needs you? You fucking abused her! You chased her and raped her and *ruined* her."

"You're right," Alexander punctuated his words with a hard grunt as he reared up to smash his forehead to Dante's nose and switch places with the reeling man, kneeling over him with a placid face that was somehow more threatening than Dante's twisted sneer. "I ruined her just as surely as she

ruined me. It's done. There's no going back. I think it's *you*
who has to learn to live with that, Edward, because Cosima
already has. This problem you have? It's yours."

They glared at each other, nose to Roman nose, gold and
black pressed together in a way that no woman could ever
think was anything other than pure masculine beauty. I was
arrested by the sight of them, by the fact that they both loved
me enough to fight for me.

I was also completely *done* with their dramatic alpha antics,
though.

"Get off your brother, Xan," I ordered, pulling at his
shoulder until he reluctantly acquiesced. "Dante, get up and
step back."

As soon as they gained their feet, I stepped between them
and pressed a hand to both their lightly heaving, massive
chests to ground the electric power charging through their
veins. They both watched me narrowly, angry with each other,
but also with me for interfering, for even interacting with the
other man.

The headiness of stepping between them sluiced through
me until I was almost light-headed. I was an organism entirely
dependent on the male mind to survive. I needed them to
want me, crave me, become enamoured with me.

The hole at the center of my being that had been ripped
out of me when I left England fed on the meat of their attention, and as I stood between the two men who had become
the center spokes of my world, I embraced my gluttony with
verve.

"You both need to knock it off. I'm a grown woman who
can make her own decisions and speak for herself. Dante..." I
turned to the man who had been my saviour the past four
years, the man who had taken the tattered pieces of my body
and soul and given them a home to recover in. He looked at
me with soft, velvet black eyes, his mouth twisted up in one
corner because he already knew he wouldn't like what I had to

say. "D, *amico mio*, Alexander came to save me from Ashcroft at Club Bacchus tonight. He didn't hurt me, and honestly, I don't think he means to hurt me ever again. I think…" I darted a glance back at the man in question and let his burning eyes fill me with conviction. "I think he wants to be with me."

"I do," Alexander confirmed in his Dominant voice, in that tone that brooked no argument. "Not that Edward deserves to know that."

"Hush," I scolded him before turning to Dante, hating the way his eyes went cold and his posture changed, his muscles tightening as if repelled by my hand on his chest. "Dante, you have to trust me to know what's best for me."

"My trust in you has nothing to do with it, *tesoro*, and everything to do with the fact that I haven't been able to trust Alexander since he sided with Noel over our mother's murder."

I winced slightly because that was the crux of the problem, wasn't it?

Dante couldn't trust Alexander, and I wasn't sure if I should.

We both turned to him, questions in our eyes like lassos ready to capture him so we could demand answers.

"I don't need you to trust me." Alexander tugged down his shirtsleeves and adjusted his cuff links, insulting Dante with his every blasé move. "I don't need you to trust me, Edward, because you never trusted me enough to come back home and tell me what you actually thought happened with Noel. You think I betrayed you? Well, *brother*, you abandoned me and left me with a man you knew to be a monster."

The air in the room went flat like stale soda, sticky with tension, but void of the angrily bumping molecules. Dante seemed suspended in it, floating on shock and uncertainty.

Clearly, he'd never thought of the past in such terms.

Honestly, neither had I.

I watched as the blood caught on Dante's upper lip from

his slightly bleeding nose and warred with whether to comfort him or shame him for doing exactly what he'd always accused Xan of doing.

Abandoning his family.

"You think Noel is a monster?" Dante asked suspiciously.

I held my breath as I waited for the answer. There was no way Alexander knew about Noel and Rodger beating me, because only those two, Dante, and Salvatore knew the truth, but there were so many other ways Noel had proved his heinousness.

Alexander stepped forward, his mask slipping to reveal an expression I'd never seen hung on his features before, one of pure and lasting agony.

"Of course, Noel is a monster." He opened his hands, clenched them around empty air, and released them with shaking fingers. "And I did monstrous things at his bidding, in his image. I am my father's son."

His wry twisted lips, self-depreciating and full of personal loathing, sliced my heart into ribbons. God, but this beautiful man thought he was uglier than his demons, and it broke my fucking heart.

I went to him before I could even think to curb the impulse, my arms slipping under his suit to press him so hard into my body it was as if I sought to absorb him into myself. Maybe my love would filter his self-disgust and leave him clean, reborn, and ready to adore himself as much as I did.

And fuck me, but I did.

So many years of lying and recrimination for my wavering emotions, and I was still exactly where I had been the day I left Pearl Hall in a bloodstained wedding dress.

Inevitably and eternally in love with Alexander.

The knowledge settled over me just as his arms did, warm and secure. I thought of how he'd taken twenty-five lashings for me, of how he'd married me against the Order's rules, and how he'd watched over me like some dark guardian angel for the four years of our separation.

I thought of all the ways the man without a heart loved me back.

My face tipped up so I could look into his polished silver eyes and his perfectly symmetrical, utterly gorgeous face, and I knew I would never feel more myself or more at home than I would exactly where I was at that moment, in his arms.

"Not evil," I whispered to him, pressing my hand to his throat so I could cup his pulse. "Just damaged."

I watched as his face went soft, as the hardest man I'd ever met exposed the hidden, tender heart of him, and I forgot Dante was in the room. I even forgot to breathe.

He leaned down to press a kiss to my mouth and then sharply bite my lower lip. "I was born and made of monsters. Nothing can change that."

"Nothing, but you," I stressed, gripping him tighter. "And you want to, don't you? You have been already."

"I have." He smiled slightly, but his eyes were still haunted. "Nothing will really be changed until the rest of them are taken care of."

"You're trying to take down the Order?" I asked, shocked despite the clues he'd already given me.

The idea of Alexander going after the most powerful scion in Britain made me hot with delight and cold with anxiety. Even though I'd somewhat foolishly decided to take them on myself, I didn't like the idea of Alexander doing the same. He was too embroiled in their world to make a clean exit, and I worried what the ramifications of his decision to end them would mean for him.

"Why do you think I stayed away, little mouse?" he asked with an arched brow. "Why do you think I ended things so brutally with you in Milan?"

"To keep me safe."

God, it hurt how obvious the truth was, how painfully it

ripped down my spine like teeth opening a raw wound. Of course, he would have been protecting me because that was what he had strived to do almost from the outset.

Use me, yes, but only for his own pleasure, his own ends.

The idea of someone else touching me or manipulating me had always driven him mad with possessive fury.

"You expect me to believe you've turned against everything you've ever known?" Dante demanded, stepping forward into our space, using his sheer mass to threaten Alexander to tell the truth.

This wasn't about me. This anger and aggression stemmed like the poisoned roots of a dead tree from the brothers' own lasting toxic relationship long before they'd met me. This was about Dante disbelieving his brother could ever be anything other than his enemy because that was what they seemed born to be.

Alexander settled Dante with a long, hard glare that shackled him where he stood. "Quite frankly, I don't give one royal fuck what you believe. The only concern I have involving you at the moment is why the fuck you haven't left Cosima's apartment yet. You clearly aren't needed, and from now on, you won't be ever again."

The words landed as they were intended to, more brutal than the physical blows he had landed on Dante's person. My handsome friend flinched with their impact, his open face closing like an agitated anemone. His eyes cut to me, searching for solace.

I bit my lip because I didn't know how to give it to him without upsetting the new balance I'd found with Xan. Without giving Dante hope when there was none.

He read into my hesitation, and in minute ways—a slump of his wide shoulders, a crease in his red mouth, a tightening of the skin beside his eyes—Dante shut down. I watched as he disassembled his emotions with painful calculation because he was an open man unused to hiding how he felt, and I hated that I was in the position to decide between two men I loved in such very different but elemental ways.

"Dante, *bello*, please, I'm not asking you to trust Xan, and I'm not asking you to help us with this, but if he really is taking down the Order and Noel, you have to know that I need to help him. Not just for Xan, but for *me*."

I tried to step out of Alexander's arms, but he wouldn't have it, and a part of me understood why. This was a stand-off about many things, and one of them was me.

"Dante," I beseeched again. "You said you wouldn't leave me alone in this."

His eyes sliced up to his brother, filled with glittering acrimony like an obsidian blade, and then back at me. I watched his fists clench and unclench as he fought with his decision.

Fear bloated under my skin like infected tissues, filling me with the uneasy belief that he might walk out my door and never again return.

"*Ti voglio bene, fratello,*" I told him.

I love you, brother.

Because the fractured brotherhood between Alexander and Dante might never be mended, but Dante and I would always be siblings of the heart.

He smiled thinly at me and turned to pick up his discarded gun before tucking it into the back of his waistband. His eyes were carefully void as they swept over me in Alexander's embrace, and when he walked by me to the door, and said, "I'm sure you know by now that sometimes love is not enough," it wrecked me just as surely as one of his bullets to my heart might have killed me.

Part Three

DISSENT

NON DECOR, DECO. I AM NOT LED, I LEAD

Chapter Sixteen

COSIMA

"If you tell me you slept with my brother, I'll kill him."

I was in the kitchen pouring a large glass of Glenfiddich scotch when Alexander said the words calmly, factually as if discussing the weather.

I ignored him, focusing on my task as I pulled two crystal cut tumblers out of the cabinet and filled them with three generous fingers of the amber liquor. Without offering the second glass to Alexander, I tipped the first to my lips and let the flaming liquid score a line of heat down the back of my throat. I dropped the empty one to the black granite countertop and tossed back the second before refilling one and offering one to Xan.

"Drink?" I asked, slightly breathless from the burn of the alcohol.

I needed the bracing pain to settle me moments after Dante had stormed out. My stomach was cold with indecision and the fear that my Dante was gone for good. I needed the heat of the scotch to burn the feeling away, if only for a while.

Alexander stared at me through the shadows of my unlit apartment, the dark making his glower dominate his forehead like a crown of thorny anger.

"Cosima, if you slept with my brother, I promise you, I will kill him," he repeated, this time with all the considerable force of his dominant personality and ire behind the words.

I wrung my hands together and wondered briefly if I should tell him the truth.

I had slept with Dante. Many times.

When I first moved to New York City, I was a mess of emotions barely contained by thin skin and brittle bones. I cried more than I spoke, and it took me weeks to smile.

Only Dante brought me solace, a hot shot of scotch whiskey to soothe my hollow belly, a velvet blanket wrapped around my shoulders to stave a cold even sharper than the one I'd felt my first few weeks in Pearl Hall's ballroom.

He held me until I slept, force-fed me, and tried everything to make me smile.

I'd substituted one Master for another, though Dante was considerably kinder and infinitely less harmful to my heart. He'd even befriended Sinclair when I'd lived with him in an attempt to rope another person into a tag team to get me out of the house and living again.

"Yes." I looked Alexander straight in the eye as I confessed, my chin tipped high, my shoulders squared. I wouldn't be made to feel ashamed for my need or my relationship with his brother. "I slept with him dozens of times when I first arrived, though neither of us really slept."

Alexander's rage perfumed the air like gasoline and hot stone. I knew he was ready to explode, to break apart into an inferno he didn't have the right to light.

I held up one hand to stop him and willed it not to shake.

It was a wonder I was even standing after everything I'd been through as of late, so I let myself have the slight tremble in my fingers.

"I had hellacious nightmares that kept me up for hours. I'd wake up sobbing and thrashing so hard, I would have hurt myself if Dante didn't hold me down, and even then, sometimes I'd hurt him. I cried so much I went cold, and my body trembled so hard from the shock of it I couldn't hold still enough to fall asleep at all. He lay beside me through all of it because he knew, unlike anyone else in my life, not even my *family*, especially not them, that I'd been through hell and come back to the world of the living something other than fully human. Something haunted and broken and dark."

I slanted a long, sizzling glance at Alexander, hating him at that moment the same way I had three years ago after he'd eviscerated me in Milan.

"If you want to condemn me for taking the only solace I could from the only man I could ever hope to find it in, then go ahead, but you'll be less of a man for it."

We stood facing off for a moment that seemed suspended in time when everything shifted profoundly, but infinitesimally from night to day. Finally, when Alexander moved toward me, I let out a heavy breath I hadn't been aware I was holding.

He reached me in three long, brutal strides and hoisted me up against his body so that my toes dangled off the floor. His mouth was on mine in the next second, his eyes open on mine as he took my mouth in a firm but searching kiss. Only when I opened the seam of my mouth for his sweeping tongue did he close his eyes and relax into the embrace, groaning into me like a man finding sweet relief.

When he pulled away, he pushed his forehead against mine, his eyes still closed as if he couldn't bear to look at me while he confessed. "I'm a great jealous cad, so I hate the very thought of him being anything at all to you. I'll admit it. Still, I know it's my own fault you had to turn to him, and so, I know I must and I will live with it. Forgive me for being a brute with my anger."

"You're a brute in more than just your anger, Xan," I said softly, forgiving him with my gentle tease.

His eyes flashed open, sparkling like diamonds in a velvet box. "Ah, but I won't apologize for brutalizing you with my body. You enjoy it too much."

The shiver that wracked my frame agreed with him before my words could.

His laughter was smoke against my face, heady and strong enough to drug me. I wanted to hear his merriment every day until I died, and I didn't care that I knew I would have to work for it.

"What now?" I asked because I was so overwhelmed by the changes the last three days had wrought on my life that I didn't know up from down or left from right.

I wanted to stay in this dizzying new reality forever, but I knew my life would never be as simple as that. There were still too many things in the way of our peace to relax for long.

Alexander smoothed one of his big, beautiful hands over my forehead and down the cloak of inky hair at my back. "Let me bathe you and wash away the greasy-eyed stares of the men at Club Bacchus while I explain some things to you."

"That sounds good," I breathed but didn't move because I was in his arms and some panicked part of me worried what would happen if I let him go for even one moment.

His smile was slight and gentle as if he knew, and he probably did, exactly what I feared. He turned me around to face the bathroom, somehow knowing where my bedroom and en suite were in the apartment and slapped me on my bottom like a rider to his horse's flank.

"Get going and start the bath. I have a phone call to make before I join you."

"Ashcroft?" I asked even as I obeyed him and walked down the short hall to my room.

"Later," he reminded me firmly before giving me his back and walking down into the living room to take the call.

I left the lights off in my room, not eager to have Alexander's discerning eyes on the red dressed bed that looked remarkably like my own from Pearl Hall or the overlapping pink and red carpets beneath it.

I flicked them on in my big bathroom so that I could find my St. Aubyn *d'Oro* oil and added it to the bathwater as it poured into the wide Jacuzzi tub. While I waited for it to fill, I stepped up to my gold mirror as I unbuttoned the top half of my shirt and looked at my tired but elated expression, trying to discern what was different in my face that made me feel truly beautiful for the first time in years.

My exposed chest was segmented by lingering rope marks, the striation pink and white like candy cane stripes against my golden skin. They looked just as edible, and for one tantalizing second, I imagined Alexander whispering his mouth across them, tracing the marks with his tongue as if they had a taste and that taste was pure, distilled submission.

And I realized what it was that made me seem so different in my reflection.

For the first time in years, my body had been satiated and my heart held hope. The winning combination set my skin to glowing gold beneath the rope marks and made my eyes as radiant as twin burning stars.

Alexander appeared in the reflection behind me, his black suited frame filling the entire doorway. Languidly, his eyes trailed down my body, taking in the ill-fit of his belted shirt on my frame and the way my hair curled in smooth loops like calligraphy against the white fabric.

"Do you know," he asked in that muted, deep voice that could move me like none other, "that you are the most exquisite woman I have ever had the privilege of laying eyes on?"

My voice was somewhere in my belly, burning on the hot coals of my banked but growing lust. I shook my head as he walked toward me, stopping just behind my back.

His fingers reached around my shoulder to trail gently down my cheek and then wrap one by one around the long column of my throat. Only then did he step flush against me, pulling me tightly by that hand until I could feel his erection hard and dangerous as a loaded gun against my spine.

"So golden, those money eyes," he murmured as he dipped his head to press his lips and then his teeth to my neck over my fluttering, stuttering pulse point. "Yet you are something more precious than gold. At least to me."

I moaned softly, tilting my ass into his hard cock, my tender throat into his teeth. "Xan."

"Mmm," he agreed with my unspoken plea, dipping his other hand in the open material gaping at my chest so that he could run one rough fingertip over the rope marks framing my tits. "I love seeing evidence of me on your skin."

My hips gyrated roughly back at his, my nipples beading obviously through the thin shirt as he continued to meticulously stoke my arousal. I'd just come harder than ever at Club Bacchus, and I was still ravenously greedy for more of him, from him.

His teeth closed almost painfully hard over my neck, and then he was gone; the cold air where his body used to be like knife points against my sensitised skin.

I stared at him with a frown of unsettled confusion as he moved away to test the bathwater as if we hadn't just been about to fuck again.

"Undress and get in, my beauty. The water is ready."

I shed the dress shirt, holding still as it floated to the ground around me because I felt more than naked under the hot gaze of Alexander. I felt stripped down the wires, dissected and inspected like a bomb maker faced with his greatest challenge. Xan's eyes swept over every inch of my flesh, hot and thorough as hot water, pinking my skin and heating my groin.

Only when he finished his visual inspection did he sit on the edge of the tub and offer his hand to me, silently ordering me to take it and step into the bath.

"You aren't joining me?" I asked as my foot sank into the sting of heated water.

I'd wanted a repeat of the only other time I bathed with him, after the miscarriage when he had held me in his arms and made me feel as if I was the most precious of all his possessions. When Alexander smiled a small, knowing grin, I ducked behind the curtain of my hair to hide my embarrassment and slid into the water, dunking my head under the bubbles so that my stuttering heartbeat was all I could hear.

When I breached the surface, he was waiting for me. His fingers pinched my wet chin so that he could tip my gaze to his stone somber eyes.

"I'm going to tend to you while I explain some necessary things to you. If I were to get into the tub with you, I fear I wouldn't have the strength to focus on the words instead of our bodies."

A hot stone of desire wedged itself in my throat. I swallowed thickly before asking, "Is that a bad thing? I've missed the way you touch me."

"I'm touching you now," he said, emphasizing his point by sliding his fingers from my chin up my sloping jawline and into the hair over my ear. His other hand moved between my breasts, up the sharp jut of my collarbones to lightly collar my throat. "I don't have to hurt you to show you how much I own you, my beauty. I own you with every touch of my hand

and press of my lips. I own you with every word we exchange and every breath we take, even when you aren't near." His fingers tightened possessively. "How does it feel when I do this?"

"Like I'm yours." I gasped lightly through the obstruction around my neck.

Lust pooled between my legs like hot sand.

He hummed in approval as he shifted to twist his torso farther over the lip of the tub and reach for the shampoo on the other side of me. I watched with a dry mouth as his big, capable hands squeezed out the gel and lathered it between his palms. My eyes were already closing as they landed on my scalp, smoothing through the thick pelt of my hair to knead firmly at my head. My sigh curled into the steam licking off the surface of the hot water and floated to the ceiling.

"And how does this feel, *bella*?" he asked again, ducking down to plant the words warmly in my ear before trailing his lips over my cheek. He placed a kiss on each of my closed lids like coins in offering to Charon.

My throat ached with the sudden desire to cry at his tenderness, but I swallowed it down, and whispered thickly, "Like I'm yours."

"And isn't that the truth?"

It was a real question, not his usual statements masquerading poorly as inquiries. I loved that he needed the words from me, that even though he had decided to reclaim me, I actually had some kind of say in it this time.

I tipped my head back into his softly churning hands in my hair so that I could latch gold to silver, so that he could read the truth in my melted butter eyes.

"I won't ever belong to someone if they don't also belong to me."

He blinked, and somehow, in that small expression, there was a flash of proud, gentle humour. Heedless of his suit pants, Alexander swung his socked feet into the tub on either side of me and leaned down so that I was almost entirely surrounded by the impossible width of him.

"Wherever you are, however far away for whatever length of time, I'm yours."

My heart clenched into a twisted mass, searing hot and throbbing like a wound. I couldn't believe him, not the way I desperately wanted to. I'd invested too much in the past four years, reconditioning myself to believe that my love for Alexander was bad, wrong, impossible. That he had never loved me, couldn't love me, was incapable of loving me.

Four years was a long time to have invested in the wrong option.

I could feel my seams bloat and threaten to rupture around the staples I'd haphazardly used to hold myself together. Faced with change, like any human, I battled against it.

"You don't even know me. Not really."

Alexander surprised me by not immediately offering a rebuttal. Instead, he used a pitcher I hadn't notice he'd brought in from the kitchen to pour clean, tepid water over my sudsy hair, careful to cup his other hand over my forehead so soap didn't get into my eyes.

Only once I was clean did he cant my chin up with his palm under my jaw, and admit, "You've changed since I last knew you, that's true."

I snorted so hard it hurt my throat. "I've been killed and reborn so many times in my life, it's a wonder I have any authenticity at all."

"You've changed," he said calmly, sternly like a parent who would not bear being interrupted by an unruly child. "But you are still fundamentally the woman you let me know in England."

"I'm not sure it was a matter of *letting* you know me. Since when have you needed permission for anything?"

He shrugged in the elegant, bored manner of a man who

was very wealthy and had never known a moment of doubt in his life. It was almost a condescending gesture; one I shouldn't have found so very attractive.

"No person is ever wholly under another's control. You still have free will, Cosima. Yes, I curtailed it, but it was you and you alone who gave me insight into your heart. Every rebellion, every capitulation, every orgasm was a window into your darkly beautiful soul. Do not doubt for one instant that I didn't take advantage of every single one of those opportunities to know you. Even when it went against my greater plan."

"To use me against Salvatore," I filled in, reminded that if I wanted to continue with Xan, I would eventually have to tell him that I'd helped to fake my father's death.

"Yes, among other things. Truthfully, I think a part of me just wanted to own something that was wholly mine and not Noel's also," he admitted with a wry twist of his full mouth. "I could never have known just how much owning you would change my life. That you would so beautifully fill all the empty places in my life until I realized that before you, I had none."

"You didn't tell me any of this when I was with you at Pearl Hall," I accused.

Another shrug limned with ennui. "There were too many things in the way of the truth for me to see it clearly."

"What changed?"

For me, the answer was simple. I knew I loved Alexander the moment he'd dismissed me in the field of poppies to go to Italy to enact his revenge of Salvatore. I knew I would never be free of the chains from that love the moment he dismissed me on the rooftop of the Milanese Duomo and told me never to set eyes on him again.

It seemed the death of something was when we realized just how much it meant to us when it was alive.

"Someone took you from me." I noted with a shiver that he hadn't said I'd run away, that he trusted in my total enslavement to him enough to know I would never have voluntarily fled. His conviction felt like my weakness, a vulnerability I wanted to wrench away from him and protect. "I realized that it wasn't the betrayal that was driving me mad as it normally would have been. It was the sheer, absolute loss of you that haunted me. I realized, as you must now, that if you were completely and utterly enamoured by me, I was just as powerless to the feeling as you were. You see, my little mouse, somehow over that tumultuous year of ownership, we became a closed loop. What you feel, I feel. Your weakness in wanting me is exactly my weakness in reverse."

A closed loop.

I could feel it even then, the circle of energy moving through the pressed points of our skin, cycling through him and into me and back. It was how he seemed to always read my thoughts, how I craved his pleasure because his satisfaction was my own. It was Master and slave in perfect harmony.

And it seemed one could not exist, at least not contentedly, without the other.

Alexander brushed his thumb over the cut curve of my cheekbone, patiently waiting as I digested his rich, meaty words.

"I meant what I said. I'm here to reinstall you at my side for good. The only thing I need from you is your permission."

"I thought you never asked for permission for anything?" I countered because the small acidic fear I still felt in my gut needed an outlet.

Wasn't this too good to be true?

"Usually," he agreed. "But for this, I'm afraid, it's a necessity."

"If I say yes, what then?" I hedged. "Nothing has really changed."

"Not yet, but it will," he promised as he lowered himself fully into the bath, sloshing water over the sides while soaking his beautiful silk shirt and destroying his trousers. He gathered me up in his arms until I was wrapped around him like vines.

"I stayed away from you for the past four years for a reason, and that reason was to take down the Order so we could be free of them forever."

My eyebrows punctured the top of my hairline. "Is that even possible?"

"It is," he promised with the sly, coy look of a predator about to stalk and corner his prey. "Let me explain it to you."

Chapter Seventeen

ALEXANDER

My earliest memory of my father was learning to play chess against him in the second library before the vast black marble hearth. I remembered how large he seemed sitting in the high-backed tufted leather chair, his broad shoulders pressed to either side of the wingback, his head crowning the top like a golden circlet. A cigar curled smoke into the air from the gold ashtray on the side table, resting beside a crystal cut glass sweating from the cold of the iced whiskey within. Everything was so adult and sophisticated. My childhood brain was seduced by the atmosphere and my father's own elegant aura of power.

I wanted with everything I had to be exactly like him when I grew up.

It was the natural inclination of a boy to admire and aspire to be his father, but looking back on my boyhood, it was obvious Noel had taken particular pains to create a sense of divinity around himself. He succeeded. For years, I worshipped at his altar, studied his philosophies like scripture so that I could recite them verbatim when asked (which he did), and believed wholeheartedly that he had been blessed by a higher power.

I wouldn't learn until later that the higher power was no God or sacred charter, but the Order of Dionysus.

At that moment, though—no more than four years of age and still the kind of blond only small children can claim, sitting in the twin wing-backed chair to my father's and struggling not to swing my legs because it would make him angry— I simply loved Noel Davenport.

I loved him so innocently that when he set about to teach me the ways of chess, I took the lessons somberly, as seriously as a monk his vows. I read books by Bobby Fischer and Yasser Seriawan, followed the meteoric climb of Magnus Carlsen, and went to bed with the golden queen from my father's chess set clutched in my fist instead of the stuffed bear my mother had given me.

Chess was my father's game and learning its strategies was our primary form of bonding.

Edward Dante didn't like the game. He had no patience for hours of thought and subtle manipulations. He was a child of action, grass-stained jumpers and ripped trousers, bruises from roughhousing with the servant's kids, and bloody lips from altercations with older boys who tried to bully the young ones at school. His bonding time with Noel was spent with a cane and his open palms, a beating each time he rebelled from our father's teachings.

I didn't rebel. I was not inclined to be different from my

father. It was both natural to love the things he loved and beneficial.

My mother loved me deeply, but I didn't have to do anything to warrant that love, and somehow, it meant more to me that my father's affections had to be earned.

It became my childhood and adolescent mission to deserve it.

For years, I did. So well, in fact, that on my ninth birthday, Noel began my introduction to the Order.

To this day, I remember every moment of Yana's beating in the dungeon of Pearl Hall. The wet scent of cold stone and subterranean earth, the heaviness of the damp air, and the creak of the old wood steps beneath my feet as I followed my father into the dark.

Yana herself was cemented in my memory like a head-stone memorializing the death of my childhood, a marble angel weeping over the grave of the love for my father.

She was so young, eighteen as Cosima had been when I acquired her, but without any of the Latin passion and fire that made my wife blaze from the inside out. She was as thin as the waifs Edward and I imagined wandered the moors of the Peak District at night in white nightgowns, their mouths wide in eternal screams, their eyes dark with nightmares. I was terrified by the sight of her, slim and wan as she was kneeling on the ground in the middle of the chamber with her head bent and her hands clasped.

She was so fragile I worried the very vibration of our foot strikes against the floor would shatter her into millions of porcelain pieces.

Noel, it became clear, had no such compunction.

"This is Yana, Alexander, but formally, she is known as slave Davenport. You see, our family has been an established member of a very prestigious society since its inception in 1655. We are the wealthiest, most powerful men in the United Kingdom, and together, we run the country from the shadows.

We also participate in a game of wits and domination. It is the practice of the Order of Dionysus to acquire a slave to break them and train them to be the best. We have annual gatherings to assess which lord has the best pet."

His words rolled over me like the morning mist on the hills, cold and opaque. My child's mind could not begin to comprehend what he was trying to explain to me. I knew the history of England and of the Greythorn dukedom inside and out, but I had never heard of the Order, only of the Greek god Dionysus, the deity of revelry, wine, and a certain kind of madness.

Noel moved with the undulating, feline gait I'd tried to emulate my entire life to the shelves and hooks of bizarre tools lining the stone walls and retrieved a long, coiled rope like the one I'd once seen in an Indiana Jones film.

My mild confusion and unease shattered just the way I'd imagined Yana doing as he stood behind her, cocked the whip, and smiled at me.

"This, son," he'd said with the paternal, warm grin, "is how you beat your slave."

What followed was too graphic to put into words. It was the dissolution of my childhood and any purity I might have inherently retained because of my age.

Noel ruined me in that dungeon just as assuredly as he ruined Yana.

My mother noticed the abuse done to my back, of course. She was a caring woman and also an Italian one—she had eyes on the back of her head and a sense for everything that went wrong with her children. She tried to tend to the open wounds, but Noel found her and forbade her from nursing me.

I'd earned the punishment. In fact, I'd *asked* for it to spare the girl I'd been sure would break apart like a human vase on the cold stone floor of my father's favourite room in Pearl Hall.

Noel would not see me coddled. There were consequences to every action, and I had to learn that, in order to avoid the consequences, I had to be the driving force behind every action.

It was the first lesson he taught me that I wasn't happy to know, but in the end, it turned out to be the most powerful.

I was reminded of the gravity of that lesson the day Noel finally discovered I was working against the Order.

It was the same day I had irrefutable evidence that Amadeo Salvatore did *not* kill my mother.

It was just over a year since Cosima had been taken from me, and I'd never been colder, inside or out. My father took it as he was meant to, as a sign that I had moved onward and upward from my fleeting mistake with an Italian slave girl. He involved me in his business dealings once more, happily plying his sudden access to my influence to make rash, ill-advised business dealings across Great Britain.

Normally, he might have questioned my pliancy, but he was too relieved by my financial and political backing to study my motivation too closely. He made his moves across the board, and I—as I had for most of my life just as he trained me to—followed.

I had just finished an important call with the COO of Davenport Media Holdings when Noel appeared in the doorway to my office, his handsome face folded into a smug smile.

"Son," he greeted. "I believe it's time for the next stage."

"Of your master plan?" I asked without inflection. The words could have been sarcastic or sincere, but if I made my tone empty, Noel was always ready to fill my intent in for himself.

I focused on the numbers on my screen instead of my father as he took a seat on the arm of the red leather chair before my desk, but I noticed in my periphery that his smile was particularly curled that day, in the way of a cartoon villain's mustache.

Foreboding played my vertebrae like piano keys.

"For both of our gains, I should think. The Howard girl is ready to be wed, and I believe you are just the man to do the deed."

I wasn't surprised by his proclamation. Martin Howard, Noel, and Sherwood had been pressing Agatha Howard into my arms as soon as I'd dropped the knife after castrating Simon Wentworth. It was understandable. She was beautiful and highborn, but more than that, the Howards were one of the Order's most dynastic families just as the Davenports were. It was a political marriage made in secret society heaven.

"Do you indeed?" I asked blandly as an email for Willa Percy appeared in my inbox labeled *Bulgari Fashion Week Party*.

My heart kicked brutally at the door of my ribcage, restless and wild in the face of possible information about my estranged wife. Willa and Jensen both kept me in the loop about Cosima through her work with St. Aubyn, ostensibly reporting on her life because she was the face of the fashion house I owned but didn't operate.

It wasn't enough to satisfy my burning need to know everything about her every day, but it was mild enough, clever enough to slide by without notice because the Order never thought to check deeply into my dealings with St. Aubyn.

My gaze cut to Noel who sat patiently with his cat ate the canary smirk.

"She's here now in the antechamber waiting for you to call on her. I took the liberty of having O'Shea prepare a tea service. You and Agatha will have much to discuss."

"Perhaps you've forgotten, but technically, I'm already married."

I hadn't forgotten, neither of us had. Noel still watched my every move, looking for the weakness I'd exposed by my dealings with Cosima, and I still worked tirelessly every day to move closer to the termination of the Order so that I could live with her as my wife once more.

"Pish posh, we can annul that sham of a marriage even if we didn't have the Archbishop of Canterbury in our back pocket. You don't worry about that. Focus on Agatha."

"Why?" I asked, finally giving my father the attention he wanted.

I sat back in my chair, crossing my legs and casually adjusting the coat of arms cufflinks at my wrists. They were too diminutive to read the writing, but I took heart from the family motto as I sat there playing the grandest game of chess I ever would against my father.

Non decor, deco.

I am not led, I lead.

"Martin owns the rights for Falmouth Port, and we need to secure him to bring in the shipments from Africa." The illegal shipments of blood diamonds my father had invested much of his fortune into.

He had everything set up—a seller, a warehouse, and a way to funnel the money so that it would end up in his hands as clean as money like that could be.

He was excited.

In fact, I hadn't seen my father that excited in years.

That was good. I needed him distracted while I worked carefully, relentlessly in the shadows. He was astute, a worthy adversary that had beat me back all my life. I needed him distracted, and this was almost too good a distraction to be true because it was also illegal in the extreme.

"Important," I told him in reply because it was, just not for the reasons he thought.

"Indeed. He wants to solidify our partnership with a marriage. You know how it's done, son."

I did. I knew better than most.

But marrying Agatha Howard was so far out of the question, I couldn't even entertain it. She was a wild factor in my carefully planned long game, and even though I was loathe to waste time on her, if she was in the parlor ready to be set up like a good little lady, it was as good a time as any to take her pulse and see how I could play her off.

I closed down my computer as I always did just in case Noel got the urge to snoop and somehow made it past my elaborate security system, and then swiveled out of my chair.

"I'll go to her, but don't expect me to rejoice over the union," I told my father blandly as I did up my suit jacket button. "If she's anything like other British ladies, she'll be a boring shag."

Noel laughed, clapping me on the back as I moved by him as if we were old boys drinking scotch in London gentlemen's club. "That's what slaves are for, my lad."

I fought the urge to shrug off the weight of his hand on my shoulder and moved through the door without acknowledging his comment.

"Proud of you, son," he said, just loud enough for me to hear it down the hall.

Once upon a time, a very long time ago, those words would have been more precious than gold.

Now, the only thing more precious than gold to me was an Italian woman by the name of Cosima who had enchanted me as surely as Circe the sorceress.

Riddick fell into step behind me at some point down the long hallway that cut straight through the center of the house like a spine. He stayed closed to me now, closer than before. I wasn't certain if it was because I'd never trusted him with my secrets before the disappearance of my wife and he felt further moved to guard me now that I'd acknowledged our friendship, or if it was because we'd entered a new, even darker and more dangerous world since then, and he knew vigilance at all times was paramount to getting out of this crux alive.

Either way, he escorted me to the antechamber where Agatha awaited behind a closed white and gold door.

"What do we know about her?" I asked as I stared at the intricate gold leaf work that scrolled over the door like vines. I knew enough already, but Riddick was the font of my information, the well other informants poured their buckets full of secrets into.

"Not much, milord. She is a society queen, but she has few hobbies other than horse riding and visiting a sickly aunt across the pond at least three times a year for extended holidays."

"An aunt?" The information rang false. Agatha Howard was known as an ice princess. I very much doubted she had an uncharacteristic soft spot for some elderly relationship she couldn't have known very well given the distance between them. "Look into that, will you, Rid?"

"Yes, milord."

I shot him a look over my shoulder and raised a brow. "Do I look presentable enough to approach a potential bride?"

Riddick's impenetrable expression cracked with the twitch of his lips into a brief grin. "Polygamy suits you well."

I chuckled softly, letting the small reassurance of intimacy scour through me. It was too infrequent these days, Riddick my only true comfort. A sad thing for a man nearing forty to realize he has very little in the way of friends.

Then I thought of James, the prime minister helping me to corral and take down the Order, and I smiled.

Few friends, I decided, but important ones.

Noel had already committed multiple felonies with my money and support. He didn't know what was coming for him, but I did.

Personally, I thought Noel would look just fucking dandy in prison orange.

I pushed open the door, prepared to deal with a vapid, bored aristocrat I would easily temper and eventually ignore.

Instead, I was greeted with an Agatha Howard I had never seen before.

She paced the room like a caged beast in grey cords and a black velvet blazer that wonderfully showcased her slim, long form. Her hair tossed madly over her shoulder in a riot of blond curls as she spun to face me, her nostrils flared, her hands clenched at her sides, and when she opened her mouth, it was to deliver words like a series of hard blows.

"Listen to me and listen well, Lord Thornton. I absolutely, unequivocally will *not* marry you. If you can't stomach the reject, tough cookies. I'm in love with someone else, and I won't be sold like cattle for the better financial interests of my family. Now, you have a choice. You can either help me get out of this snit, or you can pressure me into it and face the consequences."

I fought the urge to grin. Her ferocity reminded me so much of Cosima I felt her absence pulse in my chest like a second heart, a broken one with an out of tune beat.

"Dare I ask how you might enact these consequences on a lord of the realm? One who happens to yield as much power and even more wealth than your own family?"

She snarled at my cool tone and the blasé way I undid my suit jacket and took a seat in one of the darned uncomfortable 18th century chairs imported from France. There was so much hatred in her eyes that I nearly lost the urge to laugh.

I'd missed female animosity. It was such good fun.

"I'll make your life a living misery. I'll get every woman in my circle to spread absolutely heinous rumors about you and your laughable manhood. I'll spit in your face each time you talk to me. I'll fight you tooth and bloody nail before I ever let you bed me, but I'll also frighten away any slut willing to sleep with you. I. Will. Make. Your. Life. Hell," she spat.

I crossed one foot over the other knee and leaned farther back in the chair, lounging comfortably as a king in his throne. She growled. Again, I fought the urge to laugh the manic humour out of my inflated lungs.

Instead, I raised a cool brow, and said, "I'm afraid you'd

have your work cut out for you, Agatha. My life has been a living hell since I was old enough to cogitate." I stared at her for a long moment, watched the passion flicker like flames in her eyes, how it heated her skin to a flushed and mottled red. That kind of passion could not be banked, at least not for long. She was willing to fight and probably die for that love she spoke of, and she would not be deterred.

I could understand such passion, such verve, because it had driven me for the past twelve months.

"I'll expose your father," she barked, then hesitated, clearly surprised by her own indiscretion. Then she straightened and narrowed those big blue eyes at me. "I'll expose him. You see, *I* know something you don't. Noel took my father's private jet to Rome the day before your mother died."

Everything stilled. Even the dust motes spiraling through the air, catching in the light cast by the fire burning in the pink marble hearth seemed to freeze as I held my breath and fought through the brutal impact of the new information.

It took minutes. Long moments when I reeled internally, careful to keep my exterior façade placid before because it was instinctual after so many years and because I wasn't yet totally sure if I could trust the irascible woman across from me.

"You're sure?" I said finally, proud of the flatness in my tone.

She blinked, then frowned, leaning forward and speaking louder as if I hadn't heard her properly the first time. "Well, of course, I am. I wouldn't just go about saying such a thing, no matter how much I may not want to marry you. My father and Noel were best friends before he passed away. They did everything together, and this was no exception. Obviously, Noel couldn't fly commercial or take his own jet if he was going to do something unspeakable… something like murder his own wife."

"You can't possibly know if Noel did that or not," I said by rote because Noel truly had programmed me beautifully.

"No," she agreed. "Although, he returned the morning after her death, and he never told anyone, so far as I can tell, that he ever went to Italy around that time. Why would he keep it a secret?"

Why would he?

Well, the answer was bloody obvious, wasn't it?

My father had really done it.

The woman he had wooed and brought back from Italy, the woman he had seemed to love despite his myriad of flaws and countless slaves, the woman who had certainly loved him back regardless of those qualms, had been murdered by her own husband.

By my father.

I closed my eyes as pain tore through every layer of my being like a fissure cracking open in the earth, shifting tectonic plates and dislodging old, settled fossils and sediment so that everything was different, everything was new and aching.

"Fuck," I breathed on an explosive breath as the air punched from my lungs.

Dante and Salvatore had been right all along.

A small, shaky part of me had always wondered, always secretly suspected their truth was *the* truth. But it was so much easier in principle than in practice to turn your back on what you knew to face a new and horrible truth about what you had always believed in.

So, I had believed in my father.

What a colossal, life-altering mistake.

I fought the urge to surge out of my chair, storm down the hall, and attack him. To drag him by the hair down to the dungeon and string him up in chains like a spider's web and slowly eat away at him with whip and weapon until he begged for death.

He had killed my mother. Taken the only family member who had ever loved or nurtured Dante or me away from us, and for what?

For what?

The question resounded through my head like a gong strike.

It was only one of the many reasons I remained seated and resolved to carry out my plan to the very end. Noel would be imprisoned, not dead, and there was greater satisfaction in knowing he would rot in the slums of some dank prison with the very sort of people he'd detested all his life.

I wanted that for him.

I wanted him to experience what a living hell felt like as I had for years.

Agatha stared down at me, her face suspended between sympathy and ire. I didn't blame her for her cruelly delivered epiphany or her indecision in the obvious face of my grief. In the past year, I had been the poster boy for the Order. In the entirety of my life, I had been one of its most groomed champions.

Of course, she wouldn't know that everything was different. That everything had started to change the day Noel beat me in place of Yana, the day my mother was pushed to her death, the day Cosima saved me on the streets of Milan, and then again, the day she was taken from me.

She couldn't know I'd been fighting against the tidal flow of my preordained destiny hand and tooth for so long, I couldn't even remember what peace felt life.

Fuck me, I was tired.

Bone-deep exhausted.

I just wanted the Order gone, Noel—fucking monster of a man—punished for his myriad of crimes, and my sweet *topolina* back at my side.

God seemed determined to prove to me that I asked for too much.

I was fucking determined to prove Him, fate, or whatever the fuck might work against me cosmically, wrong.

I took a small, steadying breath and decided to risk my plan by entrusting Agatha Howard with a portion of my truth.

"My life has been a hell," I said, "since I was old enough to realize my father was a monster, and it was made once more unbearable when I realized that monster might have killed my mother. Now, poor, spoiled Agatha, it is utterly intolerable because the one woman I've ever loved with all my being has been taken from me by the very men who wishes to unite us against our wills. So, you tell me, what option of yours do you think I will choose?"

She stared at me as she deflated, punctured through the chest by my quelling words. A long, gusty sigh leaked out her slack mouth, and she suddenly seemed much smaller.

"You hate them too," she whispered, her shock robbing her voice of any strength.

"It's not a matter of hate," I explained as if to a child. "It's a matter of revenge."

She folded weakly into the chair across from me and blinked hard. "So you'll help me?"

"No, Agatha." I grinned so wickedly that she jolted upright once more. "I am the man with the plan. *You* will help me."

"Six months later, with the help of Agatha and James, Noel was arrested for fraud, embezzling, and money laundering," I finished explaining to Cosima, who was curled up on her side much like the black cat at our feet into a tight ball, a sleek black silk robe her only adornment.

Even fresh faced with wet, ropey hair, she was still so goddamn beautiful it was hard to breathe whenever I looked at her.

She blinked those big melted butter eyes at me as she absorbed my words, and for once, I couldn't read her thoughts in her expressive features. Her silence and calm deliberation unnerved me, but I didn't fidget or press into her silence with a series of blunt questions. She deserved time to process, especially given the tumultuous nature of my story.

"Noel beat me."

It was my turn to blink, and I did so hard, black spots eroding my vision when I opened my lids again to focus on her.

"That's why I left," she explained without intonation, her voice more American than I had ever heard it, stripped of the Italian and British that made her tone so lyrical. "I left because he pulled me away from the crowd, dragged me into the dungeon by my hair, and beat me the way he once beat Yana…he even had his youngest son beat me with him."

"Youngest son?" I asked hollowly.

It surprised me that after years of monumental discoveries, betrayal, and changes, I could still be so affected by new information.

But it fucking rocked me.

My bones seemed to split under the pressure, my skin so tight and hot I thought it would crack open and my entire body would shift into something less human, something bestial, and that I would remain like that for the rest of my life, deformed by treachery, cursed by the sins of my father.

Then the warm press of a hand was on my cheek and the sweet, spicy musk of Cosima's perfume was in my nose, cracking through the blackness rotting my soul like dawn light over the horizon.

I looked up and locked my eyes to her, needing that anchor to keep me from flying into a rage.

"Xan," she said softly as her thumb rubbed over the abrasive stubble covering my cheek. "Noel married Mrs. White in secret just after your mother died, and together, they had a son."

"Mary takes care of her sister and her boy, Rodger," I said, working through it, bringing the image of a dark blond-haired boy to my mind's eye.

He wasn't a handsome lad, but I could see, now that it was forced on me, how he shared similarities with Noel.

With me.

"Fuck." I tossed the bedclothes off me, overheating even in the cool room, even in my black boxer briefs. "Fuck, bloody fucking, *fuck*."

Cosima nodded solemnly. "That's about the gist of it. He told me Rodger was a contingency plan in case you turned out just like Dante."

"You mean, in case I decided to form my own mind instead of blindly attaching myself to his?"

She flinched at the arctic frost of my words, but my Cosima didn't back away. Instead, she pressed closer, her breasts softly crushed to my chest, her long legs tangling with mine.

All I could see was her beautiful face and those priceless eyes.

Nothing could have ever calmed me more.

"He beat me because he could see what we had together, and it scared him. He didn't want you to be punished by the Order or to lose sight of what he wanted for you."

"*He* didn't want to be punished through me, and *he* didn't want to lose sight of his own narcissistic, maniacal goals."

"That too," she agreed. "I didn't want to go, Xan, you have to know that."

I rolled my forehead across hers, brushing our noses together just to feel the luxe texture of her skin on mine, her breath hot and sweet on my lips. If I could have, I would have crawled inside her loveliness and dwelled there, safe and harboured forever.

In her own strange way, Cosima was my safety and my savoir. She might not have been called on to defend me bodily, but her spirit was my shield even when she'd been absent from me for years. She was my inspiration both in that I was driven by the need to be with her again and in that I admired her more than I ever had anyone else. No one was so beautiful, so resilient, and so loving as my beauty.

Case in point, she was comforting me while divulging the details of the wicked beating she had endured at the hands of Noel.

"When did he take you?"

"Just before I found you to say goodbye."

"How could that be true? I fucked you against a wall..." I read the flashback of pain in her eyes and turned to concrete. "Are you fucking kidding me? I fucked you against a wall whilst you were suffering from a torn up back? A back torn up by my own father not a hundred yards away in my very own home on our *fucking wedding day*?"

She winced. "Xan, what would you have had me do? I'd just been beaten, and he threatened me not just with my life, but yours! I dare anyone to come up with a better idea than I did in complying. Noel had just exposed how deeply deranged and extraordinarily ruthless he could be. I was not going to test that further."

"Who is your Master?" I demanded.

"Xan—"

"No, *topolina*, who the fuck do you answer to?"

I was close enough to see her pupils blow open, the black eating away at the gold until it was only a thin frame for her darkness. "You, Master."

"That's right, *me*. If you think for one moment, I wouldn't have believed you had you told me what happened, that I wouldn't have stormed into the dungeon, strung up that monster and skinned him alive for you, woven that flesh into a tapestry that you might use for fucking darts, you are madly mistaken. Have I ever done anything to make you believe I wouldn't kill for you? Even die for you?"

She bit her plush lower lip, indenting the pink flesh so neatly, I was driven to do the same.

So, I did.

I bit into that lip, *hard*, until the tang of her blood panged on my tongue. I ate her gasp out of her mouth and then pulled back to stare into her eyes.

"A threat against you is a threat against me. And I think you know this already, *bella*, but no one, absolutely no one, threatens a Davenport and gets away with it."

"Even a fellow Davenport?" she asked wearily.

"Especially then," I vowed. "I'm going to rid our world of its demons, my beauty, and then I'll show you exactly what kind of life we can have together. A safe life, one filled not just with your beauty, but the beauty we can create together."

"That feels impossible," she admitted. "Even though I've wanted that for years."

"The best kind of dreams worth dreaming are terrifying in their enormity," I agreed, cupping her face in my hands, knowing I held the greatest dream I'd ever had between my palms, feeling it resonate through my chest like a shockwave. "I'm *this* close to having enough on the Order of Dionysus to take them down. All I need is a way to find out the date of the next auction."

"By using Yana and di Carlo?"

"Yes, though I know two others who might help. I'll visit them to find out where di Carlo's poker game might be held tomorrow night. I don't need you involved in this," I started to say and then silenced Cosima's protest before she could voice it by sliding the steel of my Dominance in my tone. "I don't want you involved in this because it could be dangerous, but I also know you're strong enough to deal with this, capable enough to *help* me with this. So, my beauty, for perhaps the first time, it's up to you."

I watched something precious and warm slide over her face as she absorbed my words, as she relished her choice. We both knew what she would choose because she was the same atavistic Italian girl she had been when she'd arrived at Pearl Hall and spat in my face, but there was delight in the pause before the answer, for both of us.

"To kill our demons, first we must master them," she said in answer.

"Don't tell me you write fortune cookies now," I teased.

She blinked at me and then pressed her breasts tighter to my chest as she arched her neck back to laugh loudly at the ceiling. I held her as she laughed, felt her joy vibrate through my very bones, and knew that at the end of all the horrors of our lives, we were each other's reward.

Chapter Eighteen

COSIMA

"Mason, please, trust me. You can stop worrying. I'm fine," I said with impatient exasperation as I tossed my mascara back into my makeup bag, fluffed my hair, and then exited the bathroom with my phone in my hand to get dressed for the day.

The morning had begun as it hadn't in years, with Alexander's body tangled up in mine, his heavy weight a soothing pressure on my torso, his breath ruffling the hair over my temple. I watched him unabashedly until the lust building between my legs forced me to trace his sleep soft mouth with my tongue. Working gently, slowly, I made my way down his long, broad torso, kissing the edges of his v-shaped form, running my tongue over the square cut moguls of his abdominals, drawing my nose over the crisp trail of hair leading from his navel to his groin where I inhaled the intoxicating sweet and salt musk of him.

Only when my tongue smoothed a slick path up his hardening cock did Alexander wake up with a deep, guttural moan. The next second, his hands were fisted in my hair, his hips jerking up to impale my mouth with the hot slide of his dick.

I moaned around him, loving the taste of his heated flesh, the brine at his tip that I worked for with swirls of my tongue and hard, sucking pulls from my lips. He kept mostly still, so still, at first, that I worried I wasn't pleasing him. But when I tipped my eyes up through my lashes to look at him, his eyes were blown fully black with dark pleasure.

"Am I pleasing you, Master?" I asked, needing the validation, vibrating with tension.

He blinked lazily and pulled his hands from my hair to cross them behind his head. My mouth watered over his cock head as I studied the way his muscles bulged beneath all that golden skin, the tufts of flaxen hair beneath those massive arms, and the way his abs contracted as I tugged at his dick. A trickle of wet leaked down my thigh, and I squirmed, Xan's eyes tracking the way my ass waved in the air.

"You're doing fine, *topolina*," he praised mildly, like an unimpressed boss. "But if you don't make me come in the next two minutes, I'll have to punish you."

My nipples furled so tightly I could feel each beat of my pulse heavy in my swollen breasts.

I went to work.

Tongue whirling, hand pumping and twisting, throat working to take his long, thick pole deep inside where I could seal my lips around his root and suck so hard my mouth ached.

"Thirty seconds." Alexander's voice cracked across my sensitive skin with the pain of a whip. There was no break in his words, no hoarseness to give away how well I was servicing him.

His impassivity worked on me like an accelerant, lighting my already burning flesh on fire with lust so severe I shook with it. My hips pumped at the air, seeking any kind of friction as I slammed my mouth back over his throbbing flesh.

"Be still," he ordered. "If you're a good girl, I won't have to clamp your pussy and paddle you until you cry for me."

I whimpered as I traced a thick vein up his shaft and then sealed my lips over the head to suck hard.

A flood of precum pooled in my mouth. I lapped it up like a cat with cream, so greedy for more I was salaciously moaning and making lurid wet, sucking noises in my quest for more.

Suddenly, Alexander knifed up to grab me under my pits, haul me up, and flip me onto my back on the bed so he could straddle my chest. I panted as his weight settled, his hot balls pooled between my breasts, and he fisted his cock so violently over my face, it instantly turned a florid purplish red.

"Do you want your Master's cum?" he demanded in a voice like gravel under tires.

I shivered and parted my damp lips, my tongue aching for another taste of his seed.

"Please, please, please."

"Should I come all over these fucking gorgeous breasts?" he asked as he reached one hand down to knead one tit and then moved to brush a thumb over my lower lip. "Or inside the wet, hot mouth?"

"Mouth, please, Master," I begged, pumping my hips up, writhing against the need coursing through my body.

I was desperate, filled with an excess of energy with no outlet. One touch to my cunt and I would detonate.

Even watching Xan loom over me like a Viking plundering his female spoils made my pussy coil so tightly, I wondered if that would be enough to launch me into climax.

There was the *thap, thap, thap* of his fist over his flesh and the hard churn of air through both our open mouths and then he was groaning, head tipped to the sky, Adam's apple a hard knot in his golden throat as he moaned his imminent release.

I swept my eyes over his glistening chest and latched them to his cock just in time to see the first long rope of his semen arch out and land half in my waiting mouth, half on my cheek. The hand not on his cock found my throat and collared it as he tipped his head down to watch himself paint cum across my face.

I waited until he was spent before licking the brine off my lips, and then Xan used his finger to scoop up the rest and feed it to me.

I wanted to beg for release, but I didn't because no matter what I said, it wasn't me with the power. And no matter how sexually frustrated I was, every single part of me loved that.

Xan looked down at me, tipping my chin up so that we locked eyes, and I read the absolute tenderness in his expression.

"I rarely dream, but when I do, I dream of two inevitable things. I dream of killing my father, but my beauty, I dream the most of you." His voice was as soft as a feather floating down against my cheek and just as hauntingly beautiful. "Though, this is the first time that dreaming of you was not a nightmare because I knew when I woke, you would still be here."

"Xan," I breathed, pulling an arm from where it was pinned under his leg so I could cup his face. "Don't make me cry."

"You're beautiful when you cry. In fact, you are the most beautiful creature on this earth," he expressed solemnly. "I'm certain of it."

I tipped my chin down to skirt his hand over my cheek and

nuzzled it. "We're well matched then because I've never seen a man more gorgeous than you."

His smile was slight and self-deprecating, but he didn't protest. "Get up now, my beauty. Let me make you breakfast."

I tried not to pout, but from the twitch of his lips, I could tell I failed. I was still poised on the knife's edge of release, my pussy so slick it made a wet noise as I followed Xan out of the bed. He ignored this.

In fact, he practically ignored me as he made us eggs and bacon flavoured with Italian herbs and goat cheese. As he worked on his phone while I picked up my forgotten Cleopatra biography and then as he took a phone call from Riddick about the state of Ashcroft, who was still being held prisoner and beaten daily for his crimes against us.

I was washing the dishes in the sink when Xan finally approached behind me, wrapping his big hands over my hips so my ass canted up against his groin. His nose pushed my hair out of the way so he could trail his warm lips over my throat before he said, "Is my poor little mouse still desperate to come?"

Instantly, my poorly banked lust flared to life, and I gyrated back against him. "Yes, Master."

"Hands to the counter, feet apart. If you move a single inch, I will stop, *topolina*, so be good for your Master, and I'll eat you until you come all over my tongue. Then I'm going to fuck you so hard, you'll be aching for the rest of the day."

And he made good on his promise, eating at my pussy and ass from behind me, propped up on his knees on the floor with his rough hands holding me open for his ravenous mouth. I came twice on his tongue and twice more around the punishing invasion of his cock, the last at the same time he flooded me with another load of his hot, sticky seed. He held me still with one hand as he pulled out and played a finger in my messy pussy, watching as our juice leaked slowly down my thigh before he smeared them as he loved to do across my entire sex.

Now, I was speaking to Mason as Xan took his turn in the shower. I felt badly that I hadn't spoken to my friend since the charity gala when Alexander had shown up to usurp his bid for my date night, but life had been too chaotic to spend any time on friendships over the past few weeks.

I couldn't very well explain why that was to Mason, so I tried to be patient with his annoyance.

"That man who bought you, Cosi, he's a fucking British *lord*, did you know that?" Mason demanded. "I read online that he's from one of the most notorious families in the United Kingdom. His great-great-grandfather was called 'Black Benedict' because he would import slaves from Africa to use for his own pleasure!"

"Mason," I said, my tone warm with unsuppressed amusement. "I hardly think it's fair to judge someone based on the actions of their 'great-great' relative."

He snorted. "Still, I don't have a good feeling about him. I hope you aren't seeing him now."

"I am," I told him, happy to do it.

I wanted people to know I was in love. I didn't want to hide anymore. Alexander was the greatest man I knew, and I was proud to be with him. That didn't necessarily mean I was ready to tell my family about him, not with the drama already wracking my family over Sinclair breaking up with Elena, but it was nice to tell at least one of my best friends about him.

There was a heavy silence as Mason processed this.

"What does this mean?"

I sighed. "It means I'm happy. For the first time in a long time. I would love if you could be happy for me."

"It just...this changes things."

"With your family?"

"Well, yes. My uncle...he won't be happy I'm not with you

anymore," he admitted with a tense groan. "I don't know how I'll handle this."

"I'm sorry," I said, and I truly meant it. Mason had been such a good friend to me over the years, and I felt badly for leaving him to deal with his oppressive, old-school thinking family. But I wouldn't let anything get in the way of Alexander and me, not anymore.

I was just pulling a sheer black blouse over my lace bra when Xan emerged from the bathroom on a cloud of steam looking like a wet gold statue stolen from the Pantheon. Immediately, my mouth went dry at the sight of him.

He frowned at the phone in my hand. "Who?"

"Mason," I mouthed to him before saying into the cell, "I've got to go, honey. I hope we can get together when things are less crazy for me. If you need any help with your family, let me know."

"It would help us both if you left that guy," he muttered darkly, but when I only laughed at him, he sighed. "Fine. Take care of yourself, Cosima. I don't get a good feeling about any of this."

Xan stalked toward me, wrapping an arm around my hips to tug me against his damp body so he could place a kiss behind my ear and then a line of them down my jugular. I shivered, hung up the phone, and dropped it to the dresser behind me, Mason totally forgotten as Alexander whispered, "On your knees, *topolina*, I missed you in the shower, and I feel the need to show you just how much."

ALEXANDER

*T*he man we needed to see lived in a large home in a small town in upstate New York, and he had done since he immigrated to this country after being tossed out of the upper crust of British Society. I knew this because I had helped to relocate him and his money to the new country in order to keep him safe from further harm.

I had told Cosima the story about what happened after she disappeared at our wedding, how I'd decided to head the Order's demands and punish Simon Wentworth for the exact crimes I myself had committed. She had listened with pursed lips and sad eyes, keeping her condemnations to herself. Ours was not a world of black and white, and she knew better than to guilt me about Simon when I'd been forced in to an impossible position. We'd both made tough choices, and we both knew what it meant to live with them.

Still, I was watching her face when we pulled up the drive of the old stone house and knocked on the door. I wanted to see how she would react to the reveal.

She didn't disappoint.

The moment Simon Wentworth opened the door, she gasped.

I was right. She recognized him from the night of The Hunt.

She recoiled a step just as Simon's pale, pleasant face broke into a wide grin, and he stepped forward to embrace me in a back-thumping embrace.

"Thornton, old chap, what the hell are you doing on my doorstep?" He laughed as he pulled back. "It's been an age since you telephoned."

"I've been busy," I said, inclining my head to Cosima at my left to indicate just how busy I had been.

Simon's face collapsed like a sandcastle into the sea. He stared at Cosima for a long moment, emotions playing out behind his eyes as he absorbed the shock of seeing her standing there.

"You remember me," he breathed finally, his expression creased and stained with old memories and stale shame.

Cosima hesitated, then nodded, moving slightly toward me in an unconscious appeal for comfort. I heeded it, taking her far hip in my grip to move her into my side.

"I, well, I don't really know what to say," Simon confessed, blowing out a gust of air as he ran a hand through his thicket of hair. "I was abominable, really. Just the worst of the worst. All I can offer is that I was terrified and in love. At the time, going after you seemed the best course of action."

"Because you were worried they would find out about you and your slave?" she asked quietly.

"Daisy," he said as his face spasmed with pain, and his voice dropped to a breathless whisper. "Her name was Daisy."

"They killed her?" she confirmed; her eyes so wide and gold they rivaled the sun glaring coldly from the winter sky.

Simon took comfort in those eyes, straightening his spine as he nodded. "They did. Before they got to me, they found her, and...well, no need to rehash the details. Needless to say, I am terribly sorry for my behavior. I have an excuse, though, there really isn't any good reason I should have scared you like that."

"I think it's a good reason," she said softly, stepping forward to place a hand on Simon's arm. "I think it's the *best* reason."

Simon's lip trembled slightly before he rolled it between his teeth to stymie the show of weakness. "It's no wonder a man like Thornton would be enamoured with a woman like you."

Cosima tilted her head to the side in question.

"So much light and softness," he explained with a small, private smile. "It's an Achilles heel for men such as us."

"Dark men."

"Broken ones," he corrected her, patting her hand on his arm before stepping back up into the house and pushing the door wide for us. "Come in, come in."

Simon's home was large, but the rooms were small, the hallways narrow, and both were filled with comfortable furniture. It was a home; vastly different from Wentworth's previous residence—a small castle—back in England. Still, I recognized his joy in it as he touched his hand to the walls while he moved passed and through the photos lining the mantle place of the living room he led us into.

I was happy he had found happiness.

It was a strange revelation because I'd been a self-centered man, a callous one, most of my life. When you are taught that empathy is a weakness from a young age, what recourse do you have but to believe it?

Loving Cosima had made me considerably more empathetic, and I had to agree that it was, in a way, a great weakness. I didn't want the innocent to suffer and the guilty to flourish, so I found I had to take a stand when these things happened.

The first time I'd really done so had been with Simon,

whisking him out of the country so that the Order couldn't finish him off. I'd tried to do the same for Daisy, but they got to her before the wedding, and there was nothing to be done.

A vase of daisies sat on the mantle beside a photo of a young ethnic woman with a demure smile. I instantly knew that was Daisy, and I felt a pang in my heart knowing he still memorialized her.

She deserved that.

"Did you move here to escape the Order after what happened?" Cosima was asking as we took a seat on a pink velvet couch that was clearly not the choice of Simon, a man whose style ran toward hunting chic.

Simon frowned at her. "Surely, you know it was Thornton who brought me over?" When I only pressed my lips together and Cosima's eyes went wide as gold doubloons, he chuckled and shook his head. "Ever comfortable as the bad guy, hmm, Thornton?"

"I did castrate you," I reminded me drily.

Cosima choked on a giggle, her hand flying to her mouth. "I'm sorry, Simon."

He waved it away with a grin. "No, no, that was rather funny. You did, of course, but you also gave me a new life, and when push came to shove, you reunited me with the one person who could heal me when all was said and done."

My wife's eyebrows shot into her hairline. "Oh?"

"He's referring to me, I believe," Agatha Howard said as she swept into the room looking every inch the aristocrat even in faded denim and an old Led Zeppelin shirt.

She went straight to Simon and settled on the arm of his chair, which he instantly tugged her off of so she landed in his lap. They grinned at each other for a moment before she faced a bemused Cosima again.

"It's good to see you again, Cosima."

"*Che cavalo,*" she breathed. "Someone please explain what's going on."

Simon smiled. "Aggie and I were best friends growing up. I was a meek lad, not inclined for much but hunting and mathematics. I didn't have many friends, save her, and she was much too good for me. I never thought to like her as anything more than my friend, but when I fell in love with Daisy...well, she was my rock. She was with both of us through everything, trying to find a way to make it safe for us to be together. Obviously, you know the tragic end to that story. What you don't know, just as I didn't, was that Agatha had been in love with me all that time. When Daisy died and I...was punished for loving her, I came to America on Thornton's dollar and set up a new life. When the Order tried to force Aggie and Thorn together, they unwittingly paired the two people who could work toward their end and *wanted* to for what was done to their loved ones."

Simon paused to press his nose into his lover's hair. Agatha closed her eyes to relish his closeness and then continued his story. "When I confronted Alexander about not wanting to marry him, we made a pact to take down the Order. He didn't trust me, at first, so I told him my story, how involved I had been with Simon and Daisy. Not only did he trust me after, but he also reunited us."

"Does your family know?" Cosima asked, but her hand was in my lap locking through my fingers and her head was tipped to press against my shoulder. Her closeness was validation of my part in their romance, a sweet acknowledgment of how brave and right she felt I was in doing that.

I felt her gratitude soar through me like a shooting star.

"They know I've absconded with a hearty portion of my inheritance and some family heirlooms, but otherwise, no, they don't know where I've settled."

Cosima was silent for a moment, obviously digesting everything she'd been told. Finally, she tilted her face up to look at me, and whispered, "Not evil, not even close."

I didn't smile at her, but my eyes held the wealth of

warmth I felt for her. I liked Simon and Agatha, but not enough to reveal how desperately entangled I was in my wife.

"Which brings us to now," I said, finally ready to get down to business. "Have you heard anything I should be privy to?"

"Like what? You know I'm keeping an eye on Noel, as are you, but thus far, he's been remarkably silent in his cage at Pearl Hall. Hell, he hasn't even hired a new servant in years."

"Did you know Giuseppe di Carlo is the newest member of the Order in the city?" I asked, searching their faces for betrayal. I trusted them as much as anyone outside of Cosima and Riddick, which was to say, not very much.

Aggie winced. "I did hear that. Alan Byers told me so the other day. Are you thinking to use him to ferret out information about the auctions?"

"Do you really think he'll give it up?" Simon asked. "He's a mafia boss, Thorn. I doubt he'll give it up with a please and thank you from the likes of you."

I raised a brow. "Do I seem like the kind of man who would use such pleasantries?"

Cosima laughed under her breath.

"No, but I don't see how else you plan to get the information from him."

"Easy," I said with a slow, slick smile. "Giuseppe di Carlo loves games, and he loves poker. I'll wager him for the information. The only problem is, we need to know where his game tonight is being held. Can you help me with that?"

Simon was a computer programmer in his previous life and made a living now doing freelance security work for big, somewhat sketchy companies.

His smile was in answer to my own, a spill of sly smugness across his face. "Oh, I think I can do that."

Chapter Nineteen

COSIMA

A woman's greatest weapon when properly applied was her form of dress. The midnight black silk dress smothered the lines of my exaggerated curves like motor oil, a cool, dark spill from the points of my shoulders over the outer swells of my breasts to pool narrowly, rippling around my high-heeled feet. My hair was brushed until it floated like strands of pure night around my bare shoulders, catching in the shadowed valley of my breasts like the imaginary fingers of the men who would desire to touch me there. My eyes were lined with kohl, my lips painted a deep, wicked red, the colour of old, spilled blood.

I was sex on two legs, and that, more than the SOG Salute mini folding knife strapped to my ankle or the small pocket pistol attached to the garter in the gap between my inner thighs, was my weapon.

And I needed a weapon that night because we were going into the lion's den.

Giuseppe di Carlo owned a small, quiet restaurant in the Bronx that wasn't featured on any Zagat guides or travel sites. Even its name was scrawled in dark grey paint on a black wood awning over the blacked-out windows. It did not invite the patronage of people who didn't know exactly what they were walking into; a modern mafia den.

"They'll search us," Alexander had warned from the kitchen as I finished putting on my face in the bathroom, "but not as thoroughly as they might because it's an open table and the kind of men enticed to play aren't the kind of men who feel comfortable without their weapons."

Not for the first time since we'd planned this outing to confront the di Carlo family crime boss, I wished Dante was there. If anyone could help us with the ins and outs of a night with Made Men, it was the Camorra *capo* himself. I bit my lip and thumbed my phone where it lay on the sink basin, wishing he would answer any of the fourteen voicemails or innumerable texts I had sent him in the past twenty-four hours.

"We can do this without Edward," Alexander said, reading my mind as only he could from where he suddenly appeared in the doorway behind me.

"We can," I agreed. "I just wish we didn't have to."

His lips thinned, but his eyes were hot with more than impatience when they moved down my body. "Come here, *topolina*."

"Don't mess me up," I said, holding out my hands as if that would stop him. "I need to be just right tonight."

"You are always enchanting," he told me. "But tell me

again not to mess you up, and I'll be sure to paint your back-side as red as wine, is that understood?"

I shivered at the authority in his voice, moving toward him before I could stop myself. "Yes."

He arched an eyebrow as I pressed into his chest.

"Yes, *Master*," I corrected with sass in my eyes, but breath from my lips.

I wanted to be stronger than my desire to submit to him, but then again, I also didn't.

Xan cupped the entire side of my face in one of his big hands. "Tonight, I am your Master. Whatever I tell you to do, you will do it without question. This and this alone is the only reason I am allowing you to come with me tonight because I know just how sweetly you will obey me. If you step out of line for one instant, not only will I have Riddick take you home, but I will also tan your arse and then fuck you senseless for hours without letting you come as punishment for your noncompliance. Is that understood?"

My legs swayed, eager to collapse into the kneeling posi-tion that made me feel whole. I steadied myself with a hand over his suited heart and nodded. Not because I had to say yes, but because I understood the gravity of the situation if I deviated from his plan.

There was no doubt that with one wrong move, we would die.

"Understood," I agreed.

I understood just how profound Alexander's trust in me was; if I put myself in danger, I was automatically doing the same for him because he would step in front of a bullet if it meant keeping me safe. It was up to me to be smart enough to keep us both from harm, which meant obeying Alexander as he knew much more about navigating a situation like this than I did.

The den of inequity one might conjure in conjunction with a mafia outfit was not what we walked into after being patted down by blank, scar-faced bouncers. Nothing was dark or macabre, slick and old-fashioned like something out of *The Godfather*. Instead, it was bold and modern, a large expanse of basement transformed into a stark black and white gambling hall. The roulette wheels were matte black and silver, the poker felt was dark garnet, the floor polished concrete, and the chairs black wood topped with black velvet cushions. It was sumptuous and striking, a beautiful place to indulge in all kinds of sins.

Only the men who already sat around the large poker table in the middle of the room were not so beautifully presented. There was a huge, square-faced man with blunt fingers and greasy skin who rubbed his rotund belly until he belched. Another was handsome in the way of the wicked, sharp, hard features honed like implements meant to extract female admiration. He was dark, with dripping black curls that kissed his shoulders, a short beard over his jaw, and a suit the same startlingly icy blue as his dark-ringed irises. When we locked eyes, he smiled, and it was one of the most sinister expressions I'd ever witnessed.

The third man was one I recognized from the society pages of the newspaper. He was nothing special to look at, flaccid, fleshy features with wide pores and a loose, wet mouth that hung open and hooked to the left like he was constantly sneering, and maybe he was. He had a lot to sneer at, Giuseppe di Carlo, given he was the head of the most prolific crime family in United States history, but at that very moment, he was sneering at me.

"Look just like your father there, Davenport," di Carlo rasped in his smoked-out voice as he raised a thick cigar to his lips. "Slick cat thinks he can just stroll into my territory mighty as he pleases without even asking my leave. How's that workin' out for ya?"

I looked over my shoulder to see Alexander standing stock-still under the press of a gun at the base of his neck. There was no sign of tension in the bored set of his features, no panic in his easy, regal posture. Only his stillness hinted that he was aware of the threat at his back.

He adjusted his cufflinks and checked the face of his Patek Phillipe watch. "Quite frankly, Giuseppe, I'm surprised you let us through the door."

The *capo* frowned for a long moment and then laughed so loudly, his weak chin warbled. "*Gotzo!* What balls you have for a man in such jeopardy. You know this, that your father, he would pay me a princely sum to hand you over to him?"

Alexander scoffed. "Doubtful. I've been operating without threat from my father for years now."

Di Carlo's brows cut thick creases into his florid forehead. "I wasn't speaking to you."

Both men looked at me.

I could feel the air around Alexander surround me like smoke before it solidified to stone. Threatening him was one thing, but me, another.

In ten seconds, accompanied by a series of *smacks*, *clicks*, and grunts, Giuseppe's thug was disarmed and Alexander was aiming his gun at his own temple.

"Speak to her like that again, and I'll kill every person here," he explained calmly.

The thug hissed through his clenched teeth, and Xan pressed the gun tighter to his head.

"Oh, sit the fuck down," Giuseppe barked. "These poker nights are fucking sacred. Don't need you ruinin' that with bloodshed before we even get started. You see, fancy pants, how it works is like this. You want to threaten me, go ahead! But you do it through your wagers."

He sat back in his chair to smoke, big belly protruding like a pregnancy bump as he waited for Alexander to decide.

After a moment's pause, he took the gun from the thug's temple and handed it by the barrel back to him. "Might want to learn how to use that, mate."

He ignored the way the man cursed and collected my arm to guide me toward the table, taking a seat directly across from Giuseppe and installing me beside him.

"You are not the only unlikely guests who have arrived tonight," Giuseppe added conversationally as he slid his eyes behind Xan's shoulder. "Welcome, *capo*."

My head turned so quickly, something crunched in my neck. I ignored the flare of pain when I took in Dante standing in a black suit with a dark red shirt looking every inch the mob boss he was. Complete with a glower that could have killed a grown man where he stood.

"Dante," I mouthed, not wanting to give away my relief at his presence to the other men at the table but needing him to know I was outrageously happy to see him.

He blinked at me, but otherwise his expression didn't change. He was channelling Alexander, the mighty coldness and impassivity that made him more statue than man.

"di Carlo," Dante almost drawled as he moved farther into the room with his man Frankie at his back. "You wanted to talk so desperately that you sent men to ambush me. Well, here I am." He unbuttoned his blazer and sank into the chair with infinite grace for such a large man. "Well, talk."

Di Carlo licked his fleshy lips in undisguised glee. "So many interesting people here tonight. Tell me, Davenport and Salvatore, do you know Ren Tarsitani and Hugo Ralston?"

Dante had told me about Ren. He was the man everyone went to for information because, somehow, he knew everything about everyone in the New York City's underworld. Not just the organized crime syndicates, but also the dirty politicians, society scandals and more. Based on the way he smiled slyly as he looked back and forth between Dante and Alexander, I figured the gorgeous, sharp-featured man with the ice chip eyes was Ren.

The other, bigger man who sat in his chair like an amorphous blob, I didn't know, but on sight, I knew he was bad news.

"Pleasure," Ren said with a nod of his head to both men on either side of me before affixing his almost colourless eyes on me. "Who, may I ask, is the great beauty you've brought with you?"

"She is of no consequence to you; therefore, you don't need to know her name," Alexander said calmly in a voice as implacable as forged steel.

Di Carlo huffed a laugh, obviously delighted with the tension solidifying the air in the room like taffy, sticky and impossible to tear through.

"Oh, but I think she could be very much of interest," Ren rebutted. "We all know why you are here, Davenport, and it's not to win dirty money from dirty men when you already have an abundance of your own. No, it's to win *information*. Information that I happen to know."

Di Carlo's pleased expression creased into a jowly frown. "Now, Ren, I don't want you to go stepping on my toes."

Ren studied him for a long minute, reaching over to lift his rocks glass to his lips and take a draught of his whiskey. "If you leave us, Giuseppe, I don't think anyone would hold you accountable for what goes on here tonight."

"Why would I do that and miss all the fun?" he demanded like a spoiled child.

I had a feeling di Carlo had gotten his own way since birth, and the idea of anything else was utterly inconceivable to him.

"You do, and I'll give you what you want on the micks," Ren offered easily, but his eyes seemed to cut through di Carlo like a hot knife through butter, slicing through his shields until the heart of his desire was laid bare to Ren's calculating gaze.

I knew a 'mick' was a derogatory term for an Irishman because Seamus had taught me as such, but I had no clue why the offer of information on them made the Cosa Nostra crime boss grin almost manically.

"I want it now, Ren," he demanded.

"After the game," he countered as if he was in a position of great power while sitting in di Carlo's own hub, surrounded by his men all of whom were obviously carrying weapons.

Di Carlo vacillated, glaring at Ren, then sweeping his eyes over the rest of us before shoving away from the table. "Fine. You have one hour before I return. And Ren? If the information isn't good, I just acquired a new nail gun I'd love to demonstrate for you."

Ren waved the threat away with his hand and then slid his eyes to the nervous, waiting card-dealer and raised his brows. "Shall we then?"

The cards were dealt, and the first three laid down on the felt before Ren spoke again, his voice as coy as a serpent in the grass. "If you want the information, I'll need something more than money from you, Davenport."

Alexander didn't seem surprised by this. He merely lifted a cool brow in question as he raised the pot by fifty dollars.

"Her," Ren said, pointing a long finger at me. "She has to kneel at my side the entire game, and if I win, she must spend an hour alone with me."

Denial was written all over Alexander's suddenly concrete form. Not even his chest moved with breath. He was so still, he seemed dead and mummified sitting there with his hands on his cards and his eyes tipped to the felt.

I thought about answering for him, agreeing to Ren's conditions because I'd rather spend one hour in a room alone with a mafioso than the rest of my life being hunted by the Order who were, most likely, ten times more malicious.

I refrained, though, because I had promised Alexander I would follow his lead, and it seemed utterly imperative that I do so at that moment.

Even Dante, strung taut as a wire at my other side, did not speak for his brother, though I knew he wanted to.

We waited, the silence almost vibrating with strain.

"If I win," Alexander began to say slowly in his cultured words formed out of ice. "You will tell me the location of the next Order of Dionysus auction in the city *and* abroad. You will give me the information immediately following the game. In addition, should I need a favour from you in the future, you will be open to receiving it."

Ren's eyes narrowed at his audacity before he let out a little chuckle. "Ballsy. I thought you Brits were known for your conservatism."

"Clearly you've forgotten the ruthlessness of the great British empire," Alexander said drolly.

Ren's eyes sparkled with wicked mirth. "Clearly. Well then, I approve." His eyes slid like an ice cube over my body, leaving a cold trail in their wake as he sized me up and then smiled thinly. "I believe your service is required at my side, *bella*."

Alexander scowled at his endearment, but surprisingly, he didn't protest. Instead, he stood and helped me to my feet. I was just moving away when his hand tightened on my hand, and he jerked me forward into his solid chest. My lips parted on an exhalation of breath, and then his mouth was sealed over mine, his tongue parrying hotly with mine in a quest for domination even though he knew I'd eventually give it freely.

I moaned, caught up in the heat that bloomed between our mouths and sank roots deep into my belly, down into my sex.

When he finally pulled away, his firm, full mouth was damp with my attentions. Before I could help myself, I raised on my toes and licked across his swollen lower lip before biting the plumpness between my teeth.

His eyes sparkled like frothing champagne as I stepped back, pride and abiding lust bubbling through the silver.

He tipped his chin slightly, and I went, rounding the table

with my hips rolling, legs as fluid as honey poured over the floor.

The men watched me, and Ralston even adjusted himself in his trousers. When I reached Ren and gracefully collapsed into a kneel at his feet, I caught the lust in their eyes trained on me like spotlights, lighting me up with his desires.

I knew the dress had been a good idea.

And though Alexander wasn't usually one for blunt force, his show of ownership was apparently just the show these possessive Italians needed.

Ren looked down at me, the only man without want clouding his vision. Instead, he studied me like a bug under glass, cataloguing my attributes and reading the intent in my face.

"Beautiful," he said softly, just for me even though everyone else could hear him under the low music. "But then, that's been somewhat of a curse for you, hasn't it, Cosima?"

I slanted him a hard look, but I wasn't surprised. He was a man of information, so of course he had known who I was the entire time. It only made me curious what his end game was. Did he mean only to play havoc with the Davenport brothers by so obviously displaying me at his side?

Or was there something else he wanted from them, from me?

I knelt quietly as the men resumed their play, but I kept a close eye on Ren, watching his hands and learning the way he played poker.

I'd learned you could discern a lot from a man by the way he played a game of strategy.

Alexander was calculating and cold. His beautiful face didn't twitch out of its repose for even a moment, as if a marble statue sat in his seat instead of a human being. When the game had finally dwindled away to just Ren and himself, I still had difficulty reading his intent. I thought he might have a high face card in his hand, probably a queen as two showed on the river, and his eyes grew even colder with wicked delight.

Dante played as he lived, with a bold passion that you saw a mile away but were still helpless to counter. He often had nothing of significance in his hand, but no one could bluff like a handsome Italian assured from birth of his own magnificence. When he went out, he did so with a gruff Neapolitan curse and an impolite hand gesture.

The man named Ralston played lazily, enjoying his booze and cigar much more than the craft of the game. He was out before the game had even really begun, but he sat there, vaguely amused and growing drunker, to watch the tense game play out.

And Ren?

He played with sly acuity, as if he was a puppetmaster dabbling with his toys.

After over an hour of play, I realized where his smugness stemmed from.

The *bastardo* was cheating.

I was appalled at his balls in doing so. Cheating in the house of di Carlo was akin to signing his own death warrant in his life's blood. He did it seamlessly, though. I wouldn't have noticed if I wasn't so close, if he didn't insist on petting my hair condescendingly or leaning over to smell my skin and lick my ear. He did it to inflame Alexander, but in the end, his smugness was his downfall because I learned his trick.

I waited, my easy submission around my shoulders like a shroud, hiding my calculation and keen eye from the misogynistic Italian beside me.

Then the fifth card was flipped on the river, and I saw my opportunity.

Ren had slid a queen into the opening between his wrist and his shirt, and it winked at me as he leaned over to slide a hand through my hair and drag his nose over my face, loudly inhaling the scent of me. Instead of passively allowing him to assault me, I wrapped my hand around that wrist and tugged him farther into me so that his mouth landed on the corner of mine. Before he could right himself, I kissed him.

It was closed mouthed, my lips sealed against his invasion, but still plush enough to entice him to give in to the embrace. He softened from his shock, and his hand tightened in the back of my hair. I moaned softly as I swiped my fingers delicately over the gap in his shirt sleeve and carefully pulled the card out from his sleeve.

When Ren moved away, he studied my face closely. He was smart enough to wonder at my play but not so unmanly that his eyes were still clear of desire. I licked my red lips and watched the way his eyes tracked the movement.

Alexander was between us in the next moment, looming over Ren with such a cold fury, I could feel it emanating off his back like dry ice.

He wrapped a hand around Ren's throat and leaned into his face to whisper, "Kiss her again, I'll remove your bullocks. I've done it before, and trust me, I rather have a knack for it."

Ren rolled his eyes as he shoved at Xan's hand. "It was your woman who kissed me, Davenport, not the other way around. And I hate to shatter your delicate sensibilities, but when I win this game, I'll do much more than kiss her mouth in my hour alone with her."

Dante growled lowly from across the table but didn't move from his spot. I knew if he did, he wouldn't be able to control his loose rein over the anger inside him.

I couldn't see Alexander's face as he stared down at Ren, but I was sure it was a frozen mask of contempt and not one blink gave away the fact that I'd slid a card into the back pocket of his suit pants. I was obscured from Ralston's eyes by Xan's big body and only Dante, seated to my left could have caught a glimmer of my movement.

Of course, he didn't say anything, but when his eyes slid to mine, they were filled with our old rapport, a childlike excited that filled the black with merriment.

Finally, Alexander broke his standoff with Ren and moved back around the table to resume his seat. He did so stiffly, a muscle in the acute angle of his jaw jumping. It was easy to read that he was angry and frustrated, that maybe his hand couldn't stand up to the assuredness Ren expressed over his ability to win.

I swallowed the smile that threatened to blossom across my mouth and tilted my head farther to the ground so my hair would obscure my face.

It was amazing how men could underestimate a pretty face, as if all a woman's effort went into her good looks with nothing left for intelligence.

Ren would learn, just as the Order would, that I was no pawn.

I was a queen.

Two minutes later, when Ren went all in on the hand, I couldn't resist looking up at Alexander from across the table. Our eyes locked, resolved as a contract signed in blood. We were a team, a closed loop of energy.

No one would ever again tear us apart, and together, working like this, we were invincible.

Giddiness arched through my gut like a shooting star.

Alexander accepted Ren's bet and pushed his chips into the center and flipped over his cards.

Two queens that matched with the cards on the river, meant he had a full house.

Ren smiled like a shark, all teeth and mean intent as he readjusted his cards, slyly trying to pull the hidden queen from his shirt sleeve.

Only, it wasn't there.

Of course.

Because I had given it to Xan.

Ren's frown flashed across his face before he could curtail it, and his eyes cut down to me.

I smiled at him beatifically.

He tensed just slightly as my possible duplicity sank in, and then his jaw flexed as he tossed his cards onto the red felt.

A queen and a ten of hearts.

Without the queen laid out for Alexander, the queen he had meant to play, Ren only had a flush, which was trumped by Xan's full house.

If he'd had the queen, he would have played the most powerful hand in the game; a royal flush.

Alexander's smile sliced a red wound between his cheeks as mocking and evil as the Joker's. "Well, Tarsitani, I believed some information is owed to me. Where and when is the Order holding its next auctions? Additionally, what do you know about the relationship between di Carlo and my father?"

Ren swallowed heavily, obviously attempting to speak through his anger at being thwarted in his plan. He opened his mouth to respond, and a crashing bang resounded through the underground room.

A moment later, the back door, one we hadn't entered through, slammed open, and four masked men spilled through the gambling den dressed in head-to-toe black. They had automatic weapons in their hands, weapons that started to spit bullets before we could even make sense of the calamity.

I dived to the floor on instinct and started to army crawl around the table to get to Alexander and Dante. A cacophony of grunts, startled shouts, and gunfire ripped the air to shreds, and the poker table exploded into splinters over my head, raining sharply down over my skin.

I shouted as two hands pulled me roughly off the ground under my armpits and began to haul me toward the door.

Not the front door, though, and with gut cramping affirmation, I knew it wasn't Dante or Xan who had caught me up to save me.

It was one of the masked men.

I screamed as I was hefted over his shoulder, kicking out and punching deeply into his kidneys in an attempt to get free. He didn't hesitate a moment, spraying bullets over the area of the room where my two beloved men were hidden.

I heard Dante swear loudly in Italian and then Xan call, "You take her now, and I will end not just you, but every single fucking person you have ever loved."

The man holding me paused for one brief second, his gun silent, his feet heavy in their tread. I thought maybe the dominant, arctic voice of my Master would be enough to halt him, but even Alexander's power had limits.

A moment later, amid a hail of gunfire, he was running us across the floor under cover from the other men and out the door into an alleyway. He took the steps to the street level two by two and then wrenched open a car door before tossing me roughly inside.

I righted myself quickly, pushing my rumpled hair out of my face with one hand while grabbing the knife from my ankle holster with the other. A flicker of movement across the interior had me moving in a flash, holding the knife up under the throat of my captor, my body spilled like an oil slick over his lap.

Only then did I look up into the face of my abductor.

"Good evening, *carina*," Seamus Moore said in mild greeting. "Look how you've grown."

Chapter Twenty

COSIMA

Seamus Moore was five years older, and apparently, none the wiser. The moment Alexander and Dante discovered he had taken me, he was a dead man, which, maybe unsurprisingly, did not incite feelings of woe in my heart. Time, it seemed, did not heal all wounds. I found only an astonishing amount of hate and dread toward the man who had acted as my father—however abysmally—since birth.

Unfortunately, it seemed time hadn't touched Seamus in other ways either. His thick hair was still the gleaming colour of candlelit copper in the low light of the limousine, his handsome features strikingly Celtic to my now trained eye; from the russet freckles on his pale skin, as vaguely sweet and contrasting as cereal in milk, to the perfectly formed small rosebud of his pink mouth. He and Elena looked so much alike, especially in the low light. For some immutable reason, they both looked even more beautiful in shadow.

It was such a shocking blow to see him again, let alone know that he had orchestrated the entire holdup in the back-room just to have a private moment with me. Some other daughter might have thought of him more often, in the moments when his choices on her behalf from the past echoed into her future. But there was more than one villain in my life, and Seamus was the least pertinent and the least malicious.

Or so I'd thought.

Sitting across from him now, his long body leaning against the expensive leather interior as if he'd been born to riches, his lips half-smiling as he sipped from a glass of champagne, I had to wonder if he'd come back to ruin my life all over again.

"Celebrating something?" I asked before I could help myself.

I'd taken my knife from his neck, but that didn't mean I was eager for a chummy father/daughter catch up.

"I'm reuniting with my long-lost daughter. I would say that's reason to celebrate," he proclaimed with the same level of showmanship he always had, as if everything in his life was happening just as he wished it to.

"I believe I told you I never wanted to see you again," I reminded him, proud of my composure when my insides roiled like a washing machine filled with rocks.

"As a matter of fact, you told me never to see the rest of our family again," he corrected with that smug mischievous twinkle in his dark grey eyes. "A promise I've upheld."

"Am I supposed to commend you for that? It's the first promise you've ever kept and the only kind thing you've ever done for our family."

I felt physically ill with resentment as I stared at his creased, handsome face arranged in his coy, carefree smirk.

Did nothing matter to this man?

Was he just as sociopathic as Noel, but cut into a different shape by his emotional impotence?

"You should." He cocked his head, a thick hank of ginger hair falling into eyes the very same dark grey as Elena's. "Do you think it is easy for a father to abandon his family?"

"Do you think it's easy to be abandoned?" I shot back, leaning forward to bare my teeth at him. "And don't give me any *cazzate* about me forcing you to leave. You abandoned your responsibilities to our family long before you actually left Napoli."

For the first time, he frowned at me, obviously put out by my attitude. "Cosi, I would think you are old enough to know I did the best I could, given the circumstances."

"I would think you'd know I'm old enough not to buy wholesale into your lies. You fucked us over all our lives, and now you're back, to what?"

"I wasn't in a good…position to help you much before now, but I have the means to make a difference to your life and I want to help. Especially with the situation you've embroiled yourself in. Honestly, *carina*, I taught you to be shrewder than all this."

"All this?" The hairs on the back of my neck stood on end in the suddenly electric air. "What do you know about my life?"

"More than you might think," he said with this sly, trickster smile.

"Don't be a smug *bastardo*. You don't know anything about me."

"Oh, but I do," he said, leaning forward to rest his forearms on his thighs, the expensive material of his suit gleaming in the low light. I noted the luxury David Yurman watch on his wrists and wondered how my terminally poor father could have afforded it. "I've been watching you for years, since I had to hand you over to that British swine."

"What?" I asked, mouthing the words because my voice had fled.

"It wasn't always easy," he confided, both casually and conspiratorially, the contrast so Seamus that I had to blink away the feeling of déjà vu. "Those Davenports have some good security, but a cousin of mine lives in Manchester. Wasn't too inconvenient to drive down to Thornton and get the village gossip about the big bad Davenports up in the grand house." He paused, sliding his eyes out the window just as pain flashed through them. "Heard you lost the baby. I'm so sorry, *carina*."

Something about the way he said that abraded my flesh like nails over a chalkboard. I shuddered, biting my tongue in the process so that when I spoke, it was with blood on my teeth. "How did you know about the baby?"

My dad flashed me a sharp-toothed grin, shark-like but cartoonish as though he'd studied it. "Who do you think paid the good ole doctor to switch out your birth control?"

Thundered rumbled through my head, the rush of blood so fierce I thought I would pass out. I couldn't comprehend his words, and my body went numb with shock.

"Why would you do something like that?" I breathed, sucker punched.

Seamus finally shed the act, scooting forward on his seat to take my limp hands in his, chafing my cold skin between his rough palms. His fingernails were short and misshapen, never having healed from when Tossi pulled them out with pliers. The physical contact seeped through my astonishment and brought my riotous emotions to the surface. First, unexpectedly, was nostalgia. I'd forgotten that my dad could be affectionate when he was around to be so. I'd missed it without even realizing it, and I felt some shame at taking comfort from the very man who had set me up to need it in the first place.

"I put you in an...impossible situation, Cosi. I know it. I own it. You made the ultimate sacrifice for your family. I knew leaving was best for everyone, but how could I leave you all alone with those beasts? I did what I could from afar. Figured if you had the creep's baby, it would give you some measure of power."

The creep's baby.

I squeezed my eyes shut as molten tears swamped my ducts and scorched trails down my cheeks.

Fuck me.

Why was my reproduction such an available tool of manipulation?

Mrs. White, Noel, and now my father had all schemed against me as if a baby was a tool and not a person.

I had only known about my pregnancy for a day, and still, the death of that baby haunted me. I couldn't look at baby shoes without feeling an aching absence in my womb.

My father hadn't killed that baby, but he'd put it in peril before it even stood a chance of survival.

I opened my eyes and stared into my father's face so close to mine. He watched me with open, guileless eyes, offering his sincerity to me like a gift.

"I was trying to help," he whispered after seeing the vivid pain in my expression.

He was only trying to help.

Hadn't he always only been trying to help?

It was his excuse for gambling, for getting involved with the Camorra, for selling me to the highest bidder.

Well, the means did not justify any of the ends. Not to me. Not ever.

I pulled my hands from his and sat back, needing the space, hating that we were even breathing the same air.

Something spasmed across his face, a clenching and closing like an octopus poised to flee. "I'm in a better place now, Cosi. I have money, influence, that you couldn't believe."

"How?" I asked, both because he wanted me to and because I wanted to know where he was in life, how he could be here, and now, so that I could avoid him forevermore.

That slick smear of a smile again. "I moved to America when your mother and Elena did, just to keep an eye on things. Ended up hooking up with some old friends from my youth. Guy named Thomas 'Gunner' Coonan took me under his wing, joined me up to his successful enterprises."

Of course. Everyone in New York knew who Kelly was; the most successful Irish crime boss since Coonan in the 70s.

"You joined the Irish mob."

Seamus grinned from ear to ear, opening his palms in a gesture of smug nonchalance. "What can I say? I got a head for business, and they recognized greatness in me the way the Camorra couldn't."

"*Dio mio*, Dad," I said, forgetting myself for a moment. "Do the Camorra know you changed sides?"

"I was never part of their outfit," he argued. "Just beholden to it. 'S not a problem."

I very much doubted that. The Irish and Italian mafia in New York were *not* friendly, and they never had been. Any excuse for conflict was flame to kerosene-soaked tinder.

"Why in the world would you practically kidnap me like this from an Italian held poker game then?" I demanded. "That's just plain stupid."

Or is it? His expression countered with the quirk of a red brow and twisted lips.

Oh.

I sighed, so exhausted by my own life, I thought I would faint from the strain. "You want to go to war with them."

Seamus beamed at me, reaching out to pat me on the hand before I could pull away. "You always were such a smart girl. Taught you well, I did. Yes, things are escalating between the Camorra and the Cosa Nostra. It's the perfect time to hit them while they're down."

"So again, you're using me as a pawn." The words were flat, two-dimensional and plastic, like fake currency in a children's game.

Useless in the real world, but they still felt good to use.

His brow crinkled into a pleat like a checkmark, just like Elena's and Giselle's did. "Don't be so dramatic. Two birds, one stone, *carina*. I'm multitasking."

I couldn't stop focusing on the hate growing inside me, poison like a weed, choking out all other thoughts and feelings until I felt consumed by it.

"You aren't my real father," I said, the words so cutting I thought for a moment they might really slice through his thick skin. "Did you know that?"

By the blank, unamused set of his features, I knew he hadn't.

"Don't play silly games," he ordered, sitting back and righting himself.

"Amadeo Salvatore is my father," I continued calmly. "You know him as *capo* Salvatore, head of the Camorra in Napoli."

Seamus snorted derisively, but a muscle flexed in his jaw, betraying his unease.

I forged on, sliding my dagger between his ribs and twist, twisting. "Mama met him in the fish market one day, and they started an affair. He wanted her to leave, and she loved him, but she was too good and too scared to do it." I paused, watched Seamus as he held his breath, confused and angry, unwilling to believe. "Haven't you ever wondered why Sebastian and I look nothing like you while Elena and Giselle could be your carbon copies?"

"Not all children look like their fathers, Cosima," he said drily, but his voice lacked conviction, and his eyes moved over me with X-ray focus, as if he could read the truth in my very bones.

"No," I agreed easily. "But if you think about it for a minute, you might remember that Salvatore had very unique eyes too. Golden eyes. You might remember that despite all your infractions, the Camorra was relatively lenient with you…why do you think that was? Maybe because Salvatore had a soft spot for Mama and caved too often in to her pleas to save your sorry arse? Maybe because you were a pseudo-father, however poor, to the two children he would never be able to parent himself?"

I leaned forward, my voice a hiss, my eyes slitted like a snake to deliver the last of my venomous attack. "I know I was your greatest accomplishment, Seamus. How does it feel to know that even that was never really yours?"

"Lies," he barked meanly, but his eyes were wet with some-thing softer than rage, and his mouth was pale with desperate tension. "That bastard lied to you, Cosima."

"Yes, but not about this." I leaned back, collected myself by smoothing down my dress and tossing my hair over my shoulder before I slid closer to the door and put my hand on the handle. "I'm not your daughter, Seamus, so you can stop 'watching over' me. I'm not your daughter, so you can stop the games. I'm not your daughter, and even if I was"—I smiled meanly, feeling my lips parted and pulled into a grotesque farce of good humour—"I would never want to see you again."

Seamus stared at me, more ruined by my revelation than he ever had been by my sale into sexual slavery. His own ego was the root of his misery. I was beautiful and clever, and Seamus had taken pride in the creation of me.

I battled the urge to take out my horrible anger in violence on his flesh and instead lifted my chin and ordered imperi-ously, "Let me out here. And Seamus, if I see you again, I'll give Alexander free rein to end you in any way he sees fit."

After a brief hesitation, he knocked on the partition behind him with two knuckles. We stared at each other, watching the bond between us disintegrate into ash.

"I love you," he told me, as if it mattered.

To him, I supposed, it did.

"Do you love me enough to stop trying to instigate this mob war? I have people I care about on the other side of this, and I don't want to see them hurt. Would you save me from that pain?" I asked, not hard, just curious even though I already knew the answer.

He pressed his lips together, flatlining the conversation. "Love has nothing to do with something like that. It's a business decision, Cosima."

"You don't know this, and it almost makes me sad for you," I admitted softly as the car cruised to a stop, and I opened the door. "But *this*, this isn't anything close to love."

"And I assume you think what you have with the lord is?" he snapped back.

I knew that very moment Alexander was finding a way to get to me, hunting me down as a surely as any predator faced with the imminent loss of his prey. Seamus raised a good point, though. What made his wrongdoings so much worse than Xan's?

I decided, as I looked at my father's frustrated confusion, that the difference was choice. Alexander had been given very little rein to make his own decisions over the years, but when he could, he made the right ones even if they still seemed horrible given the dark circumstances. Seamus had liberty all his life, and he squandered it because he was selfish and weak.

Alexander had made the choice to take care of me no matter what.

Seamus had made the choice to use me for his own gains, proven even further today by his decision to steal me away from my friends in an attempt to start a mob war that would benefit him and his.

Pathetic.

But I didn't explain any of that to the man in front of me, the man who had been my father for most of my life but who I was determined to leave behind as a stranger forevermore. I didn't explain because he didn't deserve it, but also because, tragically, he was incapable of understanding it.

Instead, I smiled sadly at him, and said pointedly, "There is a difference between saying something and doing it. You do one, and Alexander does the other. Love is so much more than words, Dad. I hope one day you understand that."

Chapter Twenty-one

COSIMA

I stood alone at the mouth of an alleyway between two brick buildings somewhere I thought vaguely might have been Queens for only five minutes before he found me. The moment the sleek black car turned the corner onto the street, I knew it was him, and I braced.

Which was prudent, because the moment the car was close, the vehicle not even stopped yet at the curb, Xan was opening the door and swinging out gracefully, powerfully onto the walk. My breath caught in my throat as he stalked toward me and then expelled in a sob when he caught me up in his arms and crushed me to his hard frame, one hand sank deep in the hair at my nape and the other banded around my lower back to pin me exactly where he wanted me.

No matter how much wealth or status I accrued in this life, I knew there would never be anything more luxurious to me than the feeling of being secured in Xan's confining embrace.

"Mine," Alexander growled into my hair before moving forward, striding farther down the dark throat of the alley.

"Yes."

I gasped as he pinned me against the rough brick with his hips and a hand cradling the back of my head so that it was protected from the wall while the other dipped down to ruck up the silk of my dress so he could reach my sex. He pressed his entire palm to my pussy, cupping it as to confirm his mastery over it, and then in one breathless moment, he tore the scrap of satin from me. The lines of the thong cut into my hips, abrading my skin as they pulled away, but I arched into the sting and found Alexander hard as a steel pipe between my legs.

The sky above us split open the same moment Xan parted my folds and sank two fingers into the wet gathering at my entrance, and when I tossed my head back to the sky on a moan, the first raindrops fell on my tongue. I swallowed them, then licked one off his stubble-roughened cheek as he pumped those thick, long fingers inside me.

Just as an orgasm tightened the seams in my body until I felt near to bursting, he pulled away, ignoring my whimper to unbutton his trousers and fist his mouthwatering cock in a big hand. His other hand moved from the back of my head to my throat, wrapping firmly around it so that his thumb was on my pulse.

"No one will ever take you from me again," he vowed as he notched the thick, round head of his cock against my entrance and impaled me in one fierce thrust.

My cunt spasmed around his girth, trying to accommodate him. I relished in the struggle, loved that he didn't give me time to adjust, just pulled back sharply and then tunneled forward again and again until my flesh yielded and sucked him tight into my body. His hand found my hair again, wrapping it around his fist and tugging to the side until my throat was exposed and his mouth could press there, teeth scraping deliciously down my skin, biting hard at the junction of my neck and shoulder.

We needed no words.

His tightly leashed muscles spoke of his trauma, his body a thickly curved shield over my own told of his desperate need to protect me even in his lust-filled haze.

We required the physical joining to confirm our connection, to prove that we were still whole, still together even after another attempt by someone else to rip us apart.

I pushed back against him and groaned as he ground against me while I was impaled on every iron inch of him, my clit rasping against his coarse pubic hair. My eyes nearly rolled into the back of my head as he sucked ruthlessly at my neck, leaving proof of his ownership under my skin.

Only when they rolled back did I noticed someone looming at the entrance of the alley. At first, I tensed, worried there was another threat.

But I knew the set of those impossibly broad shoulders, the cast of the wavy night black hair pushed away from a broad forehead, glinting vaguely in the light from the lamppost behind him. I even recognized the quality of his stillness because it was so similar to Xan's when he was faced with a hazard, assessing and coiled like a predator waiting to strike.

Dante didn't move, even when he must have seen me looking at him just a few yards down the alley, stuck to the wall by his brother's hands and driving cock. I felt his gaze like another set of hands on my body, tweaking my hard nipples and sliding calloused fingers down my back. A shudder jarred through me as Xan angled his cock and rubbed it ruthlessly against the soft spot inside me that made me see stars.

I was going to come.

I was going to come so hard all over one brother's dick while the other watched with an intensity as burning and bizarre as a midnight sun.

I was soaked through with rain, rattled by not only the confrontation with di Carlo, but the unexpected arrival of my faux father, yet all that existed for me at that moment was my body pressed between a body and the brick and a pair of black eyes.

"Come for me, *topolina*," Alexander ordered through gritted teeth as he pounded into me, hands on my hips now so that he could hold me and pump into me like a sex doll built only for his pleasure. "Come for your Master."

My muscles locked against the impending orgasm, but it still wrecked me from the inside out. I thrashed, my entire body one taut line like a fish struggling against the net, but Xan kept me pinned by his hands, Dante with his eyes. I could feel myself drenching the base of Alexander's cock and balls, his open suit pants, in my cum, and I shivered as it slid down my inner thighs.

Alexander grunted in my ear, taking the lobe between his teeth in a sharp nip. "Watch what you do to us."

He reared back, pressed his hand carefully but firmly to the side of my head so I was pinned with my eyes on Dante at the mouth of the alley, and then pressed one of my own hands over his heart so I could feel his galloping pulse.

And then he came with a fierce kick inside me and a hot flood down my thighs as he pulled out to shoot his messy load all over my clit and swollen lips.

I almost came again feeling that, seeing Dante reach down to squeeze himself through his trousers, knowing I was enough to turn on two of the most powerful, implacable men I had ever met. It was so heady, I felt drunk on it, so when Xan reached down to run his fingers in the combination of his seed and my wetness then hold them up to my lips, I didn't hesitate to suck them down. I closed my eyes at the bliss of the brine and tang of our joined juices. My mouth sucked hard, licking at the webbing between his fingers so that they were nearly lodged down my throat, seeking every last drop of the evidence of our union.

A small, errant part of me knew Dante was watching, and it jolted through me like an electric current.

Sensing my unebbing lust, Xan pushed against my body and arrowed his other hand between my thighs, his fingers pinching my clit *hard*.

"If you want to come again, my beauty, all you have to do is beg loudly for the privilege," he coaxed, his voice a silk scarf wound too tightly around my throat. "Beg your Master."

"Oh God," I groaned, legs already shaking, heart running an endless sprint in my chest. "Please, yes, Master. Make me come, please. I promise to be your good slave, just, please, let me come all over your fingers."

I was babbling loudly, my mind lost to my surroundings, our public setting forgotten, even Dante lost in the fog of lust I felt around my Master.

"Such a good, sweet slave," Xan cooed, but his voice was a cruel edge, the sharp tip of it dragging along my consciousness in a way that made my sex clench. "You'd do anything to please me, wouldn't you?"

I didn't realize his voice was pitched louder than normal, or that Dante had moved closer, his face a snarl in the thin orange light of the streetlamps.

There was only the wanton, shameful sound of Alexander's fingers on my drenched pussy, my rough breaths in the cool air, and my increasing desperation to break open and come, come, come.

"Yes, Master," I keened as he twisted his hand so his thumb could dip into my entrance and rolling deep, powerful circles just inside me that threatened to drown me in pleasure. "Yes, Master, anything for you."

"Then come," he said simply, but the words cut the last taut threads holding me together, and I came, spilling out over his hand. "Come for me."

My cries pierced the night, bounced off the brick walls and came back to me so it seemed we were all so submerged in my ecstasy we might drown.

Even Dante.

I didn't remember him, though, not as I finally came down, gyrating my swollen sex over Xan's soothing, petting touch, lolling my head against the wall as I tried to catch my breath.

I didn't remember him until Xan called in the voice I was all too familiar with, the one that was cold and deadly as an icicle impaled through someone's chest, "I hope you enjoyed the show, Edward, because that is as close as you will ever get to her."

I stiffened, but Dante spoke before I could intervene, "Satisfied with your little display?"

Xan shrugged, but he wasn't looking at his brother. His eyes were on mine, dark and turbulent as a storm over the sea. His fingers caught in the hair over my temple and slid through to the back so he could hold my head as he ran his nose along mine.

"I was having a moment with my woman after thinking the worst might have happened to her. You didn't factor into it until you *made* yourself a factor in it." His tone was bland, his words cutting.

I didn't have to look at Dante to know he was scowling, wincing from the blow.

"If you're done," he retorted, his anger getting the better of him in a way it never would with Xan. "Why don't we get Cosima off the streets and debrief about what the fuck happened to her."

"All right, my beauty?" Xan asked me softly, still touching his face to mine, his affection tactile as a lion, rubbing our jaws together, his nose over my cheek. He wanted his scent on me, and more, he wanted his tenderness on me as certain as his violent passion painted marks against my neck made with his teeth.

I sighed gustily over his lips and slumped in the bracket of his embrace, knowing I was safe and suddenly unbearably tired. "Yeah, Xan. Let's go home."

Still ignoring Dante, Xan pulled back to put my dress to rights and smooth down my hair before seeing to his own trousers. Before I could step forward, I was up in his arms, held with an arm under my back and another under my knees.

"Xan! I'm not an invalid," I protested, smacking his chest. "Stop with this Neanderthal act. You're an *earl* for Christ's sake."

His mouth twitched marginally, but he couldn't hide the thread of amusement in his voice. "I am; therefore, I can do as I wish."

"It's unnecessary," I hissed lowly as we neared Dante, and he turned on his heel to power ahead of us.

Alexander's blasé shrug jostled me. "You're saying that because you're embarrassed I shamed Edward for watching us, but think of it this way, little mouse. I let him watch because desire anchors you, and you were both literally and metaphorically lost when we found you. His regard made me feel safe to give in to what your body *and* your mind needed after the trauma. I knew that, and I gave you what you needed. Dante *needed* to watch us because he is too curious about you, and that needed to be put to bed. He will never have you. It's cruel for him to waste a single moment on wishing otherwise, so I made sure he knew it. Lastly, my beauty, *I* needed to take you like that. Submission makes you feel at peace just as Domination does for me. Losing you for even an instant was unbearable. I needed to take you like that, and now, I need to carry you like this because after what happened, I don't want to let you out of the circle of my arms let alone out of my sight. Can you give that to me?"

Immediately and without conscious thought, I said, "Yes, of course."

He ducked his head to rub his nose again over mine, a new habit that melted my heart. "Good girl."

We reached the car, but Alexander didn't let me go to slide me into the vehicle. Instead, he sat with me cradled gently in his arms and ignored the look Dante gave him when he didn't put me in my own seat.

"Now, tell us what happened," Xan demanded.

I took it as a good sign that he said "us," and I could tell by the slight softening in Dante's shoulders that he did too.

I didn't want to ostracize him again.

Sucking in a deep breath, I related my rendezvous with Seamus to the Davenport brothers, powering through their grumbling growls and clenched fists to finish my story before they went nuclear.

"I'll take care of it," Dante said immediately upon my conclusion. "Don't worry about him, *tesoro*, I'll find a meaningful way to make your message known to him."

"I don't want you to start a war over this. Please don't do anything stupid, D."

His smile was red as blood smeared between his cheeks. "Don't worry about it. I can handle my own business, and Seamus just told you, he wants a part of that."

"He may not be my biological father, but he's still the father of my two sisters and the man who had some part in raising me for eighteen years. I don't want him hurt." I didn't think I could face Mama or my sisters after that.

The thought flared a memory, and I groaned loudly, thunking my head back against Xan's hard chest. "I forgot, I have Thanksgiving dinner with my family tomorrow."

My man went stiff as a chair beneath me.

"You don't want me to go," I accused, cluing into his unspoken uneasiness.

"I don't want you to go anywhere ever again without me. At the very least, not while the Order and Noel are still active, even if the latter is slightly incapacitated."

I understood. I didn't want to be away from him for any length of time either. But my family was important to me and over the past few months since my reintroduction into Xan's world, I'd been remiss at taking care of them the way I normally would.

I couldn't miss Thanksgiving.

"Drop me off and then pick me up when we're done?" I suggested, tipping my head back to look up at him.

He was so unbelievably handsome, I hiccoughed over my own breath looking at him like that. Even tired and worried, he was beautiful. I traced my fingers over the smattering of silver at the edge of his golden temples and knew that if he asked it of me, I would leave my family behind for him until it was safe for us to see them again.

He stared down at me, his intensity a palpable current in the air, but I knew the moment he decided against that course of action because his muscles softened slightly beneath me. His sigh breezed over my face as he shook his head. "What am I going to do with you?"

I smiled drowsily, exhausted from the day. "Nothing at the moment. I know there is more to talk about, but I need to sleep. Is that okay?"

"Of course," he said in a voice like a lullaby as his fingers threaded gently through my hair. "Sleep, my beauty."

And I did.

I slept through the car ride home and through Xan carrying me into the building up to my apartment. I slept when he took off my slinky dress and replaced it with his button-up, and I only woke when I heard a raised voice in the living room.

I froze immediately, then slunk out of bed and crept to the door to peek out, seeing Dante pacing powerfully back and forth in the kitchen, an agitated panther to Xan's lounging, regal lion.

"You aren't good for her, and you fucking know it," Dante was saying. "You say you've changed, but if you were suddenly the better man you claim, you wouldn't be here endangering her like this."

"I didn't say I was a *good* man," Alexander retorted drily, swirling his whiskey in his glass. "I said I had changed for the better."

"That's not good enough."

"For who?" Xan challenged idly. "For Cosima or for you?"

There was a percussion beat of silence.

"For her."

"No, not for Cosima. You understand this even if you don't want to, but Cosima is drawn to the dark. Those things which make me less like a hero and more like a villain, she is entranced by like a moth to a flame. As long as I don't let her burn up, there is not harm for her in my *badness*, only lust and passion and connection."

"Armchair psychologist now?"

"I believe that is *you*, Edward. It's hard to believe you are the same man with a master's degree in behavioral psychology from Oxford, isn't it? Tell me, does that degree help you manipulate your Made Men?"

Ice and fire.

Alexander and Dante.

One wasn't exactly better than the other, but they were both formidable, both with egregious flaws and defining strengths.

I was trapped in Alexander's icy embrace, and I was happy there, but I could understand the allure of the other's heat, especially as he fought for me.

Going up against Alexander was not for the weak-hearted.

Dante sighed loudly, raking his hands through his thick hair so that it clumped into wavy ropes over his skull. "Tore and I could give that to her in small measures. She was happy enough without you."

"We both know that's not true."

I swallowed hard at the quiet pride in Xan's voice. He had missed me too, and that small thought opened a wealth of treasure in my chest. It felt monumental that he should have missed me all that time just as intolerably as I'd missed him.

"You know," he continued conversationally, "I knew you'd convinced her to move to America years ago. I had these vivid dreams about finding you and ripping you apart with my bare hands…the only reason I didn't was because my sources told me how much she relied on you, how much you had done and continued to do for her."

There was another vibrating pause.

"Considering that and the fact that I now know for certain Salvatore did not murder Mum, I'm still loathe to do so, but I must say…thank you." I watched Xan tip his glass to his lips and drain the liquid. "Thank you for taking care of her when I couldn't. For keeping her living as much as you could when I wasn't there to take care of her."

Dante seemed struck dumb by Xan's words, even more so than I was mouth agape crouching at the door to my bedroom. He was suspended in the amber of his brother's unusual gratitude, his big body lax but utterly still, his eyes glazed as his mind worked furiously behind them.

Finally, he reanimated, and he did so to look at Xan from under lowered lids and nod once, firmly, slowly. "I didn't do it for you, and I would do it again, forever. The thanks, though…it's appreciated."

Alexander nodded once in return, noble in his graciousness.

I loved him so vividly at that moment that even the colours in the dark seemed brighter than ever before.

"You love her," he said, and it was not quite a question, but still, Dante hesitated and then responded.

"I do. Not exactly the way you worry about. Though I have to say, it's hard to look at a woman like Cosima and not covet her, let alone *know* a woman like her so filled with love and light despite her dark past and not want to fight every day to be worthy of some significant part in her life."

I fell back to my bottom on the ground, rocked by his words.

"I told her once," my husband said softly with a tiny smile tucked into the crease of his left cheek. "For the first time in my life, she made me feel like a hero, instead of a villain. She does that to people, makes them feel ten feet taller."

"You love her," Dante said, the words lined with bitterness. "You don't deserve her, but seeing as she obviously loves you back, I guess I'll have to live with it."

"I'm not capable of love," Xan admitted with a one-shoul-dered shrug as if it didn't bother him. "But if I was…"

Dante snorted, the burst of sound breaking the tension between them. He walked forward to join his brother at the island and poured some whiskey into the second empty glass for himself before taking a seat. "Not sure what you know about love, brother, but that energy between you and your wife? That's about the definition of it."

They were both quiet, looking down at their glasses before Xan's face cracked at the edges with condescending mirth. "Dante, the armchair phycologist."

I watched in awe and humbleness as the two great men laughed softly, gruffly together at my kitchen table. What I had witnessed wasn't just a beautiful conversation about two men loving me, but a détente between brothers who never should have been at war in the first place.

And that made me smile as I picked myself off the floor and went back to bed.

Chapter Twenty-two

COSIMA

The auction was held on Christmas Eve—of all places—at a bridal warehouse owned by one of the Order members out on the farthest edge of Queens. The middle of the space had been cleared, but the elegantly clad gentlemen sipping glasses filled with hundreds of dollars' worth of scotch and champagne were hedged in on all sides by rows of virginal white garments that signified a woman's hope, love, and happiness.

The contrast was not lost on me. In fact, I couldn't swallow the bile as quickly as it rose in my throat, and I had to duck between a chiffon gown and a classy silk sheath to purge my belly of acid before I could continue through the rows to the main event.

There were half a dozen platforms in the middle of the room, placed in front of a wall of mirrors so that the slaves for sale could be demonstrated from all angles to the gentlemen's best advantage.

The auction hadn't commenced yet, but I could see Sherwood, who had come all the way from England, speaking with an elderly man too old to walk unassisted let alone fuck a poor slave, beside a podium placed in the center of it all. Simon and Agatha had found out that Sherwood, still the head of the council, had come to perform a ceremony to transfer power from the American head of the organization—most likely the decrepit man he now spoke to—to his successor.

I was happy about this, if you can call the feeling of dark pleasure curling through my gut happiness. I hadn't confronted Sherwood yet on my crusade to right the wrongs done to me by the Order, and I wanted that chance before we snuffed them out for good. I wasn't exactly sure when the moment had happened, the switch had flipped, and I'd gone from suffering victim of my circumstances to righteous avenger. However, it had happened I was grateful for it. There was still a balance to maintain. I didn't want revenge to make me manic and cruel or victimization to make me weak and bitter, but it was an easier line to find now that I knew both could be had. Living four years in the perpetual gloom of my past, fighting tooth and nail to live an ordinary life under that strain had been no life at all.

Now, standing amid men who had always been predators, knowing that they were currently lambs awaiting slaughter, I felt oddly filled with peace.

The end was near.

Alexander hadn't wanted me to go at first. There was no real need for me to be there when Xan would be the one bugged with audio/visual to document the entire exchange.

But one look at the resolve hardening my expression like some grotesque Venetian mask had changed his mind immediately. If anyone knew the power of vengeance, it was my husband.

There were women allowed in the American chapter of the Order of Dionysus, but only a few milled about the warehouse, dressed to impress, haughtier than the men as if it proved their worthiness to be there. In the culture of the Order, I suppose it did.

They made it easy to fade into the background. I was outfitted in a black leather dress that parted down the front with a single zipper that started at a deep dip between my breasts and over the knee leather boots so that the only visible skin I showed was a square of tanned flesh on my upper thighs. I caught looks from some of the men, but they were wary, assuming from my Dominatrix-style outfit that I wasn't exactly to their tastes.

I wandered to the back hallway that led to the room where the slaves were kept and beautified for auction. Apparently, most of the Masters found their slaves this way and had since the slave auctions in England during the 1800s before slavery was—ostensibly, at least—abolished.

No one paid much mind to me as I snuck a peek, and I noticed some other Masters lingering amid the girls to take a brief preview of their offerings. I searched for one woman, in particular.

Yana was seated before a small mirror, her pale hair done up in curls and secured with a silly pink bow, her naked body brushed with pink sparkles in an obvious bid to make her look younger than her decades made her. She caught my eye in the reflection and blinked hard before fiddling with the collar at her throat. Something metallic caught the light and winked at me.

Good.

Yana was wearing the audio/visual device we had given her.

Unlike the ones I'd planted in Ashcroft's house—ones that Alexander had collected to add to his wealth of incriminating evidence against the Order—the one on Yana's collar ran live directly to monitors set up in vans waiting two blocks away from the warehouse.

When they had enough information from Yana's and Xan's feeds, they would storm the warehouse and put an end to the New York chapter of the Order of Dionysus.

A team in London and another in Hong Kong were about to do the same.

It made it easy to take them down in one fell swoop when they planned their auctions all on the same day.

I'd just turned on my heel to head back to the main event when strong hands plucked at me from another dark corridor, and I went careening backward into a strong, tall body. I knew by the lemon and green pepper scent of him, who it was immediately and relaxed slightly in his hold.

Dante's breath was hot against my neck, one of his big hands eclipsing my entire hip so that I felt bracketed by his body, smothered by the intoxicating heat of his hard chest at my back.

"If I asked you to run away from it all right now, would you?"

I swallowed hard, trying to hold my breath so I wouldn't breathe in his peppery fragrance and the scent of his warm skin. "Why are you asking me that?"

"Does it matter?"

"It does if you're asking me to run away with you because you love me or because you just don't want your brother to have me."

A pause, a mushroom cloud of toxicity after an explosion.

His lips pressed to the tender hollow below my ear, and he whispered, "What if it's both?"

"You know I'm broken. He ruined me for other men, and he ruined me for myself. I'm not… There's a piece of me missing now, and he wears it like a necklace against his heart. He's never giving that back."

"No," Dante agreed. "He's not, and even if he could, you wouldn't ask for it."

I wanted to protest, but I'd been fighting the truth for so many long, cold years. We both knew he was right.

"I don't love you the way my brother does, *tesoro*," he said, shifting slightly in our confined space, brushing his groin against me in a way that had my breath catching. "He is consumed by you. His dark heart sees the temptations of your beauty and your goodness, and he wants to gorge himself on them. He wants to keep you in his orbit tied so close to him that your sun will only shine for him. It's a selfish and over-whelming love."

His words should have evoked horror and disillusion. The kind of affection he spoke of was acidic, eating away at the soft linings and inner workings of a body until it was used up and wasted away.

"I love you as the dark loves the stars. I want only to hold you, protect you, and elevate you to the greatest heights of your ambitions. I could care for you, Cosi, love you in a way that was healthy if you'd let me," he continued.

He didn't understand.

It wasn't a matter of choice.

Was it ever?

My body, my spirit, and my heart had decided who I would love long before my mind had a say in the decision.

Alexander Davenport, Lord Thornton, son of the worst man I'd ever known, was it for me.

The one.

The only.

I'd fought against the truth of it for so many years until I was dog tired and weary. I knew better now.

Besides, even if there was a choice, even if I could rewind time so that I never saved Xan's life in that Milanese alley, so that I was never sold to him, I wouldn't.

I wanted to be enslaved to him forever.

And now, after all this time, I believed he felt the same way.

"I'm sorry, D," I said softly, clutching his hands over my belly so he would know just how genuine I was. "You're a good man, probably one of the very best in this world, and I love you like a brother of my heart. But you and I both know I won't run away from Xan again."

Dante's heavy sigh rustled my hair, and his big hand flexed tight against me. "*Si, tesoro.* I know. You can't blame me for trying to make you safe, though, can you?"

"The Order is going down, di Carlo is dead, and Noel is next."

His short laugh held no humour. "You have to know, life with your Alexander will never be safe, not in the way I mean."

He was right. Alexander was a creature of the dark. No matter that he was good to me and my hero in so many ways, he would never be free of his malignant past or of his deviant predilections.

I was okay with that.

I had learned long ago to love the dark.

Twisting my head, I pressed a kiss to Dante's stubbled jaw. "It's okay, Dante. Dark things can be beautiful too."

He peered down at me in the shadows. "Don't I know it."

"You'll find someone better," I told him even though now wasn't the time. I could hear Sherwood beginning the festivities in the other room. "You don't love me the way you could love your soulmate."

He shrugged because he didn't want to admit it, and I thought he knew I spoke the truth.

"Let's get this done then," he suggested with a white smile that glowed in the dark.

"*Va bene*," I agreed, pushing out of his hold to wander back into the main space.

Sherwood was just wrapping up his address.

"Now my brothers, partake of your spoils and enjoy the night as Dionysus meant men to enjoy their wine and their women, without inhibition!" he crowed over the speakers, his last words dissolving in the fervor of the crowd's cheer.

Immediately, the first women were ushered out to take their places on the platforms, naked as the day they were born but for black plastic collars hung with I.D. cards so the men would know which women to bid on.

I kept my eyes on Sherwood.

He moved through the crowds, giving back slaps and sly grins, his thin form cutting through the bodies like a needle as he arrowed back to the room where the slaves were kept.

I followed him.

My mind was filled with memories of The Hunt as I did so. I remembered the brutal feel of the cold Scottish air against my bared skin, painful as the slide of a frozen blade across my cheeks as I ran desperately through the dark gloom of the forest. I remembered how he had dubbed me the Golden Fox, the most desirable girl to rape and plunder, so that I had men falling out of the black night like demons sent from Hell to ravish me.

I remembered him ordering Landon Knox to whip me until I was a cut-up mess of blood and torn flesh.

I let these thoughts fill my sails as I hurtled down the corridor to the backroom and saw Sherwood facing away from me, his hands on the head of a young girl servicing him on her knees with her mouth.

Disgusting.

A pig, a dirty swine I would see dead before I would see him free.

As I thought this, there was a series of powerful *bangs* as the police stormed into the warehouse, prepared to lay siege to the event.

Sherwood jerked, immediately bending to do up his pants in preparation to flee.

I stepped up behind him, quick and silent as a shadow, my knife in my hand around his torso and up against his jugular.

I could feel the pound of his pulse jar the blade.

"Hello, Sherwood," I greeted lightly as he froze. "Remember me, the Golden Fox?"

I was surprised that he relaxed slightly, his voice a relieved murmur when he said, "Slave Davenport, how interesting to see you here."

"I suppose it is for a man like you who believes himself to be invincible. Why would you think any one of your abused slaves would rise up to kick you in the balls like you deserve?"

"Is that what you plan to do, kick me in the balls?" he asked with a thread of amusement in his tone I wanted to cleave in two.

He didn't take me seriously even then with a blade against his neck. He didn't respect me or the threat I represented because of the simple fact that I was a woman, and therefore, I was nothing.

Anger coursed through me lava hot and just as corrosive.

"Metaphorically maybe," I said through my teeth. "I was just going to cuff you and wait to watch the police take you away, but now I'm not so sure. Maybe I should show you the same thing you showed me years ago. A complete and utter lack of mercy."

"Don't take your training so hard, every slave must be broken. You cannot tell me you weren't happy as slave to Thornton. It seemed you were very much in love with him," he taunted.

I hadn't known hatred had a taste, metallic and chemical like kerosene spilled over my tongue. My words ignited as they left my mouth, breathing fire. "It was the threat of love that made you order Knox to whip my back to shreds and then do the same to Alexander. It was the threat of love that made you reduce women to fucking animals in The Hunt, and it was the threat of love that is holding a knife against your throat now, Sherwood. You never stood a fucking chance."

He moved them, bucking his head back against me to dislodge my hold. But he was too tall, the base of his head only crashed into my forehead, and though it hurt, it wasn't enough to disable me. Instead, I used his off-balance momentum to curl one of my legs around one of his and press until he squawked in pain and folded to the ground. I pressed my knee hard into the middle of his back, my hand still around his throat so that he buckled farther, falling on his belly to the ground.

I wrenched his hands behind his back and took the cuffs out from where I'd hidden them between my thighs so that I could lock him up.

There was a scuffling in the hall, and strong voices crackled over the radios.

I ignored them to lean forward on Sherwood's back and whisper in his ear. "How does it feel to be bested by a woman?"

He cursed at me, but I only laughed as I got up, leaving him on the floor as I stepped away and police swarmed the room.

"Hey, Sherwood? You never know, maybe someone will make *you* their slave in jail," I taunted.

And fuck, did it feel good.

*M*uch later, after the calamity had cleared and police interviews were conducted, after we'd shared a celebratory drink with Dante and Salvatore in a little bar in Brooklyn, Alexander and I had gone back to my apartment. It was vacant because Giselle had gone on a last-minute Christmas trip to Paris, and Alexander took full advantage. His mouth was on mine the moment we opened the door, my dress was unzipped down the front and my breasts were in his hand by the time we made it to the kitchen. He didn't even take me to the bedroom.

Instead, he pushed me chest down over the cold marble island with my hands behind my back and my legs spread luridly so that the cool air of the apartment brushed over my sex.

"Stay," he ordered, swatting my ass so hard I hissed.

The sharp sting melted into a pleasant ache as he moved away, walking around me to do something out of my sight. I kept my cheek pressed to the marble, unwilling to disobey him even to sneak a peek at what he could be collecting.

I knew whatever it was, even if it first brought pain, it would ultimately lead to a mind-bending orgasm.

My body was already primed with heady adrenaline from successfully taking down the Order in three separate international locations. The war wasn't over by any means—there were still criminal trials to be had and evidence to be sorted through—but the greater threat was eliminated, and I was fucking ecstatic over it.

From the way Alexander had practically mauled me in the car and on our way into the apartment, I sensed he felt the same.

He returned to his place behind me and crouched down, his breath wafting over my wet pussy, his hands finding my ass and kneading hard into the flesh there.

"So fucking beautiful," he said in his low, heavy Dominant voice. "So fucking *mine*."

I gasped as he rasped his tongue from the top of my cunt all the way up over my ass. It felt as though he'd pulled a zipper and wetness went pooling out over my cunt in its wake.

He played a thumb roughly in the new dampness and then moved away.

"Do you remember what I told you when I found you at The Hunt? I told you that you were mine to protect and comfort just as you were mine to play with and use. Tonight, after bloody years of trying, I finally succeeded in ridding the world of the Order so you could be safe. And now, *topolina*, I am going to use you. Are you ready to be fucked hard by your Master?"

I groaned as lust bubbled in my belly like lava waiting to explode from a volcano. "Yes, Master."

"Good, little mouse," he praised over the sound of something ripping. "Now hold still while I pin you down."

I trembled as something slightly sticky wound around my ankle, adhering it to the wooden leg of the kitchen island. He wrapped it over and over until I couldn't move an inch before moving to the next ankle. I didn't realize what the substance was until he used it to bind my hands at the wrists behind my back. He was using kitchen plastic wrap.

Once bound, he hummed his pleasure and ran a big hand

from the top of my head along the bumps in my spine over my ass and between my legs where he cupped my pussy, and it wept against his palm.

"Look at this pussy so wet for me, and I've barely touched you," he murmured, giving me a short, light slap that made me moan. "You've always been so greedy for my cock. Don't worry, *bella*, I'll give it to you every single way you can have it by the end of the night."

The island was low enough that my body was at a ninety-degree angle, giving him complete access to my pussy and ass. Access he took advantage of by sweeping my wetness back and forth over my groin until I was smeared in my own desire, the heady scent of arousal heavy in the air.

I panted, trying to hump my hips harder into his passing palm but unable to because of the plastic wrap gluing me into place.

"Be still," he demanded with a hard slap to each ass cheek. "I won't tell you again. Keep this beautiful arse still, or I won't do as I planned and feast on it until you come over and over again on my tongue."

I pressed my cheek even tighter to the marble as I groaned at the thought, needing the anchor of the cold stone to keep me from floating too quickly into subspace.

I wanted to be present when Alexander fucked me. I wanted to feel the victory of our union like two gladiators celebrating over their spoils.

Then he was kneeling behind me, and something viscous and sweet smelling was being poured down the crease of my ass, sliding sensuously over my folds. Before it could drop off my swollen clit, Xan caught the stream with his tongue, licking, lapping and sucking at every fold and swell of my cunt like a starving man slurping at fruit.

"I can't be sure which tastes better," he said into my slick sex. "The honey or your sweet juices on my tongue."

He went back to feasting, eating away at my pussy and

then making his way up to the crinkled apex of my ass, swirling it with his tongue until I was melted butter spilled across the countertop.

"I have it," he declared after a long pull at my clit with his closed lips, a pull that made my entire body shudder. "It's the taste of your beautiful, drenched cunt."

A stream of useless words spilled from my mouth, *yes*, and *oh God*, and *grazie e Dio*. Alexander seemed fueled by them, working hard for every whimper and groan, humming against my flesh when I spoke in Italian because he knew just what it meant.

I was losing myself to him, to this. Just us together like a closed loop of energy.

He built me up particle by particle as if constructing a castle out of sand. I was all peaks and sharp corners, echoes in cavernous, empty rooms. He built me masterfully, an architect of lust, an engineer of desire so well versed in the physics of sexuality each movement of my body felt like a natural extension, a necessary expansion.

He slicked me with my leaking sex, moved red lines over my skin with his rough fingers, and dug into me with his hard, square teeth until my entire body, the structure he had so beautifully comprised, trembled on the verge of collapse.

But that was the point of the entire exercise, not to create, but to *detonate*.

He didn't let me come.

Not even when I begged into the marble, the stone slab as unyielding as my Master.

Instead, he ate his fill and then pulled back to rub the hot tip of his cock over my clit and drag it back over my pussy up to my ass where he *tap, tap, tapped*.

"I'm going to fuck each one of your pretty holes tonight, my beauty. I'm going to gorge myself on your flesh, drench my cock in your cum, and then wedge myself into this tight little ass with just your cum to ease the way. Would you like that, little mouse, for me to use you up until you are nothing but wet, quivering flesh for me to fuck into?"

I gasped like a fish out of water, my muscles unified as I strained to welcome the looming orgasm. I knew when it came, I would thrash from tip to tail just like that fish returned to the stream.

I thought I would die if he didn't drown me in the pleasure of climax that very second.

"Yes, Master. I need your cock; I'm dying for it."

"Oh," he cooed, the one drawn-out syllable mocking and cruel. "We can't have that now, can we?"

And then he was thrusting; his cock a blunt weapon forcing open the swollen channel of my sex without mercy. He ground into me hard, then pulled out so that just the head kissed my entrance and then tunneled back inside, his hands clamped like iron braces over my hips. I tried to brace against the counter, but I had no recourse tied down as I was.

I just had to lay there and take it.

The submission he had built in me with his big hands and dirty words coalesced into a castle made of sand, of every single particle of my being, harnessed and corralled into a thing of utter beauty.

His hips canted up harshly into the front wall of my sex on his next punishing thrust, his fingers twisted my clit like the handle on a door, and everything I was dissolved back into sand.

He fucked me ruthlessly as I spasmed around his driving cock, his hand fisting in my hair to use it as leverage so that each thrust hammered at my cervix like a hammer to a gong. The pain of it reverberated through me, set my teeth on edge, and my climax, momentarily waning, somehow began all over again.

"Master, Master, Master," I chanted as he held me still and drilled and drilled at me.

I loved his animal grunts, the way his civilized aristocratic bearing fell away like sheep's skin to reveal the wolf at his center, the raving beast with the need to rut and breed the only thing motivating him.

His thumb found my clenching asshole and began to rub, polishing it with my leaking juices.

"Such a sweet arse," he praised. "Do you want me to fuck you there, *topolina*? Take my big cock and drive inside that tight hole until you're so filled you can barely breathe for feeling me inside you to the hilt?"

I couldn't speak. There were no thoughts in my head, no words on my tongue. I was just sex, the pulse of my pussy, the wild beat of my heart churning lust-drugged blood through my body, pooling between my legs so that I was a swollen, aching mess of desire.

I wanted to tell him I needed his cock the way I needed breath. I wanted to tell him I was an addict, an honest to God addict with such a fierce passion for his body, I could barely stand to be in the same room with him without some part of my skin against his. I'd been in a four-year-long drought I would never fully recover from, and when his cock was inside me, it felt like the headiest drug in the world.

"I need to hear your words. Tell me what you want, and I just might condescend to give it to you," he practically purred as his hands kneaded my plump ass cheeks and his thumb brushed over the raised mark of his brand on my skin.

"I need you to fuck me," I panted, not really cognizant of what I said, as if the words were disassociated from my body. Need flashed through my body like a flickering neon sign, and I was only able to give voice to that. "I need you to fill me up and show me how much you own my every hole."

Alexander's chest rumbled with a deep growl as his thumb popped through my tight ring of muscle and sank into my ass. When I groaned and whimpered, thrashing my head this way and that over the marble so that my hair went spilling over the white top like spilled ink, he stopped me with a fierce smack on my bottom.

"Don't move. I want you to hold still while I work myself into this tight hole."

I groaned, giving voice to desperation in the hot pit of my belly.

But I obeyed.

I held perfectly still, barely breathing as Alexander poured something with a gentle earthy scent over my asshole. His fingers sloshed in the olive oil and smoothed it over my opening and up over my cheeks, rubbing it into the flesh until I glistened. He moaned as he plumped them in his hands.

"Such a gorgeous arse and all mine."

"Yours," I agreed, my mouth expelled like a shot from my chest as he spread open my cheeks and pressed his cock to my oiled ass and thrust the tip inside.

There was a slight burn that morphed so quickly into an exquisite ache, I couldn't help but pant into the pain and whimper for more.

He slid into me centimetre by centimetre, feeding his thick cock inside my greased hole as he rubbed his big hands all over my ass and hips. I could tell by the slight hiccough in his breath that the sight of me pulsing and struggling around his girth was getting to him, but he still moved methodically with utmost control into my body to the hilt.

When his balls pressed against my soppy wet pussy, I shuddered, my entire body alive with electricity as if he had plugged me into a socket with too high a voltage.

"That's it, hush, *bella*. I've got you," he soothed as his hands curved over my flesh, a jockey comforting his over exercised horse. "You're taking my dick like such a good slave."

I quivered again as he ran a finger over the stretched skin of my asshole, tracing where he was plunged deep inside me. My body felt stretched on a rack, ready to split open at every joint and burst open on the floor at his feet.

"I'm going to use you now," he explained calmly, coldly, as his hands tightened on my slippery hips to the point of pain. I didn't feel it, not really. I was so deep in subspace that everything done to my body immediately translated into the language of pleasure and aching need. "I'm going to use you until you are a wild, thrashing, wet mess against the table and then I'm going to come all over your beautiful arse. Are you ready, *topolina*?"

I was, and I wasn't. There was true fear on the edge of my consciousness that I simply wasn't able to handle the kind of intense pleasure he was about to give me.

But he didn't give me time to respond or reconsider.

He pulled out slowly to the tip and then crashed back into me, hammering into me with his hips angled up so that his cock dragged over every inch of my sensitive channel.

I squealed on the first thrust, groaned on the second, yelled, and then finally, blissfully, screamed on the fifth as I was torn apart by the hot piston of his cock. My vision shattered, the familiar kitchen around me dissolving to fractured, distorted images spotted in bright colours like fireworks shot off through a broken window. I could vaguely sense my body shaking so fiercely, my legs gave out and the only thing holding me up were Alexander's punishing hands, but the only thing I was truly cognizant of was the lightning strike of nearly unbearable euphoria tearing me apart from the inside out.

I collapsed against the island, limp and used as discarded spaghetti, panting loudly but not so loudly I couldn't hear the slosh and churn of his balls hitting my wet, engorged sex as he drove into me.

"Such a good slave," he praised, his voice gone to smoke with lust. "Such a good slave for your Master. Do you think you deserve my cum?"

"Only if you think I do, Master," I replied between my broken pattern of breath.

He groaned so gutturally he sounded like a beast faced with his next meal. I loved the animal side of him, the one that rutted and fucked as if it was his life's purpose. Finding the last of my strength, I straightened my legs so that I could push back against his punishing thrusts again.

"That's exactly right. I own your pleasure. I own your pink cunt, and your gold pierced clit, and your lush tits, and this sweet, fucking beautiful arse. And I'm going to sign you like an artist with his painting," he growled as he thrust one last time, ground into me so deeply it curled my toes and made a second, smaller orgasm pulse through me and then there was emptiness and cold air around me, inside me and he was pumping his cock so that molten ribbon after ribbon of his seed spilled over my glistening skin.

When he finished, he lazily rubbed his thumbs through the cooling cum and kneading it into my flesh, testing the weight of my ass checks in each hand, dipping a sperm-coated finger into the sensitive rim of my opening just to test the resistance, just to feel me shudder and whimper for more even though I was spent.

"All fucking mine," he practically purred as he placed a sweet kiss to the middle of my spine before pulling away.

He began to unwrap me from the posts and then gently free my hands, massaging them to bring back the lost circulation. When he was done, he carefully peeled my sweat-sticky torso off the countertop and lifted me into his arms. I wrapped my limbs around him, tucking my face into his neck with my nose against his pulse so I could smell his cedar forest fragrance as he walked us into the bedroom. He held me reverently, a father with a newborn child, as he pulled back the covers and dipped me beneath them, fluffing the pillows at my back until I was ensconced in cosiness. After gazing at me with exquisite tenderness as he pushed back an errant lock of my hair, he turned, naked and at ease, to walk back to the kitchen to clean up.

I snuggled deeper into the covers and stifled a yawn as my cat, Hades, jumped onto the bed and moved to curl up in the bowl of my lap, already purring. I scratched his ears as I waited for Alexander to return, wondering what was taking him so long, wondering if Mama, Sebastian, and Elena were together celebrating Christmas while Giselle and I were absent.

I had wanted to be with them, but not only was the auction more important, so was spending my first Christmas with Xan. Years ago at Pearl Hall didn't count because I'd been enslaved at the time and barely able to comprehend why I loved his sexual games, let alone acknowledge that I actually *liked* my captor.

"Close your eyes," Alexander demanded from the hall. "And if you open them, Cosima, there will be terrible restitution to be paid."

I rolled my eyes.

"Do not roll your eyes at me, little mouse," he countered without even seeing me. "Close your eyes."

I closed them, my heart tapping out a strange rhythm in my chest because the air in the room was suddenly close and heavy, the way the atmosphere changes dramatically before a storm. My ears strained as Xan walked into the room and to my side of the bed. The mattress depressed under his weight and then his hand was holding mine, tugging it over into his lap where he began to play with my fingers.

"I once told you that if I was ever moved to marry, it would be to give my future wife the protection of my name and the promise of my love no matter what may lay in the future. When I married you four years ago, I did it thinking I was only providing the first; the protection of my name. I thought I was a man without a heart and therefore without the propensity to care for you in any other way than as a possession. Then I was forced to wait in the wings for nearly half a decade in order to keep you safe from the evils of my world, and in doing so, I understood that the reason I married you was much more complex. I married you because I couldn't imagine a day without you by my side, lighting up my dark world with your golden light and vibrancy. I did it because being close to you is never close enough, because I didn't feel alive unless you were with me."

I wanted to open my eyes, but I didn't dare because he hadn't given me permission. Besides, the darkness lent a tangibility to his words, as if they had their own heartbeat and breath, both pressed against my skin like a human body. I felt his love as solidly as I felt his hand cradle my own and after so many years of doubt, that was such a beautiful promise it made tears leak out the corners of my pleated lids.

"So, Cosima, my beauty, I have a different promise to give to you now that the Order is gone, Ashcroft is eliminated, and the Cosa Nostra scum who hurt you are dead. It's a simple promise, but I hope it's profound." Alexander's warm breath passed over my face as he pressed a kiss to both of my closed lids. "Open your eyes now, *bella*."

I opened them, my sight filled with Alexander's striking face, his gold-tipped lashes heavy fans over his dark, brushed pewter eyes. They were filled then with such awe-inspiring love, I couldn't stem the weak sob that blossomed in my mouth like a wet rose.

Eyes open and locked to mine like a vow signed in the ink of our blood, he dipped his head to kiss each of my cheeks and then my lips, then my chin, all the way down my neck and along my left arm at the tender pulse points as if he wanted to transplant his love into the blood there until he reached my palm. I trembled as he planted a kiss in the center, then skirted his lips up each finger to brush them over the tip. When he reached my third ring finger, his mouth opened over the top and something glinted between his teeth in the low city light spilling in through the windows.

My heart arrested, my breath like amber trapping my

emotions in my chest as he dropped a ring down my finger and then tugged it into place with his teeth. After kissing the top of it where it lay at the base, he pulled back to look in my eyes again.

"Before, I gave you the protection of my name," he whispered, the words so sacred they felt hushed and as reverent as a prayer spoken in a holy place. "But now, I give you my whole heart and hope that you will let me prove to you every day from here on out, that I am worthy of yours in return."

I was crying steadily, my breath nearly robbed clean by the strength of those cleansing, awed tears, but I needed to speak. I needed the beautiful, misunderstood man offering me his bleeding heart to know a simple truth that hadn't changed for even one moment over the years.

The air I dragged into my lungs was threadbare but enough to sustain me to say, "I will spend the rest of my life proving to you that you are the greatest man I know, and that I will always love you irrevocably, even on the days you feel more like a villain than my hero."

I threw myself at him them, hurtling across the covers so that I was entwined over his torso and lap like some choking vine. My fingers sank into his hair and twisted so that we were pressed as close as two human bodies could be. Only then did I move back enough to tip my forehead to his and look at the emotion glazed over his beautiful eyes.

"*Il mio cuore è tuo,*" I murmured in my mother tongue, because there was no other language better able to express the wealth of feeling I had for this man.

My heart is yours.

Xan wrapped his arms around me tight as a promise, and whispered against my mouth, "I'll never want it back."

"Good, it's not returnable," I said, my giddy joy making me giggle.

His eyes smiled in return, then sobered slightly. "I know before, Pearl Hall was your prison, but do you suppose one day, when Noel is long gone, that you could ever make it your home? It was only ever that, a home, when you were there with me."

That dream I'd only ever dreamed of returning to Pearl Hall from The Hunt resurfaced in my mind, that girlhood dream of a prince and a castle being her very own.

I'd never had the luxury to dream that as a girl and never had permission to dream it as a slave, but now, as the true wife of my earl, he was giving me licence to *live* it.

I nodded as I looked down between our faces at my left hand curled over his heart and caught my breath at the stunningly huge and clear yellow diamond on my finger.

"Your eyes," he explained. "Though I couldn't find a diamond as warm as your golden eyes."

"Stop it," I ordered as more tears sluiced down my face. "You're making me cry."

Alexander grinned wickedly as his hands tightened and he sent me careening onto my back on the bed. Before his mouth sealed over my own, he growled, "Don't you know, I love to see you cry."

Part Four

DUPLICITY

NON DECOR, DECO, I AM NOT LED, I LEAD

Chapter Twenty-three

COSIMA

There was a little deli on the edge of The Bronx that Mason and I had discovered one day while walking aimlessly around the city. *Ottavio's* was smaller than the bathroom in my mid-sized apartment, lined in cracked linoleum tinged yellow from cigarette smoke and stained pink in places from spilled marinara. The hum of the refrigerator filled with Italian imported sodas underscored the loud, tinny music from a portable radio Ottavio kept perched on one of the two glass display cases. Umberto Tozzi crackled through the air as I pushed through the glass door, and it reminded me of so many years ago when Seamus had driven me in our old Fiat up the Aventine hills of Roma into Alexander's arms.

If pressed, I couldn't exactly express why I enjoyed the dingy Italian deli so much. The air was stale, the prosciutto tough as shoe leather, and the ambiance entirely sad, but I loved the community of it, the way Ottavio knew everyone by name and that people came from all over town to get the one delicious thing produced in his kitchen, homemade tiramisu. It reminded me in good ways of Napoli, the run-down, nasty stretch of it filled with enough good people to make the urine shine and the stench of it a pleasant enough place to call home.

I didn't know why Mason liked it as much as I did, probably because he was Italian on his mother's side and he liked to play at being more than white, rich, and American.

I called out a loud, happy greeting to Ottavio as I swung through the door and headed straight for the fridge to grab my San Pellegrino and Mason's favourite Chinotto Neri. After ordering a huge slab of tiramisu, I claimed one of the two tiny round tables to the left of the door and settled in to wait for Mason. It annoyed me that he was late, but only because I wanted to get back to the apartment to Skype with Alexander before he left for a day of meetings in London. He had been gone for less than forty-eight hours, and I missed him so acutely it felt like a knife wound in my chest.

The door jingled open as the soft croon of Nancy Sinatra's "Bang Bang" spilled like fuzzy yarn through the radio. His wide forehead was dotted with beads of sweat so thick they looked white as pearls, and his mouth was an open, wet puncture in his creased face. There were large sweat marks bracketing his underarms through his blazer that he didn't try to hide as he powered through the door like a lost man seeking salvation in the warm shop.

"Mason?" I asked more than called out because I was

confused by his uncharacteristic disheveled appearance. "I ordered the cake already, come sit."

He hesitated, looking out the door, up at Ottavio, and then back at me as if we presented a terrible conundrum. I patted the uncomfortable metal chair beside me and offered a small smile of encouragement.

"I've been trying to get in touch with you for ages," he told me as he took the seat.

I winced. "I know. I've been a bad friend to you the past two months, but believe me, I had good reason. Now, grab a fork before I eat all this goodness and fill me in on whatever has been going on. Did you meet someone?"

It was Mason's turn to wince, and he didn't reach for a fork, instead grasping for one of my hands to clamp between two of his clammy ones.

"Listen, Cosi, I don't know how it got to this point, I really don't. At first, it was so simple, you know? They just wanted me to be involved in your life, this innocuous spy. It was easy because, well, you know, you're you, and you are beautiful." He licked a pearl of sweat off his upper lip and then wiped his damp cheek against his suited shoulder. "I mean, I started to love you, and I got why they asked me to watch you. You *are* dangerous because you're a flame to the moth of men. Really, you have to believe me, it didn't seem like I was betraying you in doing what I was. It was just reporting to them, making sure you stayed away from the Order and from the Earl of Thornton in particular…"

There was a strange ringing in my ears, as if I'd been hit upside the head and my brain clanged between my ears. I wondered if words could concuss someone because those sentences spilling out of Mason's familiar mouth felt brutishly weaponized.

"Your mother's family?" I asked even though I already knew the answer.

The uncle he always spoke of, the one who hated homosexuality so Mason had to hide who he was, the one who ran the family with an iron fist.

Mason's chin dropped to his chest; a dead weight filled with shame. "Yes. Uncle G."

Uncle G.

Uncle Giuseppe di Carlo.

There was a series of clicks as everything slotted into place. Noel had clearly sponsored di Carlo for entry into the Order, gifting his old slave Yana to the new Master in exchange for a simple favour. Keep an eye on his eldest son's runaway bride and make sure she stays away.

But I hadn't stayed away and now...

My head snapped up, the back of my neck tingling as the door's chimes sounded again. I looked to the right, but I already knew instinctively with the well-honed senses of much hunted prey who would stand in the doorway.

"Di Carlo," I greeted mildly because perception was power, and I didn't want him to know how utterly disconcerted I was by this reveal, by my friend's years-long betrayal. "What brings you out into the light?"

His flesh face parted with a slick lipped grin as he rounded the table and took the seat perpendicular to me. He wore what I guessed to be his customary suit, a pinstriped dark grey with broad shoulders that harkened make to what I was sure he thought were the "good ole days" of the late 19th century when the mafia was in its heyday. There was a gold chain at his throat, nestled in the hairy hollow between his collarbones and three thick gold rings on his fingers that gleamed in the artificial yellow lights. He seemed like a caricature of a mobster, virile but past his prime, expensive but with cheap taste.

I knew better than to take the front for granted. He was danger wrapped up in a tawdry package, but dangerous all the same.

"My nephew speaks so highly of you, Miss Lombardi," he

spoke through his smile, but his eyes were black, wet and mean. "Or should I call you, slave Davenport."

"You can call me whatever you wish," I told him graciously even as I frantically tried to find a way out of the situation. "Just don't expect me to answer to it."

Giuseppe laughed, a throaty, phlegm-filled sound that made me want to gag. "The duke told me you were a spitfire, but fuck, no fear in the face of the most powerful man in New York City is pretty fuckin' admirable or pretty fuckin' stupid."

"Trust me, I've met men much more powerful and much crueler than you."

Mason made a noise of protest, and I noticed in my periphery—because there was no way in hell I would be stupid enough to take my eyes of Giuseppe—that he was wringing his hands together.

I wouldn't do as Mason silently begged me to. I'd been docile and caged up for too long in my life, and some smug crime boss wasn't going to make me cower. My chin lifted, and I looked down at him over my nose.

He laughed again. "If I wasn't bein' paid a pretty penny to take you to the duke, I might just be tempted to keep you for myself. Already got a mistress or two, but I have a feelin' you'd be worth the high maintenance."

"Aww, shucks," I said with a thin slice of a smile served up on my cold, immovable face.

Giuseppe's smile dissolved like a pearl in vinegar, revealing the emotionless heart of him. "As it is, you're goin' to the duke, and I'm goin' to pocket the small fortune he's paid me to use to go to war against your man, Dante Salvatore. Howdya like that?"

"You hurt him, and I'll kill you," I told him calmly. "In fact, you threaten him or anyone else in my life again, I'll kill you."

"Cosima," Mason barked out, reaching across the table to squeeze my wrist painfully. "Shut *up*."

Something cold and hard pressed to my knee under the small, circular table, and for a moment, I was confused by the misdirection. Then I realized, Mason was offering up the butt of a gun against my thigh, unseen by his uncle.

We locked eyes so quickly, it was just a flash, a lightning strike of connection, but it offered up a wealth of information.

Mason didn't want this.

He was just another pawn pressed into service in a greater game being played by Giuseppe di Carlo, and he was done being controlled.

He was done because even though our friendship was based on betrayal, it still meant a lot to him, and he didn't want to see me pressganged back into sexual slavery.

So Mason had a heart then, even if he didn't have a spine.

On the table, I wrenched my hand out of his grip even as the one below it wrapped fingers around the small firearm and pulled it up into the bowl of my lap.

"Fuck off, Mason," I snarled.

Pain exploded in my right cheek so bright it robbed my vision. When I was able to blink away the black spots and turn back to the men, Giuseppe was fixing the angle of one of his gold rings on his finger, clearly having been the one to deliver the blow.

"Talk back again," he said without looking at me, instead taking the Chinotto Neri I'd bought for Mason and drinking from it. "*I* will kill *you* and screw the duke."

"Do you really think I'm just going to go quietly with you into the good night?" I demanded, indicating the busy streets outside and Ottavio behind the counter. "People will notice. The cops troll the streets of the Bronx like ants, and they'll come guns blazing if they think you're committing a crime they can pin you for."

"Clearly, your experiences in the motherland didn't teach you much." Giuseppe held up a hand and the door chimed open the next instant, a suited man stepping up to the counter to speak hushed Italian with Ottavio before blatantly handing over a thick roll of cash. The shopkeeper's eyes shot to me, his mouth a wavy line of worry.

After a moment, though, he pocketed the cash and went into the back.

I allowed myself a slow blink and a moment to swallow back the bile rising in my throat before I reaffixed my game face.

"Here in New York," Giuseppe told me with great relish, "we own everybody. Don't you worry that pretty head about anything but coming with us nice and easy so we don't have to deliver you broken up to your new master."

"In your dreams."

"No." Giuseppe leaned forward to speak into my face, spittle flying over my cheeks. "Not in my dreams. In yours. Because if you don't do what you're fucking told, I will hunt Dante Salvatore and Alexander Davenport down, tie them together so they can die as brothers, and then I will beat them into mulch so you can't tell where one guy starts and the other ends."

"You could try," I seethed, moving even closer so that my nose was nearly pressed to his bulbous, porous nostrils. "But they would take you down."

"For that, I think I'll kill them anyway," he decided, licking his wide, rubber smile.

I'd had enough.

There was no way this man was taking me away from everyone I knew and loved after we had *finally* taken down the Order and happily ever after or something like it was finally in my sights.

I pushed away from the table with my thighs, still leaning into Giuseppe to obscure his view of my lap so I had time to raise the gun and push the barrel of it to his chest. It happened so fast and without any deliberate thought running through my mind, only the survival instinct that curled my finger back over the trigger.

I smiled at him as I pulled it, as the gun jarred back into the junction between my index finger and thumb so hard I thought my hand fractured. Giuseppe was shocked in that brief pause, his eyes wide, his elastic mouth gaping open like the wound I'd blown clean through his upper left chest.

I hoped I hit his heart, I thought finally as the echo of the shot began to falter, and Giuseppe collapsed as if in slow motion to the ground beside his chair, clutching at the blood staining his breast pocket like a blooming rose.

Mason and I locked eyes, his face greasy and crumpled like a used napkin.

"My God, Cosi," he breathed in that tiny gap of peace before the calamity. "Run."

I didn't run.

Instead, I pivoted quickly and shot off at the blur of black I knew was di Carlo's thug coming toward me. He grunted when I drilled him through the left thigh and fell to the floor, raising his gun to get one off on me.

I shot him in that shoulder, and he fell back, gun skittering across the linoleum.

He was done and groaning, so I took a moment to step back to Giuseppe, looming over his body and casting a shadow that turned his pooling red blood black.

I had never wanted to hurt anyone, but this was what my life had become.

Kill or be killed.

So, staring down at Giuseppe as he glared up at me, panting through his pain, I did what I'd been trying to do for years.

I killed one of my demons.

The gun was no longer cold, but achingly hot in my hands as I cocked it and leveled the mouth of the weapon at Giuseppe's head.

Pop.

This innocuous sound followed by the wet smacking *slap* of his brain spilling out over the floor.

"Cosima," Mason yelled at me, prompting me to turn halfway toward him before I heard another *pop*, this one muffled by the glass.

Seconds later, there was a light, almost musical tinkling as the glass shattered and rained over the floor on either side of the wall, hitting me across the legs in pinpricks of fire.

Something slammed into my side then and began to burn as if someone had shoved a flare beneath my skin. I looked down dumbly to see a spot of red on my white cashmere turtleneck dress and then reeled back again when something sliced through my shoulder, jerking me off-balance so that I went careening to the floor on one knee.

I looked up through my curtain of tousled hair to see a GMC black SUV idling at the curb, two men dressed in black aiming at me with perfectly steady handguns.

And I knew with utter, eerie calm, that I was going to die.

After everything, I was going to be shot dead in a Bronx deli by the mafia. All my life, I'd run from them, and finally, maybe poetically, they were finally going to get my ounce of flesh.

I thought of all the things, at that moment of clarity before death, that had brought me to that point. My father's weakness, my mother's silence, Alexander's submission and then defiance to his malicious dad, Dante and Salvatore's interference...

The memories surged through me, riding the pain to the surface of my thoughts so that they were hand in hand. Pain and remembrance.

I struggled to focus on the one thing glinting gold in the darkness.

Xan.

Fuck, I thought as I swayed and another *pop* went off as

Mason yelled something, and I was pushed to the right by an unbelievable force less than a second before fire ripped over the side of my head, and I couldn't think anymore for the hurt that overtook me as I fell to the ground.

I blinked blearily at the cracked, yellow ceiling and then Mason was there, bent over me, the sound of a car backfiring tearing through the air as the assailants took off.

"Fuck, God, fuck. Cosi," Mason babbled, his hand fluttering around me like carrion over carcass. "Fuck, there is so much blood."

"If I die," I whispered, surprised my voice even worked through the thick surge of blood in my throat. "Tell him I loved him."

Mason cursed and tried to collect the ribbons of blood spilling from the gaping wound, but I didn't watch to see if he succeeded because blackness finally overwhelmed the searing pain, and I was *out*.

Chapter Twenty-four

ALEXANDER

I hadn't been back to Pearl Hall in years, but I'd needed to return to speak with my father because against all odds, the incriminating information the FBI and the MI-5 had found on almost every single member of the Order of Dionysus did *not* include information on Noel Davenport, the Duke of Greythorn.

I did not understand how this was possible except for the fact that he must have had someone watching me or mine to know what was going on so that he could prepare for it. Even prepared, it was only a matter of time before they uncovered enough evidence to put Noel away with the rest of them forever. I didn't want to wait any longer for that time.

I wanted Pearl Hall for myself again. I wanted to take my wife back to my ancestral lands and make that grand house, for the first time in so long I wasn't sure it had ever been recorded in our history, a fucking home. A haven filled to the brim with our love and our glorious life together.

In order to do that, I had to face the monster who'd made me.

A butler answered the door for me, unsurprised by the sight of me because the warden at the gates had clearly forewarned him. He ushered me mutely through my unchanged house into Noel's favourite library, the very one with the chess set placed before the black marble fireplace. He sat in the same leather highbacked chair he always occupied there, his fingers held in a steeple over the chess set, his face carefully void of expression. He was still handsome, even at sixty-eight years old, and it made me sick to look at him and know I would likely appear just like him at that age. His carbon copy, he used to say admiringly, as if gazing into a flattering mirror that reflected a much younger version of himself.

"Sit down," Noel ordered.

I remained standing, but I strode into the room and stopped with my thighs pressed to his palatial desk, looming over him from across the mahogany surface. Balancing on my fingertips, I leaned forward, hooking his eyes with the force of my expression.

"You've made a deal with the Devil, have you?"

My father tipped his head slightly to the side in mock shock. "Me? Why, Alexander, it's not like you to be so daft. I've been under house arrest for twenty-nine months. What do you possibly insinuating I've done from the cage of my own home?"

"You know exactly what I'm referring to you. I didn't

come here to faff about, Noel. How did you know about the takedown of the Order?" I demanded.

"*Semper paratus*," he drawled. "Always prepare, son. I taught you that from a young age."

"I want to know how."

"And I want out of this bleeding house," he countered, finally stirring from his impassivity like a dragon from enchanted slumber. "Sometimes, we simply don't get what we desire."

"Perhaps," I agreed, righting myself to smile at him the way an executioner might smile at their hapless victim. "Though lately, I've been getting exactly what I want. The Order is disassembled. After centuries of abuse and flagrant perversions, your precious society is *over*, and there will be no recuperating from it. I've cut at the heart of the hydra. James is using the dissolution as a political feather in his cap. It's all over the global news. You and yours are *done*."

"It seems, as I'm sitting here and not behind bars, that I am, in fact, *not* done," Noel retorted. "And once again, son, you forget the primary theory of chess. This is a game of mental Darwinism. If you blunder about as you have, gallivanting all over the globe trying to take down a group of monsters and save your damsel in distress, you've forgotten an important fact." He leaned forward with a sneer, revealing eye teeth pointed enough to be termed fangs. "The worst enemies are often closer to home."

Ominous foreboding rolled through the room like pastoral fog over the moors, and I couldn't bite back the shiver that crept spider soft up my spine.

"What have you done?" I asked, wanting to weaponize the words so he would feel the threat in them but feeling as if I held an unloaded gun.

He sat back in his chair, a placid smile on his face, eyes inanimate as marbles. The same butler who had open the door for me swept into the room with something glinting on a pillow and headed for the roaring fireplace. I stood still as Noel unfolded from his chair and went to the servant, plucking a familiar gold necklace hung with the massive heart of a glowing ruby in his fingers. It caught the firelight as it dangled off one fire, the burnished thorns turning red in the glow as if tipped with blood.

Cosima's collar.

The same collar I had taken from Pearl Hall when I had abandoned it to my father years ago. The same collar, until I moment ago, I believed had been locked in my safe at the Plaza in New York City.

And Noel had it.

He had sent someone into the hotel room, broken into my safe, and knowing I would visit, had prepared this portentous ceremony to drive a lance into the shield of security I had felt the past few years.

Noel might have been caged, but even a caged monster finds a way to let his evil spread.

My father smiled at me the way he had when I was a lad, gently condescending, potentially proud if only I could accurately comprehend the lesson he was about to deliver upon me.

"Love is the ultimate weakness, Alexander. The moment you foolishly fell arse over tit in love with your slave was the moment you put yourself in check, dear boy. And this?" He swung the necklace over his finger, back and forth, building speed until it flew off and spiraled into the fireplace, sinking into the flames like a boat lost at sea. "This is checkmate."

I stepped forward with a snarl marring my face, rage like an ice storm ravishing my body. "You can throw around metaphors, burn symbols, and taunt me for a perceived weakness that is truthfully a strength. You can do it all, but those are the hollow mechanisms of a fucking monster, Noel. In the end, even if it takes me an entire lifetime, I'll see you burn just like that collar."

I turned on my heel to leave, then thought the better of it and swung back. Noel was already returning to his desk, so he wasn't prepared for my tackle. He fell to the floor like a sack of potatoes and lay prone as I smashed one of my massive fists into his face. I felt the crunch of his nose under the pressure and knew that, for the second time, I had broken it.

He coughed and gurgled through the spill of blood flowing down his face, and I leaned close enough to feel the spray of pink tinged spittle against my skin. "I told you once, and I will tell you once more, Noel. You touch one hair on Cosima, and I'll kill you with my bare fucking hands. And that's a vow I take much more seriously than any I ever made to your precious defunct Order."

I pushed up from the floor and strode to the door, not hesitating even though I wanted to, when Noel whispered wetly, "Too late for that, son."

I told myself it was a bluff, that he only needed a way to save face, but I knew the moment I stepped out of Pearl Hall's massive double doors and saw Riddick pale as a sheet of paper standing beside the car that something was terribly, woefully wrong.

"Tell me," I demanded as I crunched over the gravel on long steps. I slapped the roof of the car beside him, and snarled, "Tell me, man!"

"Cosima, milord," was his response, broken up by horror and rage so that his words fell like shards to the ground between us. "She's been shot."

*S*he was in a white bed in a white room in a hospital filled with utilitarian white things. I blinked hard at the sight of my strong, passionate beauty shriveled up and utterly still in such a stark home.

She deserved beauty around her at every minute of every day. Elegant furnishings, jewels at her slim, long throat, and flowers to scent her air. She deserved to look like the duchess she would one day become as she lay there fighting for her life.

My chest felt like a cavern of ice as I listened to the monitors she was hooked up to hum and beep with more life than she exhibited herself. I wanted to be able to breathe for her, to give my life in exchange for her own if it came to that.

But it wouldn't.

I'd already put in the calls. The best doctors in the goddamn world were on their way to fix her. Riddick was at the florist demanding poppies and dahlias, exotic tiger lilies and fragrant roses, anything to enliven my sleeping beauty and help her fight even in her unconsciousness.

I walked fully into the doorframe, ready to claim my place by her side, but a red-headed woman blocked my entry.

"Excuse me," I said politely because even though I wanted

to forcibly knock her out of my way to get to Cosima faster, I was well bred.

She spun to face me, her flame gold hair catching the yellow fluorescent lights and gleaming so bright it made me blink.

Her mouth hung open as she stared up at me, curiously mute. I reined in my impatience and looked over at Cosima again, noticing the two people sitting at her bedside.

A man I instantly wanted to throttle for being so close to her until I noticed his pink and purple pinstripe suit and matching ascot.

And a woman, another redhead, though this one was dark-haired with a face cut into fierce angles.

Cosima's sisters.

Half-sisters.

I wondered if they knew that, or if Cosima had kept them in the dark.

The dark, I decided, because my beauty wouldn't want them to suffer any pain in knowing.

The one sitting blinked once, her mouth slack with admiration, before her features closed like iron shutters and she jumped to her feet, moving around the bed to block my wife from my view.

My fists curled into heavy hammers at my sides.

"You have the wrong room," she told me with her nose hiked in the air.

A brief flash of admiration cracked my manic resolve. This sister had to be Elena, the woman with more brain than soul, the one who read everything she could get her hands on in the slums of Napoli, and who handled herself like a princess even when she'd been no more than a pauper.

"This is Cosima Lombardi's room," the other sister, Giselle, told me softly.

I looked down at her, noting her curves and the stain of orange acrylic paint left over on her right hand. This was the sister of gentle affection and dreamy observation, of France and pearls, lace and fancy.

I'd known them for less than a minute, hadn't even been introduced, but after years of watching from afar, their personalities labeled for me in Cosima's own recollections, I felt as if they were my own sisters.

In a way, they were.

"Perhaps *you* are in the wrong room," I told them coolly. "This is Cosima Davenport's room."

"What?" Giselle breathed.

"Excuse me?" Elena barked at me.

I adjusted my gold cufflink emblazoned with my coat of arms and took comfort in knowing the same image was branded on my wife's buttock.

"The woman you are trying to hide from me," I said idly, "is my wife."

The bomb detonated as if in a silent movie, the room so quiet you could hear a pin drop, but the sisters' reactions were explosive.

"What?"

Giselle's entire body filled with air as she struggled to suck in a breath, then exhaled loudly, painfully as if punctured.

"Excuse me?"

Elena looked the picture of betrayal when her face collapsed with shock.

The dark side of my heart reveled in their reactions. I wanted them to know the truth, to feel it so acutely it would be carved into their hearts and minds forever.

Cosima was *mine,* and I would never tire of demonstrating my ownership over my most precious possession.

"Who are you?" Giselle breathed with reverent terror as if I was the devil.

I felt high off her fear, made invincible by my legal right to be in that room with Cosima.

"Her husband," I told them somewhat redundantly, just to

reinforce my point. "You may call me Alexander, seeing as we are family."

They gaped at me as I strode past Giselle and grabbed an empty chair to place beside Cosima's bed. My arse was barely in the seat as I leaned over her, shielding her from the others with my broad back so that I could have this one semi-private moment to grieve her state.

"My beauty." My voice was heavy and wet with sorrow as I looked down into her tragically beautiful face, her skin too pale and too cold beneath my fingers as I trailed them down her gaunt cheek. "My sleeping beauty, it's time to wake."

The sight of the most vivacious person I knew lying so still, so close to death, lit my heart on fire like a flint to stone.

Over the crackling roar of my incinerating organ, I heard a sharp voice say, "Cosima isn't married."

"She is," I said drily, focusing on my derision instead of the calamity of grief making a ruckus in my chest. "I was at the ceremony."

"She would never get married without telling us," that same voice bit out, hard and awkwardly anglicized.

I glared over my shoulder at Elena as she stood up to shake a finger in my face. "You are some *freak* stalker who has seen her in magazines and fixated on her. *Get out!*"

I stared at her, darkly amused that she attempted to hold my glare when I'd been outstaring men as twice as old and powerful as her since I was a lad.

Cosima would have told me to go gentle, to empathise with her sisters who were clearly grieving, anxious, and completely derailed by the arrival of a previous unknown husband to their favourite sister.

I didn't give a shit about empathising.

I wanted to be alone with my wife. I wanted to stroke her skin until it was warm and flushed, to wake her up with my Dominant voice and then kiss her so deeply that she would be able to taste the ash of my eviscerated heart on my tongue and know the horror of my despair.

Then I wanted to leave Riddick at the door, more men at the entrance of the hospital, and set out to find the dead man who had dared to lay a hand on my beauty. I knew that Noel must have been behind the order given his whispered admission at Pearl Hall, but I wanted the man behind the gun.

Only then, after I had blood on my hands—wet, warm, and *right*—would I bloody well consider the selfish, irascible feelings of the other Lombardi women.

"I would say your goodbyes," I suggested coldly, turning my back on them once more to take Cosima's hand between mine. "Visiting hours are over, and I am the only one who has been granted the choice of staying the night with her."

"Like hell you are," Elena snapped. "How do I know you are who you say you are?"

"He is her husband."

My shoulders stiffened involuntarily at the sound of my brother's mongrel European accent. I didn't turn to face him, hoping as I had when I'd been only a boy, that if I ignored my little brother, he would bugger off.

"They were married two years ago in England," Dante explained, perhaps purposely misleading them so they would think she had met me more recently than she really had. "If you press him, I am sure he will show you the marriage certificate."

There was a discordant, staccato pause like a note hit out of tune.

"What the hell is happening?" Elena demanded again. I was beginning to understand why Giselle found her elder sister so bloody irritating. "First you, and now this maniac who claims to be her husband?"

"Stop."

It was so soft, so hoarse, at first, we all thought it was just the rasp of the wind tousling the cheap curtains through the open window or the shift of my suit sleeve grazing the rough bedsheets.

But it was her.

Cosima.

My wife's sweet voice like the sound of fucking angels singing.

With my heart thumping and swollen in my throat, I angled my head down to look into the golden eyes I knew would meet mine.

Even though I was braced for impact, the sight rocked me to my soul.

Those huge irises were the center of my universe, twin suns that I wanted to spend the rest of my life orbiting around. I catalogued the thick, black fan of her lashes and the deep bruising on the top of her cheeks. How could someone so broken be so goddamn magnificent?

"Cosima!" Giselle sobbed, lurching forward to clutch at her sister's leg while Elena stepped up to silently take her other free hand.

"Bambina," Cosima croaked, her eyes squinting against the pain in her head and the bright, hideous artificial lights. "Water."

Before anyone else could react, I slid a gentle hand under her neck to help lift her head as I pressed the rim of a small Dixie cup to her lips. "Just a little bit, my beauty. You do not want to make yourself sick."

Vaguely, I was aware of the other strange man in the room stating he would go find the doctor. I was grateful someone had thought of that. I felt as concussed as the woman in the hospital bed after the shock of seeing her wake from a coma.

Beside me, Elena vibrated with relief and lingering anxiety.

"You scared the shit out of me. You *terrified* me, Cosima. What would we do without you?" she beseeched in a voice like a little girl.

It seemed out of place coming from a woman I knew was on track to be the youngest partner in the history of her prestigious law firm.

"You would survive," Cosima responded calmly, but her eyes were on mine, and they were filled with frantic, frightened questions.

What are you doing here? Why do I feel like death warmed over? Who did this to me?

It was only her mouth that gave away the extent of her relief. It softened the longer she stared at me, curling at the edges like burning paper as the air between us warmed with passion.

Elena was still spouting selfish nonsense. I decided to give her thirty more seconds before I kicked her out.

"You *will* survive," Cosima amended, cluing into the strained tension between her two sisters that had permeated the air since before my arrival.

"Everyone needs to leave," I demanded.

Thirty fucking seconds was more than enough.

I was a bloody saint for letting them breathe the same air as Cosima right now when every single instinct in my body told me to lock her away in a tower and guard her there like some kind of vicious monster against any and everything that might try to harm her.

Even if it was the emotional harm her sisters were unintentionally doling out.

Cosima shouldn't have to deal with family drama ever again, let alone from the very moment she woke up from a fucking coma.

"We don't need to do shit," Elena snapped.

And essentially secured my everlasting apathy.

"Xan," Cosima scolded me softly, finally ignoring her sisters the way we both wanted to. She gave my hand a weak squeeze and tilted her head so that all her black hair went sliding over the pillow to frame her beloved face. "You came."

I swallowed painfully past the knife that was suddenly lodged in my chest. It killed me to know she would doubt me like that.

Wasn't it ludicrously obvious that she was my everything?

Instead of struggling to convey the depth of my unrest, I let my voice go cold with rage and recrimination. "I am the only one who hurts you, remember?"

Her entire face suffused with peace for the first time since waking, and she leaned even farther over to the edge of the bed. I met her halfway, our faces so close I could smell the signature fragrance I'd had made for her so long ago. One of her sisters must have been brushing the oil through her hair while she slept.

She dragged a deep lungful of air into her lungs, closing her eyes as if the smell of me was as essential to her as hers was to me.

"I know," she whispered on the exhale.

I brushed my free hand over her forehead, down the side of her soft cheek, then into her hair so I could twirl a lock around my finger. The smile she rewarded me with for the familiar gesture was worth more than her weight in gold.

"Cosima," Giselle said softly after clearing her throat. "I know you just woke up, but what the actual *fuck*? You're married?"

"Yes," my wife affirmed immediately, relaxing into the bed as I stroked her hair. "I know you're worried, but Alexander… cares for me. He is here to take care of me." Her eyes flashed open and unerringly landed on Dante who still lingered like a tosser in the doorway. "And so is Dante."

The doctor pushed into the room then, frowning at the many occupants and then immediately ordering their removal. Her sisters protested, but I'd had Dr. Steele flown in specially to tend to Cosima because he was the best neurosurgeon in North America, and he wouldn't let anything get between him and a patient.

"I am the husband," I told him, standing up to offer my hand.

Dr. Steele stared at me, his face impassive but for the twinkle in his eyes.

The man had known me for years, and when I'd called him to take care of my wife, he'd almost busted a gut laughing at the news I'd succumbed to something as mundane as love.

"Fine, but stay in the corner. The rest of you, out."

"It's okay. I'm awake now. I'll see you again, soon, *si?*" Cosima said, her voice even weaker, and her lids fluttering to stay open. She'd been awake only ten minutes, and already, she was exhausted.

I burned with the need to shout at the lingering family to get the fuck out.

The sisters and the male stranger left before I was forced to take bodily action, but Dante lingered, leaning against the wall beside the door with his ankles and arms crossed like a lazy bodyguard.

And he was.

Lazy, inept, fucking useless.

Why the bloody hell hadn't he been with her?

He should have stuck to her side like *glue* while I was away.

I shot him a scathing look that promised retribution later, but he only smiled thinly and answered Elena's outraged call from down the hall, leaving the room to speak to her.

When the door clicked shut, I instantly moved. "Will I hurt you if I come onto the bed with you?"

"It'll hurt more if you don't," she promised, shifting over with a wince so that I would have a sliver of the bed.

Carefully, more carefully than I'd ever done anything, I curled myself around her, one hand on her good side, the other over her head where I could play lightly with her hair. She sighed as soon as I settled and closed her eyes.

"I could sleep."

"You can sleep, my beauty. I'll watch over you," I vowed.

"I know," she whispered. "I knew even when Giuseppe threatened to take me to Noel. I knew you'd find me no matter what."

Rage moved through me, quick and silent as a possession. I swallowed thickly once, twice to speak through the wrath lodged in my throat.

"Always. Know also that Giuseppe is a dead man for hurting you."

"Already dead," she murmured, falling quickly into sleep. "I shot him."

A moment later, her mouth softened, and her breath evened out. I lay there for a long while, listening to her breath as one might listen to a symphony, letting the sound move through my soul like a spiritual awakening.

She was alive.

Alive.

But she had been through too much, and enough was enough. From that moment on, Riddick and I wouldn't leave her fucking side. Not until Noel was taken care of and put away, because no matter that it was Giuseppe's thugs who had obviously hurt my wife, I had no doubt Noel had orchestrated it.

There was a gruff cough from the doorway, and I looked up to see Salvatore there, dressed all in black, his face a white mask of horror. There were tears in his gold eyes as he stared at the sleeping woman who shared those eyes with him.

"*Madonna santa*," he breathed in a voice that was clogged with tears. "Look at her."

"Look at you," I countered coldly. "Alive and well."

His expression shuttered, the wet glazed eyes turning cold as marbles. "As if you didn't know."

I leveled him with a cold look, but I was curious how he could have known that.

"I was not exactly subtle as I should have been, mm?" he addressed my unspoken question as he moved into the room and into the chair on the other side of Cosima. His meaty hand trembled as he linked it gently with hers. "I could not be when my daughter was so close. I knew it was probable you and others had eyes on her, but I indulged my own need to see her more than was prudent if I truly wanted to stay dead."

The age-old fury in my heart eroded under the warmth of his affection for my wife. He hadn't been there for her when she was a girl, and I resented him for that even though I knew it wasn't exactly his choice. I wanted to believe that a true man made his own decisions regardless of the obstacles that faced him, but life wasn't so simple and I'd had firsthand experience with the difficulty of overcoming your own circumstances.

The truth was, he loved Cosima with a verve that led him to sacrifice his own safety on multiple occasions in order to see her happy.

I could respect that.

Hadn't I spent the past four years doing the very same?

But my softening was more than even that rational.

Once, years ago before the death of my beloved mother, I had called this man Uncle Tore. We had spent countless occasions with him as boys both in England and Italy with our mother, learning Italian, picking olives out of his many orchards, and squishing grapes with our toes in the old way just because it was fun for boys to get messy. He had loved us too, not quite the same way he loved Cosima, but in his own deep way. We were the children of his best friend, and as was the Italian way, that made us family to him.

So, there were deep fissures in the arctic glaciers I'd built between myself and my old affection for the man, and they deepened as I saw one furious tear roll down his creased cheek.

"It was Giuseppe di Carlo and his men," I said quietly, careful not to disturb the magnificent beauty sleeping in my hold. "That is all I got before she slept again."

He nodded tersely as fury flashed over his face. "Of

course, it was. He has been trying to start a war since Dante took over as Camorra *capo*. He does not like that we will not parlay with him. He does not like that we pose a threat to his territory and undisputed reign as mafia kingpin in the city."

"Perhaps," I allowed. "But it's more than that. He made a deal with the Order, with Noel, to spy on Cosima in exchange for membership."

"More power." Tore clucked his tongue and shook his head. "Sometimes these *stronzo*, they do not understand that all power is not created equal. The taint of some, like this, will end you."

"I can't argue. He's dead."

His forehead dissected into deep lines of shock. "How so? You got to him already."

I tipped my head toward my wife, sweeping my fingers over her crown to collect silky locks between my fingers. Her gorgeous mane comforted me as much as it did her. "This one took him out before she was shot. Or so she says."

"Check on that," he said, and it was half question, half musing. I had no doubt he would check on it even though he expected me to do the same. "Still, we will kill all of the men involved."

I nodded. "That's the plan."

We locked eyes for a moment over Cosima's prone, broken body, bonding over our dual protectiveness, and our combined rage and need for vengeance.

"Where were you when this happened?" he asked, and it wasn't a reprimand, just curiosity.

"I confronted Noel," I admitted. "Once again, I think he planned this exactly right so that I would be gone, and she would be vulnerable. Though," I added in a voice like dry ice, "Dante was meant to be watching out for her."

Tore winced as he drew Cosima's hand to his face, pressing it to his cheek and closing his eyes. "This is my fault. I called Dante to a different project, something that needed doing for our organization. I didn't realize…"

I wanted to keep the wrath I felt toward Dante locked up in a pin, wild and rabid, but I knew in the same way I knew Cosima was my reason for living that Dante would never let any harm come to her if he could help it. He must have had a reason for leaving her, one I would be sure to find out quickly.

"The Order is done," I told Salvatore, needing him on my side, *our* side, more than ever. "But Noel is still locked up at Pearl Hall, free to make his maneuvers. I don't want Cosima alone for one moment until he is locked up in prison where he bloody well belongs."

Our eyes clashed, a deal struck in the lines of our vision.

"*Bene,*" he agreed. "Whatever you need. In fact, may I suggest you let her convalesce with me in my home upstate? It is very private, very secure. You will not have to worry."

"I am not leaving her." It was so out of the question that I would have laughed if my wife hadn't just woken from a coma and my heart wasn't still recovering.

The man who had once been my uncle and then my sworn enemy stared at me for a long moment with my wife's hand on his face as if to anchor him.

"I did not imagine you would. You are both welcome in my home, Alexander, if you should wish it."

I looked down at the woman in my arms, at the sweet curve of her face and the thick fan of her lashes resting on her steep cheeks, and I knew I would do anything to make her safe and happy. Even if it meant reconciling with a man I'd hated for over a decade.

"Fine. I will be there, but only when I am not out hunting down di Carlo's men," I told him.

Dante appeared in the doorway, haggard but taut with his own fury. "Hunting sounds perfect to me."

Chapter Twenty-five

COSIMA

I woke up alone with an immediate sense of where I was even though I had been struggling for weeks with memory loss and crippling headaches that robbed me of all my senses. My belly was to the bed, my legs and arms akimbo over the large mattress and sparingly covered by a white linen sheet. I moved my masses of hair out of my face, lifting my head to gaze out the French doors to the little balcony off my bedroom at my father's house in Niagara county. The sky was upholstered in grey suede clouds rubbed dark and light across the horizon so that only cool, weak light filtered through and cast the treed landscape in watery winter pastels.

My body still ached, and my brain still scrambled, but after six weeks of convalescing, I was almost as good as new. It was the gunshot wound to my head that caused me the most trouble, but the dull ache in my shoulder and left side were lessening every day.

I was ready for reality again.

Upstate New York was beautiful, and spending unadulterated time with my father was a blessing I would never take for granted. We went for long walks in the crisp air, cooked together, ate together, and read together on his big, cushy red couch before the fire. It was idyllic.

But it was not my life, and I was growing tired of the mundanity.

Alexander and Dante both came and left as they pleased, gone more often than not to take out the men involved in my shooting and to provide testimony in the trails of the more prolific Order members.

I missed them, but more than that, I wanted to help them.

It wasn't good for my spirit to be locked up in a house like a princess in a tower, unable to help those who fought to save her.

I was no princess.

I was a fucking warrior, and I wanted revenge just as much as they did.

Also, Alexander hadn't fucked me hard in weeks.

I understood why. The doctors hadn't given me the okay for intercourse until ten days before, and while he had made me love to whenever he was there, he hadn't been my Master since before the shooting.

I needed it. I needed his stern, calculating hands to leash my restless soul and bring me some fleeting degree of peace.

I sighed heavily, flipping onto my back to stare at the ceiling, remembering the last conversation I had with Elena before Alexander took me away to Salvatore's.

The only person I had really said goodbye to before disappearing was Giselle, and only then because I lived with her, and due to her taboo relationship with Sinclair, which came to light while I was still in the hospital, I thought she would understand.

She did. She would not throw stones at glass houses when she herself had been involved in an affair with her sister's boyfriend and was now pregnant with his child.

Elena, on the other hand, had not been pleased to learn more about my relationship with Alexander.

"I just don't understand," she'd argued from my hospital bedside, perched in an ugly plastic chair that she sat in as if it were a throne. "How could you marry a man and not tell any of us...not tell me?"

I understood her sadness. Of all my siblings, Elena was the closest only to me. This was her doing. She chafed against Sebastian's passionate, bold nature and secretly resented him for growing up a man in our misogynistic land and therefore having more opportunities than the rest of us. Her relationship with Giselle, of course, was a frayed wire that worked only to electrocute anyone who dared to trifle with it.

My eldest sister was a difficult woman, but I had found that it was the most difficult women who were the greatest to know. She was strong and fierce in the face of adversity, a mother bear with her cub, and smart enough to outmaneuver even the craftiest of foes. She was beautiful, as cultivated and classy as a polished diamond, and just as cold. Elena had taught me so many things over the years, like how to be a strong woman, but also, how not to be. She had allowed her past traumas to calcify her heart, and as a result, she had no room in her soul for someone new or different.

It was tragic, and I hoped one day, she would find a way to

soften, but I knew looking into her condemnatory eyes that day would not be today.

"There is a lot you don't know, and I won't tell you, Lena," I tried to explain gently even though my head pounded so fiercely it was a struggle to think at all. "The only thing you really need to know is that Alexander is my husband, and... well, I love him."

It was the first time I had said it out loud, and it felt good to feel the words perfume the air.

"Dante told me some things," she said forebodingly. "He told me that your *husband* bought out Dad's debt, so essentially, he bought *you*."

A bitter little laugh escaped my lips before I could help it. "Alexander helped me pay for your education, Lena, for Giselle's schooling, and Sebastian's plane ticket to London. How is that a bad thing?"

"He made you into a whore," she exclaimed, her low-lidded eyes flashing like lightning through storm clouds. "I never would have thought you'd stoop so low to get us out of Naples."

A snarl built in my chest and escaped with my next words. "Careful, you don't know what you're talking about, and I love you, I do, but there are some things that cannot be forgiven. You've already ostracized Giselle and Sinclair. Do not do the same to me."

My stern words deflated some of her indignation, her shoulders slumping slightly as she planted her forearms in the bed to lean over me.

"I just worry about you, my Cosi," she said in a soft, sad voice that rubbed against my skin like wet velvet. "I don't understand your life, and it worries me. You showed up at Thanksgiving dinner with *welts* on your wrists from this man, and now you've been shot *three times* because of some mess he's embroiled you in."

"You judge me because you don't understand," I told her

calmly.

She scoffed. "It's not a difficult situation to grasp, Cosima. The man bought you, beat you, brutalized you, and embroiled you in an international mess that got you shot in the fucking head."

I turned my head, my gaze searching for anything that wasn't her and wasn't white, latching onto a sliver of cerulean blue sky barely visible between skyscrapers. The cheap pillowcase was rough against my cheek and smelled like antiseptic.

Unbidden, I thought of the silk sheets on my bed at Pearl Hall, the pearlescent wallpaper that glowed in the filtered British light like the inside of an oyster shell, and the rich gold antique furniture. It was opulent and rich, a vivid setting for the riotous love I'd found within those walls.

I blinked and the memory dissipated, leaving in its place that stark room and the pinched face of my horrified sister.

I sighed gustily. "If you aren't going to try to empathise or understand, I won't bother explaining myself to you, Elena."

"How can I understand something like this? The man only caused you pain, Cosima. What could there possibly be to love about that?"

"Maybe I like the pain. Maybe I'm the type of woman who responds to calculated cruelty and animal savagery more than pretty romance and sweet platitudes. Maybe I like the kind of man most people think is a villain, and maybe I'm the kind of woman who is more dark than light." I glared at her as I spoke, my words more Italian than English, spiced with the heat of my homeland and my lifelong heartache.

I was tired of clarifying my kinks and predilections to myself. There was no way I was going to sit idly by while my sister, who knew next to nothing about the circumstances of my life, cast judgment against me.

Elena's face was twisted tight at the lips, a bulging cap on the emotions clogging her pores.

"Am I the only one in this family not screwed up with

perversion?" she asked, her words pointed, but her delivery soft as if she couldn't find the conviction to truly condemn us anymore.

My rage allayed into tender pity. I snaked my hand across the abrasive white sheets and opened my palm for her. Tentatively, biting her lip as if she was about to surrender to her mortal enemy, Elena wrapped her fingers in mine.

She had soft hands, perfectly manicured and painted in the deep, almost purple red of Italian chianti. There were two rings, one on each hand, the first a simple gold and amethyst band Sinclair had given her for their first anniversary and the second, an onyx and pearl combination I'd given her last year at her birthday.

I thumbed the gold band and looked up at her, my face suffused with a love so great it made my eyes tear. "Lena, *cara*, I know you've been through so much in the past few months. I know how heartbroken you are over Sinclair and Giselle's relationship. I know because I've been heartbroken for four years while I lived apart from Alexander. I know because in some ways, even though we're back together, the scars of that heartbreak will never fade. But please, *cara mia*, do not let this hurt consume your life. Let in the light. Discover someone new to love. You deserve happiness, but you need to *find* it because goodness rarely just falls in someone's lap."

"Oh, shut up, Cosima, you have no idea what this is like! How...how humiliated I feel. Every person in New York knows that Daniel left me for my little sister. She orchestrated the total and utter devastation of my life as I knew it!" Her face was expressionless in its grief and rage. "Little Miss Beautiful, no one would ever leave you, would they? Oh, wait..." Her smile was razor thin and cut deep into the tender flesh of my heart. "Someone has."

I suddenly felt explosive with rage. It screamed through my molten blood and clawed at my throat to escape, but the look in my sister's eyes smothered the flames and turned them into smoky sorrow.

"Grow up, big sister. Being hurt does not give you free license to be cruel. It doesn't matter that it left your heart in tatters; it happens to the best of us. You have a choice to make, and you better do it quickly because if you keep on keeping on the way you have since Sin left you, you won't have anyone left to bitch to." I disentangled my hand from hers and turned my head. "Now, could you please leave? I'm exhausted."

She hesitated for a long moment before standing up, planting a kiss on my forehead, and leaving. One week later, during my last night in the city, she had shown up at Giselle and Sinclair's housewarming party to throw a tantrum about their surprise pregnancy.

I supposed, unhappily, that she had made a choice about what kind of victim she wanted to be.

One who remained a victim forever.

I was stirred out of my reverie by the sound of voices downstairs and a heavy tread on the creaking wooden stairs. A moment later, the door opened on my Alexander, his hair wind tousled into rows of flaxen wheat, his silver eyes glittering with victory.

"We found him," he told me with cold triumph that felt like a trophy tossed between us. He closed the door and went to me, crawling over my prone body on his hands and knees so he loomed over me. "We found the bastard who shot you, and my beauty, we killed him."

"I told you, I don't need you to go on a killing spree for me," I reminded him even though the thrill of knowing the man who had tried to kill me was gone made my heart palpitate.

"I did terrible things to steal your love. Do you think I won't commit crimes even more atrocious to win you back?"

he asked, with such solemnity it felt like a preacher asked me to disavow a lesson from God.

"No," I said honestly and watched him smile. "And I can't say I don't love you for that."

His joy skittered over me like an electric current, rippling gooseflesh across my skin. I wrapped my arms and legs around him to pull him down on top of me and smiled in his face.

"Thank you," I breathed against his lips because I sealed my gratitude with a long, lingering kiss.

He took control of the embrace, hauling me even tighter against his body, his tongue plundering my mouth until I whimpered.

"One less evil against us," I said breathlessly when he pulled away.

My fingers played in the hair over his temple, stroking over the flecks of silver there that made him look deliciously distinguished. He smelled of cold, clean air and just a hint of his forestry scent. I pressed my nose to his throat to get closer to the scent.

He was curiously still against me for a heartbeat before he tipped his head to ask quietly in my ear, "If all the monsters were slayed and all the obstacles were removed and the only thing left was you and me, would you stay?"

"Would you ask me to?" I countered even as my heart began to beat so forcibly I wondered if it would crack a rib.

"Yes," he said simply as if it was obvious.

"Why?"

"Would you stay?" he reinforced with a gritted kind of determination as if he couldn't begin to answer for his motivation unless I responded first.

"I'd need a reason."

I didn't. The reason was him; it always had been. I'd learned my reason for living was *me*. No one could take my life from me again unless I let them. But my reason for happiness?

That was answered by the man on top of me, every diamond hard, brilliant cut, multifaceted inch of him.

He spoke slowly, each word had weight and substance like a physical thing polished and placed before me, a jeweled necklace of a phrase. "Would you stay…if I told you I love you?"

Every molecule of my being stopped functioning. My breath evaporated in my lungs, my heart calcified and ceased to beat, my body went numb with shock.

"I thought you didn't have a heart to love me with?" I asked carefully because this could very well be too good to be true.

Maybe he was just manipulating me, maybe he needed to use me again for some nefarious purpose.

Of maybe, just maybe, this was real.

His goodness since his return to my life was not a ruse, but a promise of only more goodness to come.

I held my breath as the dreams I'd dreamed in vapor began to solidify in front of me.

Alexander's expression was one I had never seen before, his hard features softened like melting butter under the heat of burning passion in his molten metal eyes. The fingers of one hand whispered across my jaw and then cupped my throat.

"It appears I did all along. It was just locked away from me, and the only person who could access it was you."

Tears sprang to my eyes and spilled over, a waterfall breaking through a yearlong dam. I wanted to speak, but my emotions were too big, swelling in my throat and robbing me of a voice.

Instead, I mouthed, "I love you."

He didn't smile as I thought he would. If anything, his expression grew tighter, filled with a tension I couldn't understand. "I know I'm not worthy of you. You deserve so much more than I've given you, that I ever could give, but I promise to try to earn your love and devotion every day for the rest of our lives if you'll let me."

"I'm your slave," I told him on a wet laugh. "Where else would I rather be than at your side?"

"My slave, my *topolina*, my countess, my wife." He said each epitaph like a butler announcing royalty to the room, as if each title was priceless.

I realized, to him, to me, they were.

"You are the best thing that ever happened to me," I said because it hurt me to know he didn't believe himself worthy of my love when he was the only person I could ever dream of giving my heart to.

"Don't be ridiculous. I was the harbinger of your doom."

"No. I know our story might seem black and white, you the villain and me the victim, but it isn't so simple. Before you, I had no prospects. I had a meager career as a model that provided just enough for my family to get us through with the bare minimum of provisions. I was a tool and a martyr. I had no thoughts or feelings for myself. I was, as you said, a queen who was made to think she was only a pawn. Then you came in your black chariot and pulled me into the shadows of the underworld, and I came alive."

"You almost died," he said, his voice cracked through with devastation. "So many bloody times, because of me."

"I might have died otherwise. You aren't the only bad guy in my life," I teased.

He didn't smile.

I traced a finger along the brutal cut of his square jaw up to his ear and around the perfectly formed shell of it. He was so exquisitely designed that he took my breath away.

Leaning forward, I pressed a kiss to his pulse, keeping my lips there for a moment to feel the beat quicken against me.

"You still make me come alive," I whispered in his ear. "Sometimes, it feels as if I don't exist unless you are in a room with me."

He paused for a moment, breathing deeply through his emotions as he absorbed my words. Then he pulled back only to place his forehead against mine.

"Well then, my beauty, I'll have to make sure you are never in a room without me."

He kissed the giggle off my lips and shared his own joy with me using his tongue, then later, his entire body.

Chapter Twenty-six

ALEXANDER

*E*very day my wife recovered from the shooting was one I relished like a chest full of treasure. Each time she laughed, her husky chuckle was a diamond collected in my palm, and every minute she spent walking around growing physically stronger again was a gemstone brighter than any occurring in nature. I watched, and I coveted, and when I felt there were no more gains to be had in her recovery, I decided it was time to give back some of the treasure Cosima had given me.

I leaned in the doorway of our bedroom at Salvatore's and watched my wife as she lay across the bed on her back, legs up in the air, one hand twirling a lock of her hair like some teenage advertisement for a woman's magazine. She was beautiful even in one of my old Cambridge T-shirts and a pair of her father's chunky wool knit socks, so beautiful I was happy to watch her while she finished her phone call.

"Honestly, Sin, I'm having a terrible time believing you," she said in a tone filled with the music of her laughter. "I just...you're really getting married?"

I'd only had the occasion to meet my wife's friend once in the two weeks we spent in New York after Cosima left the hospital before we hid her away in upstate New York. He was a stern man, but not the cold, implacable one Cosima had spoken of in the past. No, now happily shacked up with Giselle in a palatial Brooklyn penthouse with a baby on the way, Daniel Sinclair seemed like the happiest bloke in America. Even when Elena had crashed the evening when we painted the nursery to throw what I was beginning to understand was a classically Elena-style fit about the pregnancy, Sinclair had been unmoved in his resolve and his contentedness.

He was a man hooked deeply through the heart by the siren's song of a woman's love, and he would not be swayed from it.

Not even to comfort his estranged longtime partner.

Now, it seemed, he had decided to take their short relationship to a new level by marrying Giselle.

The man bloody well moved quickly when he knew what he wanted.

"No, no, of course I think it's a splendid idea! I'm just shocked that my friend Sinclair organized a *surprise* elopement in Mexico. I mean, who are you and what did you do with the man I once knew?" She paused with a smile on her face, her eyes sliding to me in the doorway, and that smile blooming even bigger. "Yeah, yeah, I think I know a little something about love changing you for the better."

I raised a brow at her that had her winking at me.

"Of course, Xan and I will be there," she said confidently even though I scowled. "We wouldn't miss it for anything. Just text me the details, and we will make it work. And Sin? I can't wait to see two of my beloved people have their happily ever after. Don't let the pain and consequences of your journey to this moment taint the beauty of your future together. What you two have is something very few people ever get to experience. Cherish it."

She said a few more words, laughing again as she hung up the phone. The moment she did, I was on her, hefting her off the body over my shoulder in a fireman's carry.

She squawked, hitting her hands against my arse. "Xan! *Che cavalo!* What are you doing?"

I ignored her as I took her through the house, down the stairs, and out the back door. Salvatore and Dante were out in town and wouldn't be back for at least an hour.

Just enough time for what I had planned.

Cosima had settled over my shoulder, tapping out a light beat against my arse cheeks while humming a song as if being slung over my back was normal and comfortable.

When we reached Salvatore's small stables at the back of the property, though, she stilled, and the quality of her silence turned the air static. She said nothing as I righted her, standing her up beside the blazing hearth so that she would stay warm in the early spring air.

I'd prepared everything that morning while Cosima readied herself for the day, and she caught sight of it then, her eyes widening as she took in the branding iron lying beside the fire.

"Xan..." she said slowly. "You've already branded me once. Don't you think twice is overkill?"

I nodded, keeping our eyes locked as I began to unbutton my shirt. "I'll admit, that would be excessive. Though, it wasn't what I had in mind."

Cosima's eyes burned brighter, twin noonday suns as she watched me unbutton and pull off my shirt. Her gaze raked over my abdominals before finding mine again. "What, what exactly did you have in mind then?"

"You are going to ride me while I sit on that stool," I said with a wave of my hand to said stool. "And after you've made me come, you are going to brand me." I stepped forward to take her hand and place it over my heart. "Right here."

She squirmed, her eyes flashing light and dark as she warred with her instinctual deviant delight and learned shamed. "Xan, I really don't think that's necessary."

"Well, I do," I said in the tone that meant our conversation, as I knew it, was over.

She bit her plush lower lip and then released it, the reddened flesh beckoning me like a red cape to a bull. "Why?"

"I own you, I branded you, and I married you. As far as I am concerned, we are even on two accounts, but not the third. I meant what I said, *bella*. You own me as much as I own you. I want that to be known."

She continued to prevaricate, looking at the branding iron and then back at the unmarred skin over my heart. "No one will see it unless you go to the beach or something."

"No…but just as with you and your brand, *I* will know it is there, and I will also feel the ache of it. I want that with me always. Are you saying," I asked with a cold quirked brow, "that you would rid yourself of yours if given the chance?"

"No," she snapped immediately.

I opened my hands and shrugged. "Then there we have it."

"It hurts," she admitted.

"You can kiss it better," I said drolly as I took off my pants. "Now, undress. I'm eager to come before we get started."

My wife moved like a dancer even though she'd never had any training. She made the removal of her overlarge shirt and socks look like a Las Vegas burlesque show, and by the time her perfect form was bared to me in the golden firelight, I was hard as marble.

I stood still for her, watching her move toward me as light and agile as the light of the fire against the wooden walls. She bit her lip before she reached out to touch my chest, her hand hovering with a hesitation that was a request.

I nodded my head, wrapped my hand around her wrist, and pressed her palm to the center of my chest. "Touch me as you please. Sometimes, my beauty, Domination is not about me taking over your body with control and discipline. Sometimes, it's about letting the submissive worship that which she adores."

She tipped her eyes to mine, showing me their warm, liquid centers before she concentrated on my torso, running her hands over the steep ridges and cut edges of my muscle groups. The pads of her fingers rasped over my nipples, her nails scratched through the thick trail of flaxen hair leading to my groin, and she traced the sharp line of the muscles in my groin all the way to the root of my pulsing cock. Her exploration was gentle and venerable, an artist feeling for the form beneath a block of marble, carefully mapping out the form and the emotiveness in her art.

My legs wanted to tremble at that tenderness, and my heart ached like pressure on a bruise as I struggled to believe I deserved that level of love from that level of exquisite woman.

She made me believe.

She made a study of teaching me I belonged with her by sinking to her knees and taking my cock deep down her throat. She struggled against the weight of my shaft as it pinned her tongue and dragged along the hot, warm canal of her throat. She panted at she lapped at my head, purple and big as an Italian plum she couldn't stop sucking. Her fingers played over my balls, weighing the heft of them, rolling them over her palm.

She made me crazy with desire, and I knew it was to show me how crazy I'd made her with love.

It was an exhibition in worship, and it turned the air around us warm and close as the atmosphere in a chapel. I imagined the scent of incense and myrrh as she sat me down on the stool and carefully took me into her golden body. We dipped our heads to watch my tip sink into her wet folds and then hissed in unison, heads thrown back as she slid all the way down to the root.

I loved the silken snugness of her cunt around me, the way her large breasts jiggled obscenely as she raised and lowered herself over my thick pole, riding it hard even though it stretched her nearly painfully tight. I loved the way she fisted her hands in my hair and held me still so that we locked eyes as she rode me, and I could read the love and gratitude there like an oath written on gold parchment.

I loved it so much, loved her so much, that when I finally came between her thighs, it felt like a blessing and an induction into a faith I actually, acutely wanted to join. One of beauty and surrender, one of trust and sacrifice, one that existed only between this gorgeous Italian girl and her cruel British Master.

She ate my groan off my lips, feeding her moan of climax right back to me as we orgasmed together in the firelight.

Before I could recover, she was dipping the iron pole beside us into the fire, rolling it in the heat until it glowed as brightly as her pleasure fevered eyes. She said nothing as she raised it, yet her eyes said everything.

They said, *I love you.*

They said, *I will never be without you even if you should go.*

They said, *we are a closed loop.*

And then the searing tip of the brand was pressed directly into the skin over my heart, and it felt as if the emotion she'd poured into my once hollow body erupted from that place, spilling out with agony that tangled so closely with ecstasy I didn't know where one ended and the other began.

I kissed her hard, fisting a hand in her luscious hair to keep her close while I feasted on her warm, spicy flavour. The burn was wicked, the pain so severe I wondered for a moment if I might cry out from it for the first time in my life.

I didn't.

I took solace in the woman who was my reward for a being born into such a life, and I continued to do so long after she had pulled the iron away from my body, long after our skin had cooled and the fire had died down. I held her, and I loved with only my hands on her back and my tongue in her mouth, and when we finally parted, I felt filled with a previously unfamiliar emotion.

Clean, bright hope like a bubble expanded from my gut, floating delicately to the surface of my thoughts.

I brought her palm over my wound, gritting my teeth against the pressure on the raw flesh. She dipped her head as I moved it away again, studying the stylized initials "CD" covered in thorns and poppies carved forever into my skin.

"Yours," I said gruffly.

"Yours," she agreed.

And I thought maybe, at that one moment suspended between agony and joy, an in-between place that seemed to exist solely in the gap between our bodies, if maybe our happily ever after was achievable after all.

COSIMA

e held hands as we walked across the thick grass down the sloping lawn to my father's large, airy home. It felt so mundane and yet utterly profound to be holding the hand of Alexander Davenport, Earl of Thornton and my Master. After all this time and so many tribulations, it was a simple act I didn't take for granted.

My fingers flexed between his, and he slid me a sidelong look that wasn't quite a smile but spoke of one. I couldn't help but look at the space beneath his buttoned shirt where the new brand lay, a brand he had willing offered because he wanted to be owned as equally by me and I was by him. Love and awe rolled through me like a warm breeze, and I felt filled with hope for the first time in a long time as we strolled back to the house where my father and Dante would probably be waiting with some delicious home-cooked meal and a bottle of deep red wine.

Car doors slamming around the front of the house and sudden coarse shouts in Italian had both of us freezing mid-step.

"*Vaffanculo,*" Tore growled as we broke into a sprint and rounded the house to the front yard. "What the hell are you taking him for?"

I slammed to an abrupt stop as if I'd run into a brick wall when I arrived beside the scene and took it in.

There were police cars in a row of three down the drive, their light spinning pinwheels of red, blue, and white light over the yard and the tableau of two men pushing Dante to the hood of a car in order to cuff him. They were both considerably shorter than the Italian-British man, and they used excessive force to keep him in place even though he lay passively against the car.

They read him his Miranda rights in low, ceaseless monotones that I could barely hear over Tore's ranting questions.

"As I said," a third policeman was saying to him, "Edward Dante Davenport is under arrest for the murder of Giuseppe di Carlo. If you continue your tirade, we will be forced to arrest you for police assault and impeding a criminal investigation."

"Like hell you will," Tore bellowed, shoving a finger at the younger man. I'd never seen him so angry; his face was flushed, and his voice was as rough as gravel underfoot.

Alexander stepped forward with confidence to intercept Tore's lunging body and began to calmly speak with the officer. I didn't do anything because my body had ceased to function.

I was mired in shock, my feet tangled in the roots of my own self-hatred and the muck of my confusion.

How could this be possible?

Dante hadn't killed di Carlo.

My hand still burned with the heat of the gun in my hand as I'd turned it on the Cosa Nostra crime boss, as I'd drilled a round into his black heart and one into his corrupted brain. My fingers flexed in the empty air as the memory ran through me like a physical thing, like a car crash breaking every bone in my body.

Dante was being arrested for a crime *I* had committed.

No.

That couldn't possibly happen.

Not the brother of my heart, not my saviour and best friend.

Not him.

I stepped forward like a bullet from the chamber of a gun, shooting into place between Alexander and the cop before they could stop me.

"He didn't do it," I said in a voice that clinked my words to the ground like ice cubes from a machine; mechanical and cold. "Dante wasn't even *there*."

"Cosima," Alexander barked, my name the edge of a whip slicing through the air against my skin. I jerked back from the impact and straight into his open arms. He banded them around my torso and cemented me to his body.

"You're the victim, correct?" The officer checked his small notebook. "A Cosima Lombardi?"

"Cosima Davenport," Alexander snapped. "My wife and the sister of the man you are trying to pin for a murder he didn't commit."

I opened my mouth to tell them it was *me*. That I was a murderess, and honestly, I would do it again, and again, and again if it meant the scum of di Carlo would be rid from the world forever.

But Alexander was there, holding me so tightly I couldn't draw breath to speak, and then Dante was turning, the muscles in his arms bulging as they pulled tight behind his back, restrained by the harsh bite of handcuffs. His eyes were large with solemnity, a black so absolute I felt myself being sucked into the darkness like light through a black hole.

He said so many things with that look, so many agonizing

truths that I jerked against Alexander as they pierced through me like bullets.

Don't, they said.

Don't take this from me, they ordered.

This is for you, tesoro. This is for you, and I will do it because I will do anything for you, even if you don't ask for it. This is for you, and you will not take this sacrifice away from me.

A sob exploded from the cold chamber of my chest, puncturing the air so harshly the cops all jerked to look at me.

I shook my head manically, my hair flying over my face, strands sticking to the tears trailing down the skin. "No, no, no, *fratello mio*."

Yes, yes, yes, mia bella sorella, his eyes said gently, firmly.

I couldn't bear it, but I also knew the devastation that would be wrecked on my two Davenport men if I was bound in cuffs and dragged to prison. They wouldn't stop until the rebar was twisted open, the concrete cell blasted apart so they could get to me. Nothing, absolutely nothing, would stop these men from making sure I was free after almost a lifetime of servitude to something or someone.

This was what they had been fighting for the last half decade.

Not just the ruin of the Order and the truth of Chiara Davenport's death.

But *my* freedom.

They would not, I knew in the very marrow of my bones, let me sacrifice all their gains now when we were so close to the end.

I whimpered as the realization settled under my skin and itched there.

Alexander felt the shift in my body and let out a rough breath. I felt him tip his chin down at his brother, their gazes locked over my head.

"This isn't the end, brother," Alexander promised in the

same weighty tone he'd pledged himself as my husband. "I won't let this happen."

Dante's red lips pressed into a line that was supposed to be a smile. "You're a Lord, Alexander, not a god."

My husband straightened to his full six feet five inches and leveled his haughty glare at his brother. "That remains to be seen. Let's test it, shall we? I'll have you out on bail before the month is out. Understood?"

Dante's lips twitched again, true humour flickering over his beautiful face. "Aye, aye, brother."

Salvatore stepped up in line with us, his shoulder brushing Alexander's in a show of solidarity I never thought I would witness. "We've got you, *ragazzo*."

Dante nodded once, then cut his eyes to me. "You both better take care of my treasure." My father and husband grunted, slightly offended that he even had to ask. "And you, *tesoro*, you take care of my family."

I nodded mutely, a sob lodged in my throat like a rock the size of a curled fist. Silently, we all watched as they opened the police car door and shoved Dante inside. The cops went to their vehicles, and only when the first of the convey started down the dirt drive did I explode out of Xan's arms and race to the last car. My fingers pressed to the window, smearing my tears over the pane.

Dante smiled at me and trailed his big fingers in the marks I'd left there.

"I love you," I shouted so loudly I could feel the vibration of it in my fingers on the glass.

"*Ti amo*," Dante mouthed.

And then the car was moving slow, then faster, too fast for my churning legs to keep up with, and I was falling to the ground as my fingers lost their connection to the glass. I landed hard on my hip but didn't feel it through the pain radiating from my heart, eviscerating my body like a nuclear weapon.

"Oh God, *Dio mio*," I chanted into my knees as I brought them to my chest and watered them with my tears. "He's going to jail because of me."

Alexander and Tore were on me the next moment. My father sat behind me, cradling me between his legs, his hands tenderly moving the hair off my face to lay my head against his chest. My husband moved in front of me, sliding my legs over his so only a small diamond of space was between our pelvises, and his face was in mine, his hands rubbing over my cold, shivering arms.

"Hush, my beauty, hush," he encouraged me gently, his eyes on me, inside me, sealing up my gaping wounds with careful stitches and soothing caresses. "Hush, and trust me now, wife. If it's the last thing I do, we will end Noel for orchestrating this, and we will get Dante out of jail and home where he belongs."

"With us," I declared.

He hesitated, but only to blink slowly and flash his eyes at me, showing how they turned from sorrowful smoke to absolute stone. "Yes. Home with us."

I sank deep into the bracketed embrace of my father and my husband and allowed myself to believe their strength was enough to bring Dante back to me.

I went alone to Metropolitan Correction Center two days later. Alexander, Tore, and even Sebastian, when he found out, had wanted to accompany me, but I couldn't let them. This was about Dante and me. I owed it to him to face his reality without the shield of the men in my life who loved me. I wanted to be exposed as a raw nerve when I went to him, as if my vulnerability would make the sacrifice that much more beautiful.

I didn't know about that, but when I saw him behind the glass in the prison they were keeping him in until further notice, I felt every single atom in my body keen with pain like the sorrowful howl of a wolf. He was so large, so beautiful and trapped like a magnificent wild animal in an enclosure too small and ill-equipped to handle him. Grief and rage burned in my hollow chest as I locked eyes on him through the plexiglass and picked up the plastic phone to speak with him, but I had vowed before I arrived that I wouldn't cry in front of him.

Dante hated to see me cry.

I pressed my fingertips to the glass, needing to feel at least the heat of him through the blockade to reassure myself the only way I knew how, through some kind of physical connection.

His hand was over mine through the partition in less time than it took for my heart to turn over in my chest.

"Dante," I said through the crackling phone line. "*Mio bello Dante.*"

There was a wealth of sorrow and regret in those few words, but I didn't know how to transcribe them in any other way than by saying his chosen name. In some ways, this was the life Dante had chosen for himself when he turned his back on Edward Davenport to be Dante Salvatore, from a lord of the realm to a *capo* in an Italian crime outfit. In other ways, it was grossly unfair.

I'd been the one to kill Giuseppe.

The memory of pulling the trigger lingered in my finger like scar tissue, heavy and misshapen under my skin.

I remembered the way my heartbeat had slowed, so contrary to the way I would have imagined it churning hot, panicked blood through my veins. It slowed and my vision stung, then went clear as if wiped with Windex. Nothing existed in my body, no thought save one, one golden impulse that overwrote everything else.

Di Carlo was threatening the two men who had been the centers of my universe for the last five years.

Killing him wasn't even a question.

Yet now, so many weeks after the fact, I found myself doubting my decision. If I hadn't killed di Carlo, what might have happened?

Would Dante be free?

"Don't do that." His rumbling voice cut through my thoughts, and when I looked up at him, it was to see an expression on his face I'd never seen before. He was angry with me. Some small part of me was appeased by his anger. I wanted to be punished for my actions, and previously, I'd had no one who wanted to castigate me for them. "Don't you dare think that way, Cosima Lombardi Davenport. You did what you had to do in order to get out of an impossible situation. You soiled your hands, your very fucking *soul*, to save me. If you self-flagellate yourself for that the rest of your life, what was the point of your sacrifice in the first place?"

My lips twisted to echo the wry grin I'd often seen on Xan's face when someone dared to reprimand him, and he couldn't argue their point. "While I see your point, it's only because I was going to say the same thing about you taking the fall for something you didn't do."

He shrugged cavalierly, in the way of all Davenport men. "You did it, *tesoro*. Not only did I put you in that position in the first place, but anything you've had to do or will ever have to do…I'd take your place. No questions asked, no regret felt afterward."

"Dante," I said again in that heavy voice, an entire encyclopedia of words and thoughts inside that one word. My fingers sweat against the glass and smeared over the murky plane as I pushed my hand harder over his. "How can you feel that way about me?"

"How can I not? Ask any man who knows you well—and isn't evil—if he would do the same for you, and honestly, Cosi, I doubt you would find a different response. Personally, though, my love for you is only a faded offshoot of my respect for you. I've never met a man or woman more willing to martyr themselves for their loved ones. A woman who has been through an almost endless onslaught of nightmarish events, yet still retains her warmth, her integrity, and a smile that could melt the heart of a psychopath. I envied you when I first learned about you from Tore, and then I hated you when I thought you were only ever going to be Xan's pawn, but as you always do, you proved me flagrantly wrong. I love you, and I'd die for you. I'd be in this place for you—*happily*—because there is no doubt in my mind that you would do the same for me."

"You make me sound too good to be true," I tried to sass through my broken voice. My chest was compressed with the force of tears, my nose plugged up to stop their flow. "I'm horribly flawed."

"Aren't we all?" Dante said with his trademark grin, his lips red as split cherries, his mouth so wide it punctured creases in each cheek like sharp dimples.

"I don't want you in here," I told him desperately, feeling my eyes drown in a hot flood of tears as despair filled me to the brim. "I don't want you here at all. I don't want any of this for you."

"We all make our beds, *tesoro*. I knew there was a likelihood I would end up in a place like this one day, and I thanked God I look good in orange."

"Don't joke," I snapped at him even as I smiled. "Only you would joke right now."

The amusement in his face bleached out, the ruddiness in his cheeks gone, his lips a single pale line. "Listen to me now, and really hear me. Of all the things that have happened in our lives, of all the awful outcomes that could have manifested from the greed and the hate at the core of those atrocities, my incarceration is almost pathetically mundane. I can survive this, *cara*. I can survive anything, and I think you know now, but this? This I can survive well."

He was right. Dante was a large man, a built man, so packed with muscle I could see the striations under the exposed olive skin of his forearms, bulging like rocks wrapped in orange canvas under his regulation jumper. He could kill a man with his bare hands, and he would if they tried to fuck with him in prison. He was also smart enough not to let it come to that.

Xan was not the only one Noel had taught to play chess.

"I know," I conceded, not sad but darkly proud of my beast behind the glass. "I know, but still, I won't have it. Not for long. Xan's secured the best fucking lawyers in the country, and Elena is on the team taking the case. I made her promise to do *anything* she must to get you free of this."

Dante raised an eyebrow, ignoring the clank and groan of the door opening and slamming shut behind him as another prisoner, this one with Nazi tattoos on his neck, entered the phone bay to make a call.

"Your Elena may be a smart woman, but I doubt she is a ruthless one. Getting me 'free of this' will take more than excellent legalese."

I thought of the way my sister had beaten up Christopher at Giselle's art gallery opening, of the times she had been shrewd

enough even as a child to hide the rest of us kids in our designated spots so that the local Camorra wouldn't find us and use us
against Seamus and Mama. I thought of the edge in her eyes like
a honed blade and her restless discontent despite her perfectly
ordered, socially respectable life. I thought of her instantaneous
agreement to join Dante's team of lawyers even though she
hated everything that spoke of my life without her. I thought of
the fissure in her habitually cold face as she'd held me while I
cried for the man I'd unwittingly sent to prison for me.

"She's a Lombardi woman," I told him solemnly. "I
wouldn't underestimate what she can do if you put her in a
corner."

"And why would she fight from this corner for a man she
does not know, let alone a man like me?"

I tipped my chin just as she would have with pride radiating through my voice. "Because I asked her to, and there is
nothing she wouldn't do for me."

Dante stilled at my words, impacted by the way they
echoed his own. He respected nothing as much as loyalty, and
Elena was the most loyal soul I knew.

She would go to bat for him. Hell, I truly believed she
would go beyond that to get him out of trouble because he
was a man I loved, and my sister loved me enough to never
want to see me without, not if she could help it.

Chapter Twenty-seven

COSIMA

*I*f my relationship with Alexander was like something from a dark Greek myth, Sinclair and Giselle's romance was like a fairy tale; and not one of the Grimm brothers' nightmarish fables. No, this was something even Disney couldn't produce.

It seemed the light filtering through the palm trees in trapezoids and sparkling off the calm, clear waters like fistfuls of glitter was actually *pink*, as if the very air was aware of the romance of the moment.

Sinclair, the cold Frenchman who had dated but not committed to my eldest sister Elena for years, had planned and executed not only a surprise proposal but the perfect elopement for my other sister, Giselle. It was so beautiful, the way she walked out of the waves in a wedding dress like froth over her curves, escorted by Sebastian who felt no shame in the tears that lined his eyes. It was so shocking to see Sinclair of the implacable expression and incredible calm watch her walk up to him to be his bride with a face as open and bright as a newly formed star pulled down from the sky.

We had missed so much, but there was no way in heaven or hell I would have missed Giselle and Sinclair's wedding. Alexander was in fine spirits after taking down the Order, even though his father was still free to rein over his realm of terror at Pearl Hall, so he actually capitulated to my demands. In fact, he went so far as to fly Mama, Sebastian, and Dante down to Cabo San Lucas with us on his private plane. Dante wasn't allowed out the country when he was on bail, but Alexander was rich enough to grease the right palms to make it so. Neither Alexander nor I were comfortable with him out of our sight since he'd been released the week before, and I knew Dante felt the same.

Elena, of course, didn't join us.

When I heard about Christopher's reappearance in their lives at Giselle's art show, I'd wanted to hop on a plane and take both my sisters in my arms just to feel for myself that they were safe from harm. It pained me to know that I wouldn't be seeing Elena at the wedding, which was exactly why I had pressured Xan into going back to New York to attend the newlywed's party at Osteria Lombardi.

Elena, I knew, would be there.

Something indefinable had happened when she interfered in Christopher's assault on Giselle, some transition between my sisters from arch-rivals to hospitable foes. It wasn't that they would ever be close. Like ink and oil, they belonged too much to different things, but it was the dénouement we had never thought they would achieve.

So Elena was there in the bustling restaurant that night along with everyone else my family loved; Dante, Cage Tracey, Willa Percy, Giselle's friends Brenna and Candy, Sinclair's business associates who had witnessed their affair in Mexico, and even some of my sister's friends from France had made the journey. It was an Italian party, so it was loud, filled with boisterous laughter that gleamed brightly under the strung fairy lights, and too much wine was poured and imbued.

We hadn't had a party like it since the restaurant opened two years before, when Sebastian and I had finally been able to hand our mother her dream in the form of brick and mortar.

I'd missed it, the camaraderie between us all, the way we orbited around each other, coming together and breaking apart in duos and trios of combinations every so often because we couldn't stand to be apart.

Not anymore. Not after so many years of fractured family life.

Even Salvatore was folded into the bosom of our family. Sebastian unwittingly charmed his father with tales from Hollywood, unaware that the older man laughed not only because they were funny, but because he was learning about his son's life from his own lips in a way he never believed he would. Mama lingered nearby, talking to Giselle and Sinclair, but her eyes were on her men, a small smile placed like a fading indentation in her doughy cheek.

"Theirs is a love story without an end," Dante said softly from behind me.

I turned in the circle of Alexander's arm, content to stay there while my husband spoke to Sinclair's business associate, Richard Denman, about a potential joint venture in London.

"Maybe one day," I hoped. "Maybe one day, they'll get their heads out of their asses."

Dante rewarded my coarseness with one of his loud, gravely laughs, his head thrown back so his black hair framed him like a dark crown. "What will I do without you when you are gone, *tesoro*?"

"You mean if *you* are gone," I corrected gently with a hand on his iron forearm. "We won't let that happen, though, D."

His grin was wry, and he looked so very much like Alexander in his rare moment of self-deprecation. "I wonder if it is a Davenport curse that we always believe we have the ability to control things. Sometimes, I'm afraid, *cara*, it is the things that control us."

"No, not anymore. We've come out on the other side of battle victorious and now to the victor go the spoils," I teased, knocking my wine glass against his rocks glass. "If we can take down the Order, we can certainly take down the New York City police force and district attorney's office."

Another twisted grin that ate up his full, too-red mouth. "And if that happens? If I am free, I'll still be here in the city, and where will my Cosi be? I doubt it will be here with me."

"No," I said again, this time with a genuine smile that branched off from the roots of homesickness dug deeply into my heart. "We'll go back to Pearl Hall."

"Noel is still there," he reminded me pointlessly, just because he wanted to change the topic from his own trials.

I shrugged. "Alexander thinks it will only be a matter of time now that the Order has fallen for the MI-5 to have enough on Noel to incarcerate him for good. Apparently, they've found records of transactions between a shell company potentially operated by Noel and di Carlo, so they could even pin my attempted murder on him."

"So, you really are going to leave?" Elena asked softly from behind me.

I reached back and found her hand unerringly to pull her to my side. Her familiar Chanel number 5 scent wafted over me, and the feel of her against me was so right that it felt like two puzzle pieces clicking together. I leaned my head against her shoulder, the ends of her curls soft as cotton beneath my cheek.

"I will, but I'll come back to visit often."

There was a silence between the three of us that said *not often enough. It won't be the same.*

It wouldn't. I wasn't naïve enough to doubt it. I had lived apart from my siblings for long enough to know how distance could erode a bond. I also knew that the secrets we had all harboured between us were almost at an end, that it would be easier to love across a thousand miles without those obstacles to hurdle over.

"You'll take care of each other for me, right?"

I watched as my question prompted Dante and Elena to lock eyes, flaring to life an electric almost nuclear frisson between them that made the hairs at the back of my neck stand on end.

"No promises," Elena broke the heavy silence to say, her chin at its haughty angle, her voice as English as a true American born.

"I don't think I like her enough to look out for her," Dante admitted, half-joking, half-somber as if even he couldn't tell where his true feelings about my abrasive sister fell.

I didn't blame him. The woman in my arms was more complicated than most by half, and her experiences had only hardened her further, made her incompatible with the ordinary people of the world.

It was a good thing, I thought as Dante's sidelong gaze roved over Elena's prim but oddly sexy black tuxedo-style dress that Dante was one of the least ordinary men I knew.

"You'll be fine," I surmised with more than a little smugness in my voice.

"I still think you should consider a long-distance marriage," Elena suggested. At my narrowed look, she gave an insolent shrug that could have rivaled one of Alexander's. "What? You did it before."

I laughed, but Alexander did not as he turned into the conversation with a heavy frown at my sister. He banded his arm around my hip and tugged me free from her so that I was wrapped around his side like a vine, exactly the way he preferred me.

"You'll be grateful that I will allow my wife to visit at all," he told her imperiously.

They locked eyes, one alpha to another, both so utterly indignant and so completely assured of their own superiority that I couldn't help the giggle that burst through my lips.

I hadn't giggled like that since I was a girl, since before Xan, and Seamus's downturn, since before puberty when beauty had sliced into me like a double-edged sword, both a blessing and a curse.

I giggled even harder. When I recovered, they were all staring at me with soft looks on their hard faces that proved just how much they loved me in ways so incredibly tender. It made their affection all the more precious for how elementally it went against their natures.

I leaned into Xan to press a kiss to the hinge of his jaw and excused myself to the ladies' room. It was hard not to laugh when, the moment I walked away, the three of them descended into bickering again.

As I passed Sinclair, his hand reached out to gently ensnare mine. Our eyes met, and I saw all the happiness I'd ever wanted for him shining from his eyes. It made my throat throb with tears.

"Happy?" he asked, simply.

"Almost as much as you," I told him, squeezing his hand back. "It seems you have a knack for saving Lombardi girls."

He didn't laugh with me. Instead, his electric eyes went dark as they looked at his new wife and then back at me. "No, Cosi, the Lombardi girls have a knack for saving lost men."

I swallowed his blessing like communion wine with closed eyes and a soft smile of thanks before I moved again through the jovial crowd. Something dark moved too low and quick through the edge of my vision, prompting me to look at the shadows in the hallway leading back to the bathrooms.

A boy stood there, his shoulders pressed to the wood, his hands in the pockets of his impeccably pressed trousers. He was oddly familiar even in the low light, the burnish of his flaxen hair, the way it pushed back from his forehead in a ridged crown of gold that contrasted deeply with the dark pits of his shadowed eyes. He couldn't have been more than fourteen, on the knife's edge of puberty, but not quite there, still slim in a way that looked gangly and round faced with baby fat that had yet to melt off.

It wasn't until I was almost upon him that I realized just exactly who he was.

Rodger Davenport.

Noel's third son, the one masterfully produced by Noel's secret union with Mrs. White and kept hidden from Alexander and Dante in case, one day, he was needed to usurp his older brothers.

The one and only son I had never and would ever trust with my life because he had proven the one time I had the displeasure of interacting with him, that he would be only too happy to end it.

Alexander and Dante, for all their faults and considerable darkness, were well-adjusted saints compared to the fevered evil that lurked in Rodger.

I saw that malicious intent as we locked eyes, and he grinned like a demon freed from Tartarus to wreak hell on earth. My heart palpitated brutally in my chest as if he'd reached through my ribcage to squeeze it in warning.

"What are you doing here?" I said. Even though I was too far away and the room was too loud for him to really hear me.

He read my lips, though; his thin, starched smile stretched tighter between his cheeks as he caught onto my fear.

"Come see," he taunted and then ducked down the hall.

A woman came out of the yawning mouth of the hall just as he moved into it, obscuring which way Rodger went. I decided to check the kitchen first and found it empty but for two cooks sweating and swearing under their breath as they hustled out with the last of the food to be served. I winked at Carla as she looked up at me, then ducked back out the door, hesitating in front of the men's room before I shoved through the door.

Rodger stood by the row of urinals, his hands in his suit pockets, one shiny loafer clad foot tapping a beat on the tiles as he whistled a sharp, staccato tune.

"Boring party," he noted with a one-sided smirk. "I bet you miss the Order's soirees, don't you, slave?"

I tipped my chin high. "We both know I do *not*. What are you doing here, Rodger? If Alexander and Dante see you, they won't hesitate, and I don't want to see a boy your age get hurt."

"He told me you were soft," Rodger said with a cluck of his tongue and a shake of his head that dislodged a piece of gold hair from his crown so that it swung into his dark eye. "He also told me he tried to teach you that softness would be the death of you."

"Noel didn't teach me anything but pain and regret," I retorted.

My heel was still pressed to the swinging door so that it was lodged open, the sounds from the party a soothing comfort at my back. I was facing off with the spawn of Satan, but my heroes were close at hand if anything went wrong. I wanted to see why Rodger would take the risk to come all this way just to taunt me.

He cocked his head to the side. "Those are valuable lessons, are they not?"

They were. The pain had unlocked the mysteries of my body's mechanisms, and the regret had taught me exactly what was important in my life.

But I'd had enough pain and enough regret without Noel force-feeding his own brand of misery to me the night of my wedding.

"Should we bring your older brothers in here and ask them if they agree?" I asked with a sharp smile to match his own.

Rodger was a creature of the dark. He respected boldness, cruelty, and manipulation the way a normal person might honour wisdom, courage, and empathy.

"Or maybe I could teach you something about pain?" I asked, running my hand up my thigh and pulling the fabric as I went so that the knife folded and tucked into my garter was revealed to him. "Just as you did that day with me in the dungeon."

He licked his lips, fast as a lizard and just as revolting. When he looked up from my exposed leg, he smiled his eerie, boyish grin. "That was a fun day, wasn't it? I can't wait to have more of those."

"You won't. Ever."

"Oh!" he said with a little chuckle, rocking back on his heels. "I thought you understood. Silly of me, my father told me you were stupid."

"As stupid as your father? After all, he is the one under house arrest for fraud, embezzlement, and money laundering."

Rodger's affable mask cracked and then fell off his face entirely, revealing a curled sneer that showcased his vivid pink gums and bent British teeth. "Do not speak of your betters in that manner, slave, or I will be forced to punish you before I get you home to father."

"I'm not going anywhere with you," I told him firmly. "I'm going to poke my head out this door and call for Alexander. Then he and Dante can decide what to do with you. They aren't as 'soft' as me, so I hope for your sake that they're feeling lenient. Though every time they see my back, cut up with scars you and your father put there, their eyes go black with rage, so I wouldn't bet money on it."

"No need," he said, jolly once more, bouncing on his toes as if he couldn't wait to let me in on a wonderful secret. "You're going to come with me because you *want* to."

I snorted, the Neapolitan coming out in me as indignant rage burned clean through my cultivated class. "In your fucking dreams, kid."

"I am no *kid*. You will refer to me as Lord Davenport." He ignored my scoff and stepped forward with over-bright eyes as glazed and madly rolling as marbles set loose. "And you will willingly come with me because if you don't, I'm going to blow up everyone you love right here in this slum."

My neck pained sharply as fear hooked into my spine and pulled me taut. "What?"

"It's pathetic really, how easy it is to buy items for an explosive. Ashcroft was so mad, you see, that Alexander took away his dick and bullocks, that he was happy to give us a nice and easy recipe for a homemade bomb."

I squeezed my eyes shut against the truth I saw in his face, the eagerness in his expression that told me he wasn't bluffing. I knew Ashcroft was recovering from his injuries, learning to be both a eunuch and a cripple in an expensive recovery home upstate, but I hadn't thought he would join forces with Noel to get back at us. At least, not like this.

I was sure it occurred to Alexander and Dante, and that they were keeping an eye, but with everything going on with the elopement and Dante's arrest, they hadn't been as vigilant. We had won the battle, but it seemed we forgot that we had yet to win the war.

"Where is it?" I asked him, desperately trying to figure a way out of the situation.

"The kitchen, of course. The explosive isn't very strong, so I'm counting on the gas in the room to really set it off with a proper *bang*." He smiled so wide, I thought he could swallow me whole with his big mouth. It felt like staring down a barracuda while I was prone in the water. "If I don't leave here with you in the next ten minutes, the Order acolyte we paid is going to slink into the kitchen and *set it off*."

He watched me as a bomb went off at the center of my gut, as my internal organs spasmed and collapsed, as my heart erupted in a bloody mess of deceased hopes and dreams. He watched, and he cupped himself through his flannel trousers as my pain made him hard.

"No time to say goodbye, I'm afraid, not if you don't want to say goodbye for good," he said, *soto voce*.

There was a crinkling, static sort of sound rushing through my ears as if someone was unwrapping a candy beside each ear, and it took me a long moment to realize it was the sound of my panicked heart frantically churning blood through my veins. I wished I was smarter, quicker, just *readier* to deal with a situation like this.

I had to go.

I wasn't going to put my loved ones in jeopardy and all of them, every single last one of them really, was in Osteria Lombardi that night. If I facilitated, if I called out for help, what would happen to them?

Surely, Rodger wouldn't let himself get blown to smithereens.

"No," he said, answering the questions that played out over my face. "We're close enough to the back door that I can make it in time."

Cazzo!

I couldn't bear the idea of everyone dying because of my willfulness, not when I didn't have any other plan up my sleeve to save them. My mind wheeled through options, calling the police somehow, flagging down someone after I left with Rodger, leaving a clue as to was going on so that they could at least find me quickly…but there was nothing. Not really.

"Five minutes left, but we are pushing it, don't you think, slave?" Rodger asked with wide, guileless eyes.

He was a good actor, as good as his pernicious father. If I called for help walking down the street with him, who would believe this teenage, beautifully dressed adolescent would be a threat to me?

"You're coming," he told me because he saw the way my shoulders slumped, he saw the way my heart flickered and went out like a flame in my eyes.

"I'm coming."

He nodded and then walked on his bouncing toes to my side where he offered me his arm the way a gentleman would at a ball. His gentlemanly gesture was so flagrantly contradictory to our circumstances that it made me simultaneously want to laugh and cry.

I didn't take it.

Instead, I shoved out the door and went down the hall out the back door into the stagnant, cold air of the alleyway without looking back at the crowd of partygoers. I didn't know what I would be moved to do if I saw them again and so, I denied myself even that last look.

Alexander and Dante would find me, as long as I got out of there to keep them safe.

I had no doubt of their resolve and ability to save me.

They had done it before, and they would do it again as long as life demanded that from them.

From us.

There was a nondescript black car idling outside, exhaust curling through the air and wrapping around me, the toxic fumes as sickening as the feel of Rodger's hand pushing me to the car and then into its dark interior. He grinned at me before shutting the door, a grin so young and excitable it made me cold from the inside out.

He was pure evil, and he was only fourteen. Only a boy.

It seemed where Noel had failed to make Alexander and Dante into men without souls, he had succeeded with Rodger.

It was as repulsive a realization as it was incredibly sad.

Rodger had never had the innocence that came with childhood because Noel had taught him from birth that the world was a terrible place, and if he wanted thrive, he had to be the most terrible thing in it in order to succeed.

I stared out the window at the brick back wall of Osteria Lombardi as my ears rang and my eyes smarted with tears. It was hard to believe that after everything we had been through and fought for, I was finally going back to Pearl Hall.

Not as its mistress as I had dreamed of for years.

But once more, as a slave.

I turned to look at Rodger to find him staring at me, his good humour sloughed off like a snake's dead skin.

"Was it worth it? Knowing you will die at home with us so your loved ones can live on without you?" He asked the question without inflection or any true emotional curiosity. He asked it because he didn't understand the concept. He had manipulated me, not knowing why I would ever fall for his mechanism because he himself had no heart, no loved ones he would ever have to sacrifice if called upon to do so.

"Yes," I said, and it was the truest word I'd ever spoken.

"Too bad," Rodger said and then with a flash of his little boy grin, he swiped open the screen of his phone and sent off a prepared text message.

I could see what it said from where I sat.

Do it.

My mouth was open like the wound I felt yawning through my chest as I looked up at him to confirm, "Rodger, what are you—?"

My words cut off when I heard the startled shouts begin inside the restaurant, and I forgot what I had been about to say when there was a loud hiss and then a strange hollow *pop* followed by the boom and shatter of breaking glass and crumbling mortar.

My body twisted to keep my eyes on the building as the car moved forward down the alley. I watched as fire blew out through the back door and licked its red tongue toward the sky, incinerating the garbage bagged on either side of the entry.

If anyone was inside that inferno, they would not survive.

There was a loud sucking, wet gurgle and heave of air inside the car as we turned left out of the alley, and the flaming building disappeared. I didn't know what it was until I tried to speak and realized my mouth was flapping open like a luffing sail caught in the wind, my chest ravaged with sobs so deep the keel of them dug into my gut and ached fiercely.

"Why?" I managed through the tears destroying my body like a fucking tempest.

I tried not to think of all my loved ones fried by the fire, tried not to remember my school trip to *Pompeii* where loved ones lay overlapped in futile attempts at protection, calcified by soot and black rock. I tried not to think of Sebastian and Mama, of my Giselle and my Elena, of Dante and most of all, of Alexander.

I tried to focus on the wealth of rage in my chest instead as I stared at Rodger and forced him to answer with the sheer weight of my gaze.

He licked his lips and shrugged his aristocratic shrug before leaning back in his chair to settle in for the ride. "Because," he said on a yawn. "Because it was fun."

And when he leaned over to sink the tip of a fine needle into my wrist, I let him because the only cure for the kind of heartbreak ripping me apart was the blessed relief of medically induced oblivion.

Part Five

DEATH

Chapter Twenty-eight

COSIMA

My brain was too heavy and hot in the confines of my skull. It throbbed like a metronome set to ticking between my ears, setting off a series of raw nerves throughout my body so that I pulsed with pain all over.

I squeezed my eyes shut tighter, not against the pain but the *déjà vu*.

My mouth was cotton coated as I opened it in an attempt to gulp in more of the cold, damp air of wherever the hell I'd woken up in. The ground was a frozen, unforgiving bite beneath my hip and leaden legs, but as I traced my quaking fingers along the grooves in the tile, I recognized it for what it was.

The black and white checkered tiles shot through with gold that composed the floor of Pearl Hall's ballroom.

My stomach tossed violently up my throat, and before I could stem the flow, I was leaning over painfully to throw up whatever poison was left in my system. The acrid scent filled my nose and made my stomach convulse until every ounce of liquid was wrung from my body.

I fell to the floor beside the mess, quaking and sweating as I curled in on my hollow core.

There was no doubt in my mind that Noel had dragged me back to this place to remake the hell of my initiation into the games of the Order. I knew cameras were placed throughout the ballroom, trained on me twenty-four hours of the day, watching me for any weakness they could possibly exploit.

They.

It seemed the spare had taken over as Noel's heir and was being probably groomed to take his place as Satan's living incarnate.

As if conjured by my thoughts like the devil himself, the door opened with an insidious hiss over the polished marble floors and the clack of expensive shoes echoed throughout the cavernous hall.

I didn't raise my head when the two pairs of shoes came to a standstill just inside my view. They were polished black leather loafers, the same style, but one pair smaller than the other.

Twin horrors.

Before I could even blink, one shoe lifted backward and then slammed into my stomach.

Pain erupted like an overripe fruit bursting in my middle, and I choked on my scream as I curled further into myself.

"She's not so pretty anymore, is she, Father?" Rodger asked as he lifted his foot again and aimed it at my chest.

"Settle, boy, we don't want her to lose consciousness before she understands just what is happening here, do we?"

"No, Father," he agreed with quiet, sinister delight.

He couldn't wait for what was to come.

He was only a boy, barely on the cusp of manhood, yet the joy that should have been reserved for Christmas or his first co-ed dance was displaced. I had no doubt he would take more pleasure in whipping me than he ever would from what Santa might bring.

It hurt my heart to realize that you were never too young to be a bad human.

Noel stepped forward into a crouch the very same way Alexander had the first time he'd visited me in the ballroom nearly five years ago. I watched him pinch his slacks to accommodate the muscles in his thighs, the way he flicked a piece of lint off the flannel and onto my leg. He had a broad, handsome face with a strong square jaw and thick hair he'd given to all three of his sons.

His was not a face of evil. He was handsome, charm etched into the lines beside his eyes that hinted at a life filled with smiles.

It was all such an elaborate lie.

I knew he must have studied the tapes of my time being broken in the ballroom, and this re-enactment was all part of his master plan.

And at every stage of that plan, he'd intended to administer the maximum amount of pain on Alexander and on me.

I collected the thick, metallic bile on my tongue and raised my head enough to look him squarely in the eye while I spat into his face.

The wet clot landed on his cheek and slid slowly to the crease of his mouth. I watched with acid in my gut as he merely parted his lips and licked the sludge away with his tongue.

A second later, he had lunged forward, his hands locked in my hair and twisted at such painful angles, I cried out help-lessly in pain.

"Disrespect me again and I'll let Rodger skin you alive and then nurse you back to health only to do it all. Over. Again."

I didn't say anything, and I didn't look away, but he read my capitulation at the backs of my eyes.

"Now, I want to welcome you to your new home. At the moment, it consists of these four walls. This ballroom is all you will know until you earn the right to more." A wide, toothy smile crossed his face as he recited the same lines Alexander had. His hands wrenched harder in my hair like a sticky light switch flipping on my stream of tears. He licked one and then bit into my cheek before pulling back to finish his speech. "You know, Ruthie, how to earn the right for more because this is a game you've played before. Only this time, *I* will break you, and in the end, the only thing you will know is the sound of the word *Master* on your lips as you beg me to let you tend to my needs."

"You can keep me chained in here until the day I die, and I will *never* call you by that epitaph," I vowed.

"Well then," he said with a vague smile as his hands slid out of my hair and he patted my cheek, once more the docile older gentleman. "Maybe the day you die is closer at hand than you thought."

Noel straightened and turned on his heel to walk back across the expanse of the room. Rodger stayed, his foot tapping out an erratic rhythm as he looked lustily down at me. Then he too crouched in the manner of his brother and father, so close I could smell the sweet cotton candy scent of his breath on my face. It was a deeply disturbing reminder of his youth contrasted to the ancient evil that had been passed down from his Davenport ancestors and transplanted in his eyes.

"If you fail," he told me eagerly, his big eyes grey and unfeeling as concrete burying me alive. "He said I get to kill you myself and bury you in the maze with the others."

He stood quickly, made to run after his father, and then quickly delivered a hard, swift kick to my exposed face that caught me right in the mouth. My lip split open like an over-ripe fruit, weeping so much blood I thought for a moment he had dislodged my tooth. I didn't cry out with the pain, but my body contracted tighter as if taking up less space might minimize the hurt.

Rodger laughed as he looked down at me. I tried to evade his foot as it went for my face again, but I was caught up in the chains and dazed from the first blow. He planted his loafer on my face and ground it into my wet, broken mouth with another little chuckle of glee before he finally turned away.

I licked at the blood as it trickled out of my mouth onto the black marble tile and watched as his bloody foot *squick*ed against the floor on his way out the door.

With a groan to release the tension of pain in my body, I rolled to my back and stared up at the mural of Hades bursting through the crust of the earth in his black chariot led by undead horses to spirit away the beautiful spring goddess Persephone.

I tried to breathe through the pain in my gut and jaw as I sought solace in my favourite myth. Many scholars believed that Hades had abducted Persephone against her will and that of her mother, and that, if any deals had indeed been struck, it was between Hades and Persephone's estranged father, Zeus.

Why wouldn't Zeus believe Hades was an excellent choice of husband? He was the ruler of one of the three kingdoms, the eldest child of Rhea and Cronus, and a war hero.

How was he to know what happened in the shadowy

moors of the Underworld, where demons roamed and the undead toiled away their eternities?

No matter how the abduction happened, I chose to believe the unpopular view that Persephone had been stolen away against her will, but it was she who had decided to eat the pomegranate seeds to ensure she would have to return to the Underworld for six months of the year. After years of manipulation, she had taken her own destiny into her hands and decided to have the best of both worlds in order to satisfy the duality in her soul.

Of course, the whole thing was a creation myth to explain away the seasons, but it was also an allegory for my life in a way I never would have thought it could be.

Salvatore had manipulated me into being sold into slavery.

Alexander had wrenched me from my world as I knew it into the dark domain he'd been forced to reign in since birth.

Yet I didn't blame either of them for their actions.

They were only trying to survive the lot life had given them.

And in the end, their actions had led me to a wealth of opportunities I might not otherwise have known.

I found the love of a good father, one with the defective morals of a Made Man, but with a wealth of loyalty and love for his family.

I'd discovered how utterly devastating true love could be, how it razed your soul to the ground and from the ashes, you were reborn as a new version of yourself, one with a heart made up from pieces of someone else.

Mostly, I'd learned to be the kind of woman I could be proud of; totally resilient, completely unafraid in the face of her enemies, and wholly willing to offer her heart despite the scars accumulated on it.

Tears pooled at the corners of my eyes, blurring my view of the vibrant ceiling painting. I closed my eyes as the wet raced down my cheeks. I didn't need to look at the mural to see it in my mind. It had brought me peace the first time I'd been prisoner here, and it brought me a measure of consolation now.

A sob bubbled up my throat, wet and full of muck.

I released it into the air and curled onto my side in the fetal position as I finally allowed myself to release the truth.

The explosion that had rocked Osteria Lombardi had most definitely killed some of my loved ones. There was no way everyone could have survived unscathed.

I thought of Sebastian and Mama, of Giselle and Sinclair newly married and so in love, of Elena so bitter and so in need of a new start.

They couldn't be dead.

Not my family.

Not Dante with his roguish grin and tender smile crafted just for me.

Not Salvatore so soon after I'd found him and began to love him.

It couldn't be possible, yet I knew in my bones it was.

I could contemplate the death of my family, though each thought scored through me like acid poured over a knife wound, but I could not bring myself to acknowledge the last possibility.

The one that proclaimed Alexander Davenport as dead.

It just *couldn't* be possible.

How did someone kill a man like him?

He was taller and stronger than anyone else, padded with dense muscle like a suit of armor worn beneath his skin. A bomb couldn't take that down.

Could it?

But he was smarter than everyone else too. His predatory talents would have clued him in to the wrongness in the air; the feel of the room suddenly without me and the faint, ominous pressure in the atmosphere like the sky before a storm. He would have gone searching for me, maybe even roping Sebastian or Dante into it. They could have all been outside when the bomb went off.

It was possible.

I realized too late that I was hyperventilating. The air seized in my lungs and turned too quickly to carbon dioxide. I couldn't get enough oxygen, and then I couldn't remember how to move my chest to get air into the chambers.

My vision swam as I looked blindly up at Hades, silently, insanely pleading with him to burst through the floor of the ballroom and save me from this hell so he could drag me to his own.

It was my last thought before my body gave up, and I passed out.

Chapter Twenty-nine

COSIMA

Time passed. I knew it only by the faint intrinsic sense my body had of the sun rising and falling outside the closed brocade drapes over the windows in the ballroom. They fed me at odd hours and visited at random intervals to ask for my submission, sometimes days apart and other times repeated every hour on the hour.

Noel didn't just starve me, keeping me alive—barely—on stale bread, moulding cheese, and tepid water. He employed tactics as if we were playing war games.

Bright spotlights were set up in a circle around the diameter of my chain length, and they pulsed with blinding light on timers so that I was only ever guaranteed a handful of hours asleep.

The room was glacial cold. It was late spring in Britain, and it shouldn't have been so arctic across the peaks and valley of the district, but somehow, the ballroom became a refrigerator, and I the bone-chilled meat.

I was beyond misery, but I didn't break because Noel didn't understand one basic principle.

If my family was dead—as by then I had convinced myself they were, especially because no one had come to break me free—I had nothing left to live for.

I knew that Noel's patience would run out and Rodger's excitement would kick in. That my days were numbered as long as I continued my quiet, painful rebellion.

But I wasn't willing to sacrifice my pride and my poise by consenting to be the slave of the most sadistic man in England.

I refused to desecrate the plethora of golden memories I had of Alexander as my Master by calling any other man, let alone the man who *took him from me*, the same title.

It was blasphemy.

Sacrilegious.

I didn't care if that meant my religion was chains and whips, Dominance and submission, consent and rebellion.

I had prayed too long at Alexander's altar to be ashamed now.

It was those memories of him that buoyed me in the dark, turbulent hours of solitary confinement in that frozen cage.

When Rodger grew tired of my apathy and his adolescent fists landed adult blows on my prone body, I thought of Alexander gently washing my hair, running the strands like ink through his fingers.

When Noel tried to degrade me by taking away my toilet bucket and then again when he spent his seed on my face while Rodger held me down to remind me that I was already his, I thought of all the ways Alexander had made me *his* from the inside out. How he had stamped my ass with his brand, my mind with his language of power, and my heart with the duality of his actions and intent.

I reminded myself, chanting for hours every day that I was *his, his, his*.

Not theirs.

Maybe not even my own.

Being his provided me with a mental shield I was desperate to hide behind. I couldn't be responsible for my actions because Alexander was, and if he couldn't be there, then mentally, neither was I.

I knew the moment the double doors banged open one day that Noel's patience was at an end. The air gathered around him, sucked to the magnetic force of his fury as he prowled across the marble to my side where I lay curled on the ground with my chains looped over my arms for something to cuddle in cold comfort.

I peered up into the shadows of his face, his frame entirely backlit by the oppressive light of the spotlights encircling us. He'd never looked more sinister or more apt.

"You will get up," he promised darkly.

My mouth was too dry to part with words, so I answered with my stillness and my silence.

"You will get up, Ruthie, because I know your hamartia is your good little heart. You can't stand to see people suffer, can you?"

My throat clenched and rubbed like sandpaper as I swallowed hard.

"No, you can't," he agreed with arrogant satisfaction. "So, you will get up because if you don't..." His sly, smug contempt plumed in the air between us as thick as cigar smoke. "I'll kill the servants one by one."

My eyes widened before I could school my expression.

He couldn't be serious.

Only I knew well enough by then to understand the extent Noel would go to in order to get his way. He was a psychopath who had murdered countless women in cold blood, including his wife and the mother of his children.

Of course, he would kill the servants. They were nothing more to him than automated responses to his basic needs.

He would probably take pleasure in killing them.

The urge to cry waterlogged my heart and set my pulse to a heavy, drowning beat.

I refused to give in to the impulse.

If I was going to capitulate, I'd do it strong until the end.

Alexander had taught me that.

My body ached as I maneuvered myself onto my feet, legs wobbling as they attempted to hold my weight for the first time in days. Noel reached out to slap at my breast so hard, I hissed.

"Your skin is blue. Bathe and dress in the clothes I've left with you, then go below stairs to help the servants prepare dinner. I want you serving me everything with your bare hands," he instructed with dark amusement before lifting one of my hands and sucking a finger into his mouth. "I want each course seasoned with the taste of your flesh."

"You disgust me," I told him.

I was on the floor the next instant, my cheek blasted with pain so bright it rendered me momentarily blind. Before I could recover, Noel's hand was on my chin in a punishing grip I knew would leave a bruise as dark as blackberry juice.

"Talk back to me again, Ruthie," he warned almost idly, a direct contrast to his words and his grasp. "And I'll make sure no one ever calls you beautiful again. Understood?"

I nodded, rebellion so hot on my tongue it burned.

Impossibly, his hold on my face cinched tighter. "Answer properly."

"Yes, sir," I said with the utmost respect so that he

wouldn't hit me again for saying *sir* when he would have liked *Master*.

He made a short noise of approval in his throat and then released me with a light push so that I went falling back onto the floor. "Go to your old room. Mrs. White is waiting for you there."

My throat seized up as I thought about the woman who had taken part in every single step of my torture at the hands of Noel. Anger doused my brittle body, and I went up in flames.

By the time I made my slow, painful way down the corridor to my old room, my skin was burning with the fire in my blood.

Mrs. White was waiting in the same black dress and white apron she had always worn, her curls tucked up in a habitual bun. She was older, but her face retained a girlish plumpness that made her seem younger than she was.

Why was it the worst people I knew wore the most beautiful masks?

It made it nearly impossible to see past my instinctual love of their beauty to the demons lurking beneath.

"Good afternoon, dearie," she greeted me with a genuine if tremulous smile. "It's so good to see you alive and well again."

"Well?" I asked, the air hissing from my body like steam from an overworked engine. "You think this is *well?*"

She bit her lip and tittered nervously. "No, perhaps not *well*, but alive then. I wasn't so sure after what happened in New York."

"As if you didn't know what he had planned," I accused as I stalked toward her. She took one step back for every two I progressed until she was backed against the windows, and I was pressed deeply into her soft body. "You knew back then what would become of me, and when that didn't work out, you still tried to see me killed."

She swallowed thickly, her breath hot and smelling of peaches against my face. Irrationally, the fact that she had recently indulged in sweet ripe fruit made me even angrier.

I hadn't tasted something fresh for *days*, and this horrible bitch was gorging herself on fruit in Alexander's fucking kitchen.

My hand snapped up before I even realized it and wrapped finger by finger around Mrs. White's fleshy, pale throat. She choked against my hold, her spit flying in my face. I rubbed it off with one hand and then sneered nearly against her lips, "I don't care if you didn't have a choice. I don't care if you were only trying to survive. You took me under your wing while I was enslaved here, you made me think I could trust you, and then you took advantage of that. Maybe I could forgive you for that, but I can never forgive you for taking me away from Xan. I can never forgive you or your son for k-killing him and my family."

Mrs. White sputtered, her face ripening like a tomato on the vine from sickly green to pink then vermillion red.

Still, I squeezed.

It wouldn't be the first time I'd killed someone, though it would probably be my last.

I knew I didn't have much longer to live, and if it was the last thing I did, I would be happy I'd ended Mary White's life myself.

The door behind me banged opened just before I was ripped away from her by an arm belted across my chest and shoulders. I could tell by his scent, musky and contrived, that Noel was the one dragging me away from his old slave. He pushed me into the chair before a vanity and then back-handed me so hard on my already sore right cheek that I felt the skin split over my cheekbone.

Then he was in my face, caging me in with his arms braced on the chair, looming over me like a vengeful God. "I gave you liberty, and I have no compunction taking it away again. If you can't behave, I will *make you*." He looked over my shoulder at the door where I could see Rodger in my periphery, bouncing on his toes as he watched his father take out his anger on me. "Son, fetch me my toolkit."

It turned out that Noel's version of a toolkit was like something out of Dr. Frankenstein. He had hammers, nails, and a nail gun, whips, floggers, and chains, raw ginger and cayenne pepper, clamps with teeth and weights with hooks to attach to genital piercings. First, he buckled a red ball gag around my head, securing it between my teeth so that I sat before the mirror looking like a suckling pig roast ready for devouring.

Then he opened that vicious kit and began to apply his tools to my body in punishment for attacking Mrs. White.

My arms were bound from shoulder to wrist with rough rope to the chair back and my legs from groin to ankle against the chair legs. There was ginger paste painted onto the delicate skin of my clit, igniting it with itching, burning discomfort even before he clamped it with hard metal teeth. Then Noel taught Rodger how to use adjustable c-clamps to pinch my nipples between the metal bracket and the screw head.

The worst part of the entire ordeal was being forced to watch them truss me up like a doll in the beautiful gilt mirror I'd once loved in a room that Alexander had helped make into a home.

Tears streaked down my face even after they finished, photographed me, and left with a warning to let Mrs. White ready me for dinner or else...

Her hands shook as she painted my pried open lips blood red and dried my tears as well as she could to apply bronze and blush. Sometimes, her breath hiccoughed as her eyes strayed to my bruising nipples or pained sex, but she continued diligently to pretty my face for our shared dictator.

"I know you don't want to hear it," she said finally in a voice so quiet, I had to strain to hear her even in the silent room, "but I want, no, *need* to explain myself to you...When

Noel took me as his slave, I was elated and horrified. My father was one of the last unsuccessful tenants farming Davenport land, and he owed Noel a great debt. Much like you, I was given as payment. I lived close enough to know the village gossip, so I knew what Noel did with his slaves. He went through so many, you see, and even though outsiders weren't allowed into the Hall, delivery boys could sometimes hear the wails and then some of the servants, well, they nattered when they shouldn't have. I wasn't the prettiest lass, and I wasn't very charming or classy the way I figured a *lord* would want, but I was clever."

She chuckled sadly to herself as she finished my makeup and picked up the brush to run through my hair. Her eyes locked on mine in the mirror, and even though I wanted to look away, I became mesmerised in the distressed denim of her gaze.

"I was clever enough to know I had to give more than just my body and submission to Noel if I wanted to survive him. Remember I told you before the night of the ball in London? Beauty fades, darling girl, and I needed something that would *last*. I almost wish now that I hadn't endured. Twenty years is a long time to be beaten by a man with endless creativity…but I made the choices I made to survive, and then when I had a son, so that he would too."

I glared at her, writing my own monologue in gold ink so that she might read it in my eyes.

She stared right back, her lips twisted with a conflicting mixture of pride and doubt, before she hesitantly unbuckled the gag and gently removed it from my stretched mouth.

I worked my jaw to relieve the ache before I said, "You're right, I don't care. You sacrificed a woman you should have empathised with. There were other ways to win the game, other moves you could have made."

She bit her lip and then opened her palms to the air in

benediction. "It was the most direct way I could find to checkmate."

"Well," I told her ominously because her fishing expedition for pity had not hooked me through the mouth or reeled me in. If anything, it made me hate her all the more. "The game isn't over yet."

I watched as she read the acrimony carved into my features, and then as her own face curdled like bad cream.

"Fine," she whispered. "If you want another enemy while you're here, I'll be one. But you should know, the choice was yours."

"I have never made my own choices under this roof, and I won't be allowed to now," I countered.

She pressed her lips together in a flatline as she realized just how dead in the water her efforts to sway me to her dark side were, and then with narrowed eyes, she put the ball gag back around my head.

Chapter Thirty

COSIMA

I found the kitchen the same way I'd left from the beautifully refurbished wood paneled walls to the old AGA cooker and every single kitchen servant I'd known before. Straight down to Douglas O'Shea.

The knife wound of his betrayal radiated through my back.

It might have been slightly ridiculous to think Douglas would abandon his position as head cook at Pearl Hall after I'd gone, but it wasn't a stretch to think he would have resigned after Alexander openly renounced his father.

Yet there he stood at the long worn wooden table at the

center of the room with a red apple in his hand, the peel curling over his many-freckled hand like the body of a snake. The sight of his brightly glinting copper hair, red as the tip of a flame, and the ruddy collection of freckles splashed across his pale skin made my heart ache with nostalgia.

"Ducky," he breathed, the sound of it like air leaking from a punctured lung.

He looked ruined by the sight of me. Tears pooled in his eyes, and his usually steady hands trembled as he put the apple down to brace himself against the tabletop.

"Out! The lot of you," he ordered shakily.

I realized the entire kitchen crew had paused in their efforts to stare at me. The young servant I remembered was named Jeffery scuttled toward me on his way out the door and astonished me by tugging gently on my hand in a small sign of solidarity.

The gesture brought the tears haunting my throat out onto my tongue.

When I looked back at Douglas, he was blatantly crying.

"I'm in bloody shambles. I so wanted this to go a certain way," he started between sniffles. "I wanted to be strong for you because I know how cocked-up this whole thing is, but ducky, the sight of you like that…" He waved a hand at my collared, shackled, and white corseted body. "It's gutted me."

"You and me both."

He flinched at my cold tone, and then his eyes widened as he dashed around the table only to crash into the invisible wall of my rancor a foot before he reached me.

His hands fluttered like birds without a perch as he tried to explain, "I almost stormed out the second that tosser told me you'd up and left us. There was no way my sweet ducky would just run away without saying goodbye unless he'd done something to deserve it. Had my bags packed and everything when the great lord of the manor himself graced my doorway and explained a few things to me."

He took a risk and clasped my hands in his, the chains between my shackles clicking like the tongue of a scolding Italian mother. I let him, not because I felt any less betrayed, but because after so long in the dark and lonely cold, I craved tender physical affection.

"It was Lord Thornton who asked me to stay on at Pearl Hall," he whispered frantically as voices sounded in the hall. "You see, marra, I'm a proper spy now. Alexander's eyes and ears in his enemy's home."

Relief sluiced over me like the cleansing rain of a spring shower. My knees trembled under the weight of his truth, and I was crying before I could stop myself, flinging my arms around Douglas in an inescapable hug.

He held me, and together, we cried for a good long moment.

"Have…have you heard from him since I've been here?" I choked out through my tears.

I knew before he stiffened in my arms what his answer would be. "No, love, I'm sorry. I heard about the explosion, and well, his grace seems to think both his eldest sons are dead."

Anguish roar up my throat and spilled forth like water breaking through a dam. I clutched Douglas to me so tightly, I could feel the shape of his bones beneath his skin.

When I finally had control of myself, I stepped back, but only enough to look into his dear face, and say, "Thank you."

His face juddered as he swallowed a sob, then smoothed into a tender smile as he collected one of my tears with his thumb. "You look cream-crackered. Sit down and help me with this pie while we plot your escape."

Over the sweet scent of apples, Douglas explained how he had been using Alexander's hawk Astor to send handwritten missives about Noel's goings-on to a man Alexander paid and trusted in Manchester. Sometimes, Douglas would receive notes in reply, but mostly it was an endless stream of information about the Duke of Greythorn's whereabouts, who visited at Pearl Hall, and anything to do with the Order.

"I have to say I was chuffed as a mother when I heard you'd done it," he said with a cheeky grin when we spoke about the dissolution of the Order of Dionysus. "Thought the man was mad for taking them on, but then, what better reason than you to do it?"

The other kitchen staff returned after that, so Douglas and I were forced to keep our chatter superfluous, but as we put the finishing touches on dinner, he pulled me close under the guise of needing my help with the after-dinner tea service preparations.

"You know, of course, that your favourite flower is used to create the infamous opium," he said softly, conversationally.

The hairs on the back of my neck stood on end, but I gave no outward sign of discomposure as I hummed my response.

"Well, it's a little-known fact that the seeds of the poppy…" He pulled a basket of the blooms off one of the windowsills and showed me the small bowl full of seeds he had harvested. "Can be used to make a tea that mimics the effects of morphine. They call it a 'twilight slumber.'"

I chewed my lip as I watched him crush some of the seeds and then mix them with some herbs before putting the mixture in a sieve on the mouth of a teapot.

"So, your master plan is to put Noel to sleep at the table?" I asked.

He shot me a look. "No, ducky, my plan is to make him a wee bit more pliable. They've used morphine in studies for truth serums, and it's been found to loosen the tongue. Not to mention, it'll make him a little loopy and out of his senses. Hopefully, it'll make whatever he has planned post-supper a tad more tolerable."

I laid my hand over his on the pot and gave it a squeeze. "Thank you, Douglas."

"Anything for you. Now, I won't tell you to break a leg

because I'm afraid Noel will actually do that, but I shall wish you the best of luck, love." He pressed a kiss to my cheek.

His affection and loyalty shone through my dreary future like a crack of light in the dark. As I followed the butlers up the stairs with the platters of food, I tried to keep my sight focused on that sliver of hope and not on the sucking black abyss of dread that threatened to overtake me.

Alexander and I had rediscovered each other, committed to our relationship for the first time, and taken down an entire corrupt secret society.

I refused to believe this was the end of our story.

The hero dead before the happily ever after, and the heroine murdered by the villain.

I had to believe everything I'd learned over the course of my ordeals had led me to this moment, a moment when I would outwit the smartest, cruelest man I'd ever known and— I looked down at the tea tray I held filled with poppy seed tea—give him a taste of his own poison.

Chapter Thirty-one

COSIMA

The dining hall was darker than ever before, limned only in the weak golden glow cast from dozens of gleaming candelabras set throughout the room. The effect made the entire gilt room feel like the inside of a tarnished treasure chest filled with priceless trinkets and diamonds accumulated over the centuries of Davenport canon. The way Noel looked at me as I entered the long, narrow hall made me feel like the most expensive treasure of them all.

There was glory in his eyes and a smug tension to the set of his shoulders beneath his customary bespoke suit that conveyed his wicked excitement.

He was eager to play the final moves in this game of his. I was the last piece remaining on the board, a pawn who had somehow returned as a queen. He would take such deviant delight in cutting me down, and I knew the feeling surpassed his annoyance at my resiliency.

Rodger wasn't present, and his absence concerned me. Like a mother with her child, I felt more at ease having him within sight because who knew what he would get up to without supervision.

"Ruth," Noel called out just to hear his voice echo through the high hall. "Come to your Master and present yourself."

Each step was leaden with dread, but I made it to his side without vomiting. He was so insidiously clever, Noel was, to recreate every scene of my capitulation to Xan. It confused and sickened me enough to have my body and mind swaying nauseatingly off-balance as a neophyte on a ship.

"She looks like a queen, but she is a pawn," Noel murmured happily as he looked down at me by his side, knees bent, head bowed, hands pressed together as if in prayer to him. "Now, feed me."

So, I did.

I tried to empty my mind of thought, to focus on the sound of my breath flowing in and out of my body, but Noel made sure I was an active participant in his dinner. He hummed around my fingers, sucking on the tips and biting into the pads as I passed food from the plate into his mouth with my hands. At one point, he pressed my free hand on the burgeoning swell of the erection trapped beneath his suit pants, and I shuddered so hard in revulsion, I dropped Cornish hen on his trousers.

He made me eat it off his lap without the use of my hands.

As I recovered, knees quaking and eyes leaking tears, the dinner plates were taken away and the tea service was placed on the sideboard. I swallowed the thick bile on the back of my tongue and made to get up to retrieve the tea.

"Crawl," Noel demanded as he leaned back in his throne-like chair to watch me.

I crawled.

My mind clung to questions I would ask Noel once he'd imbued the tea.

Answers Alexander had deserved his entire life and never received.

If he was truly gone, the very least I could do was glean them for both of us.

The antique blue and white Spode tea set rattled on the silver tray as I stood and clutched it in my shaking hands. I was so filled with a violent cocktail of reactions that I couldn't decipher my own emotional landscape.

The only thing I knew was this.

If I had to live one more day bound in the chains of Noel's servitude, I would kill myself.

But not before I killed *him*.

I smiled prettily into his face as I laid the tea set before him, my breasts exposed to his lecherous gaze in the flimsy white lace and chiffon corset I wore. With the black shackles at my wrists, throat, and ankles, I looked like a virginal whore.

Noel loved it.

His eyes went black with pleasure, pupils blown open to reveal the cold, depthless center of his depravity.

He liked to see me shake and tremble.

He loved to watch me move, every one of my actions puppeteered by his words.

I rolled my hips toward him, presenting the curve of my ass and the dip of my spine for his hand to sluice down. His eyes narrowed as he took advantage of my position, suspicious of my increasingly servile nature.

I fluttered my eyelids at him as if I was nervous but pleased by his attentions.

A smile pin-tucked his lips into his left cheek.

"You know, Ruthie," he began pleasantly as his hand smoothed up and down my back, dipping between my legs to pat my sex before repeating the movement again and again. It was a proprietary touch, one meant to degrade me from woman to object. It didn't work because I was pouring the tea into the pretty little cup and watching as he lifted it to his lips and swallowed. When I next smiled, it was genuine. "Women have been marginalized throughout history for a reason. You see, you *are* the weaker sex. Men are stronger mentally and physically. The argument that women 'feel more' and that makes them strong is rubbish, complete and utter drivel. Emotionality is the failure of the weak, and you, my dear Ruthie, are a prime example of that weakness."

"Yes, sir," I allowed with a meek bow of my head.

I watched through my eyelashes as he took another long sip, then another.

My heart rammed against the cage of my chest, threatening to break a rib. Cold sweat broke over my forehead, and I silently willed him to drink more.

"Come sit here," Noel beckoned, patting his thigh.

I hesitated as he squeezed his hand over his erection, drawing my notice to it.

He wouldn't force me to sit on his lap, not physically. He wanted to watch me struggle to make the decision myself, to surrender to him when I realized that he had me cornered.

I sat.

But the fire of my rage and my passion was lit deep beneath my placid expression and outward show of subjugation.

I was fire wrapped in ice, and it was only a matter of time before the latter melted away, and I was all heat. All fury.

My fingers itched in my lap as I watched Noel drink more of his poppy seed tea.

He finished the shallow bowl of tea and watched me as I poured more.

"You know he's dead, don't you, Ruthie?" he asked casually as he picked up the unused knife at his place setting and began to play the sharp edge up and down my neck. "You know your precious Alexander and Edward died…that they burned to a crisp in the time it would take me to run the tip of this right across your long, golden throat."

I swallowed hard against the pinch of the blade on my voice box and gave a slight nod to mollify him.

He hummed. "It was such a shame to kill them. The *years* that went into their upbringing and education, well, it devastates me to think of all that wasted time. Rodger is only thirteen and already more a man than the two of them together ever were."

"Your definition of man is *monster*," I bit out. "You killed your own sons. I don't know how you sleep at night, *brutto figlio di puttana bastardo.*"

Ugly son of a bitch bastard.

Only Italian will slack the viciousness of the fury pouring over my tongue like molten lead. I wanted to curse at him, scald him with the hot Latin words until he was impaled by my wrath like a pincushion.

Noel grinned as he scraped the knife's point over my lace cover nipple, back and forth like an out of sync metronome. "I have a new slave who does wonders with her whore mouth. Sleep is the only option after I've finished with her."

"You're repugnant," I said and spat on his face.

He froze as the coagulated saliva adhered to his skin, then slowly crept down his cheek, leaving a viscous trail. I was close enough, perched on his lap like that, to see how his grey eyes so much darker than Xan's silver—like mottled mercury or old led, something metallic and lifeless—went hard with displeasure.

"Rodger," he called out in a pleasant voice completely at

odds with the press of the knife to my chest and the toxic heat in his gaze. "Bring your mother forward, will you?"

Noel settled more comfortably in his chair, readjusting me so I sat perched on the rigid edge of his erection, the knife then pressed to my throat so hard, I felt blood form in a crescent moon. Together we watched as Rodger emerged from the shadows with Mrs. White in his hold. At first, it seemed familial, his growing frame just an inch taller than hers, a lanky arm wrapped around her middle, another on her shoulder under her hair like a little boy hiding behind his mummy.

It wasn't until the low light of the candles cast yellow lamination over something with a dull sheen in the hand resting on her shoulder that I realized Rodger held a gun pressed to his mother's temple.

Mrs. White's pale, trembling face was ugly and tragic, the same urine yellow of Napoli, filled with the same inescapable dread. I read what she wrote in her eyes as we locked gazes, the resignation and the terror.

She'd known all along in some dark, irrevocable place in her soul that her own tool of survival would be the death of her.

"I told you I would kill every single servant in this house if you didn't mind me," Noel prompted me. "It seems only fitting to begin in this manner."

"Noel," I said slowly, surprised by the level of horror I felt. "Don't do this."

"Kill Mary?" he asked, his face creased with mild, polite surprise as if I had offended him, but he was too gentlemanly to care. "Why, I don't intend to."

My spine softened slightly with relief. I didn't want her to die like that. No one deserved to be killed by their son and their husband, by the very people who should have loved her most. It echoed too profoundly in my heart.

At least I could die knowing the two people who had loved me most had died loving me, died after saving me.

"Rodger would do the deed, wouldn't you, son?" he asked conversationally.

A shiver ripped out my spine.

Mrs. White whimpered, but Rodger only adjusted his hold, boyish face obscured partially by shadows, but the wedge of his smile even more white in the dark.

"Happily," he responded.

"Unfortunately, that's not quite what we have planned," Noel said, as he adjusted and reached beneath his chair to produce another handgun, this one antique and so ornate it didn't seem functional.

"Do you know how to use one of these, dear Ruthie?" he asked.

I stared back and forth between the weapon and the man with growing horror. "No."

"Little filthy liar," he crowed happily. "You killed Giuseppe di Carlo with a gun. Oh? You thought I didn't know. I told you knowledge is power, Ruthie, and I have both in spades. Now, get up like a good girl and play this game for Rodger and me."

My entire body shook as Noel helped me to my feet, and I gagged as he pressed the cold, heavy weight of the gun into my hand. My stomach ached with sharp agony. My vision swam as Noel stepped to my side and dug the point of his knife into my side over a kidney. Rodger handed his mother a small gun and stepped to the side with the barrel of his weapon still at her temple.

We were pawns on the board of a father and son chess game. Noel wanted to teach Rodger what it was to sacrifice his queen.

"What does he get by doing this?" I asked softly, already knowing the answer.

"Why, my dear," Noel purred into my ear. "He gets *you*."

I swallowed around my heart where it sat lodged painfully

in my throat and tried to steady my hands as they clasped over the handle of the gun.

"What's the game exactly?"

"You have the opportunity to kill Mary right now with no opposition," Noel explained, his voice almost wispy with delight, a man high on something less tangible than a drug. Something made of pure, distilled evil.

"What if I don't shoot her?" I asked.

He *tsk*ed. "Then your poor soft heart will be the death of you, as it is the death of every weak being, because then Mary will kill *you* to save her own life, won't you, Mary?"

Mrs. White only shook harder, sweat pouring down her face like tears.

"You see, Mary knows what it takes to succeed in life. She gave me her good years, complete access to her body so I could do simply unspeakable things, and she gave me a son. She worked hard to live a long life, and I've no doubt, if given the opportunity awarded by your cowardice, she will work hard again to prolong it further."

"I won't kill her for you," I vowed.

I wouldn't.

I didn't care that Mrs. White was a traitor to womankind and that she deserved to die for all the horrible things she had facilitated on Noel's behalf.

I wouldn't stain my soul by killing a woman without recourse, even one who was the wife of the devil himself.

"So be it," Noel accepted easily. "I'd hoped to play with you for years to come, but that new slave is fresh enough to last for a while. You don't have anyone left who will miss you, so I can bury you in the maze with the rest of the women."

"Rest of the women?" I breathed as my heart started to race with anticipation.

Was this it?

The moment before my probable death and the drugged

tea or his arrogance was finally kicking in. Was Noel finally going to confess his crimes?

"Funny, isn't it? To think that Alexander spent so many years searching for the answers to his mother's death, and she was buried in the backyard the entire time."

Noel's wicked laughter echoed through the high-ceiling room. It juddered through me like an electric shock, resettling my brain chemistry and lighting up my nerves.

"The slaves, I understand," I said, surprised by the calm in my voice. "But your wife?"

"She was slumming with the dago and conspiring to run away with *my* sons straight into his filthy arms." Noel's face was twisted up like hot metal, seared with ugly hatred. "It had to end. Just as I had to end the baby Alexander so foolishly planted in your belly."

The imprint of the two hands that had pushed me down the ballroom steps and killed our baby burned at my back.

My body went hollow with despair, and then all of the sudden, filled to the brim with lava-like fury that densified into stone.

"I'm going to kill you," I told him through my teeth.

He laughed. "You can try, but if you don't kill Mary right now, you're the one who will be dead."

In a flurry of actions almost too quick to interpret, Noel signaled to Rodger with a tilt of his head and the boy took his staying hand off the gun in Mrs. White's shaking hand. A moment later, it was raised, the dark, innocuously small chamber pointed unerringly at my chest.

"I'm truly sorry, love," she whispered with tears falling into the open wound of her distressed mouth.

I wasn't.

Not any longer and not for anything.

Before I could even consciously decide, the gun in my hands was raised, and the trigger was pressed by the firm clasp on my finger. The gun recoiled in my hand, jerking my shoulder enough to jar me to the side just as Mrs. White's gun went off.

Her bullet grazed my outer left arm, leaving a trail of fiery agony in its wake.

My bullet found her brain, dead quiet in the wake of its unflinching connection with her skull. A second later, Rodger let her drop to the ground with a wet, punishing *thunk*.

Over the rushing roar of blood in my ears, I vaguely heard Noel and then Rodger laughing lightly, pleased and shocked at the outcome of our outdated duel. Before I could think about it, before I could even begin to grasp the firestorm of heart-break and fury raging through me, I whirled toward Noel and brought the butt of the gun down hard across his laughing face.

The crunch reverberated through the dining hall followed by Noel's grunt of pain as he stumbled back into the table with a crash of plates and cutlery. His arm dislodged one of the candelabras, and the flames spilled to the cloth, lighting the table on fire like a flaming throne below Noel's prone body.

He screamed.

I turned on my heel and *ran*, Rodger's following footsteps already ringing out against the wood behind me. The door at the end of the hall opened before I could even wrap my hand around the handle and Douglas appeared, his face pale but set with determination as fierce as a Celtic warrior. In one hand, he held a massive kitchen knife.

"Go," he urged, shoving me by. "Get out of here, now."

I wanted to thank him, cry and hug him for lying in wait for Rodger so I could get gone, to tell him I loved him for putting himself at risk and that I loved him for being my friend when I didn't have any left.

Instead, I ran.

I ran down the hall, not stopping or even flinching when I heard a crash and scream from behind me where Douglas and

Rodger had clashed. I ran through the dark hall harder than I'd even run at The Hunt, so hard my bare feet split against the friction with the glossed floors and my toes threatened to slip in the blood. So hard I went careening into priceless paintings as I turned the corners. So hard my lungs seemed to seize, and I couldn't really breathe, the tissues clasping around nothing but carbon.

Still, with an inevitably I felt at the back of my crazed mine like a premonition, Rodger caught me.

His hands appeared as if out of thin air, wrapping around my middle and hauling me to the ground from behind. I screamed, flipping as I fell so that I landed hard on my hip, but my legs were twisted briefly out of Rodger's seeking grip. He looked up at me with seething eyes like a rabid dog.

I reared my leg back and kicked him square in his foaming mouth.

A garbled growl sounded, but I didn't stop to watch him recover. I scrambled to my feet and searched manically for a weapon, for *anything* to use against the boy who was close enough to a man in body and corrupt enough mind to do serious damage to my person. There was nothing but a side table decorated with an antique gold phone, paintings on the wall, and… the stuffed and mounted head of a stag.

I jumped up to grasp the antlers in my hands, screaming as Rodger crawled forward and grabbed at one of my ankles, pulling me toward the ground. I leaned down into his momentum even though I knew if I ended up on the ground with him without a weapon, I was dead. His force helped me pull the large head from the wall, and I went tumbling to the ground with it, narrowly missing being impaled by one of the grand points.

Rodger grabbed at my ankle again, tugging me closer as he grunted, "You miserable, filthy whore, I'm going to fuck you with my hands around your pathetic throat until you—"

I reared up, using every ounce of my core strength to

bring the mounted head up over my head and down into Rodger's exposed, arched back.

There was a sickening soft sound like something punching into an old couch cushion and then a thud as the tip of the antler broke through his body and knocked against the floor. Rodger stared up at me in disbelief, his face so young, his eyes wide as they began to tear. His hand spasmed, then loosened around my foot.

I didn't stay to watch if he would die.

I scrambled backward on my hands and feet, then spun around to dash off down the hall again on legs wobbly with shock. Still, I ran, almost drunkenly, so fast it hurt, down the narrow corridor that cut straight through the house from front to back.

Finally, I burst out one of the back entrances to the house and fell into the damp night, the air like ice against my moist, hot skin. I stared at the haloed edge of light spilling from the house into the huge abyss of blackness beyond.

There was a sound behind me that spurred me forward like a gunshot at the starting line.

I ran blind, my eyes streaming with tears, my hair a dark cloak behind me the same colour as the intractable night. The dirt ground painfully into the cuts on my feet and shrubs tore at the bare skin of my arms as I pumped them manically at my sides.

Finally, I could make some sense of the dark, enough to realize with dread I felt like a dropped anchor in my stomach, that I had somehow made it into the maze on the east side of the property.

The same maze Noel had just confessed to burying the bodies of his slaves in.

The body of his wife.

My body too, if I didn't find a way out of the labyrinth.

Frantically, as I dodged around a bend in the hedgerows, I

tried to recall everything Alexander had told me about the property and about the elaborate maze.

Constructed by Capability Brown in the late 1700s, it was one of Pearl Hall's greatest sights and one that had stared at me through the windows of my bedroom during my entire time in captivity. There were two exits, one at either side, with a center spoke where a collection of Grecian marble statues lay. It was a massive maze, thousands of yew bushes used to make up the paths and dead ends in the pattern.

A sob exploded from my panting mouth as I continued to run blindly through the collection of twists and turns, the branches tearing at all my exposed skin, the ground eating away at the flesh of my feet.

I ran, and I bled.

I sweated, and I cried.

And over it all, I heard the distant lilting call of my name.

"Ruthie," Noel's voice carried faintly over the wind, and the wet air streaming with drizzling rain. "Ruthie, you little bitch, if you come to me now, I promise not to kill you."

Fresh panic sluiced through my waning body, kicking my gait into hyper speed. I gritted my teeth, ducked my head into the rain, and ran harder still.

Only moments later, I reached the spoke at the center of the yew wheel and crashed into the back of a statue so hard I saw stars. Reeling, I walked clumsily farther into the middle, at the center of the circle of marble carved Grecian gods, and then fell to my knees as my balance deserted me.

I pushed my damp, clinging hair out of my face and looked at the six places the maze connected to the center, trying to discern which one might lead me to the far entrance and which one I had just stumbled out of, but my mind was scrambled by the crash and overcooked with terror.

"I'm going to die here," I said to myself and the earth beneath my hands, watching the grim glimmer of my tears falling with the rain to the soft, damp ground.

I curled my fingers into the soil, fighting the urge to tip my head to the heavens and howl like a lost a wolf, crying for the rest of my pack that would never come, crying for the death I knew was close to arriving at my back.

In all my experiences, I never truly thought I was seconds from dying, not like this. I wanted to press my body into the dirt and be swallowed up in the warm embrace of the soil, die at the hands of nature instead of the hands of a monster.

And that spurred something inside me, some insanity that reared its head the more I poked at it.

I started digging.

Chapter Thirty-two

ALEXANDER

The house was lit up like a beacon, but as empty as a tomb. I slunk through the halls, disturbed by the weight of the silence, how it filled the air like amber, pinning everything in place as if it hadn't been disturbed since my last visit.

Only when I pushed into the dining hall did I find evidence of life.

Or, I should have said, *death*.

The dining room table was a half-charred, still smoking mess, and Mrs. White lay in a shroud of her own satin red blood beside it, her face tipped up to the ceiling, the faintly surprised set of her mouth open and scarlet like her head wound.

My blood went glacial in my veins.

Riddick bent to place his hand on her arm and looked up at me with grim eyes. "Still warm."

My heart kicked and throbbed in my chest, wailing with fresh, incessant terror, terror I'd known from the moment Cosima disappeared into the back of Osteria Lombardi never to reappear. I hadn't felt any of my own fear when I went to find her and discovered the crude, homemade bomb on the basin instead of my wife. I'd been driven forward by the cold wind of purpose, collecting everyone as I pushed out the doors, calling to Dante to do the same.

Everyone made it out, except for two souls who'd been in the back alley when the explosion went off and caught the debris in their bodies.

I hadn't felt fear then, nor elation, not for myself or the others who had survived.

I'd only felt the huge, palpitating terror that came from knowing someone had my wife.

It took less than twelve hours to discern Noel had been the one behind the crime, that he had sent Rodger in on the private Davenport plane to retrieve my wife and ferry her away to her own personal hell.

We couldn't go to her right away.

Not without a plan.

It seemed Noel had used the last of his personal money to hire a team of thugs and trained professionals to seal the grounds. There were so many of them, they looked like ants crawling over the fortified walls of the property from the drone's video feed.

The police told us to stay in town while they attempted to figure out the crime, and I didn't waste time. I called in Salvatore and Dante's crew, I called in Simon's anti-Order bandits and hired my own security team.

We planned, and we plotted. I saw Dante off back to jail because they briefly wondered if he had been behind the bombing. I kept mum on the truth of the event because I didn't want the police mucking it up.

And then, thirteen long days after Cosima was taken, I finally boarded a plane with my crew and my plan and set off to get my wife.

Only, after taking out the thugs and scaling the walls, after telephoning in a delayed call to the local police and to the MI-5 unit I'd been working with, Cosima wasn't there.

And Mrs. White was dead on the floor of the dining room. *Fuck.*

I jogged out the other end of the hall and nearly stumbled over Douglas who lay passed out against the wall, a bleeding, but non-threatening wound rounding his forehead. My heart jumped into my throat as I checked his pulse, and Riddick moved after me down the hall. There was blood all over the Persian rug near the termination of the endless corridor, the wet, metallic smell of it still rich in the air.

I swallowed the urge to vomit, the insatiable need to know if it was Cosima's blood I carefully avoided as I walked by, and pulled the remains of my habitual arctic calm around me like fucking armor.

I would not give in to emotions until I had my wife safe in my arms and our enemies dead at her feet like an offering to a God.

We arrived at the end of the hall, and Riddick pushed open the door to listen briefly to the night air before we continued our search of the upper levels.

Just as the wood swung closed, we heard it, faint as a ghostly moan on the winds of the moors.

Ruthie.

Riddick and I exploded into a sprint simultaneously, guns warm in our ready hands as we took off to the left of the house and plunged into the darkness, predators to the monsters that hunted Cosima through the night.

The cold wind bit at my cheeks, and the rain plastered my black clothes to my body, but I gave them no heed as I entered the narrow mouth of the maze and concentrated on following my memories to its core. I could hear commotion amid the yews, a truncated scream, and a male roar of fury.

I pushed hard, tearing around corners, feet slipping through the mud, catching my hands on branches to leverage myself upright around the tight bends. Riddick called through the radio for backup and we trundled on.

He crashed into my back as I stopped abruptly at the beginning of the last row leading to the center circle because there was a small body at the far end, watching two bodies struggle in the dirt with a gun raised and shaking, waiting to shoot.

"Brother," I called out, speaking for the first time to a boy I'd never met.

He turned slowly, gun armed and ready but quaking in his hands, and I noticed the gory hole in his abdomen, partially covered by his torn and bloody jumper.

Cosima had got him.

Pride moved through me, eradicating some of the frantic worry in my blood so that I could think more calmly.

"Put down your gun, and I won't hurt you," I told him, slowly moving closer with my gun still raised.

Riddick had disappeared like an apparition into thin air.

"Fuck you, slave lover," he spat. "You and your whore don't deserve to live."

I sighed and dropped my gun. "Have it your way, then."

"You don't have the stones to kill a boy," he jeered.

I tipped my head and smiled Noel's smile at him. "No, but he does."

Rodger turned his head just as Riddick appeared out of the maze beside him and pressed his gun to his head with a soft, anti-climatic *pop*.

Noel's false heir fell to the ground with a wet plop.

I ran and leaped over him the moment he dropped, focusing on the scrambling duo in the middle of the clearing. As I drew closer, I saw the mulch of churned up earth, their feet sank amid the dark soil, shards of white peppered up among them. Noel had his hands around Cosima's neck, forcing her into the air, her toes dangling.

He couldn't see her though, his eyes bloody and riddled with long, deep gauges from Cosima's nails. He blindly squeezed and squeezed, not carrying if he actually saw her die.

I was on him in the next second, hitting him so savagely in a sideswipe tackle that he instantly dropped Cosima and crumpled to the ground. My fists met his face before his head even hit the ground. I beat into him like a hammer to meat, pulverising his face, hating him with every smash, transferring the pain he'd inflicted my entire life through every blow to his despicable head. Somehow, he was able to raise a hand and plunge a small knife from somewhere into my thigh. I grunted and tried to steel myself, but he overpowered me, scrambling to his feet with his back to me, his head cocked over his shoulder to watch me as he started for Cosima again.

I lunged at him, grabbing at his arms and pinning them at his back, opening his chest up. I spun him, thinking to impale his heartless torso on the marble lance of the statue beside me.

Instead, Cosima appeared, dredged in rain and rolled in earth like a goddess newly risen from the bowels of hell. She had something in her hand, long and white, pointed into a danger-like edge.

She planted a palm over the place Noel should have harboured a soul, and then she looked at him with her golden eyes bright even in the dark and she sank that white weapon deep into his side.

He grunted and jerked in my embrace. I cinched my hold and braced my legs, holding Noel up as my wife stabbed him again and again in the side. I held him until his legs gave out. I held him while his breath began to stutter over his grunts and curses. I held him as Cosima killed him, and then when he died, I held him still so that she could look into my eyes as her chest heaved with exertion and her bloody hand shook in the air, the bone still lifted, so that she would know it was done, and I was proud of her for doing it.

She was a vengeful goddess, a righteous warrior, and I never loved her more than I did at that moment as her anger melted into silent tears, and she whispered brokenly, "Please tell me I've not gone mad. Please tell me you're alive."

I dropped Noel unceremoniously to the ground and caught my wife up in my arms, crushing her to my chest like a human defibrillator, needing the shock of her skin against mine to bring myself back to life after thirteen days of zombified misery.

"I'm here," I said into her hair as I pushed it back, as I planted a crown of kisses over her forehead and anointed her mouth with my lips. "I'm here, I'm here, and I swear to God and everything holy or unholy, my beauty, we will never be without each other again."

I chanted the words over and over again, the melody to the harmony of her repeated, *Xan, Xan, oh, Xan,* until the red and blue lights of police cars cut through the dark of the maze, and it finally occurred to both of us that it was over.

The demons were slain at our feet, and my spring goddess, my dead queen, was in my arms again.

I looked down into her face, into the gold eyes that had ignited my destiny and planted a heart inside my chest, and tipped it further into the air so I could kiss the rain and relief off her lips.

"You found me," she breathed into my mouth as if awed.

"I promised you I always would," I reminded her. "I always will."

Chapter Thirty-three

COSIMA

For the first time in my life, I woke up in Alexander's black and blue bedroom. My entire body ached from the neglectful abuse it had undergone for the past few weeks as Noel's prisoner and the fury of the chase through the maze three days before while my mind was its own bruise, tenderized by the pounding relief and turmoil at having killed three humans in the span of two months. I felt fragile, almost brittle like something old and worn you needed to wear gloves to handle. I was only twenty-two years old, but I felt as if I'd lived a dozen lives, a hundred years of sorrow compacted into a little over two decades. I knew it would take a long time before I achieved any kind of normalcy or stability. My dragons had been slayed, my prince resurrected from the dead, but this princess bore scars that would never completely fade. They were battle wounds, badges of victory against the many monsters of my life, but they still ached, and I knew they would periodically, spasmodically in the years to come like an old injury flaring up in the damp British cold.

But at that moment of first waking, when my lids slowly parted and my eyes focused on the long golden slope of torso under my cheek, none of the pain existed. Instead, like the sun cresting beyond the navy velvet drapes, hope and cautious happiness dawned through my chest and warmed my body from fingers to toes.

I was in Alexander's bedroom, pressed between his arms and legs like a flower eternalized in the pages of a book, sheltered from time and harm by the powerful folds of his body. He was safe and relatively unharmed, holding me like he never again intended to let me go, even in his slumber.

Pearl Hall was quiet outside the double doors, already stripped of servants loyal to the old Davenport ways and waiting for its new master and mistress to fill it with fresh souls. I imagined a lightly concussed Douglas in his kitchen, nattering with the few kitchen staff left while he worked puff pastry through his strong hands to make my favourite breakfast pastry, and Riddick in the gymnasium, already warming up for his morning fencing session with Xan and me.

It was the first morning of my new life, the last life I ever intended to live. This manor and this man were finally, irrevocably *mine*. I had always been theirs, stamped both metaphorically and literally with their possession, but it was the first time I could reciprocate that ownership and the headiness of tenure settled over me like a heavy crown.

The impossible dream I'd once dreamed of being Pearl Hall and Alexander's mistress had come to fruition and not through sheer luck or the will of others, but through my brave actions and the relentless pursuit of my goals.

I'd earned this. Earned them.

There would never be any doubt in my mind or the minds of others who might have been inclined to dissent that I deserved to be Duchess of Greythorn, wife of the great Alexander Davenport, doyen of one of the most extensive, beautiful estate in England.

Alexander's cool silken chest dampened under my cheek, and I realized I was crying. The sweet, cleansing release of tears I should have cried over the years but didn't allow myself to because I feared it would show a weakness I would never overcome. I understood, as one of the tears slipped over Xan's mounded pectoral and wound through the maze of his abdominals until it pooled in his belly button, that tears were not the sign of a weak woman.

They were the sign of a woman who was unafraid of her own powerful emotions, who was capable of harnessing that power to fuel her passionate ambitions.

It was exactly my deep well of emotionality that had given me the strength to continue loving Alexander against all odds, that had given me a small escape during the times of torture with Ashcroft and Noel, that had shielded me from and armed me for the battle I had just won.

Lying there in bed with Alexander, I didn't just feel peaceful, I felt canonized. There would never be many people who knew the true story of Alexander and Cosima, not the way everyone knew the tale of Hades and Persephone, but both of us knew the truth.

Just like the goddess of spring, I had chosen to return to the underworld, not because I was coerced, but because I found in the darkness and beauty of that wild domain that I belonged there more than I ever had above ground.

Alexander stirred under me, his arm banding tighter over

my hip, the other crossing over to stroke down my hair and tip up my chin so my face was exposed to his sleep-leaden gaze.

I felt my heart in my throat as he took his time studying me, his grey eyes soft as velvet against my skin as they swept over the edge of my cheekbones, trailed the seam of my hair-line and lingered on my lips like a kiss.

"Good morning, wife," he greeted, his upper-crust accent abraded with sleep in a way that made my pussy dampen.

The hand in my hair flexed, then tugged, forcing me closer to his face.

"Good morning, husband," I said on a slight gasp.

I wriggled against his good leg, stimulating my wakening pussy against the hair roughened, hard panel of flesh. My pulse jumped as I watched Alexander's eyes turn to smoke with longing.

His hand clamped over my hip and then relaxed as he moved to place his hands behind his head, the muscles in his arms flexing in a way that made my mouth water.

He looked every inch the indolent lord as he ordered, "I don't have long this morning for idleness. If you're really so desperate to come, little mouse, you'll have to ride my leg. I have emails to attend to before I shower and leave for London."

I pouted at him even though I'd been particularly insa-tiable since he'd returned from the "dead." We had spent the first two nights after the maze debacle in a small inn in Whaley Bridge, being interviewed by local police and a few visiting members of MI-5, but every free moment otherwise, we were tangled together in the paisley bedsheets.

There were no scenes, no blatant Dom or sub behavior, just the natural twisting of hips and twining of limbs as we reconnected in the most fundamental way we knew how.

It would have been easy to blame it on the exhilaration of a near-death experience or the high of vanquishing our foes, but it was much simpler than that.

We were safe, and we were free. The worries that had weighed down our thoughts for years had evaporated and left in their place like crystalized salt after the going of the tide were lust and love.

So, we indulged.

We indulged so much my pussy was still puffy, and my skin was riddled with red marks and bruises like the spring fields of poppies and blossoming bluebells exploding over the British countryside.

I couldn't really complain that Alexander didn't have time to fuck me when that was essentially all he'd done for the past three days, but I was still put out.

"Please," I breathed even as I tilted my hips and began to churn against him. "If you have to be gone all day, I need you inside me one more time."

Alexander ignored me, leaning over to grab his phone from the nightstand and then grabbing a silk grey pillow to prop behind his back before he resettled. His eyes were on the screen, his face utterly expressionless as he finally said, "Either come like this, *topolina*, or not at all."

His disinterest lit a box of matches in my groin and before I could censure myself, I was gyrating, grinding against him. The scrape of his leg hairs against my clit and the hard heat of his muscled thigh pressed flush to my wet and blooming sex coupled with his relentless passivity had me orgasming before I knew it. My soft cry punctured the air as I shuddered against him, arms wrapped tightly around his narrow waist to hold me steady while I spasmed.

While I lay there, my panting breath rippling gooseflesh over his torso, Alexander continued to read his email, fingers moving rapidly over the screen. There was a whoosh as an email was sent off, and then all of the sudden, I was under him, his body so heavy it stole my breath.

His face was in mine, his impassive expression broken open with the inflexible cast of his lust. I gasped into his mouth as he pressed it against mine, as his hand found my swollen, achy sex and pressed deliciously hard against it.

"Does your pussy hurt yet, *bella*? Does it ache from the stretch and thrust of my cock? I think I fucked you fifty times in the last thirty-six hours, and I want you to feel every single one of those fucks in this pretty cunt."

I was moaning before he'd finished speaking, panting for more like a shameless wanton. There was something extraordinary that happened to a well-used pussy; the more you fucked it, the better it felt, and the more it wanted.

Or maybe that was just me.

And I was finding, as Alexander wedged the crown of his big cock into my nearly swollen closed folds, that I was okay with my insatiable desires because Alexander was an insatiable man.

I walked the entire house three times. The first time was leisurely, touching everything as I passed, feeling the texture of the 15th century tapestries and the smooth curves of the carved wooden antiques, squishing my bare toes in the Persian rugs, and spending long moments gazing into the collection of priceless artworks lining the walls. None of the remaining servants bothered me as I walked like a wraith in my white silk robe through the haunted and hallowed halls of the house that I vowed to make into a home. They seemed to sense that I needed the freedom to roam after so long confined to one place, specific rooms. On my second pass, I delved deeper, finding the keys in the study that opened some of the locked doors I'd always wondered about. I found what must have been Rodger's room, decked out in antique weaponry and European football posters, and Noel's collection of rooms, all dark and musky with his scent, a fragrance I associated acutely with evil.

Those rooms would be stripped to the bare necessities and revamped entirely.

If this was to be my home, as I assumed it would be given that lords usually lived on their estates and Alexander's business was based in London, it was going to be one exorcised of ghosts.

So, when I found a room decorated in the soft mauves and nearly translucent blues of a dawn in a tropical paradise, I designated it as Giselle and Sinclair's future escape when they visited. Then again, when I found a bold black and red room with an oriental theme that seemed strong and bold enough for my Elena, and once more with the small, but beautifully cozy room abutting a long-ago used nursery that I knew would perfectly suit Mama.

On my third pass, I barely opened my eyes. I counted the marble steps as I took them, feeling the cold, smooth rock under my feet, the way my hand fit perfectly to the carved curves of the bannister as my palm slid across it. I breathed in the yeasted, damp scent of the kitchen and the wet, close air of the greenhouse perfumed with hundreds of exotic flowers and the slightly acrid tint of the pond water there. I imagined scenes of laughter in the den where I'd once played chess with Noel, transposing an image of Alexander and I playing there instead, shedding our clothes each time we capitulated a piece to the other. I thought of the massive Douglas fir Riddick would cut down for us from the forest in the back that we would decorate for Christmas and place in the corner of the main living room, and of the stockings we would hang from the famous black marble fireplace with its demons and angels intertwined up the columns.

When I reached the kitchen, I stopped in the doorway to watch as Douglas gave a sound little speech to some of the new staff Alexander and Riddick had already hired.

"I run a tight ship, lads and lasses." Douglas gestured grandly to his kitchen wearing the bandage over his cut head like a crown. "This is a serious place of business because food and pastry are serious undertakings. I won't have any of you cocking up my schedule, so adapt quickly or you'll be sent packing, you hear? The duke and duchess have been through…a lot in the last fortnight, or really, in the last two decades. They don't need willful or imbecilic servants making shambles of their happily ever after."

A young boy, no more than sixteen, tentatively raised his hand. "'S true that the lord killed his own father in the back garden, then?"

Douglas's boyish face contorted with a glare as he rapped his wooden spoon over the boy's knuckles where they lay on the table. "Ask another impertinent question again and you'll be gone from here. There will be no idle gossip about the master and mistress of Pearl Hall, not where I can hear you if you know what's good for your knuckles and your bellies, and not where his Grace can find out, if you know what's good for your safety and your pocketbooks."

I was tempted to laugh at Douglas's threats, but instead, I arranged my face into a polite mask and stepped up to say, "Chef O'Shea is correct about one thing." I waited as the staff all whipped toward me with varying awed and terrified expressions. It was clear they had all heard about Noel's and Rodger's deaths, about the pall over Pearl Hall, but I wouldn't have them being scared of Alexander and me. "He is a fear-some beast when he's angry."

I winked at them, and they all shifted awkwardly in their seats, sharing looks that questioned whether they were meant to laugh or not.

Douglas stepped in with a shake of his wooden spoon at me. "You're one to talk. I've not met a woman so grumpy as you when you've not eaten."

I shrugged. "Happily, you keep me well fed."

Douglas preened for me, and I laughed, moving over to press a kiss to his rosy cheek. I'd always been affectionate, but in the wake of the latest events, I found myself unable to see Riddick and Douglas, two of the knights who had risked their lives to help me, without touching them. It was only one of the myriad of ways I sought to show my gratitude and love for the next few decades.

Some of the staff looked horrified by my closeness with Douglas, so I decided to nip that in the bud before I continued my tour of the house. I sat on the edge of the table even though Douglas swatted at me and smoothed my robe so that it covered my legs as if it was a priceless gown.

"Listen, I've no doubt you heard the stories about what has happened at Pearl Hall recently...and maybe not so recently. As with any place of history, there are many stories here, both good and bad. What I want to promise you is this: there will be no more bad stories here. At least, not while Xan and I live. The past is done and, quite literally, buried. If you wish to stay on at Pearl Hall, know that you do it not just as a servant but as part of a family. We will expect you to do your duties, but we also expect you to contribute to the positive atmosphere of the home. You see, we have loads of new memories that need planting in these gardens and hanging on these walls. If you don't feel you can keep mum on the past and any strange goings-on, you may find happen here, then no hard feelings, but please leave. If you think you'd be happy in a home, however grand Pearl Hall may seem, please stay and I'll be so happy to know you as the opportunities arise."

Collectively, the group of twelve or so servants blinked at me, but none of them rose to leave the table so I took it as a good sign. With a sigh, I stood and pressed another kiss to Douglas's cheek in farewell.

He stilled me for a moment with a hand on my arm. "Not mistress more than a day and you're already the best duchess Pearl Hall has ever seen, ducky."

I blinked away the sharp sting of tears and squeezed his hand before I dropped it in a mute but poignant thanks. Then I swept from the room and continued my third walk of the house.

I ended my third pass in the gymnasium and found Riddick waiting for me there, his eyes closed as he meditated seated on the ground in the middle of the mats.

Smiling, I crept toward him, not so much as a bone creaking or a joint popping as I made my way toward him and prepared to startle him out of his wits.

He cracked open an eye just as I reared back to scare him, and drily stated, "Heard you before you crossed the threshold, duchess. Even silk has a sound."

I scowled down at my robe and then back at him. "One of these days, I'm going to scare the pants off of you, Riddick."

He raised his brows as he unfolded his long, wide body and stood. "I doubt very much that my employer would be pleased his wife had seen me starkers."

I blinked and then burst out laughing, holding my stomach to contain my glee. "Riddick," I gasped. "Did you just make a joke?"

His face was expressionless as he said, "I wouldn't dream of it."

I giggled again and had the immense satisfaction of seeing his lips twitch at the corners. I followed him as he led the way to the fencing equipment and didn't say a word when I noticed he had laid out some of my old fitness clothes for me to change into. I knew thanking him for his thoughtfulness would only embarrass the quintessentially British stoic man.

But when he said softly, in his coarsely accented voice, so different than Xan's posh English, "You were right brave, you were, Cosima. Never been prouder of a body in my entire life, and I was in the army," I caved.

My arms were around his square torso in a second, my cheek pressed just under his rock-hard pectoral muscle. I felt as if I was hugging a boulder, and for a long moment, he was as still as one.

Then one arm wrapped gently, tenderly around my back, and the other found my head where it rested for a moment before patting me awkwardly.

"There, there," he grunted. "No need to get all wound up. Everything's sorted now, and you can finally have some peace, hmm?"

I looked up, up, up at him with my arms still locked, barely, around his middle, and I gifted him with one of my megawatt smiles. "You know, Riddick, that I love you very much, don't you?"

A blush lay waste to his pallid skin like a forest fire, and his eyes shifted uneasily through the room as if he worried Alexander was in wait to accuse him of putting the moves on his wife. I bit back my laughter at his discomfort but decided to put him out of his misery by breaking free of my hold. I turned my back to give him a moment to compose himself and selected my rapier from the wall of weapons.

"I'm a bit out of practice," I said over my shoulder as I took my things to get changed. "But if you lose, you have to go riding with me. I miss Helios."

I left the room laughing as Riddick grunted his disapproval. He hated horses, and he was too much fun to discomfort not to make the most of the bet and win our little wager.

A few hours later, I was laughing again as I flew over the

acreage of Pearl Hall on Helios, her sleek, powerful body churning up the earth in our wake. I peered over my shoulder to see Riddick as a speck on the hill behind me, his mount moving at a jerky, slow pace under his large form. There was no doubt in my mind Riddick had let me win purposefully. My left arm still burned slightly from the bullet graze and my feet were tender as I executed my footwork, slowed slightly by the pain. But Riddick had given me the victory as his own way of telling me he loved me too, and I appreciated it even as I giggled at his uneasiness on a horse.

I buried my laughter in Helios's soft, hay smelling golden mane and kicked her into a soaring gallop. We transected the field of poppies Alexander's mother had planted to remind her of her girlhood home in Italy, and dodged through the tight weave of trees in the forest before bursting through the clearing and up over the tallest peak so that I could survey every inch of the Davenport estate from atop my steed.

Helios and I were both panting, my monotone cream riding set saturated with sweat like my mare's pale gold coat. My body would ache even more tomorrow after the unfamiliarity of the long, hard ride, but I knew I would relish it.

It was worth the ache and more, every single thing I'd been through to know every inch of the land I could see—the purpling heather over the far moors, the last of the morning fog swirling in the bowl of the valley near the little village of Thornton, the dark shadowed forest stretching horizontally over the estate like a belt cinching it all together—was all ours.

His and mine.

Mine, because I was his.

And by his own repeated declaration, he was mine.

Riddick plodded up the hill on his dappled grey mare, his forehead beaded in sweat, his short hair plastered to his head, and his expression deadly.

"All right, Rid?" I asked jauntily with a tip of my riding hat.

He scowled, his heavy brow compressed over his glittering eyes, but he didn't say anything until he drew abreast of my mount. Then, he reached out to tug one of my thick plaited pigtails hard enough to make me wince but not enough to hurt, and he vowed, "I will never, ever go riding with you again. Alexander will have to buy a utility vehicle if he wants me charging off after you across the grounds."

I tipped my head back to laugh at the great blue bowl of the sky, and when I recovered enough to tilt my chin down again, Riddick was riding off down the hill. I frowned as I made to call after him, but a voice beside me startled me into paralysis.

"I've seen you in some magnificent postures," Alexander said mildly as if we were in the middle of a conversation already. He sat atop his great black stallion with his gloved hands crossed over the tooled leather pommel of the saddle. With his long, muscular thighs encased in stone-coloured riding pants and tall glossy black boots, and his wide shoulders and narrowed waist cinched in a velvet black blazer, Alexander looked every inch the lord of the manor. I took in the stubble lining his jaw like flecks of pure gold and noticed the strain in his cheeks from biting back a smile. "But it has to be said, Cosima, you are a sight to behold right now."

Warmth suffused my chest and split my lips into a smile so wide, they ached. "It may be because I don't think I have ever been so happy. I feel as if I could float away."

"The threats that have weighed you down for so long are gone, so I'm not surprised you feel that way. Though"—he urged Charon closer to me so that he could snag my chin between his cool gloved fingers and force my eyes intently to his—"you will always have me to tether you."

I used my chin to urge his hand over my cheek and leaned into him. "I've always been partial to you holding me down."

Xan's face broke into one of his rare, beautifully creased smiles that made his eyes gleam like polished silver. I reached over to trace my thumb over the shape of that smile and then chuckled when his teeth nipped at the pad.

"You're happy too," I told him because even though he seemed the same staid, regal man with a face like a mask and eyes like two cold stones, I could sense the shift in the air around him. He too seemed lighter.

"I've been happier with you in every moment we've spent together than I have ever been in the entirety of my life without you," he admitted easily as if his words didn't mean absolutely everything to a girl who had never been loved so candidly in her life by a man other than her brother.

"Do you think…?" I ventured before halting the stream of words by biting my lower lip.

Alexander glared at me when I didn't continue and then carefully unhooked my teeth from my mouth. "Do not hold anything back from me, my beauty. You are a mystery I've spent too long waiting to unravel, and the process begins now. I want to know everything."

"I don't want to jinx it," I said with a wince because it was ridiculous to believe in such trivial superstitions after everything we'd been through.

His face settled feature by feature, brick by brick, into a stone wall of somberness. I gasped as he twisted to fit his hands under my armpits and half-dragged, half-lifted me from my saddle onto his where he settled me with my legs draped over his thighs, a diamond of space between our groins, one powerful arm around my waist and the other wrapped in my pigtails so that my head arched back and my mouth bloomed open just under his.

Alexander spoke with a wry, almost nervous twist to his lips, an energy in his eyes that spoke of nearly boyish eagerness and vulnerability. "The tale usually goes, there is a desperate princess locked away in a tower in need of a valiant knight to slay her dragons and spirit her away to a happily ever after, but our truth is different. It was me who needed you, Cosima. I sensed your bravery the moment you stepped in to save the life of a man you didn't know in a random Milanese alleyway, and I knew it for sure when you refused to break for me, when you promised I wouldn't win your heart or your spirit unless I could earn them. You saved me from an eternity of hell I wasn't even perfectly aware I was living. You gave me reason to slay my demons, reason to doubt my own villainy, and now, that part of our lives is over."

The arm around my waist shifted so that he could rub his smooth leather-clad thumb over my cheek, and he rested his forehead against mine. The wrinkles in his forehead smoothed out as he closed his eyes and released a sigh like a man atoned for his sins by God.

When he moved back an inch to lock eyes with me, his blazed with the fury of an inner flame. "But hear me when I say that time is over. I don't need you to save me anymore and neither does your family. You have martyred and battled enough. It's time to hang up your sainthood and your sword because if something ever comes for us again, it will be me who pays the toll, me who takes up the lance. I will never *ever* let anyone touch you again. You see, my beauty, you taught me what it takes to be a hero, so I'll be prepared if the mantle ever has to be taken up again."

His thumb continued to move across my cheek, wiping away the tears as soon as they spilled from my lids. A hiccough worked its way up my throat, a precursor to heavy, bloated sobs that wracked my entire body with shudders and gasps.

Alexander held me as I cried, crushed to his chest so tightly I could feel the steady, heavy thud of his heart against its cage. It was that beat that finally soothed me because it reminded me that Alexander was the greatest man I'd ever known, but more than that, there was a dark, dangerous beast inside his chest that would break free if anyone tried to fuck with us again.

And I would never bet against that beast.

I knew he would keep me safe from harm.

"I was going to say," I whispered through my snot and tears, my voice so thick it seemed I spoke through a cotton-filled mouth. "Do you think we get our happily ever after now? I mean, what happens after this?"

There was something utterly poignant about the way Alexander tilted my chin up with his big hands, their strength subtly reined so that they could brush tenderly over my wet cheeks, collecting my tears. His face was serious as I had ever seen it, features heavy and almost stern as he stared down at me, but it was his eyes that drew my focus. They were wide, dark and light in equal turns like sunlight filtering through storm clouds, and so sincere with love it made my breath catch.

"What happens after this?" he mused as he took my hands in each of his and methodically bit the pad of each finger before kissing each knuckle. "What happens after this is we move you properly into the house. We put your books in the library, your clothes beside mine in our closet, and your portrait next to mine in the Hall of Mirrors. I go to work in the city, you go to work wherever that may take you, and we both come home to each other here. We're already married." Alexander pressed his lush mouth to the enormous canary yellow diamond on my left ring finger. "But I see a proper honeymoon in our future, wherever my bride desires. And children. When we are ready, as many children as you're willing to give me."

Tears were falling again, but I was never able to think about our miscarriage without them. It hadn't been the right time or place to have a child, but the devastation was still very real. Knowing that I once again had the chance to have a baby with Alexander's mercurial grey eyes and gorgeous British accent filled every empty space inside me with unequivocal joy.

"But for now," Alexander said, an impish grin twisting the

left side of his firm mouth. "We must return to the house so that I can give you a very belated wedding present and an early birthday gift."

Quickly and effortlessly, Alexander was hefting me out of his saddle and twisting me back onto my own.

"If you'd like to attempt to beat me back to the stables, you're more than welcome to," he continued mildly, the tiny curve of his mouth belying his arrogant amusement. "The loser will be punished, of course. I think a spanking with a riding crop sounds fitting, don't you?"

Before he was even finished speaking, I was off, Helios leaping into motion so fluid it seemed that we spilled down the hill and into the valley as easily as water through a stream. My laughter was high and breathless as I pressed my torso into Helios's warm body, buried my nose in her sweet mane, and galloped across the estate, no demons or monsters giving chase behind me, just the man I always knew would find me if I ran.

Still, somehow, probably due to nearly four decades of horseback riding, Alexander drew abreast with me, grinning like the innocent boy he had never been, and then quickly overtook me with a loud, freeing *whoop* of joy.

He beat me soundly, arriving at the stables two minutes before me, and then he beat me soundly again with a riding crop while I braced myself against the same fireplace he'd once branded me against. He held my ass when he finally thrust into my wet, clutching heat, his thumb digging into the flesh over my brand as if he could rebrand me through touch alone.

It was that thought and the belief that he could, that broke the bloated seal on my orgasm.

I was still panting, my hands linked around Alexander's neck, the only thing keeping my wobbling knees from collapsing, when he started to laugh his gorgeous, rumbling laughter against my neck.

"What?" I asked, pulling him by the hair so I could see his creased, happy face. "Why are you laughing?"

An imperious shrug. "I'm allowed to laugh, am I not?"

"You are," I agreed slowly. "You just don't very often."

His amusement softened into something far more intimate as he gently nipped my chin with his teeth. "I have the sense that will change now."

I beamed into his face, and he clucked his tongue at me. "Infatuated, the both of us. I hope Riddick has a strong stomach because he doesn't much like public displays of affection. Most Brits don't."

"Good thing you're half Italian then."

"Good thing." He slapped my ass sharply, reigniting the burn from the riding crop. "Now get inside and go to your room. Some of the gifts I spoke of are waiting for you on your bed."

I opened the door of the room that had been my haven the entire first year of my stay at Pearl Hall with more trepidation than I ever had before. A surprise from Alexander could mean anything from a horse to the piked head of a former enemy staked to the floor still dripping blood.

At first, as the ornate gold and cream painted door swung inwards, I didn't see anything out of the ordinary. The pink and red carpets still overlapped in pleasing disarray, the gorgeous draperies over the bed tied open with golden ropes to reveal the deep red satin coverlet and mounds of goose down pillows. It was opulent and homey, and even though I would be spending my nights with Alexander in his room in the future, I would always consider this room my own sweet escape.

Distracted by nostalgia, I almost overlooked the small black blob on the duvet, but the floor creaked slightly under my booted feet and a little head peeked up, gold eyes the same colour as my own popping open amid the inky fur.

"Hades!" I cried as I dived onto the bed and grabbed my little demon cat into my arms.

I rolled onto my back, holding his warm, soft body on my chest with my hands under his pits so that he sat between my breasts and we could look each other in the eye. He blinked at me sleepily and yawned, exposing his little pink tongue, before finally greeting me with a croaky meow.

I hugged him tenderly to my chest and threw my head back against the duvet to smile into the canopy, my cheeks aching with the spread of joy on my face.

There was a creak in the hall that signaled the arrival of someone at my door, and I laughed without looking over to see Xan standing smugly there.

"You wonderful, sly man. Thank you so much for getting Hades here. He means everything to me."

There was a light scoff and then the smooth, lyrical lilt of my brother Sebastian's voice. "I'm deeply wounded, *mia cara*. Here I was, always thinking *I* was your favourite."

I shot into a seated position and blinked at the sight of my brother, Giselle, Sinclair, Mama, and Salvatore in the doorway.

"*Cazzo*," I cursed through the sudden onslaught of tears. "I've cried more today than I have in five years."

My family laughed and filtered through the door to surround me on the bed, peppering me with kisses and enfolding me in hugs. We settled with my head on Mama's soft chest, Giselle's on my stomach with her legs over Sinclair, and Sebastian's on my thigh. Salvatore sat at my feet, smiling alternatively at me and then at Mama, his big, thick hands on my ankles.

"I thought you were all dead," I tried to explain through my incessant tears. "I thought you were all dead because of things I did, and I imagined the rest of my miserable life without you all, and I wanted to do more than die. I wanted to stop existing."

"Ah, *piccola*," Mama cooed as she stroked my hair back from my face. "Your husband and Dante got most of us out before the bomb exploded. Alexander, he followed you when you went to the back because he had a sense of danger, and when you could not be found, he pushed everyone out."

"It was a sight to behold," Giselle admitted, giggling softly. "These two huge men grabbing people as they went, pushing and yelling for everyone to get out of the restaurant."

"Two killed," Salvatore muttered darkly. "Your mama's sous chef and one of Dante's boys."

"I'll go to the funeral," I said immediately. "Xan and I will pay for it."

"You won't. It's done, and I took care of it," my dad said, his thick brows nearly obscuring his furious eyes. "Just as I will take care of the di Carlo scum who involved themselves with Noel."

"Tore," Mama soothed. "*Calmarsi.*"
Settle down.

I was surprised by the empathy in her soft mouth and her gentle words. Mama hadn't had a kind word to say to the love of her life in decades, and now, it seemed, she was condoning the violent thoughts and future actions Salvatore planned against a rival mafia syndicate.

"Whoa," I breathed, making wide eyes at Sebastian who chuckled.

"Elena isn't here because she's keeping her promise to you," Sinclair interjected, picking up my hand to clasp it between his own. "She and the rest of the legal team are looking after Dante."

I closed my eyes at the sharp sting of relief and deeper pulse of agony in my chest. The vision of my gorgeous, big man Dante in an ugly orange jumpsuit caged in a drab room of concrete all day made me physically ill. He didn't deserve to be there.

I did.

Maybe even Xan did.

But not Dante, not my beloved best friend.

"She's going to get him out," Sin promised. "Trust me, she's a shark."

I nodded but didn't give voice to my lingering fears because I didn't want them out there in the universe manifesting.

My eye snagged on Riddick lingering just outside of the door, forever my sentry.

"Rid, come in and meet my family," I called out.

He scowled.

"Come," I demanded.

He moved slightly into the door on leaden steps that screamed how reluctant he was to socialize, revealing Douglas behind him, carrying a large silver tray loaded with his gorgeous pastries.

"Enough of the heavy," Douglas announced. "Time for treats and a good chinwag. Giselle, love, Cosima tells me you lived in Paris. We must talk about all the places where you ate."

"Riddick? I hear you taught Cosima how to fence. Think

you have time to teach me a thing or two? You see, I have this film coming up…" Sebastian launched into discussion with the large, stoic man as if they had been friends for life.

I laughed as Douglas swept into the room followed by two servants carrying tea and champagne, and I continued to laugh, as I hadn't for years, while my two families co-mingled.

Chapter Thirty-four

COSIMA

The surprises didn't end there.

Riddick unearthed a large white box from my closet tied with a note from Alexander requesting I wear its contents that night. Giselle ripped the wrapping apart with me, both of us giggling as we hadn't done since we were girls. We stopped at the sight of the white silk dress cushioned by mountains of gold tissue paper. The fabric was cool and slippery as I held it up to my body, and it shone in the light like a saltwater pearl.

"Stunning," Giselle murmured as she fingered the fabric. "I have to paint you in this one day."

"Here," Riddick had said, thrusting another smaller hat box at me.

Inside lay a golden crown of thorns intermingled with fresh, fragrant flowers.

And I knew without needing confirmation that Alexander wanted me to look like Persephone in her maiden white, plucking flowers from a meadow when the Dead God broke through the earth to abduct her.

"Look at her," Mama whispered, her voice thick with tears. "She looks so much in love."

"*Si*," Salvatore murmured back. "Just as her mother once looked at me."

I bit my lip, refusing to look over at them in an attempt to give them some privacy. I'd never harboured delusions about my parents getting together again, but I knew they still longed for each other.

I also knew longing wasn't love.

"Let me do your hair," Giselle ordered, pushing me into the chair before my vanity.

I liked seeing her in the reflection where I used to see Mrs. White. It made the memory of sitting there all the less painful. It made me realize this was exactly what Alexander had predicted when he invited my family to visit. They were the only ones who could perform an exorcism on the many poltergeists in the Hall without even whipping out the Bible and sage sticks.

God, but I loved that man.

"I'll miss you so much," Giselle said as she dragged the gold brush through my hair. "New York won't be the same for me without you there."

"I'll visit," I promised.

She bit her lip, her eyes finding Sinclair in the reflection. "Cosi, I have my own alpha male, so I speak with authority when I say, I don't think that man is going to willingly let you out of his sight for a very, *very* long time."

She was undoubtedly right, but I still said, "He'll let me visit my family, *bambina*. He knows how much you mean to me."

"Um, would it be cowardly of me to request you don't use me as an excuse. Honestly, the man kind of scares me."

I'd laughed so hard, my stomach cramped.

Even now, walking down the hall by myself in search of my mysteriously disappeared family two hours later, I chuckled at the wide-eyed look on my sister's face.

I couldn't blame her. Alexander was an extremely terrifying man.

It was just one of the many reasons the dark side of my heart adored him.

The familiar strains of a Verdi symphony tickled the inside of my ears as I swept through the Hall of Mirrors and down the corridor to the ballroom. I frowned as I drew closer, the clatter of feet on the tiles and the low hum of chatter underscoring the swell of music.

Riddick appeared beside me so silently, I startled.

"Allow me, your grace," he said formally, dressed to the nines in a perfectly tailored suit that made the somewhat crudely constructed man look entirely dashing.

I nodded, so many questions on my tongue, it felt cemented to the bottom of my mouth.

He stepped in front of me and pushed open the wide double doors to reveal the secret of the cacophony inside.

The ballroom was transformed.

For once, the drapes were tied open, the windows glimmering black mirrors in the night, reflecting the fragments of light from the many chandeliers like constellations of stars. The warm light made the gold leaf glow like luminous vines covering most of the room's tall walls and my beloved mural of Hades and Persephone seemed to spring forth from the ceiling in a three-dimensional rendering.

It was gorgeous and so completely contrary to my history

in the space, I felt momentarily bemazed and bamboozled. Had this loveliness been lurking in the dark of my cage the entire time? Had I been kept captive in a place of beauty, like a ballerina trapped in a closed music box, unaware of the gorgeousness around her, too haunted by the dark?

I blinked, wondering if I was imagining the warmth, hallucinating the many loved ones punctuating the space as I had in my loneliest hours being broken by Xan and Noel on the cold, hard black marble floor.

I wasn't. Giselle and Sinclair stood in gorgeous refinery, his hand on the back of her neck in a claiming hold, Sebastian beside them with his head tipped to me but his suit-clad body angled toward my old friend Erika Van Bellegham's stunning figure. Salvatore and Mama stood close but not touching, their hands both loose and twitching slightly at their sides as if drawn to each other by some invisible magnetic force. I caught sight of Agatha Howard holding Simon Wentworth's hand, Jensen Brask standing beside Willa Percy, both peering at me with slight, smug grins as if they knew this would be my life all along. The staff was there too, in their humble finery, their smiles wide as they watched their lord and master carve a path through the crowd to collect his duchess.

To collect me.

My mouth went dry and my sex wet as I took in Alexander's long, powerful gait eating up the floor, his stride purposeful, but somewhat unhurried as if he couldn't wait to get to me, but he knew he had all the time in the world to reach me. His silver eyes caught in the warm light and reflected like diamonds from his golden face, one of Hephaestus's perfect automatons come to life.

As he stopped before me, his face stony with tender solemnity, and took my hand, I felt for the first time ever as if my life was a fairy tale. Not one of the Grimm brother's gruesome stories without optimism and filled with monsters, but something pure. A Bildungsroman meant to inspire hope, with the lesson that if you persevere through your times of trouble, you can come out the other side with a spine of steel, the heart of a worthy man held in your palm, and wisdom around your shoulders like a royal mantel.

"*Topolina*," he said with a small kick of his upper lip that belied his amusement at my stunned silence. "Take your husband's hand."

Mutely, I did, my hand sliding into his like a key in a lock.

He tugged gently, leading me through the crowd to the middle of the room. He stopped me with my feet on the black marble tile scarred and punctured from the impression of the spike that had held me down in chains.

I looked up from my stilettoed feet on that wounded tile, and Alexander's face was suddenly up against mine, his eyes everything I could see, his mouth moving against mine.

"You will always be my slave, my beauty," he whispered just for me. "But you will also always be my duchess." A kiss pressed like a notary stamp to my lips, legalizing his words, and then he pulled back to face the crowd. "Everyone, may I present to you, Cosima Ruth Lombardi Davenport, Duchess of Greythorn, and my gorgeous bride."

Everyone clapped, Sebastian throwing in a whistle and Giselle a soft whoop.

My skin was too dark to show a blush, but my flesh caught fire with gentle embarrassment and pride.

"You are the greatest treasure I will ever know," Xan continued as Riddick stepped up with a large, flat velvet box and handed it to him. "But I wanted to belatedly commemorate our marriage with a gift worthy of you."

There was a collective gasp as Alexander popped open the jewelry case and countless diamonds erupted under the multifaceted light. My hand flew to my mouth to contain the immensity of my emotions as I stared at the necklace of diamonds constructed to look like thorny leaves and the absolutely sumptuous yellow gold diamond at its base.

To everyone else, it looked like an extravagant present from a lord of the realm to his new(ish) bride.

To me, it looked exactly like what it was—a replacement collar for the one Alexander had told me Noel had cast into the fire.

"Something incomparable for my incomparable bride," he said as he lifted it in one hand, smoothed my cloak of hair off my shoulders, and settled the heavy, cold weight around my neck.

The weight of the diamonds was so acute, I knew it was deliberate. So that I would always feel the force of his possession around my throat.

Alexander turned me to face him after clasping it closed, his face impassive as he stared at his collar around my neck. He lifted a finger to run the back of it over the smooth rectangular yellow diamond in the hollow of my throat, and then he looked up at me with softly pursed lips to say, "Even L'Incomparable pales next to your money eyes."

"Only because you love me," I told him, trying to tease and failing because the words were hoarse with unshed tears.

He shrugged his insolent schoolboy shrug. "Undoubtedly. Now, slave, dance with me."

Collecting one hand in his, wrapping the other around my waist, Alexander spun me into movement, music flaring to life like the kick of my skirt the second he whirled us into motion.

"Wagner wrote this symphony for his wife, Cosima, for her birthday," Alexander told me as we danced, and everyone else began to dance with us.

I pressed my cheek to the fabric over his heart. "Why are you doing all of this?"

His chin rested over my head, his hands drawing me closer so that we were flush together, barely dancing. "Because I wanted to show you how serious I was about replacing all the nightmarish memories in this house with new ones, brilliant ones. I wanted to somehow illustrate how sorry I am for all the things I've put you through. I want you to understand even when I cannot measure the fathomless depth of love I have for you at the heart of me, how very much I desire you to be happy in this life with me."

"Xan," I said, pulling back to tip his head down to me with a hand at his neck, hard over his pulse just to feel it beat. "I would dance with you forever in the dark if it meant being with you. I don't need the light or the diamonds, I hardly even need my loved ones. You could have dragged me into the cold, dim ballroom, clasped that old chain around my ankle, and I would still love you. I don't regret the things you've done or the events of the past five years. They brought us together and cemented our bond. They made me strong, and they made you worthy."

"Ours isn't exactly a romantic story," he admitted wryly.

I arched a brow, pressed my palm over the brand I knew he wore on the skin over his heart, and dragged one of his hands down my back to my ass where it rested over my own brand. I thought of Helios and my collar, of Xan pulling strings to get me a job with St. Aubyn, of the years he spent longing for me but denying himself to keep me safe. I thought of the way my body felt when I was away from him, like a form without a shadow even in absolute sunlight.

I thought of the way he would have died for me, and the way I nearly died for him.

"Isn't it?" I asked softly. "I think it's romantic as hell."

"Literally," Alexander quipped with a roguish grin that made me tip my head back to the mural of Persephone and her Dead God and laugh and laugh and laugh.

And when I looked back down at Alexander, my once Dead God was laughing too.

Epilogue

COSIMA

The courtroom vibrated with hushed, anticipatory chatter as the gathered waited for the venerable Judge Hartford to take the stand and begin the proceedings. I could hear the cacophony of press and spectators outside the closed doors to the chamber and even outside on the street. It was the biggest trial against a supposed mafioso since the Mafia Commission Trial in the eighties, and it was sensational news throughout New York City and beyond.

This was helped, of course, by the fact that the man on trial for first-degree murder, racketeering, and illegal gambling was the gorgeous, charmingly incorrigible, and dangerously intense Edward Dante Davenport.

The noise rose tidal strong as the side door opened, and the man himself was ushered through by two guards and his law team. He wore all black even though it made him look wickedly sinful and sinister, his hair pushed back from his face but for one wavy lock that draped over his forehead into his black eyes.

He looked like an ad for *mad, bad, and dangerous to know.*

I shook my head as I caught eyes with Elena, who stood behind him with the rest of his law team with her red-painted lips pressed together in a line that underscored her fury at losing that particular battle with her client.

He should have worn a white button-up, at least, to soften his appearance and make him seem like your average businessman.

But of course, Dante didn't care to look innocuous, and I was certain he had argued wearing such a getup would only make it more obvious that he was a lion dressed as a lamb.

"Bloody idiot," Alexander muttered at my side as he glared at his brother.

My husband was not in a good mood.

Not only because his brother was on trial for murder but also because his being so made it necessary for us to be in New York.

Alexander *hated* the city.

It was the symbol of our years apart and my refuge when I'd been lost without him.

If he had it his way, we probably would never again set foot on Manhattan island again.

But Dante was on trial for murder, so here we were, sitting in the first row reserved for his family, lending the weight of the Davenport name and Greythorn rank to Dante's case.

It was hard for the public to believe the brother of a duke would resort to becoming a mafioso.

"*Tesoro*," Dante murmured with a small smile as the guards slotted him between the railing and the table he would sit at and then pushed him down hard into his chair.

My heart twisted up in my chest, turning my reassuring smile into a wince.

"*Fratello*," I offered softly, leaning forward to place my hand on the railing where he could see it and know I wished it was on his arm or around his back in a fierce embrace.

The hard cast of his face softened for a moment as he stared at me, his love shining out from every pore. He had sacrificed so much for me over the years, and I refused to believe he would be punished for it by spending the next twenty-five years in prison.

"We will win." Alexander cut into my thoughts with his strong, sure words. "I won't let them do this to you."

Dante's grin turned wry as he looked over at his brother, his twin in form if not colouring. Gold and black, bad wrapped up in a pretty package and good trapped in bad boy form.

They were a yin and yang pairing I didn't want to ever again think about living without.

"You think you can do anything." Dante shook his head fondly. "You know the entire world does not bow down to your grace, *sì*?"

Xan raised one cool brow in silent rebuttal.

Dante laughed, and the visual was captured by the court reporters many flashing cameras.

I had no doubt it would grace the headlines of all the popular newspapers tomorrow.

Mafia capo laughs in the face of his crimes.

"Shut up and face forward, Edward," Elena snapped, pinching his leg hard as she took the seat between him and her co-counsel. "For once in your life, do as you're told."

"Make me," he taunted her before shooting me an invet-erate wink.

I smiled at him as he wanted me to, but I didn't feel light-hearted.

Elena locked eyes with me, and her prim, professional mask shifted for a moment to show me her quiet worry. She had made me a promise to fight for Dante as she would fight for *me*, but I could see at the moment how much of a long shot it was that Dante would be found not guilty.

He wasn't guilty, of course.

I'd been the one to kill Giuseppe di Carlo.

But after years of living under the influence of the Order, I knew how powerful manipulation could be, and right now? The public wanted Dante to go down for these crimes.

"I won't let it happen, my beauty," Alexander swore, leaning down into my ear to whisper the words there like a prayer. "I will go to the ends of the earth to make sure he does not suffer any more for us."

I smiled thinly at him but took his hands in mine for comfort and rubbed the golden band on his ring finger. "You once told me that not everyone deserves a happy ending. Can you honestly say we do? That the brother you hated for the last two decades does?"

He tipped my chin with his knuckle and fused his gaze to mine. "If anyone deserves a happy ending, it is the people who suffer while finding it. I promise you, wife, this too will pass, and one day soon, we'll all be drinking together and reminiscing about this exact moment. Do you believe your husband?"

I looked into the eyes I'd memorized the first time I'd seen them in a back alley in Milano, the ones that had been waiting for me when I woke up for the first time in Pearl Hall's ballroom, and I thought about how he had promised me both times that he would be there waiting for me.

He was not a man who gave up, no matter the circumstances, and I knew this was just one more obstacle for him to cut his teeth on.

He was the hero of my story, but as any good reader knows, the hero would always become a villain if his loved ones were threatened.

And Alexander was all too willing to go to war for his brother and his wife.

"I believe you," I told him.

And even though it took years and twisted turns we never could have predicted, in the end, I was right to.

Two years later.

I had never been in so much pain before. Not in my entire life.

God only knew that was saying something.

My entire body felt like a building burning down, the seams aching to hold up the increasing weight of walls as it threatened to cave in, the wood sweating from the heat as it rose higher and higher.

It was pure agony.

But I gloried in it.

Not because my Master was using one of his many wicked toys to draw whimpers and sighs from me. Though he was, in essence, also the reason for this pain.

But because I was sweating and heaving and splitting apart at the seams between my thighs to give birth to the baby we'd made together.

"Why in the bloody hell is she in so much pain, Doctor?" my husband snarled at the country's most renowned obstetrician. His handsome face was screwed up tight, his skin red with the force of bottling up all his considerable rage.

It went without saying that after everything we'd been through together, Alexander didn't like to see me hurt.

"This is a completely natural process, your Grace," Dr. Reinhardt promised, totally unfazed by the large, angry man scowling at him from my bedside. "Your wife is doing amazingly well considering the size of the baby."

This placated him slightly. It pleased some manly sensibility in my husband to know that he had produced a big, healthy baby, and more, that I was doing so well under stress.

Praising me was the quickest way to get on Alexander's good side.

As long as that praise was platonic.

Even then, if it was from a man who was unattached or in any way handsome, he might make a point to threaten him as a friendly reminder that I was, and always would be, his.

Pain ripped through my groin and up my spin to resonate in my brain like a radioactive strike.

Alexander cursed bloody murder at the guttural groan that sprang from my ravaged throat, but he took up his position by my side once more and let me grip his hand so hard his joints ground together in protest.

"You are so beautiful," he told me in a broken voice as he leaned over to press his forehead against my sweat-soaked one. "You are so beautiful to me. At this moment, more beautiful than any other. No one has ever been prouder or more in love with their wife than me, do you understand that, my beauty?"

I nodded, my teeth gritted so tightly I could speak as another contraction rippled through me.

"Okay, time to push, Lady Greythorn," the doctor encouraged me from his intimate position between my legs.

It had shocked me that Alexander had allowed a male

doctor to be my obstetrician, but he was the undisputed top doctor in the United Kingdom.

And he was also gay, happily married to his childhood sweetheart.

Which explained Alexander's willingness, though he did make Dr. Reinhardt interview with us three times before he gave him the position as the Duchess of Greythorn's doctor.

"I'm ready," I told him, my smile twisted like hot metal on my face.

My entire body felt like an overloaded electrical wire ready to explode. I was desperate to push and release the tension even though the pain as I bore down was nearly unbearable.

"I love you, my beauty, my *topolina*, my duchess," Alexander chanted as he propped my back against his torso and held both my hands so I could squeeze them hard enough to break them as I struggled to push our child into the world. "You are my greatest treasure."

I tilted my head back, muscles strained tight enough to pop and let the scream boiling in my throat erupt into the air.

A moment later, a piercing wail underscored the last notes of my scream.

I blinked slowly through my sweat-stung eyes, trying to focus beyond the pain as I'd become so adept at doing so that I could focus on the being Dr. Reinhardt held aloft in his hands.

"My God," Alexander's voice broke as he smoothed my wet hair away from my forehead and then softly laid me back down on the bed so that he could accept the clippers from the doctor and cut the umbilical cord. "My good God."

My eyes burned, and my body felt like a deflated balloon, incapable of animation as I gave in to the impulse to close my lids and rest for a moment.

"My beauty," Alexander's soft voice pulled me gently from slumber. "It's time to meet your son."

Instantly, adrenaline coursed through my body, and my

eyes snapped open, my vision clear and brilliant as I locked eyes on a pair of silver-blue irises I knew would turn into Alexander's grey with time.

Our baby.

A sob lodged itself in my throat as my heart pounded hard and heavy in my chest. I felt swollen to bursting with love, overripe and vulnerable.

Baby Davenport was eight pounds, eleven ounces with a thick thatch of black hair and a perfectly formed bow-shaped mouth that was puckered as he fussed slightly in his daddy's arms.

He was the most beautiful thing I had ever seen in my life.

I looked up at Alexander through my tear slicked eyes and saw in his expression the same prodigious tenderness that had overtaken me.

He sat on the edge of the bed and moved the baby so he could lay on my naked chest. The room was cleared, obviously ordered so by my domineering duke, so we could both watch in awe as the baby snuggled into my swollen breast and curled a fist over my heart.

"I never thought in all my life to dream this kind of dream," Alexander murmured softly, aware of the sweet, secure cocoon we were enrobed in. "I never believed I would be free of my demons, let alone at liberty to share my life with a woman like you at my side, with beautiful children at our feet. Even if I was free from those chains that bound me, I never would have thought I would be worthy of such a future as this."

The sob stuck in my throat fell from my lips as I turned my head into his shoulders and let my tears of gratitude anoint his black button-up.

He let me cry even though I know it pained him to watch me. His hand was in my hair, stroking it back from my hot, damp face in a way that soothed me to my ragged core.

I shifted my head back to press a kiss to the strong, steady pulse in his throat and then turned again to look down at the sweet bundle on my chest.

He was warm and quiet, sleeping against me as if he knew just how safe he was in my arms with both of us in the arms of his father.

Alexander would never let anything bad happen to either of us. We were bringing our child into a world without the Order, without Noel Davenport, and without the threat of the mafia hanging over us.

"This is our era of happiness," I reminded Alexander as I placed a kiss gentle as a butterfly against our son's soft head. "All he will ever know is joy and light."

"Yes," Alexander promised, one of his thick, long fingers uncurled against the baby's plump cheek. "Though your family is undoubtedly crazy, *bella*, so I hesitate to say it will be without drama."

I let out a watery laugh as I ran my nose over the top of the baby's head so I could drag in some of his sweet infant scent.

"Do we have a name for our future duke?" Alexander asked.

The pregnancy hadn't been an easy one for either of us emotionally. Even though Noel was gone, he still haunted Pearl Hall and our memories of my truncated first pregnancy like a hellish spectre. Alexander was overbearing and viciously protective the entire nine months, barely letting me out of the house, let alone out of the country to visit my family or work out my existing contracts. I was just as loathe to be parted from our home and my husband. It had been two years since the end of our horrors, but it still felt as though no time had passed since I'd been back home at Pearl Hall as its mistress, and I wasn't ready to be away from them for any real length of time.

I had morning sickness the entire pregnancy, horrible nightmares that lingered long after I woke, and terrible hot flashes that had Alexander installing a ceiling fan and four Dyson floor fans in our bedroom just so I could scrape together a few hours of sleep at night.

It was grueling, but we loved every minute of it. And by some silent agreement, we were careful about making too many plans for the baby once he or she arrived. We didn't learn the gender, we didn't pick out names, and we only had a crib back at home because Riddick had built one for us as a baby present.

It was stupid for two mature adults to believe it was possible to jinx it, but we'd lived through such trials and heart-break for so long, we didn't want to take any chances.

So, we didn't have a name for the little earl that lay in my arms.

But as I peered down at his perfect, handsome little face, I thought of a name that was all too perfect for him.

"What about Aidon?" I asked, tilting my head back to look at the man who had burst into my life and dragged me through hell in order to give me a kingdom we could one day call our own. "*Aides* or *Aidoneus* is one of the lesser-known names of Hades."

Alexander's beautiful, strong face melted into one of his rare open smiles as he chuckled. "Only my wife would want to name our child after the Greek god of the Underworld."

"Only your wife would understand just how much the story of Hades and Persephone means to me, to us," I countered. "Hades is a misunderstood god, but he maintained balance and harmony between good and evil. He was a fair and just ruler with great responsibility, just as our son will be one day."

I looked down at our gift as he shifted his little furled hand into his mouth, and I knew in a newly discovered chamber of my heart where motherhood sat and pulsed that the little man on my chest was going to be one of the greatest men who ever lived.

"Aidon," Alexander tested, his accent carving the name smooth and clean like sculpted marble. "Aidon Dante Joseph Davenport, seventh Earl of Thornton and heir to the Dukedom of Greythorn." He ran his big hand gently over the baby's head as if metaphorically crowning him with his titles. "Yes, I think Aidon will suit him just fine."

"I love you," I told him fiercely as the feeling brutalized my chest and made it difficult to breathe. "If I had to go back, I would choose to be your slave again and again. I don't want our enslavement to each other to ever end."

My husband leaned down to press his forehead to mine, one hand still cupping the back of Aidon's soft head. I kept my eyes open, gaze sank deep in the perforated silver of his gorgeous eyes.

"Thank you for giving me a gift I never thought to ask for," he said quietly, his tone so genuine it made my heart ache. "I promise to prove myself worthy of it, of you and our child, every single bloody day for the rest of our lives."

"I know," I said before I sealed his promise with a kiss. "You are the best man I know, and I'll spend the rest of my life proving to you that I already know just how worthy you are."

ALEXANDER

Four years later.

Pearl Hall echoed like church bells in an ancient tower with the peeling, silver laughter of many children dancing, playing, and racing through its halls. Theodore and Genevieve Sinclair took turns sliding down the great, curving bannister of the staircase in the Great Hall as Riddick looked on as a stern supervisor, only cracking a smile when Genny demanded he stand at the bottom and high five her on her way down.

Two of the Davenport triplets giggled ceaselessly as their aunt Elena and uncle Dante blew kisses into their sweet baby rolls of fat and tickled the swell of their little bellies from where they lay inside their playpen set up in the informal living room. The adults argued good naturedly over which of the brothers was cuter, Edward or Dorian, and both babies screamed in delight as if adding their own opinions to the debate.

Mama held the only Davenport girl, the last triplet born, a small thing made of golden skin and curling ink-stained hair with eyes already turned a brightly polished silver. She cooed to little Poppy in a serious tone, imparting wisdom in dialect Italian the eleven-month-old girl couldn't yet understand. Still, Poppy pressed her little fist to Mama's softly creased cheek as if she comprehended each word.

Giselle sat on the loveseat before the fire curled up beside her husband, who read from *'Twas the Night Before Christmas* aloud for the benefit of the preteen girl lying belly down on the Persian carpet with her chocolate-stained face cupped in her hands as she listened. When she interrupted the story to protest, Elena shot her daughter a long, lingering look that spoke volumes and shut down the girl with a grumbled apology as she settled back in to listen.

I stood in the doorway between the Great Hall and the living room with my shoulder against the jamb, and my arms crossed as I took in the happy family tableau occupying my ancestral home.

It was our first Christmas as a family in years, and my wife had somehow convinced her clan to travel across the pond and spend it here at Pearl Hall. Every year previously, we had flown to the States for the occasion, but Cosima was tired— three newborns would test a literal saint—and she wanted her family in her home to celebrate.

I hadn't properly understood her inclination until the current moment, watching my in-law's children scurry around the imposing estate as if it was a playground, seeing my wife share the love of our home with her sisters and brother, and woo their partners with our history and amenities.

Pearl Hall had felt like a true home the moment I'd rein-stalled Cosima at my side as its mistress, and it felt like a palace once more the moment we'd brought Aidon home from the hospital, but this was the first time I understood that together, my wife and I were creating a new legacy for the place.

It would never again be a cage for slaves or a prison for its heirs. Our children would grow up knowing it as a home as much as any other, a place of love and warmth with a new history built on loyalty and emotional generosity. They would impart this adage on to their children and from them their own, on and on until the legacy that had ended with Noel would be long forgotten and washed from the walls and grounds of Pearl Hall by many, many years of *my* family's laughter.

The scent of crushed autumn leaves and warm spice heralded her arrival before slender arms wrapped themselves around my middle, and Cosima pressed herself to my back.

"Hullo, husband," she said in a jaunty British accent.

Her voice would never forget those last traces of her homeland, but more and more over the years, she had adapted to my British-isms and manner of speaking. I enjoyed the traces of my country in her speech. It was yet another reminder of all the ways I'd made her intractably mine.

"Hullo, wife," I replied, tugging her around to my front so I could take her face in my hands and look into her beloved golden eyes.

In the first years of our reunion, I'd harboured a secret, horrifying belief that our love was too good to be true. That any minute, she would recognize the mistake she had made in choosing me and get the hell out of my life.

But that moment never came.

Instead, every day that I woke up beside her, it was to a particular look in her eye I'd come to understand was crafted only for me. It was a look that turned her eyes from solid gold to warm, honeyed butter, soft and pliable with love and submission for me.

That expression was echoed in her money eyes then as I looked down into them, and I felt the mirror of that feeling take up inside my chest.

"How did I get to be such a lucky bastard?" I asked her before taking her lips in a firm, punishing kiss.

When I finally had my fill—for the moment— I pulled back and watched with wholly male satisfaction as she blinked dazedly a few times before recovering. She reached up to wrap her fingers around my wrists as they still held her face, and she smiled her million-dollar smile.

"You know perfectly well how you managed it, Xan. You paid the price for me."

"Cheeky," I scolded with a click of my tongue before I sobered and bent my knees slightly so that I was eye-level with her. "I paid the price not in wealth, but in sacrifice. Nearly four years without you was worse than any punishment had by Sisyphus or Tantalus."

"Agreed," Cosima said with a firm nod before collapsing once more in a beatific grin. "Are you happy now, husband?"

I looked over her head into the living room again as Cage

Tracey began to play the piano, and Sebastian stood up to invite his mother to dance with him. Dante and Elena bickered over the game of chess they had started in the same spot Cosi had once played Noel before the fireplace while Aidon and Giselle carefully painted the trainset the former had received as an early Christmas present.

It was so perfect as to be nauseating for a man who had not believed in love for the better part of his life.

I told my wife that.

She tipped her head back and laughed her raucous, genuine laughter. I let it wash over me as I held her in my arms, and when she righted herself, I gave in to the impulse to kiss her once more.

The doorbell trilled throughout the house, causing everyone to pause in the revelry.

We were all together, not a loved one forgotten, so it was curious that anyone would arrive on Christmas Eve to the closed estate.

I was surprised the guard had let whoever it was through the gates without permission.

That was until my wife smiled like the cat who was about to eat the bloody canary.

"*Topolina*," I drawled dangerously. "What have you done?"

Her smile was wicked as she ducked out of my arms and scurried away to answer the door, impatiently shooing away Riddick as he tried to take the duty from her.

I caught eyes with Sebastian as he stood with his mother in his arms, and we shared a moment of apprehension.

We both had an inkling who Cosima might have invited into our home.

Not *who*, but *whom*.

A moment later, a male and female voice sounded from the Great Hall, and a moment after that, Giselle and Sin's daughter and son were dragging in two people by the hand with Cosima following in the rear.

"Look, *Papa*," Theo crowed to his dad. "Adam and Linnea are here!"

The air in the room went flat, the jovial atmosphere doused with gasoline before it lit on fire a second later when the tall, admittedly gorgeous woman holding Theo's hand said softly, "Hi, everyone."

I didn't have to look at Sebastian to know he was bursting with rage and run through with hurt. Everyone else unfroze from their shock and gave in to their impulse to be polite despite the awkward situation. I remained standing in the door as the others greeted Sebastian's ex-best friend and ex-lover, offering my solidarity to the brother-in-law I'd grown to respect and love.

His eyes cut to me, and he tilted his head slightly in thanks.

"Sebastian," Adam Meyers said, his voice strong and confident as he stepped forward after exchanging hellos with the rest of the family, eyes locked on the man across the room. "Come here and greet us."

"We just came to wish you a Merry Christmas, Seb," Linnea said in her soft, lyrical voice, beseeching where Adam was commandeering.

They made a striking couple standing there. Adam's regal, stern bearing a result of his British aristocratic upbringing, whereas Linnea was faintly exotic and entirely beguiling with all that blond hair and bombshell physique tucked in a cashmere dress.

Sebastian's dark looks were a perfect foil and complement to the two, but standing across the room as he was, it was impossible to tell how physically or emotionally compatible they could have been together. Then or—if the two newcomers had anything to do about it—now.

"Sebastian." Adam's voice cut clean through the air between them like a bullwhip. "Come here."

Instantly, Sebastian moved forward even though his

posture spoke of recalcitrance and humiliated anger. He reminded me of Cosima when I'd first brought her to heel, defiant and noble but deeply drawn to domination.

I looked for her behind Adam and noticed her twin expression of bewilderment.

Adam and Sebastian clearly had a greater history than we'd previously understood.

"*I hope you know what you're doing,*" I mouthed to my wife.

She bit her lip and shrugged.

Sebastian reached Adam, stopping toe to toe with him in belligerent defiance. They stared at each other for a long moment, energy crackling in the room so profoundly even the triplets were quiet in their crib.

Finally, Linnea stepped forward, placing a hand on each of their vibrating chests like a lightning rod grounding them both.

"Stop," she ordered quietly. "You're both making a scene, and this is Christmas. Give me a kiss, Sebastian, and then a tour of this gorgeous house."

The men stared at each other for another long second before Seb's shoulders rounded slightly in defeat, and he turned to press a brief kiss to Linnea's cheek.

"Start with the east wing," Cosima suggested, sweeping closer to place a comforting hand on her brother's arm. "I'm sure they'll both enjoy the chapel."

Sebastian gave her a tight nod and then made forward with Linnea's hand tucked into his arm. Adam reached out and clamped his fingers on Sebastian's shoulder so that he froze in his tracks. Without looking back at him, Seb stepped slightly out of the way and let Adam take the lead even though he didn't know his way through the Hall.

Cosima and I shared another look as the trio left the room and the air flattened like stale pop.

"Well, *cazzo*," Dante said, shattering our shocked silence.

"That was more sexual tension than I've seen since Elena first met me."

Elena socked him in the arm and then laughed when Cage nodded in agreement.

We'd all had our fair share of romantic turbulence, and apparently, according to my meddling wife, it was time for Sebastian to finish out his.

I lifted an arm so she could fit into my side when she came to me and then pressed my lips into the fragrant hair over her ear to murmur, "I think I'll have to punish you for that little stunt, my beauty. We were looking forward to a peaceful Christmas."

The love of my life looked up at me out of the corner of her golden eyes, a cheeky smile creasing her cheek as she said, "Do you think the only reason I did that was for Seb? I was looking for a reason for you to punish me. I was tired of being good."

"Ah," I said as Aidon called out for me to look at his trains. "When everyone is tucked into bed, I'll have to tuck you into the St. Andrews cross and remind you just what happens when you're bad."

Thank you so much for reading ENAMOURED!
Sign up for my newsletter to keep up to date on all things

Giana Darling and the words I write. You can even download a *free* short story!

If you loved reading about Cosima's dark love story with her enigmatic Master Alexander, you'll want to find out what happens to his mafioso brother, Dante!

Add Dante's upcoming book, **When Heroes Fall,** to your Goodreads TBR now so you don't miss his epic mafia romance!

You can also read about Cosima's sister Giselle right now for a chance to uncover the mystery of her affair! Find out what happens when Giselle takes a vacation before reuniting with her family in New York City, and meets the French billionaire Sinclair. He is everything she never knew she wanted, but he's also taken…
One-click **The Affair** now!

5 HOT STEAMY AFFAIR STARS!! Get ready for a hot steamy one-week holiday affair with twists and turns. Sexy Sinclair knows what he wants which is beautiful Giselle and he goes for it. These two will heat the pages up and suck you into their story. — Goodreads reviewer 5 stars

Thanks etc.

Alexander and Cosima's story is a complicated chaos of dualities merging and disassociating constantly. Some may say that Alexander doesn't deserve Cosima, but I would argue that as long as she loves him and he spends the rest of his life striving to be worthy of her, that is enough for them both. We don't always fall in love with the best person or a good person, but as long as they are the *right* one, none of that really matters.

Before I continue to the acknowledgments just a quick disclaimer, I do not in any way support human trafficking. This is a fictionalized version of a very scary and real problem that still faces our society. If you need to talk to someone about the realities of the social issue, please contact your national human trafficking center to learn more.

Allaa, I can't imagine writing without you. You've made the process that I've lived for since I was a child even more incredible and I will always honour you for that.

To Ella, every day is better with your voice in it. You're my ride or die.

To my #dirtysoulsister Michelle Clay. Your tales of real-life romance constantly inspire. I've always wanted someone to divulge the craziness of my life to and know that I will never be judged for it. I am unbelievably grateful to have found that in you.

Jenny from Editing4Indies, you are my saviour. Thank you for polishing this manuscript from a diamond in the rough into a polished gem.

Thank you so much Ellie McLove for sweeping in to do the proofing of this document.

Candi from Candi Kane PR, you make releases ten times less stressful and any author knows that's worth everything.

Najla Qamber from Najla Qamber Designs, is the only woman I have ever worked with on a cover. She is my wizard and the creator of all my gorgeous graphics.

I love thanking my Review Team because without them, no one would know about my words.

Giana's Darlings, you are the best reader's group on the planet and my safe, little happy place on the interweb.

To my sister Grace. Your constant support is the cornerstone that inspired me to write a story about sisterly love. Thank you for loving me the way you do.

To Fiona and Lauren, you two have provided me with enough solace, adventures, laughter, and love to last me a lifetime in the decade plus that I've known you two, and it thrills me every day to know we have so many more decades of fun and friendship together. I can't wait to one day dedicated a book to Mrs. H and Mrs. A, because that's obviously going to be one of my wedding presents to both of you!

To my Armie. It seems ridiculous that we've only known each other for three years, yet we have enough shared memories to last a lifetime. You make each day even more beautiful to me simply by existing.

As always, to the Love of My Life. In every book I write, I try to find the words to explain how deeply one person can love another. In every book, I fail to bring to life the complexities of a love like ours. I'm so grateful that I have a lifetime to try to do justice to that emotion and commitment. You inspire me every day.

Other Books by Giana Darling

The Evolution of Sin Trilogy

Giselle Moore is running away from her past in France for a new life in America, but before she moves to New York City, she takes a holiday on the beaches of Mexico and meets a sinful, enigmatic French businessman, Sinclair, who awakens submissive desires and changes her life forever.

The Affair
The Secret
The Consequence
The Evolution Of Sin Trilogy Boxset

The Fallen Men Series

The Fallen Men are a series of interconnected, standalone, erotic MC romances that each feature age gap love stories between dirty-talking, Alpha males and the strong, sassy women who win their hearts.

Lessons in Corruption
Welcome to the Dark Side
Good Gone Bad
After the Fall
Inked in Lies

Dead Man Walking

A Fallen Men Companion Book of Poetry:
King of Iron Hearts

The Enslaved Duet

*The Enslaved Duet is a dark romance duology about an eighteen-year old
Italian fashion model, Cosima Lombardi, who is sold by her indebted
father to a British Earl who's nefarious plans for her include more than
just sexual slavery… Their epic tale spans across Italy, England,
Scotland, and the USA across a five-year period that sees them endure
murder, separation, and a web of infinite lies.*

Enthralled (The Enslaved Duet #1)
Enamoured (The Enslaved Duet, #2)

The Elite Seven Series
Sloth (The Elite Seven Series, #7)

Coming Soon
Fallen King (A Fallen Men Short Story)
When Heroes Fall (Anti-Heroes in Love, #1)
When Villains Rise (Anti-Heroes in Love, #2)

About Giana Darling

Giana Darling is a *USA Today*, *Wall Street Journal*, Top 40 Best Selling Canadian romance writer who specializes in the taboo and angsty side of love and romance. She currently lives in beautiful British Columbia where she spends time riding on the back of her man's bike, baking pies, and reading snuggled up with her cat, Persephone.

Join my Reader's Group
Subscribe to my Newsletter
Follow me on IG
Like me on Facebook
Follow me on Goodreads
Follow me on BookBub
Follow me on Pinterest

www.ingramcontent.com/pod-product-compliance
Lightning Source LLC
Chambersburg PA
CBHW072009020726
47501CB00006B/1742